A DRUID STONE

MÓRDHA STONE CHRONICLES, BOOK 5

KIM ALLRED

STORM COAST PUBLISHING, LLC

A DRUID STONE
Mórdha Stone Chronicles, Book 5
KIM ALLRED

Published by Storm Coast Publishing, LLC

Copyright © 2020 by Kim Allred
Cover Design by Amanda Kelsey of Razzle Dazzle Design
Print edition November 2020
ISBN 978-1-953832-00-9

OTHER BOOKS BY KIM ALLRED

For all those we've left behind...

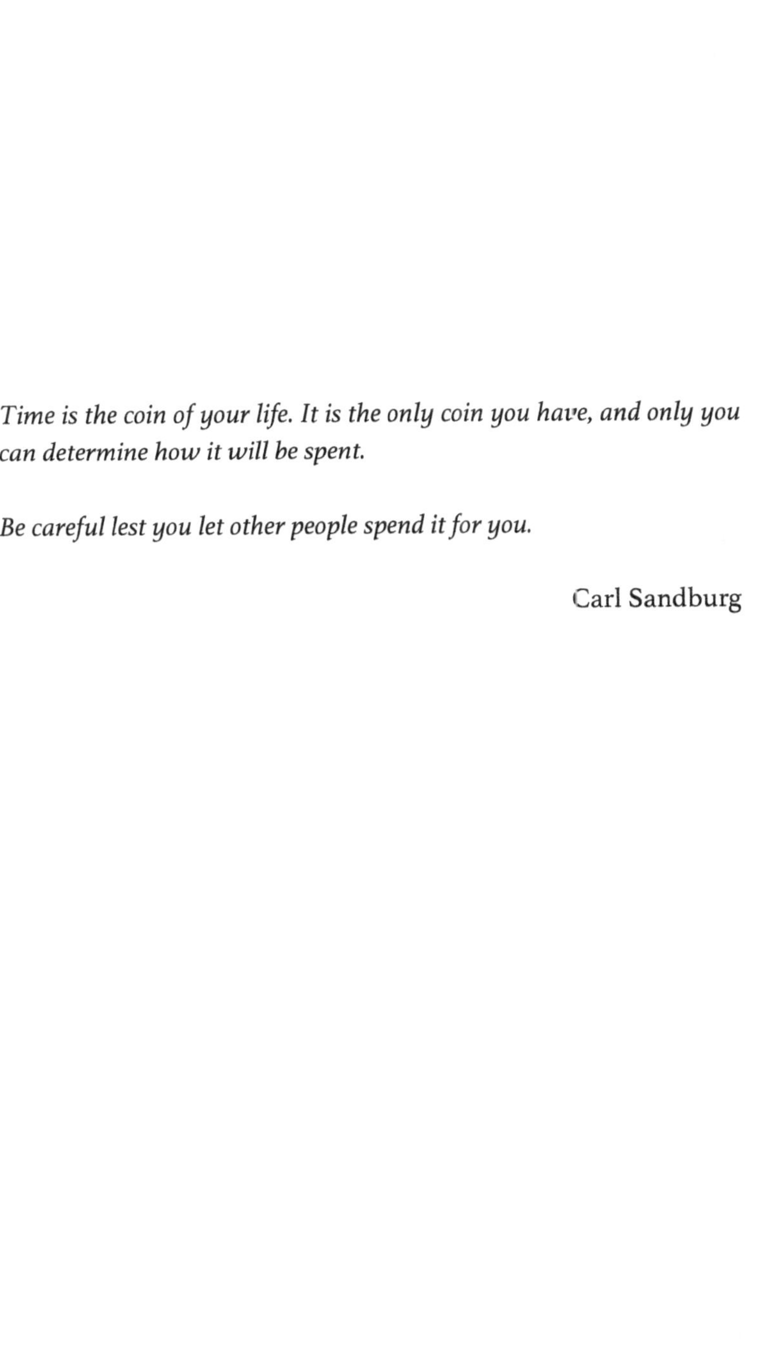

Time is the coin of your life. It is the only coin you have, and only you can determine how it will be spent.

Be careful lest you let other people spend it for you.

Carl Sandburg

1

AJ Moore was going to be sick. Passionately and thoroughly ill. The fog swirled around her, its thick white tendrils reaching out like skeletal arms in a horror movie. She doubled over, clenching her middle. Her stomach twisted like someone was squeezing every drop of moisture out of an old dish rag.

The dead weight of Beckworth—the Viscount of Waverly and deceitful bastard—hung over her left shoulder. Somehow, through the horrible nausea she was aware of his sticky blood staining her shirt.

She smirked. If she survived the time jump, she'd stab him again, if for no other reason than he irritated her.

All thoughts vanished as the pain intensified. The brightness of the mist overwhelmed her senses before she fell into blessed darkness.

When she opened her eyes, disoriented after the jump, the heavy body sprawled across her triggered a claustrophobic attack. She shoved against it until she was able to twist away. She managed to crawl two feet before the remains of her lunch returned. That was when she noticed it was raining—correction

—pouring. The vomit disintegrated into a pool of water, turning it into a gray gruel.

She backed away before she gagged. Water streamed off her forehead, and she scraped the saturated hair from her face.

Where the hell were they?

She crawled back to the body and turned it over, hoping he'd drowned in the puddle of mud he lay in. Unfortunately, Beckworth stirred.

When his eyes fluttered open, she screamed at him. Partly to ensure he could hear her, but also because, short of repeatedly stabbing him in the neck, it was all she could think to do. "What the hell were you thinking? Why did you do that?"

He either couldn't hear her or didn't care to answer.

She grabbed his shirt, heedless of the blood still seeping from his wound, and shook him. "Why couldn't you wait? We could have all come back together."

Tears mixed with rain, and her chest heaved as she cried out her anger and frustration. When it didn't appear Beckworth would answer her, she beat on his chest, then fell back to pull herself together.

The landscape was difficult to make out through the steady rainfall, yet it seemed familiar. She had expected to arrive in England at the Earl of Hereford's estate. Realization dawned. That would have required Ethan's incantation. The new and improved version from Maire's more recent translations. Instead, Beckworth had interfered and grabbed the Heart Stone she'd foolishly worn around her neck. Although he'd whispered an older incantation, it hadn't mattered. Just the act of him touching his stone with the Heart Stone was enough to carry them back to the location of the torc.

They must be on the knoll in France, and the only remaining question was the year. At least the monastery would be close— that was something. Full of despair, she sank back in the mud.

What would she find when she went to town? Would Ethan and Maire be at the inn as she'd last left them?

Finn.

Her heart filled with longing and a deep, aching sense of loss. Less than twenty-four hours ago, they had married and promised never to leave one another. Now he was two hundred years away. Or was he?

Ethan still had a stone. They never discussed Maire's updated incantations, but Ethan would have the translation to follow the Heart Stone. AJ had no idea how accurate the travel would be or the timing. It could take months for them to connect, assuming they arrived in the same time period.

Distorted mumbling drew her attention back to her current dilemma.

"You."

She crawled over and rose to her knees so she could stare down at him.

"You." His head rolled from side to side. He paused after each word, waiting for his labored breathing to subside. "You," he attempted for the third time. He heaved and almost gagged. A line of spittle formed at the corner of his mouth, and even scrunched in pain, his soaking-wet face was beautifully handsome. His normally cornflower-blue eyes were dulled, his face pasty as he forced out the word, "Stabbed." He sucked air but couldn't seem to squeak out the next word.

"Me," AJ finished for him. "You stabbed me. Is that what you're trying to croak out?" When his half-crazed eyes rolled to her, she nodded, her eyes narrowing, her voice laced with controlled rage. "Yes. I did. And I've a mind to stab you again. So lie still while I think."

There were dozens of reasons to stab him. For kidnapping her months ago. For holding Maire hostage for two years. For torturing Finn when he was held in the duke's dungeons. For blindly following them back to the future. For stalking her and then kidnapping her again. Hell, he deserved to be stabbed just for being an asshole.

She considered the real reason she'd stabbed him. In those last few seconds before the fog claimed them from the inn parking lot, she'd remembered Finn having difficulty after their jump back to the future. He'd been injured from torture before they'd left. Though he'd mostly healed, Finn had mentioned that injuries made the travel more difficult. Finn had floated in and out of delirium for hours upon their return. It required an entire day before he could hobble around the bedroom, and three days to fully recover.

Beckworth had confessed to being unconscious for two days after the sisters had found him. His injury, the first time she'd stabbed his shoulder, also hadn't healed before he was pulled into the vortex of her jump home with Finn. The two days of Beckworth's stupor might have been from medication the sisters had given him, but AJ didn't think so.

Tired of being wet, she scanned the area. The bushes were closer than the trees and would be sufficient for her plan. She pulled herself up, but a brief bout of nausea made her stagger. After gaining her balance, and with several false starts, she used Beckworth's partial moments of awareness to aid their movement across the clearing. She tucked him into the underbrush. The ground wasn't entirely dry, but it provided some reprieve from the torrential rain. She discovered the backpack during their long crawl. Beckworth must have grabbed it as he raced to get away from the inn with her in tow. She pulled the pack from him and pushed her arms through the straps, allowing it to fall against her back.

If her suspicions were correct and they were in France, she had some options. The only question was the year. Based on the rain and the leafless trees, it was winter or maybe early spring. Then she remembered the possibility of war and groaned.

Beckworth had passed out again. She left him as he lay. It was doubtful anyone was walking about in this weather. She considered stabbing him again, just to be sure he wouldn't wander off, or maybe just because. Instead, she stood, kicked decayed leaves over his legs to cover him, and turned toward the direction of town.

She followed the trail until she reached the main street. The docks were to her left and Guerin's Inn to her right, just as she remembered it.

She was almost to the inn when she noticed the first soldiers. Two of them leaned against a building. If they spotted her, they didn't care, but it confirmed one thing—it was no longer 1802—and England's war with Napoleon was alive and well.

When she knocked at the back door of the inn, she tried to remember the innkeeper's name. She didn't remember anyone calling him Guerin.

The door opened, and a gruff voice spoke in French. She panicked. She could only guess what the innkeeper thought of the drowned rat that stood before him. No words came to her; she didn't know French. Everyone had spoken English the last she'd been there. If they were at war, it made sense that French would be the first words spoken.

She stood, struggling for what to say, when the man grabbed her by the arms and dragged her in. He yelled, "Sofi." AJ almost cried with relief. Sofi was the innkeeper's wife.

Before she knew it, she was pushed into a chair in front of the kitchen fires. A minute later, a blanket was thrown over her drenched summer blouse and jeans. She shivered. Another minute later, a towel fell over her shoulders. Another was wrapped around her head as someone vigorously rubbed her hair in what she assumed was an attempt to dry it.

"Miss Moore. Is that you?" Sofi's worried question made AJ sigh in relief. They remembered her.

She nodded and pushed the woman's hands away so she could look up. Husband and wife stared down at her before glancing at each other.

"This is a very dangerous time to have returned. It looks like you swam across the channel." The innkeeper shook his head and wiped flour from his hands. He'd been baking bread. That explained the heavenly aroma that filled her nose and made her stomach grumble.

"I can explain. But first, I have a large favor to ask." She spoke slowly, watching their anxious expressions. When the pair glanced at each other again, AJ added, "And I can pay you."

AN HOUR LATER, Beckworth lay on a bed in the smallest room the inn had available, a fire blazing in the hearth.

AJ huddled in front of another fire in an adjacent room. Her clothes hung over the back of a chair positioned close to the hearth, next to her shoes and socks drying on the heated stones. Sofi had loaned her a dress, and though it was short at the ankles and arms, the rest fit well enough. Beckworth's backpack perched next to her on the couch as she slowly sifted through the contents.

Her concerns about finances were immediately relieved when she found the silver coins and jewelry they'd planned to return to the sisters. She'd save what she could, but her survival came first. She never met the sisters and didn't know why they'd taken in Beckworth, but everyone paid for the risks of their decisions. She would require transport to England, and with the war the innkeeper confirmed had begun last summer, the price would be high.

Her second request of Henri Guerin, the innkeeper, after retrieving Beckworth, was to send a message to Sebastian at the monastery. He promised to send someone as soon as the rain let up. All she could do was wait.

She'd expected to see several soldiers at the inn, but there were only three. Henri said the soldiers rotated their visits to the inns. Two dozen troops stayed in the barracks by the dock at any given time. Most of them preferred the inn across the street, which Henri was grateful for. Soldiers discouraged customers.

Feeling secure for the moment, she stared into the fire and considered her plight. If Finn and Ethan had followed her through the vortex, they should have arrived in France and shouldn't be too far from town. Not that anything had been written on how the stones worked. It was all trial and error. Her greatest fear was them landing in the middle of French soldiers. The one thing she hated most about this time period was no cell phones. Communication with England could take weeks, and with the war, possibly months.

Her mind raced with possibilities until a headache crept up her neck and pounded at the back of her skull. She couldn't jump back home without the proper incantation. She'd written it on a piece of paper that she'd stuffed in her duffel. The one she'd left in the library at home. Finn had asked her to memorize the words, but the ability to correctly pronounce the Celtic words without the instructions eluded her. Sebastian had the translations and could reconstruct the incantation. For now, she had a different mission. Find Maire. The best place to start would be Hereford. When Ethan and Finn arrived, that would be their destination. She was certain of it.

She closed her eyes, unable to focus. A short nap and she'd be good as new.

When a soft tapping from the door woke her, she groaned at her body's stiffness. She pulled the dagger strapped to her leg.

When the knob began to turn, she scurried to stand behind the door before it opened. Was Beckworth awake? She couldn't imagine him knocking. And the soldiers had ignored her when she'd run downstairs earlier for hot water.

A figure emerged, and she swung the dagger to bring the hilt down on the stranger's head. She pulled back at the last minute. The figure, shrouded under a familiar hooded cloak, was her height but with a larger girth.

When the man turned, AJ almost leaped into his arms.

Instead, when Sebastian stared at her with his whimsical smile, she slumped into his arms with a sob of relief.

2

"Your hands are cold, child." Sebastian rubbed her hands, then guided her to the sofa. "Sit. I've asked the innkeeper to bring hot tea and something for you to eat."

AJ followed him without question. She could use something to warm her. As good as it was to see the monk, she couldn't dispel the inner chill that clung to her.

Once seated in front of the fire, Sebastian lowered his hood and held her gaze for a long moment before nodding. "I had a feeling I'd not seen the last of you."

AJ laughed. "Has *The Book of Stones* given you a glimpse into the future, or have you been playing with the stones?" She said it in jest, but the monk's curious gaze made her wonder if she wasn't far from the truth.

"All in good time. Perhaps you should start with the man in the other room." He lifted an eyebrow. "The one tied to the bed."

She smirked. "You know about him."

He nodded. "Henri apprised me of the hours since a rain-soaked woman appeared at their kitchen door. I must admit, I was expecting Captain Murphy."

"It should have been." Her words, whispered softly, couldn't hide the bitterness or the longing. She wiped away a tear and blew out a shaky laugh. "It seems trouble follows the stones. I'm not quite sure where to start."

A soft knock interrupted them, and Sebastian patted her shoulder on his way to the door. A young lad scurried in, setting a tray on the table before rushing out, closing the door behind him.

AJ didn't think she could eat, but the smell of fresh bread made her nose twitch with interest.

Sebastian brought her a cup of steaming tea. "Drink this first, and then we'll have some food. Sofi told me you haven't eaten since your arrival."

She warmed her hands on the mug and stared into the fire, her thoughts whirling as she reflected on the last twelve hours. Her gut clenched whenever she remembered the last time she'd seen Finn. His fear, his anger, and his love etched on his face. They still had Ethan's stone. She had to believe they would find her, and she absently reached for the necklace that held her wedding ring.

Sebastian tried again. "Why don't you tell me what happened when you left us all those months ago."

AJ released a small chuckle. "To you, it's been over a year, but to me, only a few months have gone by." She shook her head. "I can't explain it, but time passes differently between our jumps. I don't know why."

Sebastian considered it for a moment and shrugged. "Who can explain everything we've read or experienced? Some things shall always remain a mystery. Did you arrive where you thought you would?"

"Yes. Back to the same spot we'd left." She sipped her tea and, as suggested, told Sebastian everything. Their arrival, Finn's reaction to the jump while still injured, and the life they were building. The words flew out of her mouth, and she didn't stop until the mug of tea was cold in her hands. She sipped it and grimaced.

"It sounds like a wonderful life."

She stood and took his mug, dumping the remaining cold tea in the washbasin before refilling them. The pot of tea was still warm, but she preferred her tea hot. She placed it on a ring by the hearth to heat it before settling on the sofa and pulling her legs under her.

"Our life wasn't perfect, but I was happier than anyone could be." She smiled at the monk and grasped the hand he held out.

"Except for the man who followed you to your time."

She looked up, startled by his words.

"I was at the knoll too, if you remember. I witnessed his disappearance in the fog. Maire worried about it for weeks until Ethan convinced her everything was all right."

Her smile faded, and a slow anger burned. "I won't rest until I find out how he's connected to Maire's disappearance."

The monk sat back, startled. "Maire disappeared?"

She nodded. "I realized it was Beckworth who'd been following me. Before I had a chance to tell Finn, Ethan arrived." The words tumbled out as she walked Sebastian through the events of Ethan's arrival. When everything came out jumbled, the monk made her repeat the story, this time slowing down to recount Ethan's story from when Maire and Ethan had sailed from France on the *Daphne Marie*. She told him of their arrival at the earl's estate in Hereford, their time in London, and their return to the country. It felt good to talk about Maire, and though it was a false security, it made her feel closer to her missing friend.

"The last anyone saw of her was when she departed for Peterstow, supposedly to purchase medicinal seeds she couldn't find in Hereford. When her guards returned to say she'd been taken, Ethan spent two months searching, but neither he nor

Thomas could find a trace of her or who took her. With nothing left to lose, he jumped to the future to see if we could find something from history..." She stumbled over the words, then tried again. "I know it sounds weird, but Ethan hoped that something that occurred during this timeline might have been written down, and we'd be able to find it in my time." She shook her head. "I've lived it, and it still seems strange."

She released a sigh and sat back. She hadn't stopped talking once she began, and other than getting her to repeat the story, Sebastian never interrupted. Now that it was all out, she wasn't sure what to do. She assumed she was numb from the events of the last two days, starting when she found Beckworth standing in the kitchen at the inn. Her struggle with him before being tied up, Finn and Ethan rescuing her, Beckworth's capture and surprising escape, and her misfortune of Beckworth discovering the Heart Stone dangling from her necklace. Then zap—the two of them landing two hundred years in the past. And worst of all, arriving in France at a time of war. Numb didn't even begin to cover it.

When she glanced at Sebastian, he gazed into the fire, but if she had to guess, his thoughts were miles away, hidden behind a solemn poker face. He finally glanced at her and smiled. "I could use another cup of tea." He stood, and for a moment, he appeared more fragile than she'd ever seen him. Had it been a mistake to get him involved again?

But what other choice did she have?

"Come drink some tea, child, and I'll tell you what I know of the druid book."

She jumped up. "Ethan said Maire might have been taken because of that book. What do you know?"

His eyes twinkled as he held out a hand to the empty chair. "You've haven't touched Sofi's soup. I think you'll like it."

AJ grumbled at his transparent attempt to get her to eat, but when her stomach growled loudly enough for Sebastian to give her a knowing smile, she complied.

"Fine." She sipped the soup, grudgingly admitting it was tasty. When she broke off a piece of the remaining bread and pointed it at him, she said, "Now that I'm eating, tell me everything you know. Every time I hear the book mentioned, I get this nagging feeling I should be remembering something."

He nodded but cautiously changed the topic. "You never mentioned if Ethan ever discovered a link to Maire's whereabouts."

AJ finished chewing a bite of bread, then washed it down with tea. Henri's bread was as good as she remembered it. She smiled at the monk. "It was your journals."

"Mine." His shock lifted his eyebrows until they almost touched his hairline.

"I'll have to tell you about the historians." She thought about it. "Well, maybe I shouldn't. I guess it doesn't matter. But in two hundred years, historians will find part of *The Book of Stones* and your journals."

He smiled. "So Ethan was correct to search the future to reveal the past."

AJ snorted and tore off another piece of bread. "It doesn't get any easier to hear, but yes. You received a letter from Elizabeth Ratliff." She sat up. "Or maybe that hasn't happened yet. What's the date?"

He placed a hand on hers. "It's mid-February, 1804. I received her letter months ago. I'm aware that Sir Ratliff was killed, and I worry about the fate of the Heart Stone."

She shrugged. "It must be okay. I still have it, so it must still find its way through the keepers."

"The keepers?"

"Just one more thing to share with you, but that will keep for now. Tell me about the book. I assume it's as Ethan said, that it was written by the druid who time-traveled."

Before Sebastian could say a word, a loud crash sounded from the room next door.

AJ jumped up. "Beckworth."

3

———

Beckworth woke with a start, the room stifling, the sweat drenching him. When his vision cleared, he moved an arm and found it bound to the bed. Not tightly. He had some movement, a few inches. His legs were free, for whatever good that did. He glanced around and tried to recall what happened.

Bits and pieces of images flitted through his aching head. Rushing out of the inn with AJ. Fear of Ethan catching him. The fog returning and the painful white light. Lying in the rain, pain radiating from his shoulder. She'd stabbed him again. He cursed and refocused on his surroundings.

The room seemed familiar, but after so many years and so many inns, they all did. The hearth blazed with a fire, and the walls were aged. He remembered voices—French. Was it possible he was at the inn near the monastery? He relaxed and sighed with relief. He might be bound, but he was in his own time. Step one accomplished.

Why was he bound?

Then he remembered AJ yelling at him. She'd kicked him. Repeatedly. That would explain the pain in his side, but his shoulder hurt worse. He growled. She'd stabbed him again as the fog arrived. It had been a mistake to bring her, and now it was too late.

He stared at the ceiling. How did she get him to the inn? He snorted. What story had she weaved that would keep him trussed up? Another thought hit him. Murphy's men had stayed at the inn for some time and had probably paid well. Would they remember the little wench? AJ was difficult to forget, but most of the time she'd been dressed like a boy.

What year was it? Maybe Murphy and Hughes were already here, following behind through the mist.

Panic set in, and he lifted his head. Mistake. His vision blurred, and nausea clenched his stomach. Then he noticed the tray on the bedside table. A teapot and mug. A bowl. There had been short bursts of wakefulness when someone fed him. A young girl, eyes wide, her hands shaking.

He remembered AJ. She had run a towel over his head before spoon feeding him. For one awful second, he pictured Edith and then Louise peering down at him, their smiles cloying as they fed him their magical elixirs.

He must have been delirious, probably suffering from an infection. He remembered the anger in AJ's eyes as she drove the knife into him. After all the months trying to get home, and now that he was close, he'd die in an old French inn tied to a bed.

A terrible thirst overcame him, and for the first time, he noted something else. Besides his need to quench his parched throat, his stomach ached for sustenance. He reached for the tray, but the rope binding him wasn't long enough for him to grasp the mug. It had taken every bit of energy to raise his arm. He'd never be able to hold a mug without both hands.

He tried again, his fingers stretching to touch the tray. He grasped the edge and managed to move it an inch before he fell back, trying to catch his breath. A laugh choked out. Even a cup of tea didn't come easy.

Unwilling to give up, he shifted his body to his right and gained another inch, the mug almost within his reach. He leaned forward, the rope around his wrist digging into his flesh. His hand trembled from the exertion. He smiled when his fingers touched the mug, then it slid as the tray lost its balance and tumbled.

It clattered to the ground before he could stop it. He fell back on the bed and shouted with frustration.

A minute later, the door burst open. AJ stared down at him and the tray of broken pottery.

"Damn it, Beckworth." She knelt to pick up the tray. "Why didn't you just yell for help like the last time?"

He was too tired to lift his head, but he rolled it to one side to watch her. She wore a simple brown dress, and her hair hung loose. Even in a dowdy gown with shadows under her eyes, she couldn't hide her allure.

She set the tray and remnants of his last meal on a table by the window.

"Thirsty." His voice was scratchy. He swallowed, though it was difficult with his dry mouth. "Thirsty."

She stared at him, one eyebrow raised as she assessed him. Somehow satisfied, she found a mug that hadn't been broken and poured water from a pitcher. She bent over him, the mug near his face. "If you don't lift your head, you'll be wearing most of this. I doubt you'll enjoy lying in wet clothes."

He obeyed and almost cried when the cool water trickled down his throat. After only a few swallows, she pulled it away.

"More." His voice sounded stronger.

She shook her head. "Give it a minute. If you drink too fast, you'll throw it up. You haven't eaten or drank much since we arrived."

He laid his head back and noticed the older man hovering just inside the door. Beckworth had seen him before but couldn't remember where. The thick, plain robe suggested he was one of the monks from the monastery.

"Are you ready for more?" AJ brought the mug to his lips, and Beckworth drank as much as she offered.

"Should I have them bring up another tray?" The monk's words were low and soothing. If he thought it strange for Beckworth to be tied to a bed in an old inn, he gave no sign of it.

"Maybe a bit of stew and a chunk of bread." AJ returned to the water basin while the monk retrieved the tray. She carried a small basin that she set on the bedside table. "What do you remember?"

She squeezed out a wet towel and wiped his brow. The cool rag felt good, and he closed his eyes.

"You stabbed me."

"And you dragged me back in time with you. I'm not sure I'd call that even."

He chuckled and opened his eyes. He expected to see anger or loathing. Any sign that reflected her distaste for him, but her expression was void of any emotion. "It seems we are fated to be together."

She snorted. "Not hardly. It's more like I stepped in something I can't quite scrape off. I wonder what that says about you."

He smiled as she wiped his face. "Story of my life, I'm afraid." He lifted his arm with whatever slim strength had returned. "Is this necessary?"

She quirked a brow and smiled. "Absolutely."

A light knock sounded, and they turned to find a young lad standing in the doorway.

"Hello, Marcel," AJ cooed. "Do you mind refreshing the water?"

"No, Miss AJ. Shall I bring more towels? Maybe some food?"

"The towels would be wonderful. Sebastian is seeing to the food."

Marcel nodded, grabbed the pitcher and soiled towels before disappearing.

The two remained in silence until Sebastian returned. Beckworth's mouth watered and his stomach growled as he lifted his head to see what was in the bowl.

Sebastian gave him a smile that seemed more an apology. "The stew has been watered down. I think it will settle better until you get used to it."

AJ fed Beckworth like a small child. After several mouthfuls, his stomach protested the greasy meal, and it lurched. He thought he was going to be sick. AJ set the bowl aside and forced him to take two bites of the bread. She then demanded he drink water, even though he was positive it would urge everything back up.

"Now lay back. Your stomach should be fine. We'll try again after you've slept." She placed the leftover stew by the fire to keep warm then checked his restraints. "You need more rest. You have a slight fever, but it seems under control for now. The shoulder is healing, and unfortunately, it appears you'll be good as new in another day or two."

She stood over him, and the barest hint of a smile suggested she was pleased with his situation. "I'm in the room next door, and Marcel checks in every hour. Try not to break anything else."

AJ swept out of the room, but the monk remained. He stared down at Beckworth, a hand rubbing his chin. He fussed with something on the tray, then lifted a mug toward him.

"I'm sorry to see you in such a state. I've mixed a few herbs to help. Drink this."

The monk helped Beckworth raise his head to drink. The

concoction tasted sweet until a bitter aftertaste made him grimace.

Sebastian nodded. "It has a bit of an unpleasant bite. You won't notice it for long."

Beckworth's vision blurred, and the monk split into two separate individuals. The room turned fuzzy.

"Sleep well."

Beckworth tried to stay awake, but his lids grew heavy, and then the edges of his vision turned dark as the room faded away.

AJ LIFTED her head when Sebastian returned. She'd been studying a timepiece she'd discovered in Beckworth's backpack. The watch would be considered vintage even in this time period. "Is he sleeping?"

The monk chuckled. "Oh, yes. He should sleep through the evening."

"Are you sure the monastery is the best place?"

Sebastian settled into a chair by the fire and took the proffered cup of tea from AJ. He wiped his brow and sipped. "After Maire and Ethan left, General Clermont arrived to oversee the running of the monastery. When the conflict with England started, it was assumed he'd remain here because of the port, but within a month, he was called away. He left his second-in-command in charge.

"Fortunately, with the war, the monastery is no longer of import to Napoleon. Major Frain, who has a fondness for drink, set up lodging at the inn across from the docks. We're on our own, so it won't be difficult to install you in a room below the main floor. With your plain dress, you'll fit in with the staff, and the kitchen and yard should be available to you. Several of the staff remember you with great fondness."

AJ dropped her gaze. She wondered how fond of her they'd be when they discovered she was keeping a man tied to a bed. Even hidden downstairs, it wouldn't take long for word to spread. The question was how long they would have to stay. "I'm going to need passage to England. Is that possible with the war?"

The monk scratched his head. "With the troops at the dock, Major Frain believes their mere presence is keeping the smugglers away."

AJ could understand their position. "That makes sense. What smuggler would sail into a port held by French troops?"

"Exactly. Yet, the port remains busy, and very little happens other than drunken fights for the troops to break up. However, many of the ships run contraband, but when they arrive at port to take on fresh supplies, they keep their holds empty of illicit cargo."

AJ snickered. "Smart. Once they have supplies, they stop someplace else for their cargo." She considered her options. "Do you know any of the captains that run the English blockades?"

Sebastian's grin was the one he saved for when he was planning something. Her spirits rose. "I have a thought or two on that. First, we must leave the inn." He stood and brushed off his robes. "Get some sleep. I have a few arrangements to make but will return before first light. Be ready to leave."

AJ glanced around the room. Other than Beckworth's backpack and her jeans and shirt, there wasn't much to pack. "I'll be ready."

After Sebastian left, AJ returned to Beckworth's room and found him fast asleep, spittle at the corners of his mouth. He was going to be hopping mad once he could think clearly. She double-checked his bindings then went downstairs to find Sofi. Since she arrived without her prepared duffel, AJ would need a few things. If she was leaving before the stores opened, she would need help with the shopping.

Once back in her room, she crawled into bed and turned on her side to watch the fire. She didn't know how Sebastian would get her on a ship, but she had to be ready at a moment's notice. But should she leave? She'd been in France for almost a full day, and she'd hoped Finn and Ethan would have arrived by now. Where were they? Still at Westcliffe? Maybe they jumped to a different time.

She pushed down her rising panic. The one thing she wouldn't do was become as paralyzed as she'd been the first time Finn had brought her back in time. She had a mission. Find Maire. If she could get to England, she could get to the earl in Hereford. She had money, all she needed was transportation. And above all else, she required protection. She already had several ideas on how to hide her dagger, but another thought occurred to her. The man in the next room. As much as she loathed and distrusted him, they bore a mutual objective—to discover what was happening at Waverly. What would she do about him?

AJ HAD TOSSED ALL NIGHT, waking to turbulent thoughts she couldn't quell. Beckworth dragging her out of Westcliffe, the jump, finding herself back at the inn without Finn. Where was he? Sebastian was the only person capable of holding her together when doubts crept in. Unwilling to relive the last twenty-four hours one more time, she dragged herself from bed, added wood to the fire, and curled up on the couch, a thin blanket covering her. She'd concocted a skeleton of a plan the night before. As she stared into the fire, she reworked her idea as Finn did, walking through various scenarios and creating alternatives for the sketchier areas. She eventually dozed until she heard the tapping at the door.

She opened it cautiously, pleased to see Sebastian. Now that she had a working plan, she was anxious to get to the next step.

The monk glanced at her makeshift bed on the sofa and the messed bed. "Are you packed?"

AJ lifted the backpack, where she'd stuffed her jeans and shirt along with Beckworth's original items. She gave the room one last swift glance before following Sebastian to the next room. Two young men stood by the door.

"This is Tomas and Jules. They'll help with your friend. I've already been in to check on him, and he's still quite groggy." Sebastian opened the door, peered in, then waved for the men to follow.

AJ moved in behind them and walked straight to the window. She opened it and let the chilled winter air wash over her. The rain had left a clean earthen scent behind, and she sucked it in. She was ready. She could do this.

By the time she turned back to the room, the men were already moving Beckworth out, one carrying his feet, the other his shoulders, Beckworth's head bent toward his chest, tipped to one side. If he was faking, he was doing a good job of it. Sebastian followed close behind while AJ did a final sweep of the room before shutting the door behind her.

The smell of Henri's fresh bread made her sorry she hadn't eaten more the night before when she had the chance. The main room was quiet, but a large fire blazed in the hearth. The men carried Beckworth toward the main door, but AJ veered for the kitchen.

"Henri, are you there?" She stepped hesitantly through the door, not wanting to intrude.

The squat man appeared from behind another door, probably the pantry, and smiled. "I see you had early visitors."

AJ stared at the floor, not sure how much this man knew. She also didn't want him getting into trouble with the French troops.

"Don't worry, Miss AJ. You have safe harbor here. We are a close community, even with the uncouth men that come through our doors. We think the world of Sebastian. And you and Captain Murphy have always been kind."

"Thank you, Henri. I don't want to be a burden."

"If you want to see a burden, that French major is all the further you need to go," Sofi responded for her husband, stepping out from the pantry, carrying two flour sacks. "We'd all like to see him gone, but then we might get someone worse." She set the sacks down and crossed herself. "Is your guest gone?"

"Yes. Sebastian just had him carried out." She smiled at the couple, who continued their chores as they spoke with her.

Henri pulled a tray of fresh bread from the oven while Sofi stirred a pot of porridge. A slab of bacon sat on the counter, ready for cooking. AJ could almost smell the cooked bacon while her stomach grumbled. The back door creaked open as Marcel ran in with a basket of eggs, nodded at AJ, and rushed through to the main room.

"I was wondering if I could ask for another small favor. I have some items I need, but it's too early for the shops. I don't know when I'll be able to get back here. I don't have transportation from the monastery."

Sofi wiped her hands. "Tell me what you need."

AJ handed her a list that she'd scratched out before Sebastian arrived.

Sofi studied the page. "I can send Ella to the mercantile when it opens. Then Marcel can bring it with the other supplies we send to the monastery. Will mid-morning be soon enough?"

"More than enough. Thank you so much, Sofi." She hugged the woman and kissed her cheek. While Sofi was hugging her back, AJ tucked a small package in the woman's pocket. Sofi would never have accepted the silver necklace if AJ just handed it to her. The necklace would fetch a good price and more than pay for her requested items. The extra money would make a nice addition to what she knew Sebastian must have paid Henri. They'd both done so much for her, not just in the last day, but when she'd been here a year ago. And she was fairly certain this would be the last time she'd ever see them.

4

———

They traveled an hour west of town to reach the monastery. Sebastian pulled the wagon into the side courtyard. This was the same courtyard where Finn had killed the duke in his own ornate carriage, or so AJ was told. The two lads removed Beckworth from the cart and hustled him inside. Sebastian shuttled AJ through a side door that led to a hall. They took a right, walked through a busy kitchen where inquisitive eyes lowered when she passed, then down a short hall to a door that led to the subbasements.

The monastery had been built on the edge of a rocky cliff that overlooked the Celtic Sea. The main structure was two stories, but under the monastery, three additional floors had been carved into the stone. The main basement held several small rooms that had been used by the novitiates—those in training before taking their vows—back in the early days of the monastery, before its decline during the Revolution. Anyone who found their way to this floor would assume it to be the lowest floor in the building.

The lowest two floors were only accessible through secret passages and doorways. While these floors had been widely known three hundred years ago when the monastery had first been built, time and changes in political powers had erased the knowledge of this part of the monastery to only a small handful. Not even the duke had been aware of the passages until one of his men had stumbled upon a hidden door by sheer luck. With the duke and his men dead or returned to England, the passages were once again safely concealed.

Sebastian settled AJ into a familiar room. She'd only been in it once, for about two seconds. The monk had led Maire and AJ through it the first time he'd popped his head out from behind a bookcase in an upstairs sitting room, taking them down a dark staircase leading to this room. The passageway on this side was also hidden behind a bookcase, although simpler in design and make. The room provided AJ an avenue for either hiding in the staircase or escaping through the upper-level room if she was unable to make her way into the subbasement passages.

The room held few amenities—a single bed, a table with two chairs, and the bookcase. As soon as Sebastian left to gather more lanterns and linen, she collapsed onto the bed and fell asleep. When she woke, a lantern shone from its perch on the table next to two wrapped packages.

Being in a room with no window, she had no idea what time it was. She didn't think she'd slept the day away, and since she'd barely eaten the day before, her growling stomach didn't tell her much. After quickly unwrapping the packages to see what Ella had bought for her, she retraced her earlier steps back to the kitchen. She slipped silently through the halls, unsure who she'd run into. When she entered the kitchen, a stout woman, with thick arms and gray hair sticking out of her loose bun, dropped a kettle on the table and smiled.

"Ah, Miss AJ, Sebastian asked me to keep a tray ready for you."

Jeanne, the cook who had been hired during the duke's

tenure in the monastery, was a no-nonsense woman who seemed to have a strong loyalty to Sebastian. If she thought it strange that Sebastian was keeping a woman and an unconscious man in the basement, she kept it to herself. AJ scanned the tray as she returned to her room. A large pot of tea and food that would last throughout the day. At least she wouldn't starve. She had a busy day planned.

She began by sorting out Ella's purchases, first laying out one muddy-brown dress and one the color of dark jade. They weren't fine enough to wear to Waverly, but they were more than a servant would wear. The rest of the items included a pair of pants sized for a young man, a small shirt, an overcoat, a hat, shoes and underclothes, a small bolt of fabric, and a sewing kit. The last item was a canvas bag for traveling.

When she opened the bag, AJ discovered a package of bread, cheese, dried meat, sweet treats, and a skin of wine. Sofi's way of saying she'd found the gift AJ had left her. She laughed. They all seemed to be fattening her up. She placed the food back in the canvas bag. It would store well in the basement's cool temperature. Hopefully, she wouldn't find herself hiding in the dank hidden staircase with nothing but her bag of food and wine to keep her company while French troops scoured the basement.

Returning to the clothes, she tried on the shoes. They fit reasonably well and were functional. Next, she reviewed all the underclothes, deemed them satisfactory, and set them all aside with the shoes except for the chemise, which she laid on the bed. She tried on the shirt. The shoulders hung an inch beyond her own, and the sleeves were too long but could be rolled up. She folded the shirt and placed it with the undergarments.

The pants were loose but manageable and would hide the fact she was a woman. They were laid next to the chemise on the bed. The dresses didn't fit any better than the one she wore. The bodice fit well enough, but the sleeves were too short and the hem too high. There wasn't anything she could do about that, and it wasn't as if she were going to any parties. They only needed to be passable. If necessary, she could find some boots that might distract from the short hemline.

Once the main table was cleared, she laid out the bolt of muslin. Using shears that Jeanne had lent her, she began cutting the fabric. For the next few hours, she sewed the fabric into six pouches of various sizes. After careful consideration, she stripped ribbon from one of the dresses to use as a drawstring for each pouch. By the time she'd finished the pouches, her neck ached, her eyes were crossed from staring at stitches in the dim light, and her fingers smarted from where she kept poking them. Sewing didn't run in the family, but as she munched on her left-over breakfast and washed it down with cold tea, she reviewed her handiwork. The edges looked horrible, but they were strong enough for their purpose.

Sebastian brought a fresh pot of tea in the afternoon. When he advised her that Beckworth was resting comfortably, she'd been so busy fussing with her mediocre sewing that she'd simply snorted at the monk's news. She barely noticed him close the door quietly behind him.

Her afternoon was spent tacking the pouches into the clothing so they were strong enough to hold but easy enough to cut or rip out in an emergency. The larger pouches would hide her dagger and were sewn behind the pockets of the pants and dresses. She slit a small hole in each pocket so she could reach the pouches without too much hand movement. The smaller pouches were sewn into the chemise and dresses. She touched the necklace around her neck. Before she left the monastery, she would tuck the necklace, strung with the Heart Stone and her wedding ring, into one of the small pouches. She would move the necklace whenever she changed clothing. The dagger and necklace would never leave her person. Not willingly.

At the end of the day, Sebastian returned.

"Dare I ask what all the sewing was about?" He'd brought a tray of roasted pork, potatoes with onions and herbs, cabbage, and fresh bread. He laid out the plates and cups while AJ poured wine from a jug.

"I made secret pouches for some valuables I don't want to lose. I don't know if they'll work, but it was the only thing I could think of." AJ savored a slice of pork, then licked the juice from her fingers. She'd barely touched the food from her morning tray and was starving.

Sebastian shook his head. "Very smart indeed." He chewed a bite of bread and studied her thoughtfully. "I think one more evening of a sleeping potion, and then Beckworth needs to get on his feet."

AJ picked at the cabbage. "Is he well enough?"

He nodded. "The shoulder will hurt for several days, but it's healed enough. There's no sign of infection." He hesitated as she pondered his statement.

When she looked up, her brow rose. "What else?"

"We should untie him. He'll stay locked in the room. I have two men who would be happy to guard his door. He needs to regain his strength."

AJ sighed and finished a few bites before glancing up at Sebastian. "He's dangerous."

The monk nodded. "And he wants to get to England."

"About that. What are your thoughts? I imagine it won't be easy getting two English people past the blockade."

"I've been considering your options." He tapped his fingers on the table in between tiny sips of wine. "After dinner, I want to show you something. Then you can make up your mind how quickly you need to get to England."

She wasn't sure she liked the sound of his cryptic statement. He knew she had to return to England. It wasn't until after he'd left to finish some monastery business that she began to worry. The last thing she needed was Sebastian trying to talk her out of her plans.

BECKWORTH RAISED HIS HEAD, waited for his vision to clear, then scanned the room. He was still tied down. He'd tested his range of freedom when he'd woken earlier, still groggy and weak, but had been unable to keep his eyes open. His mind was clearer now, enough to notice that his accommodations had changed. The bed was harder than the last one, there were no windows, and it smelled of mildew. None were good signs.

He wasn't at the inn anymore.

Except it was still the monk who fed him and forced him to drink the drugged tea. The tea must have been a sleeping potion. It was the only thing that made sense with his inability to keep track of time. Yet, he grudgingly admitted he felt better than he had since arriving in the fog. His shoulder still ached, but it was more a dull throb. And though he hated to admit it, even if he hadn't been tied down, he didn't have the strength to roll over.

He took a deep breath and caught the slightest hint of salt in the dampness. They were close to the sea. If he had to guess, he'd bet they'd brought him to the monastery.

He closed his eyes when the door opened. He peered at his guest through slitted eyes and recognized the monk. He carried a tray that probably held another bowl of soup and a mug of tea. But as the tray grew closer, he swore he could smell savory meat. The tray was placed on the table next to his bed, and Sebastian pulled a chair over.

"You can open your eyes. I know you're awake." Sebastian placed a napkin across Beckworth's chest. "I have some stew for you. I think it's time to eat something more substantial to gain strength."

Beckworth chuckled as he struggled with his restraints to a more upright position. He grimaced at the stab of pain in his shoulder. "I thought you wanted me weak." His voice came out gravelly, and he coughed to clear the phlegm. "I'll be less trouble."

The monk laughed, which surprised Beckworth. All the time he'd been in the monastery with the duke, Beckworth hadn't seen much of the quiet monk.

"We need you healed as quickly as possible, and you required rest. From what AJ tells me, the transport through the fog takes the strength out of the healthiest of people." Sebastian shrugged as he stirred the bowl of stew and handed it to Beckworth. "That knife wound took quite a bit out of you."

Beckworth set the bowl in his lap, and with a shaky hand, slurped the first spoonful, surprised at how good it tasted. The simple effort drained what little strength he had, and he rested his head against the wall. "The woman keeps stabbing me."

Sebastian raised a brow while he poured a cup of tea from a small teapot. "I admit, I haven't heard your side of the story, but have you considered that your actions may have warranted some reprisal?"

He snickered as he worked another spoonful of stew in his mouth, sloshing meaty juice onto the napkin. "I try not to analyze my actions. What's done is done."

"There you have it. Without proper reflection on past actions, it's impossible to recognize the correct path forward." He handed the mug to Beckworth.

When he didn't take it, Sebastian set it down and waited for him to take another few swallows of stew. Then, with some pitiful resistance, took the bowl away.

"I wasn't finished."

"Let that settle. It's been a couple of days since you've had solid food. You can have more after you drink some tea."

"With more sleeping potion? I don't think so."

The monk pulled his chair closer to the bed. "Let's consider your situation. You're an Englishman in France. France is at war with England."

Beckworth opened and closed his mouth, then nodded.

"The year is 1804. The month is February. You've been injured and can barely move. Do you understand?"

"I've been gone almost two years.' He'd ignored everything Murphy and Hughes had mentioned about the timeline. He hadn't cared; his only focus had been on getting home. He was weak as a drowned rat and without a schilling. His gaze flickered around the room. "I had a pack with me."

The monk smiled. "That must be the pack AJ keeps with her."

Beckworth closed his eyes and dropped his head into the pillow. Damn that woman. "I have no funds and no way to get to England."

"Now you're beginning to understand the full weight of your predicament." When he offered Beckworth the mug again, he took it.

"So how long do you plan on keeping me drugged and compliant?" He sipped the tea, which smelled of mint, but there was an earthy aftertaste. Valerian root mixed with some type of mint and a bit of honey. At least he was familiar with the effects.

Sebastian patted his arm. "One more evening of the tea. You'll need to regain your strength. In the morning, we'll remove your restraints so you can take a few steps. I'll warn you now, it will take some time before you'll have full mobility in your arm."

"You want me to gain my strength?"

"I may just be a monk, but I have many duties and can't keep nursing you."

Beckworth ate his stew and drank his tea as he considered his situation. He needed to get to England. He was forgetting something. Murphy and Hughes had been ranting about something while they beat him. What was it? Maire. Something about her being kidnapped again. That would mean AJ would want to get to England. He groaned. Would he be forever plagued by her?

Once he finished eating the stew, his stomach gurgled, but he felt better. The tea was already having an effect, so he meekly settled back down as the monk picked up the tray.

"You should have a peaceful sleep. We'll discuss your situation in the morning."

Before he lost consciousness, Beckworth returned to his earlier thoughts. Maire was missing. When had Hughes returned to the future? Hughes had been here with Maire when he'd been caught in the fog with Murphy and AJ. Had Ethan traveled to the future because Maire had gone missing? What would that accomplish? Unless he wanted to bring Murphy back to hunt for her. He snorted. Maire probably just wanted to get away from the insufferable bore.

His eyes drooped. If AJ wanted to get to England, that was a good thing, right? His thoughts grew fuzzy, yet something else nagged. Why would someone kidnap Maire if the duke was dead? If only he could get his thoughts in order, but the monk's tea was working faster than he expected. Her disappearance must have something to do with those damned stones. Everything came back to them, and he wished, not for the first time, he'd never heard of them.

Another thought, darker than the rest, flitted across his groggy consciousness. Dugan had gotten away from the battle at the monastery. If Beckworth wasn't already pale from his injury, the color would have surely drained from his face at his next thought. There was a slim possibility. No. Dugan wouldn't do that, or had the duke set something in motion before his death? Dugan was fanatically loyal to the duke's family. Well, most of them. His ugly laugh was no more than a puff of air and spittle on his lips. If Dugan had fled to Austria, then the game had definitely changed.

5
___

AJ stretched her muscles, closed Maire's journal, and stared out the window to the sea beyond. She'd missed a day of fresh air while bent over her sewing. AJ had watched Maire perform minor mending while they'd gotten to know each other at Waverly, and she'd been the inspiration for AJ's pouches. Maire's luggage had hidden compartments everywhere, and AJ had watched Maire repair one. She laughed. She'd even watched Finn mend the sails.

The laughter died, and a deep, mournful ache filled her. *Where are you?* It had been over a day since she'd arrived and not a word from him or Ethan. They would have followed, but where—and when—had they landed? The urge to reach for her cell phone added to her deep frustration. She would have to renew her patience for the slow communication in this century.

She ran a hand through her hair. Unable to cope with wondering where her husband was, she stood and gazed around the small chamber. Sebastian had left her there to read while he finished other business. She brushed her fingers over her dress. Without reaching into the pocket, she couldn't feel the Heart

Stone or her wedding ring through the thickness of the fabric, but it calmed her to know they were close.

Sebastian had given her Maire's journal to read. She hadn't learned anything new about *The Book of Stones*. However, there were several portions of text that caught her attention. AJ confirmed her suspicion that Maire believed specific information about the incantations had purposely been left out of the book. Maire had also marked her single reference to the torc with a question mark in the margin. What it meant, AJ had no idea.

The most intriguing part of Maire's journal was her sparse references to a second book. Maire never called it by name nor mentioned it being written by a druid. If she knew Maire half as well as she thought, she'd have to admit that Maire hadn't been truthful in her journal. No. That wasn't right. She'd been more secretive than untruthful. Her friend had become as skittish as the druids—unwilling to leave too much in writing.

AJ left the room, journal in hand, and wandered down the hall to stretch her legs. Sebastian found her after her second wrong turn.

"Ah, there you are. I'm sorry I took so long." Sebastian wiped his forehead with a handkerchief. "Without proper stewardship, I'm afraid the running of the monastery has fallen on me."

"It's nice to see you have other monks here."

Sebastian smiled. "All we've ever wanted was to get back to our mission. Though I'm not sure it will ever be the same."

She followed him but was disappointed when it appeared they were going back toward the basement.

"I thought you might want to stretch your legs after being cooped up in your room all day."

Her spirits rose, thinking he would take her to the courtyard. "I thought you wanted to keep us hidden from the troops."

He gave her a sly grin. "I was thinking more of an underground stroll."

Her shoulders slumped, but she dutifully followed him back toward the door that led downstairs. She remained quiet as he passed the cell where Finn had been tortured, and she sighed when she noticed they were heading to his secret room. The room where Sebastian had first shown Maire and her *The Book of Stones*. Maire had spent weeks and eventually months transcribing the book from there. When she saw the statue that hid the entrance, a wave of nostalgia overcame her. She could almost hear Finn's raspy voice and feel his arm around her when she helped his broken body stumble from the room. She'd been so afraid, not for the battle raging upstairs with the duke's men, but for Finn and whether he'd heal. At the time, she'd thought she'd have to leave him. Now she was back but without him.

Sebastian stopped long enough to take Maire's journal from her and deposit it in his room. Then he took her elbow and steered her left down another hallway. After two more turns, she recognized the path. By the next right turn, dampness seeped into her bones, and the smell of wet earth grew stronger. This passage led to the outer iron door. The door that opened to a small landing and a cliff that stretched down to the rocky ocean below and up a path to the main road. Maybe she'd get some fresh air after all.

Sebastian stopped at an intersection of stone corridors. His torch was a blessing, but she still wrapped her arms around her to ward off the quickly chilling air. She should have asked Sofi to buy her a shawl.

"If you remember," Sebastian began as he pointed with the torch, "To go to the outer door, you would make a right here."

AJ nodded, refusing to stare at the menacing shadow the

torchlight created behind Sebastian. The tunnels had always creeped her out, even with Sebastian at her side.

"If you were to go straight, there are a number of smaller chambers, but the passage ends about a hundred yards farther up. We're going to the left."

That raised AJ's curiosity. *What was he up to?* Not that she didn't enjoy the walk, but hustling down dark passages didn't compare to a stroll through scented gardens. The rocky ledge outside the iron door would be preferable. They couldn't have walked more than fifty feet before Sebastian came to an alcove with a simple stone bench. It seemed an odd place to put a bench. Maybe it was meant for someone to rest after walking for hours, lost in the tunnels. She grimaced at the thought.

Sebastian reached beyond the bench to a stone motif on the wall. He ran his hand below it to the third stone and pushed in. A rush of air blew out from her right where part of the wall had been pushed in a bare inch. Sebastian and his secret doors.

She followed him through the doorway, and Sebastian lit several candles. This room was larger than his personal secret chamber, but sparser. A wooden table dominated the room, running its entire length. Over a dozen chairs fit around the table and a long sideboard occupied one wall. Several sconces lined the walls, but they were empty except for two unlit torches. The only light came from Sebastian's torch and the candles on the table.

"This is where the syndicate meets."

AJ wasn't sure she'd heard that right. "The syndicate?"

Sebastian pulled on the bottom of his ear, seeming to select his words carefully. "I imagine there's a better way to say it, but it's easier to just get to the point." He stared at up her. "The syndicate is a network of smugglers."

She laughed. "Smugglers?" When he responded with a

simple grin, she sank to one of the chairs. There were dozens of rooms that ran throughout the tunnels, including the floor beneath them. When she'd been here the last time, Sebastian told her of the cargo and political refugees that had been hidden in the rooms. But that had been decades, even centuries earlier.

"I'll tell you the rest of it over a cup of tea, but I wanted you to be aware of this room in case you required another place to hide."

"Why don't you use your own chamber?"

His jovial laugh filled the room. "My dear, they're smugglers. You don't think I'd give them access to the treasures of the monastery."

AJ wasn't sure whether to laugh with him or question his sanity. When he touched her shoulder, she stood and followed him from the room and back to the intersection. Instead of turning to go back to the monastery, Sebastian continued straight toward the outer door. They walked to what she remembered as being the halfway point. Sebastian stopped in front of an aged, wooden door and reached into his pocket, retrieving an iron ring filled with skeleton keys. It took only a moment for him to find the correct key to unlock the door. When she stood on tiptoes to look over his shoulder, her eyes widened at the number of crates stacked within.

"There are several rooms filled with crates like this. We're expecting a ship in the next day or so."

"I don't understand."

"This is how you'll get to England."

<hr>

ONCE BACK IN Sebastian's room, AJ stared at the bookshelf that once held *The Book of Stones*. Sebastian had since disassembled it and hidden it deeper within the monastery. The monk set a cup of tea in front of her and placed a knitted wrap around her shoulders. The chills had begun somewhere in the tunnels, and she'd been visibly shaking by the time they reached his secret room.

"You're telling me Jamie is on his way here with the *Daphne Marie*?" AJ asked the question once her teeth stopped chattering. The temperature in the tunnels had been cold enough to store food, but reality settled in at the mention of her old friend and Finn's ship. She was really here, and this was all really happening. And now smuggling.

Sebastian sat next to her, a mug of tea in his hands. "Not long after the war started, word spread of smugglers transporting goods between England and France. It hadn't taken long for merchants to feel the squeeze of the war on their own profits. The French patrols are persistent, and the Royal Navy retains a large presence, but the channel is vast. Talk in the taverns mentioned myriad routes and ports used for running the blockade."

AJ nodded. "That makes sense. Each side stays focused on their enemy. If a smuggler runs into their path, that's one thing, but I doubt they'd be actively pursued."

"The traffic has only increased." Sebastian opened a ledger. "These are the stores that have run through the monastery over the last several months."

He'd been busy. AJ recognized Sebastian's concise writing over several pages of inventory. "All of that ran through here? But how? The stairs to the sea were destroyed by weather."

"We've restored them. From the road as well as to the sea."

"Why would you take such risks? And right under the nose of the French army."

"The war has a long reach, and already many suffer, whether

you're a soldier or a farmer trying to put food on the table and clothes on your children." He flipped through the pages. "For every crate that goes through the monastery, the village benefits. Either from trading their own goods or by earning wages through labor—building the stairs, moving the crates, and so forth."

She laughed, sitting up to get a better look at the list of goods. The chills had been replaced by excitement at finding a way to England. "Most of these items aren't made or grown locally."

The monk shook his head. "No. Some of our local products are included in shipments to England, but most move through trade routes established throughout France, including Paris. We move perishables first and then the hardened goods. Most are smuggled within carts filled with other stores. The townspeople make good money, but we're very careful to not overspend. While the troops stationed here might be drunk more often than sober, they're not complete dolts. However, with them stationed at the port, we have an advantage."

"How often do ships come through here?"

"About once a month. We have a strong syndicate with quite a lot of cargo coming and going. We have to be careful to not draw attention with the number of carts that travel back and forth from the monastery. We use the route that bypasses the town as often as we can, but the roads can be difficult for the carts."

"I don't understand why Jamie would go through this risk."

"Jamie works for Mr. Hensley."

The mention of Hensley brought a new wave of mixed emotions. She'd spent her first night in England with Finn at Hensley's estate. His wife, Mary, was a perfect match for him. The couple was warm, welcoming, and they were complete chatterboxes. But it had been in Hensley's library, eavesdropping on

Finn and Hensley that she'd gotten her first whiff of a larger mission. She'd discovered that Finn had a secret, and her blundering into that knowledge had put their relationship at risk. She'd been foolish, and the fresh pain stabbed her heart. She noticed Sebastian's glance. While this all happened in 1802, almost two years ago in this timeline, for her, it was a mere five months ago. So much had happened since.

She shook her head and grasped Sebastian's hand. "It seems our Mr. Hensley always has his fingers in something."

Sebastian patted her hand in turn. "More than you can know, my dear." He scratched his head and stood to refill their cups. "So now, you must make a decision."

AJ knew what was coming. "How often does Jaime come here?"

"About every two months, if the weather and blockades permit. He's one of our main contacts with England. Most of the syndicate moves cargo through the rest of the continent."

Two months. Could she wait that long? It had barely been two days, and she itched to move on. Finn and Ethan should have caught up by now. If they'd followed in her wake from the fog, they should have arrived within hours of her jump. That's if she followed Ethan's logic. He'd recounted that when she and Finn had been taken by the fog the first time in Baywood, he'd been swept up soon after. Information gleaned from Beckworth's interrogation at the inn supported that theory. Beckworth had been swallowed up by their jump back home and had been in Baywood almost three months, the same amount of time she and Finn had been back. It made sense that Finn and Ethan should have followed her through the mist.

But they may have landed miles away. Still. How long should she wait?

Damn. What a choice.

"So, I either leave with Jaime when he returns to England, or take my chances and wait two months for his return?"

Sebastian pulled at his ear. "There are other ships, but none that I would trust more with your safety."

A sentiment she agreed with.

"Then let's hope Jamie is late. I need time."

6

The next morning, AJ woke tired and cranky. She'd tossed the entire evening, considering the decision she'd need to make. The question was simple. Should she wait for Finn or leave without him? She knew the answer. She just didn't like it.

After pacing her room, she decided to chance that dawn had long passed. She scoured the rooms in the basement in search of Sebastian but came up empty. The kitchen was her last option.

"Ah, you just missed him." Jeanne rolled out dough and stopped to rub her arm across her forehead. "He's gone to town and will be gone most of the day."

AJ found a corner to munch on bread and cheese, needing something to settle her rumbling stomach. The kitchen was busier than she would have anticipated for the breakfast meal. A group of young women, baskets swinging from their arms, scurried on their way to the gardens. She realized the staff had been wrapping and packing food to place in the baskets. AJ set down the last of her breakfast to investigate.

Jeanne noticed her inquisitive perusal of the group. "We sometimes have a surplus of food, so we make up baskets. There are families that live farther away from town that struggle more with the war." She placed a flattened piece of dough into a pan then began rolling out more dough. "One of our missions is to help those in need."

AJ nodded toward two more girls collecting baskets. "Do they need help?"

The cook studied her with an odd expression. "I think Sebastian would want you to stay close to the monastery."

AJ moped back to her chair and stared out the window. If she didn't find something to get her mind off her problems, she'd end up biting someone's head off.

"Although..." Jeanne mumbled. "There's a small group of kinsmen south of town. They keep to themselves because of their English ancestry. They don't want trouble from the soldiers."

"Why would the soldiers even know to bother them?"

The cook clucked her tongue. "Some of those so-called soldiers are nothing more than mercenaries with too much time on their hands. There isn't any fighting up this way, and the English know to stay away from port. The soldiers have nothing else to do but travel the countryside and steal from the farmers." She scowled, and AJ couldn't be sure but thought Jeanne might be rolling the dough harder. "They usually just steal bread and cheese, maybe some dried meat and a jug of wine if they find it. But some have gotten bolder and take sheep or goats." She almost growled. "They care not for a family's livelihood, and anyone the soldiers suspect of English descent become easy game." She heaved out a sigh and laid her roller to the side. "We try to make sure those families get more food when we have any to spare."

AJ jumped up at Jeanne's weakening stance. A trip to the countryside was just what she needed. There might be French patrols, but she could stay in the background, head down, minding her own business if they were confronted along the road. "You don't send the women on their own, do you?"

The cook looked appalled. "Of course not. Luis will go with this next group."

"What if I promise to be quiet and not get in the way? I might be able to help with herbs and such." AJ was stretching her abilities, but she'd watched Maire work magic on basic cuts and scrapes. She felt comfortable enough to help with the simple stuff.

"We could use a hand. There are two pregnant women who need to be checked on." Jeanne shook her head. "Sebastian won't be happy."

"I'll deal with any repercussions from Sebastian."

Two hours later, AJ sprawled in the back of the cart, grinning from ear to ear as the unexpected winter sun warmed her face. She breathed in the smell of earth, grass, and the remnants of an evening rain. Two older women and three young women chattered in French, with AJ only able to pick up a word or phrase. Once at the farm, she spent her time with the children, helping with salves and ointments, taking instruction from one of the older women who AJ deduced was the nurse at the monastery.

The families spoke French and English, so she was able to converse easily with the children. She found it difficult to watch how they lived and not be able to help them more than she had. On the way home, she worried about whether they would survive the war.

They were an hour from the monastery when three men on horseback approached, traveling from the direction of town. Luis made the women tuck AJ toward the back of the cart, partially hidden under a blanket. Luis didn't slow until the soldiers drew nearer and forced him to stop by blocking the road.

Huddled beneath the blanket, AJ stayed quiet and monitored the faces of the two youngest women. Their huge eyes made AJ want to drag them under the cover with her so they could all hide. She couldn't understand the conversation between Luis and the soldiers, but she understood the tone. The slurring of speech meant the soldiers had been drinking most of the morning, and only one man stood between the soldiers and the terrified women.

She reached into her pocket and opened the hidden pouch, her hand gripping the dagger. The pounding of her heart sounded like war drums in her head as the men approached the cart. They peered into the near-empty wagon, the baskets gone in exchange for half of a freshly slaughtered lamb. The families had been too proud to take from the monastery without some form of trade.

Luis bristled, his tone harsh when one of the soldiers played with the scarf around one of the youngest woman's neck. AJ caught enough of the soldier's expression to know what was on his mind. Concern for the women outweighed her own safety, but Finn had taught her patience, and she waited to see if the situation would resolve on its own. The soldier worked his way from woman to woman, finally reaching AJ. She kept her head down, and when the soldier lifted her chin to get a better look, she kept her eyes downcast. Based on the lilt in his voice, he'd asked her a question, but she didn't understand. She kept her mouth shut, willing him to go away as she tightened her fingers on the hilt.

One of the older women spoke with frantic harsh words as she pulled the blanket over AJ. The soldier appeared confused and then undecided. He shrugged and turned toward one of the younger women. When he grabbed her wrist, she screamed. AJ drew her dagger, but Luis caught the man's arm. When the second soldier roughly pulled Luis away, Luis swung and hit the man square in the jaw. The man fell. The first soldier swung his sword, hitting Luis in the back with its broad side, sending the young man sprawling into the dirt.

The third man stepped forward as if he'd waited long enough for his turn. He appeared ready to give Luis a beat-down while the other two soldiers advanced on the cart. AJ readied herself, waiting for the men to get closer. She'd have to wait for them to do something before she'd be close enough to make an impact.

Suddenly, a shout yelled above thundering hooves. The soldiers stopped when they saw who approached and ran back to their horses. Words flew in frenzied French, and Luis stood, brushing himself off, his shouting the loudest of them all. The women had pushed AJ back down so she could only listen. When the horses stormed off and the cart began to roll, AJ slid the dagger back into its pouch.

She pushed the blanket away to find two of the young women crying as they were consoled by the others. Her own nerves were rattled, and a new understanding became apparent. Soldiers at war with idle hands made for dangerous men. Would the same be true in England?

By the time they reached the monastery and got the frightened girls to the kitchen for hot tea mixed with calming herbs, AJ was mentally exhausted. Sebastian hadn't returned, though it was almost time for dinner. She stayed in the kitchen, sipping a mug of ale that Jeanne was thoughtful enough to suggest. Her mind raced as she sorted through her options, but only one kept resurfacing.

While everyone was busy repeating the events of their perilous journey, AJ tiptoed from the room and hurried down to the tunnels. She eyed the two men at the door, and taking a deep breath, spoke quickly and decisively, brooking no argument. They shook their heads but allowed her to pass.

She knocked once, then opened the door.

Beckworth sat on the bed, back against the wall, reading a book. She idly wondered what he was reading. His restraints had been removed, and his complexion appeared healthy. He glanced up before taking a second look, clearly surprised to see her.

His smile was more of a sneer. She understood. She had stabbed him and then repeatedly kicked him. Not that he hadn't deserved that and more, and she swallowed her tinge of guilt. Squaring her shoulders, she strode in, shutting the door behind her, leaving the men in the hall.

He quirked a brow, and after carefully marking his place, set down the book. "Now what do I owe for the pleasure of your company, Miss Moore?"

She glanced around the barren room before glaring down at him. "It's time to discuss our next steps."

He looked bored and waited patiently.

"I have a proposition for you."

He said nothing, but her stomach twisted when she noticed the sparkle dancing in his eyes.

BECKWORTH PACED THE ROOM, which had to be making him dizzy with his long strides and the minuscule dimensions of the room. AJ dragged the room's only chair to the other side of the chamber, waiting for him to either laugh in her face or angrily toss her out. She was betting on the risk-taker in him overshadowing his irritation with her stabbing him—again.

After several tense moments, he stopped and turned to her.

"Let me get this straight." He leaned against the wall, beads of sweat shining on his brow. His pacing had been the most exercise he'd gotten since the jump, and it was obvious he'd need more time to get his full strength back. He would barely make it to the iron door without stopping several times to catch his breath.

His gaze was steadfast, and he lazily scratched at his wound. "You want me to be your traveling companion through England. Am I posing as your betrothed or your older brother?"

She stared at him, already questioning her sanity, but without Finn or Ethan, she wasn't left with much choice. She wouldn't scavenge off Jamie's crew. "Your role is my bodyguard, nothing more and nothing less. And we're not vacationing through the countryside. I need to get to Hereford. I understand why you won't agree to that, so I'm not asking." She poured tea for two and waved at the bed. "Sit before you fall down. You're not impressing anyone."

Beckworth hesitated. He was either waiting for the strength to stumble the two paces it required to sit or wanted to prove he wasn't ready to melt into a puddle. She patiently waited until he was seated on his bed before handing him the mug.

"I'm asking for escort as far as Waverly. I'm not sure where we'll dock in England, but I doubt it will be too far north. Even if it's close to Bristol, Waverly isn't far from my path to Hereford."

He drank his tea, once again making her wait. She understood the game, and she sat back with her own tea.

"What are your plans at Waverly?" His bland expression never changed.

"Surveillance." She met his gaze and held it. "Nothing more. If you want to go in and play viscount again, I don't care. I only want to confirm whether Maire is there." She fingered the end of her wrap. "But if she is there, I would expect you to release her. If you choose not to do that, the knowledge that she's there is all I need."

"And then once in Hereford, you'll bring the earl's men to force her rescue." His tone didn't hold judgment. He seemed to be working through the rules.

She shrugged. "If Maire is there against her will, what do you think?"

He studied her, and once again reached for his wound and scratched. She had no doubt he trusted her with as much faith as she placed in him.

Then he laughed. Not a chuckle or an evil guffaw, but a deep belly laugh that made him shake as he doubled over, drops of tea splashing on the bed. He had to set the mug down before spilling it. She was ready to release her own laugh, but it was more of the hysterical type. She flicked a glance to the door, wondering what the men outside must think.

They had both lost their minds.

Once Beckworth cleared the tears from his face, he picked up his tea and slurped it down. He wiped his mouth with the sleeve of his shirt. "How far we've come, you and I." He repositioned himself on the bed to make himself taller. "But it's obvious we have a common goal. If you can find me passage to England, then it only seems fair I do my part by getting us to Waverly." He tugged at his shirt sleeve and AJ winced, the gesture reminding her of who she was making a deal with—the devil himself.

He smiled. It wasn't a leer; it was his pleasant smile. The smile he showed to his invited guests while greeting them in the halls of Waverly. "We have a deal. If Maire is there, and it's within my power, she'll be released. Otherwise, I'll expect you'll travel on to Hereford and return with the earl's army in tow."

And there it was. A deal she couldn't trust but had no other choice than to make.

She stood, happy to let her irritation with him slip out. "You need to ask Sebastian about getting some exercise. You're sweating like a pig, and at this point, won't be able to stumble down the hall to get to the ship. Or worse, you'll break your neck on the stairs, and I'll have to find a new bodyguard. I imagine you have a day, two at the most. Make them useful."

When she opened the door, his chuckle made her turn for a last look.

He leaned against the wall, arms folded against his chest. "Don't worry, love," he said in his best cockney English. "You and me make quite the right pair. They'll never see us coming." He winked as she shut the door on his mocking smile.

She nodded at the two men outside his door and rushed down the hall, eager to put distance between her and Beckworth. She might have her bodyguard, but it was like having a rattlesnake at her side, ready to strike at the slightest provocation. He'd have his own plan, and he'd only work with her as long as their goals aligned. Her spidey sense nagged.

His last statement bothered her. He said he'd release Maire if it was within his power. Why wouldn't it be in his power if he was the viscount? Beckworth knew or suspected something but wasn't sharing. She may have made a deal with the devil, but would she discover again, as she had with the duke, that he was only a bishop and not a king?

7

———

T*hree days earlier*

FINN ROLLED across the sodden grass, and Ethan dropped beside him. When they came to a stop, they staggered before standing.

"What were you thinking?" Ethan yelled as the fog dissipated. "That was cutting it close."

"That doesn't get any easier the more times we do it." Finn bent over, waiting for the nausea to subside. "I had to get both duffels. You said I'd have five minutes."

"I said maybe five minutes. Maybe. I don't believe we're working with exact science here."

"There must be some science to it unless you have Irish blood and believe in the wee folk." Finn peered through the rain, assessing their surroundings.

"This rain may work to our benefit if we've ended up in France instead of England. I don't recognize the landscape."

Finn nodded. "Not many will be out in this weather, but it doesn't help with determining which way north is."

They gathered their duffels and ran to an outcropping to get out of the rain.

"Were you able to say anything to Stella before running for me?" Ethan pushed his wet hair out of his eyes and checked the duffel for damage.

"No. I just ran when the fog returned. I figured she'd understand."

"I noticed Adam was still holding Isaiah back."

Finn nodded. "I'm sure he remembers when AJ and I left with the ship, and then a couple minutes later, obviously not five, you disappeared."

"Am I going to have to listen to your complaints during our entire mission?"

Finn shrugged as he searched the duffel for a knife and his pistol. "Depends on how long it takes to find a place to get dry and evaluate our situation."

Ethan turned his head. Finn tensed, ready to run or attack, but Ethan shook his head. Finn ruffled through his bag but kept his attention on Ethan's movements, his knife at the ready.

With speed Finn hadn't expected from Ethan, the man jumped up and raced around the outcropping, his boots silent in the mud and wet grass. A few minutes later, he returned, dragging a squirming boy by his collar.

"Settle down. I'm not going to hurt you." Ethan grabbed the boy's arm and tried to make him stand still.

Finn repeated the command in French, and the boy stopped his struggles. "Do you speak English?" he asked in French.

The boy shrugged.

Finn glanced at Ethan with a look of annoyance. "Damn Beckworth and his old incantation."

"I suppose the next question," Ethan responded, still not ready to let the boy go, "is to find out how far away we are from the monastery."

At that, the boy lifted his head.

Ethan and Finn shared a glance, then spun on their heels when the sheep bleated.

"A shepherd boy." Finn noticed Ethan's grip lighten. The boy's struggles seemed to have been replaced by curiosity.

The boy looked nervously between the men but said nothing.

Finn squatted and ruffled the boy's hair, earning a scowl from the lad as he stood taller. Finn chuckled. "So, it's a young man we've stumbled upon."

The boy seemed to like that, and with a quick glance at Ethan, he nodded.

"Well, then. If you promise to sit and talk with us like men, we'll let you go. Agreed?"

After a few seconds, the boy nodded and relaxed his shoulders.

Finn sat then glared at Ethan, pointing at a spot across from him, until Ethan relented and released the boy's arm. Ethan sat across from Finn as requested, leaving a space on either side for the boy to sit. The boy would be within reach of either man should he decide to bolt. Finn hoped a little mutual trust would go farther than bullying.

When the boy continued standing, Finn thought for a moment then scrounged in his duffel again. The boy stepped back, but Finn held up his hand in a gesture to wait. The boy held his ground.

Finn slipped out an energy bar and broke it into three pieces. He handed one to Ethan, who immediately took a bite, then offered a piece to the boy. "My name is Finn, and this is my friend, Ethan. What's your name?"

The boy hesitantly took the offered food, sniffed it, then took a small bite. His eyes lit up, then seeming to realize his mistake, tried to frown, but it was hard to hide his persistent dimples. After he swallowed, he whispered, "Michel."

Ethan nodded. "A strong name."

With that, Michel sat with the men, his back to the rocks.

Finn handed out small portions of cheese, bread, and nuts. They remained in silence as they ate and sized each other up. A sheep bleated, and they all glanced around. When Michel settled back, so did Finn and Ethan. The boy would have fled had there been danger.

After several minutes passed, Finn attempted to gather some information. "We've lost our way and need to get to the monastery. We're friends of the monk there."

Michel studied each of them, still wary, and Finn could only guess at what the boy must be thinking. He and Ethan had materialized through the fog, showing up out of nowhere. But the monastery meant something to Michel, enough for him to have the courage to sit with them and learn more.

Ethan pulled out a bottle of water and drank, handing the strange bottle to the boy. Michel studied the bottle then took a sip. Then he guzzled.

Finn smiled at Ethan. They were getting somewhere.

"Our friend's name is Sebastian," Ethan tried. "He would be very happy to see us."

"How do you know Brother Sebastian?" Michel scratched his foot, but his flinty stare remained suspicious.

Finn thought about it. "This might seem a strange question, but what year is it?"

The boy stared. "It's been almost a year since the war started."

Ethan looked around. "This could be early spring, but with the chill, I'd say a month or two earlier. Probably six months since I left, give or take."

Finn turned to Michel. "We met him a year ago, before the war."

The boy tilted his head, then dropped it as he ran his fingers through the soft, muddy dirt. When he lifted his head, his expression was filled with such defiance, Finn almost scooted back. "That was when the bad man was there."

Finn laughed out loud, making the boy jump. "Yes. We helped Sebastian chase the bad man away."

Michel looked doubtful. "Maybe you were working for the bad man."

Finn glanced at Ethan for help. How could they convince this young lad, who obviously knew of the monk and held him in high esteem?

"Michel, do you remember stories about that day?" Ethan asked.

The boy nodded.

"Did anyone tell you about the ship that sailed the coast and shot cannon at the monastery?"

The boy's eyes grew round, and he nodded again.

Ethan pointed to Finn. "This is Finn Murphy, the captain of the *Daphne Marie*. His ship fired that cannon as a diversion so we could surprise the duke. Do you understand diversion?"

Michel's face turned red. "Of course."

Finn laughed again. "Then I think we can be friends too." He rubbed his jaw, glanced at Ethan who shrugged, apparently out of suggestions. The boy was smart and had seen the fog. How far would the boy's beliefs run? "I know our arrival was not normal. The fog is deceptive. This may be hard to believe, but it helped us travel a long way, but we weren't able to bring our horses. Do you understand?"

Michel thought about it, then replied with a simple, "No."

This time both men laughed so hard that Michel began to laugh as well.

Finn held his side until his laughter quieted. "We don't know how it works either, but here we are, and we need to find a way to the monastery. How far away is it? What direction?"

Michel thought about it and pointed to his left. "North. It's a full day's ride by cart. When Sebastian or one of the other monks visit, they arrive after dinner and stay the night."

Finn felt some relief. If they walked hard, they could get there in two days. By horse, they could be there in less than a day.

"Is there a town close where we can get a room and rest for the night?"

"Only Saint-Malo if you're going to the monastery. There's another one closer, but it's south of here. It only takes Papa half a day to get there."

Ethan grumbled something under his breath.

Michel continued to run his fingers through the mud, creating circles and then long wiggly lines. "There's an old farmhouse not far from here. No one lives there anymore, so it's in need of repair." He shrugged, but it was obvious he was trying to help. "It will give you a place to sleep. Papa is gone with the cart and won't be back for another few days. I'm sure he'd take you to the monastery when he returns."

"That's too long. We could walk to the monastery by then." Ethan picked up his duffel. "Let's try the farmhouse. We can at least get out of this rain and figure out our next move."

"How do we get there?" Finn asked.

Michel jumped up. "It's on the way home. I can take you there, but you have to follow me, we need to bring the sheep with us."

8

Finn rolled onto his back and stared at the patchy roof. He was grateful he'd found a spot away from drips or that didn't pool with water. Ethan had settled on the other side of the small shelter and appeared to have his own struggles with sleep. If Finn had ever thought in the last three months that he missed his own time, all he had to think about was their large bed at the inn with AJ nestled in his arms. What had they been thinking to follow Ethan back? They should have handed him the Heart Stone and wished him luck.

That would have meant abandoning his sister. Again. That woman got into more trouble than all of them combined, always needing someone to come to her aid. His parents had coddled her too much. He couldn't help but smile. He'd done his fair share of spoiling her. What if he'd never returned with the Heart Stone the first time? As much as he worried about his sister, she always landed on her feet. Truth be told, of all of them, Maire would be the survivor of the group. Yet, here they were, rescuing her from whatever she'd gotten herself into. Assuming they could find her.

Now that he was back in the eighteen hundreds with time on

his hands as they calculated their next move, he considered the change in Ethan. He'd been surly and impatient from the moment he'd knocked on their door in Baywood. His behavior worsened when they hadn't been able to find a trace of Maire. Ethan had taken a large gamble jumping to the future. He understood Ethan's anxiety, but was that all it had been? He didn't want to admit it, but Ethan might not be sharing the entire story.

A day's ride from the monastery, and he felt as helpless as a babe.

AJ.

Where are you, my love?

As dangerous as this world was, he'd always believed the two of them could face it together. Their separation tore at him, and he ached to be on his way, caution be damned. Ethan's gruff behavior these last couple of weeks began to make sense. It was difficult to be separated from someone when you had so much to lose. If they had to hoof it to the monastery, then that was what they'd do. If they found transportation along the way, so much the better. He didn't want to walk in the rain, but the weather would keep most people off the roads, and even the soldiers would reduce their patrols.

The creak of a door brought Finn out of his musings, and he realized he'd fallen asleep, the predawn light now revealing the shabby room with patches of holes in the walls that matched the roof. He slowed his breathing and glanced across the room at Ethan, who remained motionless, either in sleep or performing his own survey of who had opened the door.

A small figure tiptoed in, a large bag at his side. Michel had returned as promised.

Finn heaved himself from his spot, twisting to relieve a knot in his shoulder and neck.

"Good morn, young master, Michel."

The boy blushed. "I'm no master." His eyes flicked to Ethan, who had rolled to his side, grunting as he ran a hand over his face.

Ethan picked at the corners of his eyes and groaned again as he pushed himself up. "A few weeks in your time, and I've become spoiled."

Michel eyed them but said nothing as he laid out small packages of food wrapped in brown cloth.

"I did believe my days of sleeping on the floor to be far behind me." Finn scratched his chin, wondering when he'd be able to shave again. They hadn't packed much for personal hygiene, believing they'd arrive at the earl's estate. Another basic necessity out of reach. He should be grateful he hadn't been gone for years, or his basic survival skills might have eluded him.

"What fine fare did you bring us?" Ethan asked as he stood, stretched his back, and walked to the circle of food Michel laid out for them.

"Mostly fruit from the orchard, but I found some cheese that hasn't yet spoiled, and Mama made extra loaves of bread. I don't think she'll miss one." He opened one of the smallest packages. "This was all the meat I could get." His voice became small, as if the bounty he'd brought was too meager.

Finn patted his back. "This is a fine haul you've brought us."

They ate in silence, nibbling more than anything else. Finn and Ethan knew to hoard what they could. They had a two-day walk, and without knowing what lay ahead of them, they needed to preserve the food.

Michel handed them a waterskin, and they drank heartily after Michel told them a small river followed the road they'd be traveling.

After they ate, Michel used a stick to draw a map of where

they were, pointing out the direction they needed to travel, the places to avoid, and which farms might be friendly.

"We'll have to skirt the town. Too many soldiers." Finn drew a line leaving the road just before town and circling south to a point on the far side of town and the road to the monastery. "We can take this road. It adds several miles but would be less risky."

"This would be a lot easier with a couple of horses or at least a cart." Ethan stared at the scratches on the dirt. "Is there any place along the way where we could buy horses?"

Michel shook his head. "Just Saint-Malo."

Finn stretched out his legs, his muscles sore from the hard floor. "If the rain lets up, we'd have a better chance of finding a ride along the road. We just have to avoid patrols."

"Which may not be as easy as it sounds if there isn't sufficient cover along the road," Ethan replied.

Silence descended as all three heads lowered to study the dirt map for answers.

"Michel. You said your papa took the cart. Does your family own other horses?" Finn studied the young lad, hoping they overlooked the obvious.

He nodded enthusiastically before his shoulders dropped. "It's just an old plow horse."

Finn pulled one of the duffels closer and rummaged through it. AJ had ordered a metal lockbox shortly after Ethan had arrived. It was no larger than a journal and three inches deep. He rolled a few dials to match the combination, and the lid popped open. He shoved objects around with his finger before picking up the smallest nugget he could find.

Ethan understood Finn's action and broke out in a laugh. "Not the most elegant ride, but he should be strong enough to carry the two of us."

Michel looked worried until Finn laid a hand on his shoulder. Then he took the boy's hand and turned it over to drop the nugget in his palm. It was half the size of a pea.

"Do you know what this is?"

The boy's eyes lit up before raising them to Finn. "Gold?"

"Aye. This could buy a couple of horses and probably feed you the rest of the year." Finn glanced at Ethan, who nodded in agreement. "I need you to run and ask your mama if she will trade the use of your horse for a few days in exchange for this. You can retrieve the horse from Sebastian once we arrive at the monastery."

Michel's face screwed up in confusion. "You only want to borrow the horse?"

Finn nodded.

"And you'll give us gold for that?"

Finn folded the young boy's hand into a fist. "This is very important, Michel. We have urgent business with Sebastian and must get there as quickly as we can. We can walk it, but it would be much easier if we had a horse."

Michel jumped up. "I'll go get him now. He's old, but he's strong. I'm sure Mama will agree."

Ethan grabbed the boy's sleeve. "Be careful with that nugget. Make sure you give it to your mother to hold onto."

He nodded vigorously and slipped through the remains of the back door, which hung askew.

"Could it be that simple?" Ethan asked.

Finn's tension along his shoulders and neck had eased with Michel's eagerness, but nothing ever went as planned where the stones were concerned. He shook his head. "At this point, I'd say we should prepare for the worst."

Ethan chuckled. "Maybe we've finally found some luck."

Finn released a sigh and shook his head. "One thing we Irish learn early on, there's no pot of gold at the end of a rainbow, and luck only comes to those who work for it."

"No wonder the Irish are always drowning their sorrows in a pint. You're a morose lot."

"You've mistaken drowning our problems with..." Finn stopped when Ethan jumped up and ran to his duffel.

Before Ethan could reach it, a man walked through the back door holding Michel in a bear hug, the young lad's feet kicking at the air and occasionally making contact with his captor's knees, which earned him a sharp shake.

The men turned to the front door when they heard the metallic click of a flintlock. Two soldiers had crowded through the front door.

The smallest of the men smiled. "We are in luck, men. Our ride through the rain has turned up a couple of rats. Or should I say spies?"

ETHAN SHOOK his head after a fist connected with his jaw. He spat blood, and when he took a breath, a sharp stab poked at his side. Not the ribs again. He didn't think they were broken, but they were definitely bruised. The soldiers must have been bored because an hour with Finn and him seemed to have resolved their pent-up frustration.

He was surprised the men had been able to catch them unaware. They were a sloppy lot, but their leader was smart. They must have seen the boy bringing them breakfast and wondered why the boy would visit an abandoned building. Three soldiers on patrol after a rainy night, probably seeking their own shelter.

Finn hadn't fared any better. The fool kept baiting the men with his dumb Irish wit. At first, Ethan hadn't understood why Finn would encourage the extra punishment. Then he caught Finn glancing at Michel. He was held by a soldier, the one who liked to heckle during the interrogations. The soldier had held the boy tightly, but as the beating continued, he'd gotten lazy. Michel appeared terrified, but the boy continually scanned the room. If Ethan had to guess, the youth was looking for a way to escape. Smart lad.

When the soldiers had first entered the farmhouse, their guns drawn and Michel in their grasp, Finn and Ethan had quickly capitulated. The soldiers shouted with glee at their discovery of weapons stuffed in the duffels. Unfortunately for Finn and Ethan, it just confirmed the soldier's suspicions they'd caught themselves a couple of spies.

The leader was the shorter of the men. His rank was only that of a corporal, but he had all the swagger of a commissioned officer. The second soldier stood a couple of inches taller than Finn and Ethan and seemed to enjoy the role of punisher. While his punches hit all the right places, he was slow and lumbering. Nothing he or Finn couldn't handle if they got loose. The one holding the boy was all talk, which seemed to rile up the punisher. Even with their prisoners, the men preferred to gripe at each other. A small opening Ethan might be able to fester.

"This would go much easier if you would just tell us who sent you and what you're doing in France." The leader kicked the duffels. "You've come armed, yet you have no horses."

"I told you before. They fell from the sky," Michel yelled, his eyes wide with fear. "They were sent by the devil."

The men laughed. The corporal pointed to the soldier that gripped a struggling Michel. "I told you the boy was simple. That's why he's the one tending the sheep."

"Then why did he bring them food?" the soldier asked, casually moving Michel to the side as the boy's arms swung out.

The corporal pointed a finger to his own head. "Think about what I just said. The boy is simple. If he thinks they fell from the sky, then he probably thinks they have magic powers."

With that, the three soldiers broke out in laughter, and the punisher landed another punch, forcing Finn to double over.

Finn's head rolled to the right, and he squinted through a bloody eye. "Exactly how much more talking are you fat blokes going to do? I'm feeling ignored."

Ethan cursed. What the hell was Finn up to? As the corporal and the punisher moved in, the third man loosened his grip on Michel. In an instant, the lad stomped down on the soldier's foot, which produced a yell. The man raised a hand to slap the boy, but he wasn't fast enough. Michel was out of his grasp and racing for the back door before anyone could catch him.

"Let him go," the corporal screamed.

The third man stopped at the edge of the door and turned back. "I can catch him."

The corporal shook his head. "I told you, he's nothing but a simpleton. Who's he going to tell? We're soldiers of the national army. No one will question us."

He turned back to Finn and nodded at the punisher. The punches began again.

9
———

A flash of light hit Finn in the face, forcing a groan, the brightness increasing the intense pain in his head. At first, he didn't understand why his head ached, but when he shifted to avoid the light, the events of the day rushed back as thoroughly as the agony radiating throughout his body. The fog, rain, France, the shepherd boy, and the soldiers. The last one explained the pain. The soldier had some weight behind him, but didn't throw his punches half as well as Dugan had. He'd call that a silver lining.

He managed to roll his head to survey his surroundings and caught the first whiff of roasted lamb. Then his stomach registered the smell, and his hunger howled. The enticing aroma was worse torture than the beatings.

The corporal sat next to a crumbling hearth. The smoke from a fire drifted through the holes in the patchy roof. His back was to Finn, but based on his short stature, there was no question about his identity.

The soldier, who'd caught then lost Michel, lounged on the other side of the hearth, mumbling into a metal cup that was probably filled with wine. The sound of splintering wood explained where the bruiser was.

Finn twisted his body to the left and spied Ethan on the other side of the room. He lay on his back, but his head was turned away from the fire, either asleep or feigning it.

His gaze flicked back to the window to determine the time of day. He had assumed morning, but when he considered the placement of the sun and the direction the window faced, he realized it was late afternoon. That made sense. The soldiers had questioned them most of the day, but the beatings decreased as the soldiers began to drink. Finn didn't remember it getting dark. It was possible that his body had just shut down and he'd slept through until morning, but he didn't think so.

The door banged open against the patchwork wall. Finn groaned at the shooting pain from the momentary tensing of muscles.

A quarter leg of lamb slammed down on the table. The bruiser wiped his face, then ran his hands down his stained pants. "That's the last of it. If we want more, we'll have to steal a lambie from that crazy shepherd boy."

The corporal stood and studied the lamb roasting on a spit in the hearth then back at the last raw quarter of meat. "We'll cook the last of it then head back to town."

"We should have started back right away." The complainer scratched his balls, belched, then went back to staring into the fire.

The corporal glanced at Finn, who'd quickly shut his eyes. "But first, we'll need another horse. I have no intention of sharing a saddle with a spy." He turned to the bruiser. "Why don't you ride to the neighboring farms and see if you can commandeer a horse for the national cause."

The soldier grinned, happy to inflict havoc on a poor farmer. A farmer the soldier was supposed to protect. But if the bruiser left, the beatings would stop, at least for a while, and for that, Finn would be grateful. The cooked meat made his stomach grumble, and rather than suffer through that, he shut his eyes and thought of AJ.

When he woke, the room was dark, flames of a fire shining through the patchwork of holes in the farmhouse. The men had built a second fire outside, but the smell of smoke and roasted meat still overwhelmed the old farmhouse. Finn's stomach twisted with nausea instead of hunger. He stretched his arms and legs, testing for both the health of his limbs and internal organs, but also for restraints. His wrists were tied behind his back with rope. His legs were also bound. His ribs ached, and he felt a shortness in his breath, but he didn't think anything was broken. The bruiser hadn't focused his punches, preferring to punch at different spots as if slamming Finn around was just great sport. He'd be sore for a while, but once out of these ropes, he'd be able to hold his own with this lot.

He swiveled his head toward where he'd last seen Ethan. A man-sized lump lay in the shadows, but when a breeze created a spark of flame, Finn saw enough to know it was Ethan. He was in a different position than last time, so Finn assumed he was alive.

While keeping an eye on the door, he listened to the sounds from outside. The soldiers words slurred with drunkenness, but they were still awake, still dangerous. Finn worked at his bindings, twisting and stretching to loosen them. He rolled to his side and tested his strength in an attempt to rise. He fell back and stifled a grunt. He waited five minutes and tried again. Better, but not enough.

He'd expended his energy, and, deciding on a five-minute rest, he rolled so he could stare at the stars through the broken thatch. He wondered if he could see Boötes from here, and whether AJ thought to search for the constellation.

A scraping sound caught his attention. He swiveled toward Ethan and saw him sitting. He was rubbing his wrists and his hands were free.

Then a hand covered Finn's mouth, the hushed words flowing quickly, "I'm Alex, Michel's brother. Stay still, and I'll cut you loose. Understand?"

Finn nodded, and when the hand fell away, he curled in and rolled over to give Alex more room to cut the ropes. Seconds later, the ropes fell away. He turned around and shoved his bound legs toward the young man, his ribs protesting at the sudden movement.

When Alex looked up, Finn determined he couldn't be more than a few years older than Michel. But enough of a man tonight for what he'd done. When he stood, he reached for Alex as his body collapsed. Then Ethan was next to him, Michel silent as a mouse behind him.

"Take a minute to catch your breath," Ethan whispered. "The duffels were piled in the corner." He handed Finn a cutlass and a knife. He nodded toward Michel and his brother. "You two need to go home."

The boys glanced at each other, and when they turned back to Ethan, Alex shook his head.

Finn would have laughed if their lives weren't on the line. "At least go out the back and stay out of sight. You can't be caught if this goes bad." When it appeared the boys weren't going to give in, Finn added, "Your mother needs you. Who will help her if you're arrested for treason?"

That did the trick. Alex nodded and grabbed Michel's hand as they disappeared through the back door as quietly as they'd come.

Finn straightened and grabbed his chest. He glanced at Ethan. "I'm not sure I can raise the sword."

Ethan stared at him for a moment, then ran back to the

corner of the room. He was back in seconds, holding one of Finn's shirts. He glanced toward the front door, and when someone laughed and the fire popped with sparks, Ethan ripped the shirt down the middle.

"Sorry about the shirt," he whispered as he tightly wrapped the remnants around Finn's chest. "It's not perfect, but you'll feel better. Try to make them do all the work."

"Wouldn't a pistol be better?"

"I doubt you can reload fast enough. Besides..." Ethan raised a pistol. "I'll take out the bruiser. If you can't take one of the others, even in your piss poor state, I'll have to do some serious rethinking about your skill sets."

Finn grunted and twisted his body back and forth. He had to admit, he did feel better. He raised the sword. Not the strength he would need for any sustained defense from the right. He shifted the sword to his left hand. Much better. He was almost as good with his left, certainly enough for this evening. He'd be able to hold his knife with his right. He took a step, then a second.

He nodded to Ethan.

Ethan led them to the door. Finn found a spot next to him with a hole large enough for him to scan the fire and all three men. The bruiser, as Ethan had called him, sat squarely in the middle. The best of all targets. Finn shook his head and scratched his chin. Their luck did seem to be changing.

Ethan held the cutlass in his left hand, the pistol, already primed, pointed toward the fire. He stepped out to the porch, his steps light and firm, testing the board before committing his full weight. As he planted his feet to take the shot, the bruiser began to rise.

At first, the large man teetered, but he pulled himself upright. His friends laughed, and he laughed with them. He continued to weave, and as he stuck his hands into his pants he looked up. And froze.

His two friends stopped laughing and stared at him. It took them several seconds to register the surprised, vacant expression, and they turned to follow his gaze. When all three focused on Ethan, and the two companions began to stand, Ethan fired. The bruiser, who still had his hands in his pants, too drunk to understand his peril, pitched backwards. He appeared to have been hit in his right shoulder. If treated in the next day or so, he should live, but for this evening, his fighting was over.

The other two stumbled over their feet, and that was when Finn could have broken out laughing as he joined Ethan on the porch. Neither man had a weapon. Ethan advanced on the complainer. When the soldier backed up, hands raised in surrender, Ethan ran to him and, using his full body, swung the butt-end of his pistol across the man's head. He dropped like a rock, and Ethan hit him again for good measure.

The corporal glanced toward his horse, where he'd foolishly left his sword. The man pulled a knife from his boot, and Finn shook his head. At least he had some spine, but with drink and poor fighting skills, the corporal was hardly worth the challenge. The corporal buckled quickly from the broadside of Finn's blade. When the corporal tried to stand, Finn knocked him out by bringing the hilt of the sword down on his head. He almost laughed until he tried to hitch a breath and a bolt of pain seized him. Finn kicked the soldier in the ribs, not regretting the payback. They were at war, after all.

***

Ethan reloaded the pistol and handed it to Finn, then tied the two men with the rope that had previously been used on them. They dragged the first two soldiers inside and bound their legs.

It required a bit more stamina to drag the bruiser into the house, and Finn made Ethan stop halfway there so he could catch his breath. Once they got the bruiser in the farmhouse, Ethan checked his wound.

"The ball's buried just below the shoulder. The bleeding has slowed, but it's going to hurt like hell. He'll need attention soon." Ethan looked around the room. "We should check the saddle-bags for something I can use to bandage the wound."

"Grab all three saddlebags. Let's see what they left for us. If these two dolts aren't as slow as they seem, they should get themselves loose soon enough. That should leave plenty of time to make it to town, or they can remove the ball themselves. If not..." Finn shrugged. "Napoleon is better off without them."

When Ethan left through the front door, Finn crawled through the crooked back door to find Michel and his brother. It wasn't hard. Michel stood, shuffling from one foot to the other, the reins of a large brown horse in his hands. The plow horse. Michel would grow into a fine man someday, as would his brother.

Finn handed them a sack. When Michel looked in, his eyes widened, and he showed Alex.

"You didn't have to do this," Michel said. "Mama was happy to help. She's tired of the soldiers taking what they please."

Finn nodded. "I kept enough of the lamb to keep Ethan and me fed until we reach the monastery. We have plenty, even if we have to hide for a day or two." He laid a hand on Michel's shoulder. "You and Alex took a large risk coming back to save us. You have our gratitude for putting your faith in us."

Alex grasped his brother's other shoulder. His voice was deep, already having changed, so perhaps a little older than Finn first thought. "My brother said you were friends of Sebastian. That was good enough for me."

Finn gave the boys his lopsided grin. "Aye, good men you are.

Now leave, so the soldiers don't know you helped us. I wouldn't want to see anything befall your family." They turned to leave, and Finn began to hobble back to the farmhouse when Michel ran up to him. He opened his hand with the small ball of gold.

Finn shook his head. "No. You earned that. Take care of your family." Then he turned and walked back to the farmhouse.

They feasted on a good portion of the lamb, then wrapped the rest to take with them. The soldiers carried light packs on their horses with basic staples and weapons. Ethan found the pouch of money the corporal had taken from him and shoved it in his pocket.

By the time they stirred the embers and restarted the fire in the hearth, Ethan's gaze had grown heavy.

"Get some sleep." Finn elbowed him. "I'll wake you in a few hours to relieve me. We'll head out at first light."

Ethan stretched out, using the blankets he'd found in the saddlebags.

Finn stared at the fire. They couldn't take the chance of running into more soldiers before reaching the monastery. That meant they'd have to take it slow or find back roads where possible. He checked on the soldiers every hour. Between the hits to their heads, the gunshot, and their drinking, they'd sleep until dawn.

When Ethan roused to relieve him, Finn crashed to the bedroll with a groan. His ribs ached, and he would need Ethan to retie the bandage before he got on a horse. As he began to doze, he sent a thought to AJ, hoping his wife was close enough to feel him. *I'm coming.*

After what seemed only minutes of sleep, Ethan kicked his foot. When he stood and stretched, the pain in his ribs hurt but was manageable. The light tinges of dawn broke on the horizon. Time to leave.

They checked the bounds on the two men and replaced the

bandage on the bruiser. He had slipped in and out of consciousness, but so far, there was no sign of infection. The wound looked angry, but the bleeding had stopped and barely seeped.

After stripping the horses of any army adornments, they packed two of the faster-looking horses and released the third.

Finn looked around, "I thought the corporal asked the big guy to find another horse."

Ethan shrugged. "Guess they couldn't find one."

Another thing to be thankful for; the soldiers hadn't hurt anyone else. It didn't give him much relief. The soldiers may second-guess their actions next time, but it wouldn't be long before they were up to no good. Some men just didn't change.

When they returned to the farmhouse, Ethan kicked the boots of the trussed-up soldiers. They were groggy and confused until they focused on Finn and Ethan.

Ethan stood next to the corporal. "Your friend needs a doctor, but he has some time before any infection takes hold. The ball is still in his chest, probably along with some of his shirt. I suggest you spend your time figuring out how to get out of your binds so someone can walk to town for help." He squatted next to the man and leaned in. "It's possible you might be able to catch the one horse we've left you, but we're taking the bridle. I hope you learned to ride bareback." He continued to stare at the corporal until the soldier looked away.

Seemingly satisfied, he stood. Finn thought Ethan might kick the soldier again, with a bit more force in a place more sensitive. Instead, Ethan's smile turned cold, and he whispered, "Long live the King of England." Halfway to the door, he turned to Finn. "Let's ride for Normandy."

Unable to say anything more insightful or deceitful, Finn followed him out.

Ethan checked the ties on the duffels and brought a horse to

Finn. "You might be feeling better now, but you'll think differently after a couple hours in the saddle."

Finn rubbed his shirt. "This seems to remind me of another time one of us had injured ribs."

"Why is it we're always chasing a woman?"

Finn laughed, then clutched his side. When he could speak again, he spit out, "They're going to be the death of us."

Ethan slapped him on the back and helped him mount. "Let's hope we're both gray-haired by then."

By the time Finn was seated, he knew this was going to be a long day. Between his aching ribs and having to skirt risky areas to avoid soldiers, it would probably be morning of the following day before they made it to the monastery.

When they'd walked the horses several yards from the house, Ethan stopped. "I'm not sure how long they'll believe we've headed east. A single man riding will be less noticeable than two."

"Aye. Why don't you take the lead? I'll follow along since I'll need a slower pace. Stay on or as close to the road as possible. We'll meet up for a break."

"Hour out?"

Finn grunted. "To begin with." He looked up to study the gray sky. "It looks like the weather might hold, so more people will be out. Let's be cautious, especially if anyone is out searching for their missing patrol."

10

———————

The knock came in the middle of the night. AJ moaned and rolled over, believing she might have dreamed the sound. She listened for another sound while she cleared away the cobwebs of sleep. A few seconds later, a second knock. She shoved the blanket away and ran to the door. Sebastian stood on the other side, a small lantern in his hand.

"It's time. Pack and meet me in the meeting room I showed you. Do you remember how to get there?"

She nodded and managed a hoarse, "I'll be right behind you."

There wasn't much she had to pack. She kept most of her items in her canvas bag, wanting to be ready at a moment's notice. She'd already decided pants were the best choice for the ship. Jamie wouldn't expect her to work, and she had coin to pay him, but she didn't want to be a hindrance. There had to be something she could do, even if it meant cooking.

She was out the door of her chamber in less than five minutes, Beckworth's pack over her shoulder and canvas bag by her side. She used the lantern from her room to guide her down the dark tunnels. Fortunately, the secret meeting room was on the same path as the outer door. After Sebastian had walked her past the statue next to his private room, her memories had returned. To reduce her building anxiety, she had spent yesterday wandering the passages. But it did little to reduce her concern for Finn, wherever the hell he was.

When she turned left instead of right at the intersection deep in the tunnels, the first doubt scratched at the back of her head. When she crept toward the stone bench, the hallway was silent. If anyone was in the room, they were either keeping quiet, or the soundproofing was amazing. Not a drop of light leaked from where the door should be.

Not sure if she was meant to wait or go inside, she touched the stone motif, then ran her hand down to the third stone. She pushed. A click, the whoosh of air, and a slim line of light shone through a small crack. A murmur of voices shut off like water from a tap.

Bingo.

Sucking up her courage, she pushed through and quickly shut the door behind her. The room was lit by a single lantern close to the door, leaving the back of the room in darkness. Several figures shuffled in the shadows. She raised the lantern to get a better look until Sebastian moved into the light. She breathed a sigh of relief. He was smiling.

She set the lantern on the table and dropped her bags.

"The good Lord in heaven, it's true." Jamie came forward, and AJ gaped. This was not the boy she'd left behind just a few months ago. Though from his perspective, it had been almost two years. He had sprouted into a ruggedly, handsome man. His dark brown curls framed his face, and he carried a day's worth of beard. He'd filled out with what appeared to be sheer muscle and four inches of height.

He stalked toward her, and she almost stepped back before he grabbed both her arms and turned her until she stood in the light of the lanterns. "My God, but it's good to see you." He appeared shocked as he continued to scan her, from her shoes to her head. Then he grinned. "Some things never change."

She had grasped his forearms, feeling the hard muscle beneath. "I can't say the same for you. The ladies must be piled up in the ports waiting for the *Daphne Marie*." She still had the ability to make him blush, and snorts sounded from around the table.

"Quiet," he commanded the men, though it was in jest. His expression turned wistful. "I wish it was under better circumstances. We were saddened to hear Maire had gone missing. But when we arrived, we didn't believe Sebastian's wild tale of your return. Though nothing surprises us anymore."

When he stepped back, a large man with dark skin and darker eyes picked her up in a bear hug.

"Lando," she squealed with delight. She hugged him like a drowning woman to a life raft. He'd always made her feel safe, partly because Finn had made him her bodyguard, and because he'd taken the time to teach her the use of her dagger. He always seemed to have faith in her.

"It's good to see you, little one. Though why is it only when danger surrounds you?"

She laughed and hugged him again. "I do seem to have a dark cloud following me around."

"More like a stain on the bottom of your shoe. Is it true you returned with the viscount?"

Grumbling circled the table, and she glanced at the other men. Additional candles had been lit, but she only recognized a couple of faces.

"I'm afraid so."

"Where's Finn?" Lando found a chair for her.

She blinked back the tears she kept in check. She knew he was out there somewhere, and she expected a damn good reason for him being late. Each day he didn't show could only spell trouble, and the only thing keeping her sane was the belief that he and Ethan were together. They'd found her before, and they would do it again. Any other thoughts would take her down a dark path that would do no one any good, least of all Maire.

AJ spent the next twenty minutes sharing a condensed story of how Beckworth got caught in the fog's vortex and had unknowingly been sucked into the future with AJ and Finn. She continued with Ethan's return and the news of Maire's abduction. She skimmed over pieces of the story, specifically around Ratliff's death, preferring to keep select portions for when she was alone with Jamie and Lando. When she finished the part about Beckworth escaping Ethan and forcing her to jump without Finn, she immediately noted that hadn't been the wisest thing to share. For better or worse, Beckworth would be needed for part of her journey.

"Aye, we'll take him with us. The sea is a good place for him to be." One of the sailors she knew growled out. A few others nodded in agreement.

"What's your plan, lass?" Jamie had kept silent through her story, and she knew he'd want to hear the rest once they were on their way.

"I know more than most of you that Beckworth can't be trusted. My goal is to get to the earl in Hereford. Wherever Finn and Ethan are, they'll eventually travel there. I'm not sure where you plan to dock in England, but I'm assuming Waverly won't be far from the road to Hereford. That means Beckworth and I have a similar goal. If any part of what he's told me is true, he desperately wants to return to his estate."

"And you'll be traveling with the devil himself." Lando shook his head, clearly not liking the plan. He rubbed his chin and glanced at Jamie and then turned to Sebastian. "Could you not talk her out of it?"

The monk shrugged. "You'll have a few days to make the attempt yourself. I've learned long ago to not waste words in vain."

"So when do we leave?" AJ asked.

"We've already dropped our cargo, and the holds are almost refilled," Jamie responded. "As soon as you say your goodbyes to Sebastian."

She nodded. "So soon?"

"Aye. We let you sleep until we were ready to leave. We need to sail while we still have the darkness and the tide." He stood, and the rest of the men rose. They clasped the monk's hand before leaving the room, their voices hushed before disappearing altogether.

"What about Beckworth?" she asked.

"The worthless baggage is with the rest of the cargo. Nicely stored." Lando beamed. "Nothing to worry about."

AJ didn't like the sound of that. It was what he deserved, but she needed him cooperative. But until they were safely at sea, she couldn't argue the precautions. She didn't want him jumping overboard and finding his own way back to England. She nodded. "Can I have a few minutes with Sebastian?"

After Lando and Jamie left, she surprised Sebastian with a tight hug. "Thank you for being such a good friend."

He chuckled. "You and Maire have been the highlight of my life." He tightened his grip on her arms. "I have sent word through the region to see if anyone has spotted Finn or Ethan. If they show up here, we'll find a way to get them to England as quickly as possible. I've also sent two missives with Jamie. One for Hensley and one for the earl to be sent by messenger as soon as you dock."

"Why?"

"It's best to have more than one plan, don't you think?"

She snorted. "I can't argue with that. Our plans always seem to go awry."

"You must be watchful at all times. Beckworth will have his own agenda."

"Believe me. No one knows that better than me. I'm not the same woman who was here before. I'm better trained, and pretty good at taking care of myself. If he can get me into Waverly, this all might be over by the time Finn and Ethan catch up."

11

Finn and Ethan spent the day using the same pattern. Ethan rode ahead with Finn following at the best pace he could manage. During the morning, there were fewer people on the road than they expected. One cart and one single rider, neither seeming interested in Finn, shared nothing more than a small nod as they passed. By afternoon, a few more people had ventured out, but there wasn't a single trace of soldiers. But even with an open road, the going was slow.

They stretched the breaks to every two hours, but by late afternoon, Finn's pain became intolerable. Ethan found a creek a quarter mile from the road and tied his horse behind a small copse of trees. Finn would have fallen to the ground after dismounting if Ethan hadn't been there to catch him. After guiding Finn to a spot by the water, Ethan cared for the horses.

"I know we haven't been moving fast, but we've put some miles behind us. Town is close." Ethan dropped the bag of food and began collecting sticks.

"Aye. I thought there would be more people on the road." Finn untied the makeshift wrap and felt his side. Tender, and when he raised his shirt, the purple marks of a bruise were forming.

"I was thinking it might be better to get some rest now, then push for town. It will be dark soon, and the road should remain clear of most travelers."

Finn leaned against a stump. "I'm not going to argue." He let Ethan refill his waterskin, and he sucked down half the bag. His portion of lamb was swallowed almost as quickly. "Why are you building a fire?"

Ethan fiddled with one of the soldier's packs and brought over two tin cups, a pot, and a bag. "Coffee."

"I thought we'd left the coffee obsession back in Baywood with Stella and Adam."

"If I could have packed the espresso machine, I would have."

Finn laughed. "Then we'd just have to find electricity."

"Feel free to laugh, but once we catch up with AJ, I won't be alone in my madness for coffee."

They stayed for three hours, each getting their share of sleep. Finn couldn't argue Ethan's decision to brew coffee. The smell alone invigorated him. As they rode out, without explanation, a sudden urgency to get to the monastery hit Finn in the gut. He urged his mount on, but the faster pace increased the pain, and he was forced back to a steady, if slower, pace.

Once they saw the dim lights of town, Finn and Ethan decided to ride together. They'd been lucky to avoid soldiers, but town would be a different story. Finn breathed deeply. The smell of the sea touched something deep in his bones, and a sense of home washed over him, relaxing the unease that had been building.

They huddled together where the road split in two and listened for riders. When nothing but an owl could be heard, Finn grew impatient. His side ached from the long day. Their afternoon rest had helped, but the miles on horseback just couldn't stop the jarring impact to his ribs.

"Change of plan." Finn muttered.

"Oh?"

"We've ridden through most of the night. We're still an hour from town, and it's only a couple of hours before first light. Rather than taking the back road, let's walk the horses through the far edge of town. We'll have to go slow, but if we stay away from the docks, we should avoid most of the patrols."

Ethan took a moment, considering their options. "It would save time. The back road is safer, but it's longer." He patted the horse, his eyes searching the darkness, but what he searched for, Finn had no idea. "All right. Same pattern. We move out separately. This time you go first, set the pace. I'll follow close until I see you dismount. Then I'll wait fifteen minutes to let you get ahead. If you run into trouble, whistle."

"If I have the breath. You remember where we held up Beckworth's coach?"

Ethan snorted. "A memorable moment."

"We'll meet up there." Finn nudged his horse into a trot, keeping alert to everything around them. Darkness gave a false sense of safety, but he speculated there would be a higher concentration of troops at the docks to monitor the ships and their cargo. Though they'd already tasted the wrath of French soldiers, getting by them to board a ship would be more difficult than getting to the monastery. One step at a time. They had to reach the monastery.

As he neared town, he slowed the horse to a walk. He'd lost track of Ethan quickly. When he stopped to listen, he heard nothing but the muffled sound of the sea and the barking of a dog. He stayed on the horse until he got as close as he dared, then he slipped from the saddle.

He rested a few minutes, waiting for the pain to recede, then turned down an old trail that wrapped around several small cottages. Dawn was more than an hour away, but lights flickered in several windows. With luck, if anyone heard the horse, they'd think it someone on an early morning errand or a soldier on patrol.

The walking eased the stitch in his side, and his breathing became easier. But halfway through town, another intense sense of urgency flooded him. He couldn't explain it, but something urged him to move faster, that time was of the essence. At one point, he leaned against the horse and counted to ten like AJ had taught him. Whatever was happening, it had to do with AJ. He felt her slipping away, but he couldn't rush into danger. The incident with the soldiers had proved that. They had to be careful until they were out of France, then they could play loose with the rules.

What seemed like an hour later, but was only half that, Finn passed the last house. He'd only run into one drunken sailor who'd probably taken a wrong turn from one of the inns. He snored against a storage building but never woke. Since he never heard a whistle, he assumed the sailor hadn't given Ethan any trouble.

When he had walked a good distance from the last house, he mounted and rode for their meeting place.

Ethan arrived a half-hour later.

"What took so long?" Finn asked, the earlier urges to hurry had abated as quickly as they'd come.

"I ran into a bit of a distraction."

"A soldier."

He nodded. "He came out of one of the houses. Scared the wits out of me."

Finn waited. When Ethan said nothing more, he asked, "And?"

Ethan picked at his shirt, and resettled himself in the saddle, a smile brightening his dark features. "He was still tucking his shirt in his pants. Let's just say he'll be sleeping off a sore jaw."

Finn chuckled. "He'll probably think the husband or father came home early."

The men laughed as they moved their mounts faster for their last leg to the monastery.

"We'll need to find a way in," Finn said after a mile of silence.

"And you have a plan?"

"There might be troops at the monastery. We'll need to find someone that can get a message to Sebastian."

Ethan glanced around. "I'd say we have less than an hour before daybreak. If we leave the horses at the outcropping where Thomas held the men the last time we were here, we can have Sebastian send someone to sneak them into town and leave them by one of the inns."

"Once we get past any troops, we can duck through the side court."

Ethan nodded. "The kitchen is our best bet. If it's the same staff, they'll find Sebastian for us."

"Let's hope he's still there."

When they reached the outcropping, they removed their duffels but left the soldier's packs as they found them, minus some coffee and a handful of dried tack. They crept down the road to the monastery as a single unit, stopping at the stone wall to the courtyard.

Finn inched forward and scanned the yard. "I don't see anyone at the main entrance. The army must not consider the monastery to be of importance."

"They would consider the port more important. They probably send a couple men to check the monastery every few days. They certainly aren't waiting for us."

Finn couldn't argue with Ethan's assessment since it matched his own. They tiptoed along the outer wall of the monastery, eyes watchful for any movement, ears primed for sound.

Light blazed from the kitchen window, and Finn smelled the wood fire. The cook would be preparing the ovens for bread. When Ethan met him at the door, they both heaved a breath and nodded. Finn opened the door slowly, his hand on his knife. He inched his way in, Ethan on his heels.

When he'd entered far enough to get a complete view of the kitchen, he stopped. He heard Ethan's intake of breath when he stepped next to him.

Four men sat around the table. Finn knew only one.

Sebastian scratched his balding head, forcing wisps of white hair to flutter. "You couldn't have worse timing."

12

Two cloaked figures wove through the crowd in the smoke-filled room that stank of unwashed men and the stale odor of vomit. The inn, while similar to Guerin's in size and style, carried a shabbier, less friendly feel. The place hadn't changed since the last time Finn had entered the establishment, searching for men to switch sides in their fight against the Duke of Dunsmore. Not willing to take a chance on missing the man he sought tonight, he and Ethan had first stopped at Guerin's, but it had been the waste of time he'd expected.

Guerin imposed a strict policy against fighting in his establishment, so smugglers came to this inn where fights weren't stopped until a clear winner was determined. With the two ships that arrived earlier in the day, the inn was overrun with brash men who flirted with the barmaids and made shady deals under the noses of the French troops who were equally boisterous with drink.

For the last two days, Finn and Ethan had worked out their frustrations of being stranded at the monastery by hauling cargo from its underground stores. The process, though well planned, was laborious, with only a handful of carts loaded each day. Once the carts were loaded, Finn and Ethan traveled with the wagons to a mountainside cave where the cargo was stored for easier distribution. Out of sight from most travelers who had no reason to traverse the thin rocky path, carts could come and go as the cargo was moved out of the cave at random intervals to other cities. Since exports traveled the same path, Finn and Ethan moved the newly arrived crates off the carts before reloading the wagons for the return trip to the monastery. Money exchanged hands along the way, which explained the town's willingness to support the illegal trade route.

When the town heralded news of a newly arrived ship, Finn would don the robes of a monk and ride to town with Luis to investigate. On their first morning at the monastery, Finn argued with Ethan, who wanted to arrange transport on the first ship that docked. Finn finally talked sense into the man. Smugglers were a tricky lot, and most couldn't be trusted past whoever paid them the most coin. If the smuggler thought they could earn extra by handing someone over to the French, they could pocket a good sum of money and evade a more thorough inspection of their ship.

Finn understood Ethan's impatience, but finding the right ship was a dicey gamble. He felt the same restlessness since learning they'd missed AJ by mere hours. The band around Finn's chest released when he heard she was well and sailed with Jamie and Lando. He was beyond furious when Sebastian revealed, somewhat hesitantly, that she took Beckworth with her. Finn had enough sense not to throttle the monk, who didn't have a prayer of talking AJ out of anything. But he would have a few words with Jamie if they ever caught up with him.

A part of him, that piece of his soul, of his heart that beat only for her, that bonded him to her, wished she'd waited for him. He understood the decision she made. She made the correct choice, but it would have been easier to accept if Beckworth weren't part of her plan.

Finn pushed his way deeper into the inn, where they found a sailor wrapped in the arms of a busty prostitute, another pastime not found at Guerin's. Ethan brushed past Finn, probably eager to have this night over, and picked the sailor up by an arm.

"Oi, I'm in the middle of somethin' here." The man staggered as Ethan helped him stand while the scantily dressed woman tried to pull the sailor back down.

Ethan flicked her a coin which she caught midair. "Take him to a room."

The brunette's eyes went wide when she saw the coin. She turned it over several times, studying it with a practiced eye. Satisfied with her inspection, her demeanor changed, and she pushed the sailor away. "Why don't you join me instead?"

Ethan eyed her with appreciation and a pleasing smile before shaking his head and pushing the sailor toward her. "Not tonight. I have business."

The woman pouted, but she understood his meaning. Finn chuckled when she patted Ethan's backside before dragging the sailor away.

"You're getting good at clearing a table." Finn pushed the empty mugs aside and sat with his back to the wall.

Ethan grunted in response, pushing his chair close to Finn so his back was also to the wall. "A few kind words and coin go further than using a stick. Are you sure he'll be here?"

Finn eyed the men at the bar before scanning the room. "Aye. Valentin always shows himself, even if it's only for an hour. His mates will gather information from their own connections, but Valentin didn't get where he is by working on second-hand news. He'll perform his own reconnaissance for the latest on the patrols and blockades."

"Wouldn't it have been easier to get a message to the man?"

"I don't know his crew, and the soldiers have a keen eye on who boards and leaves the ships."

"And this is the man you trust to get us to England?"

A grimace crossed Finn's face, his finger worrying at a grain in the wood. How did one go about explaining Valentin or any smuggler? "Trust is hard-earned amongst most smugglers." With Ethan's dour-faced response, Finn chuckled. "It's more a code they follow. You have to rely on others to keep their end of a deal. If a smuggler earns a reputation for not delivering what's promised, or for too much double-crossing, he'll find himself without cargo, friends, and sometimes, without his life."

"A rough crowd you ran with."

Finn shrugged. "If you trade fair and pay attention, it's a good life for most." He swigged ale from fresh mugs a barmaid had dropped in front of them and gave Ethan his wide-slanted grin. "And it pays good coin."

Ethan shook his head, studying Finn before turning away to scour the room. "And I suppose you practiced some of that craft during your time jumps?"

Finn refused to apologize for his actions while jumping through decades in search of a stone necklace only rumored to exist. "A man has to earn a living."

"I couldn't agree more." The words were deep, gravelly, and carried a thick French accent.

The man appeared wider than he was tall, his massive upper body that of a brawler, the sleeves of his pristine jacket straining over heavily muscled biceps. A scar ran down the left side of his face, from his hairline to just below his jaw. Otherwise, he had a pleasant face, touched with wrinkles across his forehead and at the corners of his eyes. His full head of black hair, streaked with touches of gray, was pulled into a fashionable queue. He shoved a man from the chair of a neighboring table and dragged it to

Finn's table. The sailor, half in his cups, struggled to his feet, ready to take the man on until he raised his head and squinted into the stranger's face. Mumbling some form of apology, he nodded to the stranger and moved to find another spot several tables away.

The man turned the chair, so the back braced against the table. He sat and crossed his arms over the back of the chair. "Finn Murphy. I heard you were dead."

"Valentin. The same could be said of you."

Valentin rested his gaze on Ethan, giving him a long perusal. A barmaid dropped another mug on the table and giggled when the smuggler grabbed her waist, pulling her in for a kiss. He whispered in her ear, then patted her backside as she sauntered off. He turned his attention back to Finn. "I didn't see your ship."

"It has a new captain now."

Valentin's brows lifted. "I didn't think to see the day that the *Daphne Marie* would sail with a different captain while you still walked the earth."

"Better circumstances presented themselves."

"Indeed. So what brought you to this sleepy port?"

"We need passage to England."

The old smuggler gave Ethan a quick slide glance. "That is a very dangerous and a very expensive proposition."

Finn nodded. "My friend has urgent business there." He rubbed his jaw and studied Valentin in turn. The man hadn't changed much since Finn had last seen him. The gray streaks were new, and his eyes crinkled with deeper lines from his natural humor, but in all, he was the same rogue that found more than his share of beauties in ports on both sides of the channel. The man shared the same innate skill as Finn to make influential and powerful friends. "We were supposed to meet another ship but we were..." Finn glanced around the room before lowering his voice, "temporarily detained and the ship couldn't wait."

"Did someone tell you I was coming?"

The words were spoken lightly, but Finn could hear the edge in his tone. He shook his head. "I've been watching the docks, waiting for someone I could trust with my coin.' Finn caught Ethan's smile and shake of his head at Finn's choice of words.

Valentin laughed. "Trust comes at a high price these days." When Finn only smiled, the smuggler drank from his mug. He rubbed his chin as he gave Ethan another hard stare. "You have the coin?"

Finn nodded.

"This isn't the best time for me to be taking on English." Valentin drained his mug before staring into its empty depths.

A minute went by, but Finn waited, keeping his eye on Ethan, who had the good sense to stay quiet.

Valentin barked out a laugh. "Do you remember that small village just west of Calais?"

It was Finn's turn to take a moment before the memory returned. He grinned like a schoolboy. "I remember a certain lass who clobbered you over the head and left you for dead for trying to leave without paying."

The smuggler's gaze took on a dreamy state. "She was a fiery one. One might think she had some Irish blood in her." He leaned close. "She still keeps my bed warm on cold winter nights."

Finn slapped him on the arm. "You always liked the feisty ones."

Valentin dropped his smile. "I'll make an exception for you, Murphy. But this will set the books even."

"Agreed."

"Do you know where the smithy is?"

Finn nodded.

Valentin stood. "We leave at dawn. Be there an hour before." Without another word, he strode off as quietly as he'd arrived.

Ethan lifted a brow. "I don't have a good feeling about this."

Finn's signature grin returned as he stood. "It's not Valentin we need to worry about. It's the French inspection if my old friend hasn't paid the toll."

13

AJ squinted into the wind as she braced herself against the bow of the *Daphne Marie*. Her hair caught the mist of the sea as the ship sliced through the water. She clutched her necklace, Finn ever-present on this ship that she'd always think of as his. Even if they hadn't been split apart as abruptly as they had, standing on his ship, remembering the times they'd shared on her decks and below, he would always be foremost in her thoughts. She continued to second guess her decision to leave the monastery. Would it have been so bad to wait a few more weeks in case they had followed her wake through the fog?

Her final discussions with Sebastian and Jaime on the rocky shore of France had made sense. It was equally possible that Ethan had used his newer incantation, and he and Finn had landed somewhere in England. If they didn't meet somewhere on their journey, they would all gravitate toward the earl's estate. Assuming she made it across the channel. A sharp whistle broke her concentration, and she turned to see Fitz, Jamie's second mate. A smile lightened his gruff face as he pointed up. She nodded and tucked the necklace back in her secret pocket before pushing her hair back as she secured her hat with thin leather strips under her chin. Fitz had helped her sew on the straps so the hat wouldn't fly off while protecting her skin from the deceptive winter sun.

She repositioned the small leather pouch Lando had given her over her shoulder and reached for the nearest rigging. She glanced up once before she began her climb, crossing over a yard toward the mast. One of the younger sailors nodded at her as he worked his way down, and she continued up the shroud until she reached the barrel used as a crow's nest. She picked up the spyglass tied to a nail in the barrel and swept the horizon in a slow, methodical circle. She used the spyglass for her first pass of the horizon because she'd noticed several of the men watching her at the beginning of each of her shifts.

Most of the men trusted their captain with his decision to give AJ the critical job of spotting French or English patrols. However, a few of the newer men didn't want her on board at all, and after Jamie had given her free rein to run the ship, she'd heard the grumbling. It bothered her the first day, but after Lando assured her they'd get used to it or be off the ship at the next port, she paid the men little heed.

After her first scan with the spyglass, she reached into her pouch and pulled out the binoculars Beckworth had stashed in his backpack. She'd found them when she'd searched his gear that first evening at the inn while he lay bound and hazy in his own room. Jaime and Lando had marveled at the field glasses. Jamie agreed that, as long as she was careful, the glasses were worth the risk if it made their channel crossing safer.

The four-hour shift reminded her of early morning climbs in Baywood, watching the sea from the top of the cliff. On her first watch, she couldn't think about anything other than Finn. By her third shift, she'd turned her focus to her plans for when they made land. Jamie withheld their destination until after they set sail. His announcement they would dock at a small port west of Southampton didn't change her agenda. The new location aligned with her decision to stop at Waverly on her way to Hereford.

Everything was coming together with only one possible flaw —Beckworth. They both had an interest in Waverly, but AJ began to wonder if Beckworth would be greeted with open arms on his return. He'd grown pensive since boarding the ship, even distracted. It had been over a year since he'd been home, and it was possible the place had been abandoned. Had he thought to leave anyone in charge when he'd planned to be gone for a month or two? Or maybe his thoughts were more sinister, and even from a different century, he had somehow played a role in Maire's disappearance. Taking her cue from Finn, she could either worry about it or prepare for it.

Returning to her duty, she scanned the area and spotted a ship due east of them. She focused on the masts and sheets as Lando had taught her and guessed the ship to be Royal Navy. She couldn't be sure until they were closer, but Jamie preferred to play it safe. She signaled the alarm by ringing a bell before pointing east then watched the men scramble. Her pulse quickened as Jamie instantly gave the word. Canvas cracked as men scrambled to the rigging to change their course westward.

When she peered down at Lando, she caught him tucking his own spyglass away. He looked up at her with an expression that seemed to be approval, though he was too far away for her to be certain. Either way, her cheeks flushed with excitement as the *Daphne Maire* turned to chase the setting sun. With the ship's speed, the other ship would never catch her. Not one to shirk her duties while still on watch, she scanned the horizon of their new direction to make sure they weren't being flanked. Seeing nothing for miles, she lowered her hat and went back to planning her journey to Waverly.

Beckworth leaned against the bulwark, arms shackled in front of him. He watched the men hustle as they shifted the sails to a new heading—all on the say of a mere slip of a woman. Not all the men appreciated having AJ on board, but in his brief conversations with a few of the men, he'd discovered many of the sailors knew her from a previous sail. They gave no further explanation, but he'd heard enough to know they respected her, almost as much as Murphy, their previous captain.

He shouldn't have expected any less. A captain demanded obedience on a ship, their lives might well depend on it, but respect was earned not given. And though he despised Murphy on so many levels, he'd heard the reverent tone the men used when mentioning their previous captain. Beckworth assumed the sailors' respect for AJ stemmed from her association with Murphy, but after watching her with the men, the way she offered her assistance and pulled her weight, her actions gave him pause.

The first time he'd seen her climb the rigging, he'd almost laughed until he noticed her skill. In one instance, when she'd glanced about for where to place her next step, her expression was nothing less than sheer delight as if she searched for the most difficult climb. Damn, if she wasn't a sight. Once she was in the nest, all she had to do was keep her eye on the horizon. He knew the task to be boring and easy for someone to fall prey to the roll of the ship before nodding off. Yet the men didn't hesitate when she signaled the alarm and pointed.

He grudgingly admitted that his own respect for her had grown when he'd stumbled on deck one evening and found the rain pouring down as the ship bucked against the angry waves. When he'd squinted up through the fierce storm, he'd noticed someone in the nest. It wasn't until he'd spotted a glimpse of long hair and a long slim arm bracing the rim of the nest that he'd known it was AJ.

When he'd mentioned it to Lando, the man had only grunted a response before moving on. "Don't worry about the lass. She's tied on."

Now Beckworth glared up as he watched AJ swing a pouch across her back before stepping out of the barrel. An arm jostled his, and he glanced over to find Jaime studying him. The man was young for a captain, but it seemed he'd learned much from Murphy.

Beckworth lifted his bound hands. "Where am I going to go out in the middle of the ocean? Can't you give a man a break?"

The captain had an infectious grin when he showed it, which was too often. Damned Irishmen. Always smiling like they have a secret. Jaime followed Beckworth's gaze to where AJ was crossing a yard to cut across the deck rather than take the simple path down the shroud.

Jaime kept his grin in place as he watched the sprite crawl across the rigging. "Acts of sabotage aren't always an immediate threat. I'd rather know where your hands are at all times."

Smart bugger. Beckworth scratched his chin and tried to pull at a sleeve, but his fingers couldn't quite reach. "Why do you make a woman climb up to the nest?"

Jaime laughed. "I'd have thought you knew her well enough to know one doesn't exactly make her do anything."

Beckworth smiled in return and rubbed at his shoulder as his gaze flicked up. "She is quite the little monkey. I should have remembered she knew how to climb when she escaped Dugan. That was no small feat."

"You mean the first time she escaped?" The smile on Jaime's face disappeared, and Beckworth could almost feel the brotherly protection roll off him. "And now you have the second answer as to why your hands are cuffed and why I'm wasting a man guarding you around the clock. Be happy you're not still shackled in one of the cargo holds." He edged closer and pulled himself up to his full height, which was an inch taller than Beckworth. "If I had my way, you'd be tied to the mast for the entire journey to enjoy the winter weather. It's only for AJ's wishes that you're being treated as fairly as you are. Remember that the next time you slight her."

The captain strolled away, his gaze darting about, assuring himself the men had the ship in order. When AJ reached the deck and walked to him, he put an arm around her shoulders, and she laughed at whatever he said.

Beckworth dropped to get out of the wind while he considered Jaime's words. He had to admit. AJ had proven herself resilient from the first time he'd met her. Perhaps he should rethink his plans for when they landed. AJ was beside herself with worry for Maire, and though AJ assumed he could swagger his way back to Waverly, he wasn't so sure. Dugan was up to something, and Beckworth had no doubt it had to do with those blasted stones. He needed to alter his plans. Instead of taking a gamble on entering Waverly himself, why not use the curious Miss Moore to suss out what was going on at Waverly? The webs they wove. The only question was, which of them was the spider and which the fly?

14

———————

On their last night at sea, the crew grew restless, and few slept. Laughter could be heard through the hatches from those gambling below. A handful of men wandered the deck or found a spot to quietly watch the stars. Though close to the shores of England, everyone stayed alert.

AJ's last watch had ended at dusk, and she'd lingered in the barrel to savor the last panoramic vision of the sea. She doubted she'd ever view the spectacular image from a place as wondrous as the nest. She'd spent the next two hours assisting the cook before finding her own corner of the deck to eat.

The same uneasiness of the crew settled in her bones. Though the journey across the channel had been dangerous, she felt safe. The next part of her trip wouldn't be as easy. She ran through all the possible scenarios one last time, and while she could ask Jamie to send someone with her, she couldn't see the point. She could take care of herself.

Neither he nor Lando had said another word on the topic of Beckworth. If they were worried, they would have spent the trip cajoling her to take an additional person with her. They knew her to be stubborn, but that never stopped anyone from giving her unwanted advice.

Maybe they believed her promise to not go to Waverly. That was an easy enough promise. She simply wanted to skirt the area and ask about Maire in town. She knew Ethan and Thomas had already done that, but women had a different touch when seeking information. While her reporter skills were beyond rusty, she'd watched Maire and Stella nurse the best secrets out of people.

Beckworth would be a handful on the road, but if he could get into Waverly after all this time, there was an outside chance of discovering what happened to Maire. A long shot at best, but she had to try. Then she would continue on to Hereford, possibly finding other travelers heading that same direction.

She considered how to use Beckworth to her advantage. Her best option would be to use the skills he seemed best at. In Baywood, he'd been a ghost for months while tracking her, all without her knowledge. Even when Finn and Ethan agreed he must have traveled to the future, Beckworth was still elusive. Unfortunately, his deceitfulness canceled out his benefits. Yet, she had become obsessed to know if Maire was at Waverly. She was so close.

AJ stretched her back, squirming within the hard folds of the canvas tarps. Clear skies followed them all day, the first since leaving France. They were running dark to evade the coastal patrols, but the quarter moon provided enough light for her task. She rolled the handle of the dagger in her palm and reached for the whetstone one of the sailors had loaned her. Footsteps shuffled across the deck, and a massive figure blocked the moonlight.

"Why are you not in your cabin?" Lando smiled down on her, a bushy brow raised. He kept his hair shaved close, which added to his menacing appearance. Only a handful of people knew the teddy bear hidden beneath the surface.

"It's the first night I've been able to enjoy the stars."

"You've caught the restless nature of the men."

"Maybe." She patted a spot next to her, and after a moment, Lando sat beside her. "We haven't had much time to talk."

Lando pulled out a knife and an apple. He carved a slice and offered it to her. After she took a bite, he sliced another and popped it in his mouth. His crunching mingled with the sounds of ropes rubbing against wood, the rustle of the sails, and creaking of the ship. When he finished the apple, he tossed it over the side and wiped the blade on his pants.

"Why are you still working on the ship?" AJ asked. "I would have thought you'd return to London."

He stretched out his legs and peered up to the sky. After a moment of silence, she caught the barest hint of a shrug. "I was paid well for being a bodyguard, but the gentlemen's clubs?" He sighed. "Stiff collars, standing for hours at a time. It wasn't for me."

"There must have been other work in a large city."

"In a factory or livery, maybe, but there's no freedom in that."

"Or the rush you get when we spot another ship?"

He laughed, the sound deep and comforting. "I thought I'd cured my wanderlust. Then Finn showed up in London with a crazy tale and stirred my belly. Once I walked out of the club, my spirit reawakened. After you left, I thought I'd sail back home, help Jaime where I could, then return to London."

"But you couldn't do it."

His expression was hidden in shadow, so she couldn't tell if his thoughts were wistful or regretful. The tone of his response told her everything she needed to know. "We'd only left port an hour earlier, and the alarm was sounded. My blood stirred with the thought of battle. It was then I knew I'd never return to

London. At least not to stay. If Jaime didn't need me, I'd find another ship. This was the life I was meant to live."

"Don't you ever want to settle down?"

He laughed so hard, she was sure there'd be tears of humor though it was impossible to tell in the shadowy light. "Someday, little one, I'll arrive in port, and she'll be waiting for me. But that day isn't yet." He looked down and held out a hand, nodding toward her dagger.

She handed it to him, nervous about what he'd think after all this time. He'd been the first person to teach her how to use it.

"You kept it in fine condition." He ran a finger along its single edge. "It could be sharper." He reached for the whetstone. He repositioned his seating, and AJ edged closer to watch. After a few swipes of blade against stone, he handed both to her.

AJ rolled up her shirt sleeves and settled the knife against the stone. She glanced up, and when he nodded, she went to work, studiously altering the position of the stone when Lando suggested changes to her technique. When she slid the dagger in her pocket, he stood and pulled her up so quickly she almost flew into his arms. They laughed as they walked a few steps before Lando turned her toward the wall of the forecastle.

"Let me see your blade stick."

Nerves ran along her spine as she dug in her pocket for the dagger. She'd become comfortable with Finn and Ethan's watchful gaze, but Lando made her squirm. She didn't understand why his opinion held more importance than Finn's but assumed it was because Lando had been her first instructor. She wanted to make him proud.

She steadied herself and widened her stance. The ship rolled beneath her. She acclimated to its movements as she relaxed her shoulders and blew out long breaths. She aimed and released the dagger in a single movement. The blade stuck a few inches left of the rigging.

Lando grunted. "And where were you aiming?"

She grinned. "A few inches to the right."

He beamed. "You've been practicing."

She shrugged and shared a devious smile. "You should see me with a bow."

IN THE SHADOWS, several yards from AJ and Lando, Beckworth rested against the bulwark. He'd talked the captain into allowing him time on deck, and the men had graciously bound him to the rigging. He'd be there until they made port.

He couldn't take his eyes off AJ. She listened to Lando after each throw of the blade, then made the appropriate adjustments with immediate results. If her suggestion that she was better with the bow had any truth to it, she'd become more deadly than he imagined. She might prove useful after all if he could mold the conditions to his favor. He rubbed his shoulder. Assuming she didn't find a reason to stick him with that blade again, though she never seemed to require a reason to do that.

This next stage of their journey would be interesting. He almost wished Maire was at Waverly. It would be like old times with the three of them at his dining table again.

15

Ethan tossed the thick stack of blankets aside, then braced for the chill of the room. Sleep had been impossible, and he doubted he'd get a decent night of rest until he reached England. He had a bad feeling about this Valentin, but their choices were limited. He'd understood AJ's unwillingness to wait another two months for Jamie's return. Time pressed in, and with little to do but wait, his impatience grew.

After lighting the lantern, he dressed and checked his bag, though he'd repacked twice before he'd gone to bed. He sat and stared at the shadows that played against the wall. Unable to resist, he reached into his pocket and pulled out the frayed letter. He'd kept it close since he'd received it several months ago. It was the last letter he had from Maire.

She'd been in Peterstow for less than a day and had quickly found the person she'd left Hereford to meet. He held the letter close to the light, mesmerized by her delicate handwriting, so clear and precise. She could have been a scholar had she lived in a different age. She spoke of working at the Trinity Library in Dublin, but Ethan doubted she would be happy there. As a woman, she'd be nothing more than a housemaid—able to look at the books but never touch.

He laid the page on the table, scared to hold it too long. Maire had instructed him how to handle the delicate pages of *The Book of Stones* without damaging it. Her letter wouldn't be considered sacred to anyone else, but to him, they might be the last words he'd ever have from her.

He read past her normal opening, her apology for leaving without telling him her true intentions, and her strength of conviction that she was on the right path. When he reached the last few paragraphs, he ran a hand through his hair, his breath hitching as he read.

"I spoke to the young girl, her name is Hannah. She's no more than fifteen, yet on her own, though she's found a good family that owns the apothecary here. At least I didn't completely lie before I left. The merchant has several herbs that would benefit the earl's stores. I've purchased a few samples to bring back with me."

He reread the last line several times. She planned to return to Hereford. It was the one light that kept him going. He cleared his throat and kept reading.

"Hannah had been terrified when I mentioned Waverly. I thought it might require days to convince her to talk to me. Yet, even through her fear, she shared her story. In the end, she had little to tell me. She was a housemaid, working mostly in the kitchen. On occasion, she cleaned the hearths. It was during one of her cleanings that she overheard two men talking about something called *The Mórdha Stone Grimoire*. She asked the cook about it, and before she knew it, another servant had packed her belongings. The cook told her she had to leave for her own safety. Before leaving, Hannah confided in Ella, the young woman who'd been my lady's maid while I was at Waverly.

Hannah left for Peterstow the next day and moved in as a maid with the local apothecary.

"When Ella wrote, I tried to ignore it. The duke was dead. Beckworth had disappeared into the mist, and the Heart Stone was with AJ somewhere in the future. All should be well. Yet her words haunted me. We know the Mórdha Stone was what *The Book of Stones* called the Heart Stone. We also know the druid book is out there. What if this grimoire is what we've been searching for?

"Here's the part that troubles me. It's silly of me to be writing this letter at all when I plan to leave soon. When I pressed Hannah for who she thought she'd overheard in the east wing, she insisted it had been the viscount and his bodyguard. The whole house had confirmed the viscount had returned. How could that be, Ethan? We saw the fog take him. What does this mean for Finn and AJ? I need your help, my love. I don't think this is over."

Ethan bent his head, his eyes misting over his loss of Maire and the weight of lies he'd sown with AJ and Finn. He should have told them straight away about Maire's letter. If Maire hadn't given the letter to a guard before her last visit to the apothecary, Ethan would never have known what happened. Yet, by the time he arrived at Waverly with Thomas and the earl's men, there had been no sign of Maire or the viscount.

His first thought had been to lay it all out for Finn. He hoped Finn would see something he missed. When Ethan had learned Beckworth was in the future, everything Maire had written became suspect. Had Hannah been a ruse? The girl had seemingly disappeared as quickly as Maire had.

He folded the letter and returned it to his pocket. He almost laughed when he thought about the secrets Finn and AJ had each kept. Even Adam had kept his gambling debt from others. Everyone tried to protect someone they loved through lies. And now the secrets had come full circle. He'd wait until they reached England, tell Finn everything, then take the right cross he justly deserved, assuming Finn didn't run him through with his blade.

He picked up his duffel, blew out the lantern, and raced down the tunnel to reach the warmth and light of the kitchen fires. Sebastian and Finn sat at a table, their heads bowed in deep conversation, mugs of coffee steaming in front of them.

"It appears you couldn't sleep either." Finn's smile ate at Ethan's gut, but he gave Finn a slight grin as he turned to search for a mug.

"I wanted to make sure we don't miss the ship."

"I've arranged for Luis to take you to town. I think it best I not be seen with you." Sebastian sat back and scratched his head. "I wish I had more information to help you." He glanced around the kitchen. "Cook, where are you? We need another bowl of porridge and some meat for Ethan."

"I think you've done more than enough by giving us shelter and ensuring AJ's safety." Ethan sat with his mug and nodded to the cook when she dropped a bowl and small plate of meat, cheese, and bread in front of him.

He ate quickly, and when done, Sebastian walked them to the courtyard.

Ethan tossed his duffel in the cart after Finn's, then climbed into the back with the bags. Before Finn joined Luis on the bench seat, Sebastian rested a hand on his arm.

"I'll review the translations from the book once again. If I find anything that we've overlooked, I'll forward it to the earl with one of the next ships. Godspeed in your journey, but I have faith you'll find both women."

The monk's last words revived Ethan's spirits, but when Luis dropped them at the outskirts of town, his previous concerns about the ship's captain returned.

Finn glanced around, slung a duffel onto each of his shoulders, then turned to Ethan, his voice terse. "Let's hurry." Then he broke out in a quick jog toward a back alley.

Ethan kept his eyes open for early morning patrols and hoped Finn's heightened apprehension had nothing to do with mistrust of the captain. They moved like ghosts in the early morning hours. Finn kept the pace as he ducked down alleys and made a detour toward their destination. Whether Finn was concerned about being followed or had seen someone, Ethan didn't ask.

Even with the circuitous route, they arrived at the smithy within ten minutes. Finn ducked behind a row of barrels near a building across from the smithy. "We wait here."

Ethan crouched next to him, both of them facing the street as they searched the darkness for movement. "How long do we wait?"

"Until they find us."

Those were the last words Ethan heard as something hit him in the back of the head.

16

AJ stood on the bow of the *Daphne Marie* as the crew guided the ship into the cozy port of Poole, some distance from Southampton. The last part of the voyage into this small village had been uneventful. It seemed once past the main fleet of the Royal Navy, few ships patrolled the shores this far west. Strong memories assailed her from the last time she'd sailed into England on this very ship. Finn had been with her. She reached into the pocket of her pants and squeezed the necklace that held the Heart Stone and her wedding ring. Instead of tears, a powerful resolve settled over her.

He was out there somewhere. She could almost feel him drawing nearer.

She turned her focus back to the task at hand. During the last hours of the sail, AJ had practiced different holding positions with her dagger, using both her right and left hands. The evening before, when she'd practiced with Lando, learning to use the weaker side of her body, she'd kept an eye on Beckworth. He'd been conveniently tied to the rigging in plain sight of her and Lando.

When throwing with her weaker left arm, her aim went to

hell. By the end of the first short session, she'd improved her distance. She continued to work on her aim during their journey north. Whenever she returned to her resting spot, she found Beckworth watching her, a touch of something in his gaze she thought might be admiration. Unwilling to participate in whatever game he might be playing, she responded with a cold smile. She always made sure to face him when she sharpened her dagger, and whenever she glanced his way, he turned his head. First step of intimidation accomplished.

Once the ship was moored, AJ waited for the men to remove the cargo before she picked up her canvas bag and backpack to disembark. Before leaving the ship, she glanced back along the deck of the *Daphne Marie* then up to her sails. The last time she'd left the ship, she hadn't thought she'd see it again. The ship wasn't the same without Finn. Then she turned to the sleepy town of Poole. It was nothing like the busy Southampton port. One other ship rested on the opposite dock, its sails stowed, only a handful of men on board. Carts and people moved about, but there seemed to be no hurry to get where they were going. The town smelled of the briny air and wood smoke from the chimneys.

AJ sucked in a lungful of that scent, held it for a count of ten, then blew it out as she descended to the dock. Lando was waiting for her and guided her to the single inn. It was only mid-morning, but her stomach grumbled when they entered the establishment. Fresh-baked bread and cooked meat made her eyes water and gained another growl from her belly.

A young woman, her hair tied back in a long braid of raven-colored hair, stopped in front of them, sharing a pleasant, if distracted, smile. She offered a bowl of stew along with a plate of bread and cheese. AJ nodded enthusiastically and almost sighed with pleasure when a mug of ale followed the plate.

AJ turned an eye to Lando. "Aren't you eating?"

He shook his head. "I took an extra ration at breakfast since we'll be restocking the stores."

She closed her eyes as she chewed the beef from the stew. The warm meal was a delight after two days on limited rations and hardtack on the ship. The men would be well fed once they finished their final chores and were released for a day of shore leave. She nibbled at the cheese and studied Lando, whose gaze swung to the door each time it opened. "I would think Jamie could use your help."

"I'm doing my job." He glanced away, watching a gruff man leave the bar and stumble to the door.

"I thought we'd been through this. If you can't trust me to be safe sitting at an inn, a mere two hundred yards from Jamie's crew, what are you going to do when I leave town and you go back to the ship?"

Lando crossed his arms and said nothing.

She chewed her bread and followed it with her ale before returning to the stew. "I could use your help with something else."

After a moment, he finally turned an eye toward her.

"I need two good horses with stamina for long days." When he didn't comment, she reached into her pocket and placed a small bag of coin on the table. "And I'll need a well-balanced bow and a full quiver."

With that, he lifted a brow. He watched her eat her meal, scratched his ear, then mumbled something that sounded like a curse before stalking out.

17

The gentle sway and creaking of boards forced a smile from Finn. He nestled deeper into the warmth of canvas as the smell of sea, old wood, and oil tickled his nose. An old longing of wind filling sails and the chatter of seabirds as they chased the *Daphne Maire* out of port filled his sense of adventure. His inane curiosity of not knowing what lay ahead quickly morphed into a sense of urgency. A great loss pitted his stomach and jangled his nerves.

He slowly raised to consciousness, and a blast of pain stabbed his head as he pried his eyes open to nothing more than a slit. When he moved his legs, they hit a hard wall. Something poked at his side before he remembered his ribs. A deep ache from where they'd been battered by fists soon followed.

After the pain subsided, he opened his eyes again to a dim light from a lantern swinging in rhythm with the ship. Even if he'd been blindfolded, he'd have recognized the pitch of a ship as it matched the roll of the waves. He stretched his body, performing a physical inventory. Other than the stitch in his side and the ache in his head, he was whole. When he tested the spot where his head hurt, he felt a slight bump. Then he noticed the hooded, silver gaze, filled with anger, following his movements.

At least he wasn't alone. He cleared his dry throat before whispering, "It appears we made it on the ship."

"Perhaps you should have been clearer on the accommodations." Ethan's tone matched his angry stare.

Finn untangled himself from the old sail that had covered him and gingerly pushed himself to a sitting position. Ignoring Ethan for the moment, he scanned the area. They were in a massive iron cage within a cargo hold. Based on the bulkhead and height of the ceiling, he guessed somewhere in the aft of the ship. Whether it was Valentin's ship, he couldn't say, but they would know soon enough. Crates and sacks of unknown inventory filled the room. Several narrow paths curved out of sight between the crates and into the darkness. Finn presumed they led to the door of an inner passageway since he couldn't see a ladder or opening to the upper deck.

When he noticed smells, his nose wrinkled in distaste at the odd mix of foreign spices and something wickedly foul. Inside their cage, most of the space was taken by short stacks of crates and bags of flour and grain. There was a narrow six-foot aisle to stand or pace. Once he settled back against a stack of grain sacks, he took stock of Ethan.

The man didn't look any worse for wear, though his squinting gaze spoke of more than anger. Finn assumed Ethan suffered from a matching lump on his head. An old sheet of canvas wrapped around Ethan's feet, and he sat on his own stack of bags. Finn let him glower as he took in the rest of their cell. A tin sat on top of a crate in one corner, and a crate in the opposite corner held a jug with two mugs. Water and place to piss. He'd laugh if he could confirm which ship they were on. Nothing about this jump had been simple.

He turned his attention to Ethan. "Have you seen anyone?"

Ethan shook his head. So it was going to be like that. Finn had gotten them on a ship. It could be worse.

"Are you going to pout the entire way to England?" Finn rolled his neck, and after a short snap, his head felt better. "Someone will bring us food. Eventually."

"Why do I feel more like a prisoner than a guest?" Ethan's question wasn't far from Finn's own thoughts.

If this was Valentin's ship, why were they stuffed into a hold? Something the captain had mentioned at the inn scraped at Finn's memory, but he couldn't put his finger on it. He'd have to wait until his head cleared.

"Until we know more of the situation, we could speculate the entire journey. And while we clearly need to consider our situation, can it wait until my head stops spinning?" Finn slid from his perch and tested his legs. They immediately registered the movement of the ship, and his body fell into rhythm with a natural sense of being one with a ship. He doubted that instant connection would ever leave him after years of walking decks.

He picked up the jug. It was full. He poured liquid into one of the mugs, sniffed, swirled the water, then tossed it onto the floor outside the cell. He filled the mug and offered it to Ethan, who accepted it with a slight nod. After pouring another mug for himself, Finn returned to his seat.

They drank in silence while Finn waited for the water to hydrate him. Ethan set down his mug first, his earlier sulk replaced with a thoughtful look. "If we are in the hold of your friend's ship, why would he lock us in a cell?"

Finn shrugged. "Maybe to hide us from French inspection."

Ethan considered the possibility. "And if it's not your friend?"

"I'm not sure anyone else would leave us a jug of water." He scratched his chin, just as confused as Ethan. "We shouldn't discount that another smuggler grabbed us, but if so, why not hand us over to the French?"

Ethan shook his head, then winced when he rubbed the back of his head. "None of this makes sense. I'd feel better if I knew we were traveling to England and not the far east."

"Agreed."

The scraping of wood announced an opening door. Both men dropped into low crouches. With nothing but a mug in their hands, they were as threatening as toddlers, but the instinct couldn't be helped. The door quietly closed, and footsteps approached, but shadows blocked the man from their view.

Valentin stepped from the darkness and gave a slight bow. "Hello, my friends. Welcome aboard the *Gypsy Runner*."

18

Before leaving the inn, AJ had the innkeeper wrap a few days' worth of food. The ride to Waverly would take two days, assuming no trouble. With Beckworth in tow, she planned for it. She had one idea that might keep her traveling companion in check until they reached Waverly, but she'd require just the right setting.

When she returned to the ship, new cargo was being loaded. She found Jamie and Fitz standing off to one side. Fitz carried a ledger and watched the men remove a crate from one of four loaded carts. He squinted at the writing on the side of the crate when the men stopped in front of him. He ran his finger down one page and then a second one before he placed a mark next to the item. He nodded to the men, and they shuffled off to the ship.

The crates that had been removed earlier, and the carts that had been waiting for them, were gone, already on the way to their destination. AJ imagined illicit cargo would draw unwanted attention; instead, she was impressed by the organization of tasks.

When Jamie saw her approach, he flashed an easy smile. "Lando says you kicked him out of the inn."

She snorted. "I never knew him to exaggerate." She stopped to watch another crate go by. "I just thought his time was better spent elsewhere."

His tone matched his serious expression. 'You know Finn would skin me alive if I didn't watch out for you."

Fitz slid her a sidelong glance. She sighed. "I'm sorry to have put you in this situation. But you don't have to babysit me, regardless of what Finn might think."

Fitz barked out a laugh before turning to hide his grin.

Jamie tried to retain his stern expression. He rubbed his chin, where a nice day's worth of stubble accentuated his roguish appearance. "I would call it security, but let's agree to disagree."

She gave him a quick hug. "Absolutely." She glanced over at Fitz. "Do I even want to know what the two of you are up to?"

Fitz's grin turned into a knowing nod, and he scratched his ear. "It's probably best if you don't know, Miss AJ."

"You're right. I have other things to focus on."

When silence returned, AJ released another sigh and waited for it. She'd barely taken a breath when Jamie cleared his throat.

"About that. I think I should send someone with you."

"As a bodyguard for me? Or for Beckworth?"

Fitz's chuckle snuffed out when Jamie gave him a quick shake of his head.

"If Finn..." Jamie started.

"Yes, yes. If Finn were here, but he's not." With fists planted on her hips, she held back a grin as she stood her ground. She'd noted the resigned look on Jamie's face, and the steam went out of her. Jamie was only concerned for her safety, and it endeared him to her even more. But the approach to Waverly required stealth. Too many in her group might send alarms. That could explain why Ethan and Thomas found Waverly apparently empty when they stormed up to the front door of the estate.

AJ dropped her arms and wrapped one around Jamie's arm. "I'm not the same woman I was when you last saw me. I think you know that. I'm better trained, and believe it or not, Finn has taught me a thing or two about patience and planning." She stuck a hand into her pocket and gripped the lump of necklace. She drew strength, not from the Heart Stone, but from the small band nestled next to it. "I know the next couple of days will be dangerous. I know Beckworth can't be trusted. Something else is going on. Something he won't divulge but has him worried."

The minute she said it, she knew she'd made a mistake.

"Damn it, AJ. That's the exact point I'm trying to make." Jamie huffed out a breath and kicked a rock.

She raised her hands in an attempt to calm him. "I know, but I have no plans on going anywhere near Waverly. I'll let Beckworth gather information while I wait in town. My only point was that I believe he needs me as much as I need him." She blew out a breath, as frustrated as Jamie at having to depend on the slimy bastard.

Before either could continue, the sound of approaching hooves made all three turn to find Lando walking two horses toward them. AJ inwardly thanked Finn for his continual training as she watched the two beasts shake their heads at being tugged along. She should have reminded Lando she required a gentle horse.

As if he'd read her mind, Lando clucked at her. "Don't worry. They just need a short run. I think they've been in the stalls too long."

His reassurance didn't help, but she wasn't going to argue while Jamie stared daggers at her. He didn't need another reason to lock her away before she carried out her half-baked plan. In truth, she could barely stop from talking herself out of her crazy idea.

AJ strode up to the horses and stared each of them in the eye. She screwed up her courage and reached for the more spirited one. Lando said nothing as he watched her give the horse a more thorough appraisal. Thank heavens she'd paid attention to Finn's handling of their horses back home. She had to smile when she noticed the quiver of arrows and matching bow hanging from the horse's saddle. When she glanced at Lando, he nodded his approval.

A warmth spread through her, and she squared her shoulders. "Let's get the bags strapped on, then you can bring Beckworth." AJ lifted her head and waited.

The men glanced at each other. With nothing more to say, Jamie whistled for one of the men to bring her bags. They tied Beckworth's backpack to his horse and AJ's canvas bag to hers.

They all turned to watch two crewmates walk Beckworth from the ship. His arms hung in front of him, and his hands were covered with an overcoat. He held his head high and his back straight as he strolled in front of the men. A smile graced his lips as he took in the town, the horses, and the four people waiting for him.

"I say, it's a beautiful day for a ride." Beckworth stopped next to the riderless horse.

AJ rolled her eyes before giving him a pointed look. "Be thankful you can see it. I was tempted to have a cover thrown over your head."

He eyed her playfully. "So I wouldn't know where we're going?" He laughed.

"No. I was hoping it would muffle the sound of your voice." AJ moved away to check her saddle and bridle.

The other men laughed as Jamie nodded. The guards pushed Beckworth toward his horse.

AJ stepped toward Fitz and gave him a peck on the cheek. "May the wind always be at your back." She thought she saw his eyes water a little before he gave her a wink. He returned to his inventory, shouting at the men to hurry along.

Her lips twitched as she turned first to Jamie, who glared at Beckworth, then to Lando, who watched her with both arms crossed in front of his thick chest.

"I'll expect you in Hereford within a week." Jamie's tone brooked no argument.

The statement caught her off guard. "And how will you know I've kept my word?"

"Because I'll be there. And if you're not, I'll be coming for you."

She held back a grin and eyed Lando. "And I suppose you'll be there as well."

He paused for a second, then nodded.

AJ studied him, but unable to put her finger on what troubled her, she ignored his hesitation and turned to Jamie. "If Hensley approves it, you mean."

"I don't work for Hensley." Jamie's retort was sharp. "I may run cargo and missions for him, but my schedule and ship are my own."

AJ laid a hand on his. "I didn't mean to offend."

He shook his head. "It's not you."

She understood. It wasn't easy to prove one's worth after Finn's departure, and Hensley had a way of taking over. "It was my poor choice of words." She leaned in, and before placing a kiss on his cheek, whispered so only he could hear, "Finn would be proud."

Satisfied to see the moisture collect in his eyes, she turned and gave Lando a hug. Her goodbyes accomplished, she mounted her horse as if she'd been doing it for years.

She gazed down at Beckworth. "Are you going to ride or just walk behind your beast?"

The men laughed, and the overcoat fell away as Beckworth attempted to mount his horse with tied hands. After several tries, Beckworth found the best approach and settled into the saddle. One of the guards threw the overcoat over his hands and stepped back.

"See you in Hereford." AJ kicked her horse. It tossed its head several times before AJ guided it into an easy trot. She turned to see Beckworth right behind her, the rest of the men silently watching them leave.

"Best behavior, Beckworth. I know your backpack is within easy reach, but the only thing you'll find are extra clothes and food rations. No weapons."

He didn't appear pleased, but he put on his best face. "And what if we're set upon by highwaymen."

AJ laughed, and before kicking her horse to set a faster pace, shouted back, "Don't worry. I'll protect your worthless life."

19

Finn's shoulders eased when Valentin stepped out of the gloom, but he couldn't hold back the anger in his tone. "Is this how you repay your debt to an old friend?"

Valentin studied him before sparing a glance at Ethan. "These are dangerous times." He nodded at Finn. "As I mentioned at the inn."

"And you didn't think you could trust me?"

Valentin considered the question before looking around, his gaze resting on a short barrel a few feet away. He dragged it in front of the cage and brushed his overcoat aside before perching on the drum. Crossing a leg over his knee, Valentin flicked open a knife and slowly twirled it as he reflected on Finn's question.

"What would you do if you had a rat on your ship you couldn't find?" Valentin continued to play with his knife but managed to pin Finn with a curious gaze.

Finn understood the captain's concern. A spy aboard a ship during peacetime was one thing. But during war? That required stealthy footwork to stay one step ahead of the enemy. And to catch them? Suddenly it all made sense, and he barked out a laugh, followed by his signature grin.

"I imagine I'd find a treat too tasty to pass up."

Valentin smiled in return and pointed his knife at Finn while speaking to Ethan. "This is why I like your friend so much." He pointed the knife to his own head. "He thinks things through. Sees beyond the trees."

"So, we're bait for your trap." Ethan leaned against a sack of flour but kept his eye on Valentin's knife.

Valentin laughed and turned to Finn. "You have no idea how stimulating it is to have wise men to speak with. Since this war has begun, I have very few I can share intelligent discussions. Everyone keeps to themselves, heads down to avoid notice from the soldiers. Most of the French troops are left to their own devices at ports." He shrugged. "They are either too lazy or too easily bought."

Ethan glanced around the room. "You seem to have enough money."

"Oui, but money is only as good as the next person's offer. And these noses..." He waved an arm, continuing his condemnation. "These so-called snitches, will switch loyalties with a promise of a fatter purse."

Ethan nodded, smart enough to know the answer before he ever asked the question.

"How long have we been at sea?" Finn asked.

"Only a couple of hours. I apologize for the rather abrupt meeting at the smithy. But I have to say, the two of you made an enticing package when you were brought aboard."

"And you had no trouble with the inspection?"

Valentin growled. "No. Which makes me question who this man works for."

"We must have seemed a godsend for you to ferret out your spy." Finn held the captain's gaze.

"Or perhaps we were a trap ourselves," Ethan added.

Valentin gave Ethan an appraising stare. "Yes. It was possible the two of you were a convenient ploy. If I didn't know Captain Murphy for as many years as I have, I may have turned down the tempting gift fate laid at my door. But for all his smuggling, the captain here is an honest man. Always true to his word."

"So now what?" Finn asked, pleased that he had been right to trust this man. If he and Ethan had to suffer a little discomfort to capture a rat, so much the better. There was nothing worse than vermin on a ship who could destroy the trust the sailors had for each other. It could get them all killed.

Valentin shrugged again. "This is the first step. I made no secret of coming down to check on my personal cargo. The men know this room is off-limits to anyone other than me or the first mate. They also know we brought two people on board. Now you know why you must stay. I think you'll be comfortable enough. I'll see food is brought down."

He stood, pocketed his knife, and strode to a stack of crates. When he returned, he held two well-turned daggers. "I believe these belong to you." He handed them both to Finn.

Finn recognized them immediately. They were the ones he and Ethan carried on their person. "Yes. And our bags?"

He nodded to the far corner of the room. "I've hidden them well, considering what they contain."

Finn grinned. Valentin was referring to the arsenal he and Ethan carried with them.

Finn handed Ethan his dagger then nodded at the captain. "Thank you for these."

"I can't leave you defenseless. You have my leave to kill the rat yourself if you must. However—" He pointed a finger at Finn. "You know I prefer to clean out the garbage myself."

Finn nodded before Valentin made his way to the door. "You'll see the sun again once the rat has been caught, or when we make England, whichever comes first."

After he departed, Finn glanced at Ethan. "Sorry about this."

For the first time since they'd met Valentin at the inn, Ethan laughed. "I always wondered what your life was like running cargo. Now I can honestly say I haven't missed a thing."

Finn had no comeback for that. Life at sea wasn't for everyone. As he glanced around the hold and listened to the comforting creak of the boards under his feet, he no longer doubted his future. He knew without a doubt, that while his life as captain of the *Daphne Marie* had been a good one, those days were well behind him. And, God willing, so was this century. His life was with AJ back home at their inn. He settled into his spot, the canvas sheet at hand should he need it, and considered how they might lure a spy.

20

———————

A J and Beckworth traveled for two hours, mostly in silence, until she turned off the road to a small glade. At first, she'd led the way out of town but soon realized her mistake. With Beckworth behind her, she kept glancing over her shoulder to see if he was up to something. They hadn't ridden more than a mile before she slowed and let him catch up to ride next to her. After thirty minutes, his endless banter and teasing made her want to punch him.

She considered that he might take off and leave her, or that he'd find a way to escape the ropes before she was ready. The only option left besides knocking him out, was to let him lead. Before doing that, she had to prove a point, knowing he wasn't taking her seriously. After being stabbed by her twice, he should have learned, but she didn't trust his better judgment to prevail.

She stopped fifty yards from the road and tied her horse a branch. She turned and noted his frown. "Get down."

"We've barely started. If we're going to stop every few miles for crumpets, it will take us days to get to Waverly," Beckworth grumbled as he considered his dismount. "Besides, I think we're close to a small village where we could get a warm meal."

"We're not stopping in any towns. We'll ride straight through. I don't want to take a chance of someone seeing us."

He landed on the ground more gracefully than she'd expected. "We're miles from Waverly." He continued to mutter as he sat on a rock underneath the shade of birch trees and stretched his back. He lifted his hands. "And I don't see a reason to keep my hands bound. I certainly can't go into Waverly or ride through towns like this."

AJ tossed him a small package filled with meat, cheese, and bread. "Don't eat it all. You'll want to save some for this afternoon. Then you'll have to wait for dinner." She dropped a skin of water near his feet.

When he turned his back to her to stare off across the glade, she left him to pout while she returned to the horse. Keeping an eye on him, she slipped the bow from her saddle and two arrows from the quiver before she melted into the trees.

BECKWORTH HEARD her slip away and assumed she'd gone somewhere to relieve herself. He grunted. The poor thing must have strained her neck from keeping an eye on him before she got smart enough to let him ride next to her. He couldn't blame her for her mistrust. She wasn't wrong. Her distrust of him would soon be validated, he just wasn't sure how until he knew exactly what was happening at Waverly. It made no sense to leave her behind without knowing for sure whether he'd need her.

Trouble brewed at Waverly. He'd felt it even without the scant clues he'd overheard. He knew the moment he discovered that damn book and received the first stone that his life would never be the same. He thought Murphy had given him a reprieve when he killed the duke. If only Murphy or one of his minions had killed Dugan as well. He'd have done it himself if he thought he could get away with it. But if he missed, he would the one looking over his shoulder with Dugan on his trail. That man never let go of a grudge.

Once Murphy showed up—and Beckworth held no false notion he would; the man was worse than a bad penny—he might be just the man to rid the world of Dugan. All of Beckworth's worries would crumble like a house of cards if that single task could be accomplished.

He bit into the makeshift sandwich he'd made. He almost missed the BLTs the sisters had made for him. What had they made of his disappearance? A shiver ran through him. If he could last three months with those two, he could certainly spend a day or two watching the lovely backside of Miss Moore.

He'd just taken another bite when he heard a buzz. An arrow struck the tree behind him, inches from his head. Leaves, severed from their branch, floated around him. He dropped to the ground, his body crushing his sandwich as he scanned the area. And here he was, defenseless and bound. Where the devil was that woman? She'd ridden them right into some sort of an ambush.

When nothing else happened, he rose to one knee as he peered about. He turned at the sound of rustling grass, ready to dive for the ground. AJ strolled out of the trees, a bow and an unspent arrow at her side. Her wicked grin enraged him.

"Are you daft?" His screech echoed through the glade. "You could have killed me."

She simply nodded as she replaced the arrow in the quiver and strung her bow around it. Her silence disquieted him, and after retrieving a package of food and joining him on a nearby rock, she continued to ignore him.

"You aren't going to say anything? Perhaps apologize?" Her nonchalance irritated him more than her threat to shoot an arrow between his eyes.

She unwrapped her food, slowly chewed a thick slice of bread, and washed it down with water before running a sleeve across her mouth. "I haven't had a chance to practice the bow since being dragged away from my home. I needed to make sure my aim was still true." She placed a piece of cheese on a slice of meat and took a bite. "Besides, I'm still working on my accuracy at farther distances."

Beckworth stammered then shut his mouth until he could control the building rage. When the blood stopped pounding in his ears, and with a tone still underlined with stilted anger, he barked, "I'm not a bloody target."

She gazed at him with a coldness he'd only ever seen in Murphy. And that had been when Beckworth dangled the man's sister as bait.

"That's the point I'm trying to make. That's exactly what you are. You're only here for one thing—to help me determine if Maire is being held at Waverly. I want you to feel that bull's-eye on your back. If you run, I'll track you down. And one thing I can assure you—you won't see me coming."

Though there wasn't a hint of a breeze, Beckworth shivered as if a cold wind had swept through him. If he thought he'd only teamed with a feisty woman, one who'd gotten lucky with a dagger, albeit twice, he'd been wrong. He glanced down at his crushed sandwich and let it drop to the ground. The game had changed. He'd made a bargain with a pit viper.

21

After leaving the glade, Beckworth took the lead. When they approached the first town, AJ kicked her mount to move up next to him. They rode through town without slowing down, and AJ couldn't help but smirk. The man had been filled with a silent rage ever since she loosed the arrow.

She would never forget the look on his face when she returned with the bow. His handsome face pinched in purple rage. To be honest, she never felt so relieved. He would think twice before crossing her. Not that he wouldn't eventually.

When they first left Poole, AJ assumed they would sleep under the stars. The more she thought about it as she shifted in her saddle, the more she wanted the comfort of a bed, regardless of how lumpy it might be. That decision led to another problem. How would she deal with Beckworth and an overnight stay at an inn? Beckworth seemed to have been thinking the same thing as he slowed his horse for her to ride alongside.

"If we want to be inconspicuous, we should play the married couple and get one room." Beckworth gave her a wink, obviously pushing past his earlier irritation with her. If he thought to get a rise from her, he'd have to try harder.

"I agree." She urged her mount to a trot, forcing him to do the same.

"Aren't you worried about what Murphy will think?"

She snorted. "Hardly. It's obvious we have to share a room. How else can I keep an eye on you?"

He raised his bound hands and gave her a wink. "And what will the innkeeper think of the ropes? Or are we newlyweds?"

"I'll cut your bindings before we enter town. Don't worry, the innkeeper will have no doubt that it was an arranged marriage."

He laughed, but they continued their ride in silence.

AJ spent the rest of the day considering her options once they reached Waverly. While she plotted and planned, she knew Beckworth did the same. If he'd planned anything for that evening, he changed his mind. The evening had been uneventful. He played the respectful husband, ensuring the innkeeper's son took their horses to the stable for food and water. She kept her dagger close when she fell, fully clothed, into bed. Beckworth curled on the sofa in front of the fire.

When she woke the next morning and found him gone, she couldn't decide whether it bothered her. His escape wouldn't help her plan, but she was so eager to be done with him, she was almost thankful he'd run off.

She was finishing her sponge bath when Beckworth waltzed in with a tray. Though she was fully clothed as she wiped a washcloth under an arm, he had the good manners to turn away as he poured coffee and laid out their breakfast.

"I thought it best we eat in the room." He spoke over his shoulder as he sat with his back to her. "We should arrive at Waverly by midday."

She sensed his eagerness to get moving and, after brushing her unruly hair, joined him at the table. Breakfast was a simple meal of porridge and bread. When done, she sat back and studied him while he finished his second bowl.

"What's your plan?" she asked.

"We need to establish a base. Most everyone knows me in Corsham. That's the town just southeast of Waverly. I think we should try stopping by an old friend's house first. It's a couple miles west of Waverly. We need information before we can proceed."

AJ munched on a slice of freshly baked bread then savored the strong coffee. She finally nodded. What he planned made sense. "Then, once we're settled, we'll sneak in for reconnaissance."

He perked up. "Exactly."

"And why don't you just ride up to the front door?"

Beckworth set down his spoon, wiped his mouth with a napkin, and studied her. Would he tell her the truth or some fabrication? How would she know the difference? But she suspected he'd stay somewhere in the middle, telling her just enough to garner her cooperation.

"I suspect that Dugan has his men guarding the perimeter." He sat back, his mug in his hands, and despite his worn and wrinkled clothing, and the meager surroundings, the two of them could be back at Waverly. Only at that time, they had been glaring at each other, rather than planning a joint reconnaissance mission.

"Dugan?" She felt the blood leave her face. They had suspected he might be involved. She had hoped otherwise. "What makes you think he's involved?"

He shrugged. "If Maire has been kidnapped, and we assume it has something to do with the stones, Dugan makes the most sense. He was close to the duke and knew how the stones worked."

Maybe she should have accepted Jamie's offer to send someone with them. If it was Dugan, one additional man wouldn't help. She would have to reconsider her plan—as soon as she came up with one.

He held her gaze. "While you might think Dugan and I are of the same mettle, you'd be wrong. Dugan was never my man; he was the duke's."

Could that be true? She wanted to believe he was lying, but allowing the thought to sink in, she somehow knew it was the truth. Beckworth was a manipulator and a liar. A man only willing to play the game if there was something of value to gain. But the look of distaste that slipped across his face each time Dugan's name was mentioned appeared to be a subconscious response. Like the way his upper lip curled when he was angry.

"Dugan was sent by the duke when I first took possession of Waverly. I'd assumed the duke sent him to help organize the few men I had employed for security. When the duke urged me to allow Dugan to build a stronger defense force, I realized his purpose. The duke needed someone to watch me. Make sure I stayed the course."

"You're telling me you were a hostage at Waverly?"

Beckworth laughed with true merriment, then his gaze fogged over. "I'd never thought of it that way." He sat up and tugged at his sleeves. "You'd have to understand more than we have time for now. The bottom line is that I was never a believer in the stones. I simply wanted to live a better life."

"I'm guessing you've changed your mind on that subject." AJ had pushed her bowl aside and set her elbows on the table, head resting in her hands, fully interested in his story. Now that she had him talking, she wanted to see if she could find a weakness, something she could use as insurance in case she needed it.

Beckworth had grown silent again. He shivered. "I'd rather not talk about the stones."

AJ sympathized with him. She hadn't been happy the first

time she'd learned of the stones. But at least she hadn't been alone. Finn had been with her through most of it. Beckworth had lived through a nightmare—stuck in a future century with no friends, no money, and no way to make sense of it. Though he'd had help of a sort from the sisters.

"I'm back home now—or will be soon. The only question that remains is whether Dugan is back at Waverly. And of course, whether Miss Murphy is there."

"And why do people think the viscount is back?"

"We don't know if that's true. If Dugan returned, the townspeople probably just assume the viscount is back as well."

She hated to admit it, but that seemed plausible. "We still need to know what's going on. One way or another."

He continued to study her. Not the way he had during their time together at Waverly, like she was a bug under a microscope. This seemed different. As if he wanted to share something more if he could trust her. But when his gaze slid to another point in the room, she understood he couldn't make that leap any more than she could.

"I suppose we'll find out soon enough." He stood and grabbed the backpack with his meager supplies.

They were on the road to Waverly before she released a silent curse. After all his talk at breakfast, she learned very little about Beckworth himself. Dugan had been the duke's man, and if she were to believe it, there was no love between him and Beckworth. If Dugan held Waverly, then everything she'd endured with Beckworth had been wasted effort.

Perhaps she'd made a mistake bringing him along. Too late now. One thing she had confirmed. The closer they got to Waverly, the more introspective Beckworth became. Whether his reflective mood was from worry or hatching plots, she'd have to wait until she understood his true role—her path to Maire or her worst nightmare.

22

By the end of their second day trapped inside the ship's cell, Finn and Ethan had run through dozens of scenarios for what they might find at Waverly. Each idea became more outlandish than the last with nothing but time and imagination to keep them occupied. Valentin had been true to his word. They ate well with plenty of ale to wash down the meals, yet not enough to get them drunk or unruly.

Finn had been surprised by Ethan's steady demeanor. Neither man liked being stuck in a cell, especially running through blockades. If a battle ensued, the last place they wanted to be was trapped like rats in a sinking ship. But Finn had faith in Valentin. He didn't have a choice. Fretting over it did nothing but agitate his already frayed thoughts over AJ and the danger she was in with Beckworth.

At the end of the first day, Valentin had given them a deck of cards to help pass the time. Armed with the knowledge that with each passing hour, they grew closer to England, the two men managed to not snarl at each other.

When they spent time in their own corners, Finn thought of AJ. Not where she was but memories of their time in Baywood.

Their climbing adventures. He marveled at her natural instincts for finding the next hold, and her strength of purpose to reach the top. He remembered the light sheen of sweat on her brow when she saddled Seraphina, her breathing tempered and focused as she fought her fear of spooking the horse. He smiled when he pictured her running around the backyard, filling bird feeders in nothing but her bathrobe. Her hair shimmering in the predawn light, and the coastal breeze ruffling the edges of her robe, exposing tanned legs. The morning feedings only led to mischief when she returned, her skin damp from the morning dew. Finn couldn't help but draw her close when she batted her lashes like a vamp. Some days they would make love on the living room floor, a thick quilt as their bed. He could still feel the warmth of her honeyed skin, her legs wrapped around his as she chattered about some new antique she'd found. He had to believe they'd make similar memories once they were home.

"Tell me something of Maire." Finn sat up from his makeshift bed. They'd rearranged the crates in their cell to provide more comfort and some privacy. Finn perched on top of a crate and grabbed an apple from their leftover breakfast. He waited for Ethan to untangle himself from the canvas sheet they used as bed coverings.

Ethan's hair stuck up in clumps, and he ran his hand through it, which only made it rise more. Once Ethan found his own preferred seat, tucked between two smaller crates he used as armrests, he shook his head. "We've walked through everything I can remember."

"I don't mean about her kidnapping or the events leading up to it. I mean something about her. What was she reading? What was her favorite past time? We've spent so much time apart, and when we were last together, everything was about those damn stones and book. I don't even know her favorite color anymore."

"What did it used to be?" Ethan asked. He'd placed his hands behind his head, elbows wide as he stared at the ceiling as if he were watching clouds float by.

"Green. Although Mam thought it was brown since Maire's dresses were typically covered in mud." He laughed. "Da even tried to get her to wear pants like the stable boys. He thought it might save her dresses, but Maire wouldn't budge. She was determined to do everything a boy could do while wearing a dress." Finn chuckled, then shook his head.

"Tell me," Ethan encouraged.

Finn's smile turned whimsical. "We'd been riding, and the rain caught us halfway home. Not the typical Irish drizzle but a steady downpour that had us thoroughly drenched by the time we made the stables. We'd just put the horses in their stalls when I suggested that her soaked state made her cleaner than she'd been in weeks. We were halfway to the house when she looked down, her brows furrowed in deep thought. Then she got a twinkle in her eye. That's when I knew I'd made a mistake, but I was tired and hungry. So I left her standing in the rain. I'd only taken two steps when the first handful of mud hit me square in the back."

Ethan barked out a laugh. "She didn't."

"Oh, aye, she did. I tried to ignore her until the third one smacked me in the head. Well, what could I do? It was all-out war." Finn wiped at his eyes, his own gaze years away. "I had no choice but to retaliate, but she didn't just stand there and wait for it. She was already on the move, filling both hands with mud. By the time Da pulled us from the mud, we were both thick with it. He made us sit in the rain on opposite ends of the porch until we were washed clean."

They smiled at their own vision of an irritated Maire, sitting in the rain, a smirk of satisfaction on her face.

Finn tossed the apple back and forth in his hands. "So tell me a story of Maire."

The words had barely left his lips when the outer door scraped open.

A minute passed before a man stepped out of the shadows. Finn swept a glance to Ethan, who remained sitting but leaned forward, leaning on the makeshift armrests, ready to strike if needed.

"I thought this might be where the two bodies had gone." He spoke in English, but his accent shouted French native. "Two pigeons in a cage. Or should I say English spies?" The man stepped closer, peering in to get a better look. "I'm not usually interested in passengers. I must admit, the way you were brought on board piqued my curiosity." He began searching the crates. "Where are your bags? I saw them carried in with you."

Finn studied the man. This had to be Valentin's spy. His outward confidence suggested he'd done this type of work dozens of times, but Finn noticed the light sheen of sweat on his brow though the cargo hold was chilly. The spy leaned over a crate, a hand braced on one edge. The hand trembled, which might be from a medical condition or too much drink. Finn didn't believe either.

The spy scanned the cargo hold before sitting on the barrel Valentin had left in front of the cage. Finn assumed the man had lost interest in searching for the duffels. The spy braced his hands on his thighs and leaned toward Finn. "What if I said I had a deal for you?" His gaze darted between Finn and Ethan. "Just tell me why the captain has you locked in the cage. I can make your trip more pleasant." He didn't wait long before sneering. "I can also make the rest of your journey more painful. Nobody watches this cabin. The captain is so arrogant, he stopped caring what's in this hold some time ago."

"And why would you believe that?" Ethan asked the question, surprising Finn. Though he'd been about to ask the question himself.

The man's laugh was high-pitched. "I've been stealing from this hold for months. Nothing big. Nothing overly noticeable. With each port, the inventory grows, and I take my share."

"You hide it somewhere and then sell it when you reach port." Finn grinned and nodded, encouraging the man to speak.

The man nodded along. "That's right. If I can provide some additional information, I get a bonus."

Finn considered the statement then let his eyes round as if he just figured it out. "You're gathering ship movements and the smugglers' port of calls."

"You're turning on your own," Ethan added.

The man shrugged. "I saw an opportunity. That s all."

"You're a traitor." Ethan's accompanying sneer enraged the man.

The spy stood so quickly, the barrel tipped over and rolled toward the darkness until a boot stopped it. It took him a couple of minutes to note the silence. Finn and Ethan understood because they'd seen the men at the edges of shadows. The spy had only the abrupt stop of the barrel to clue him in—they weren't alone.

Three men stepped from different paths through the crates. The spy turned, and when he saw the face of Valentin and two barrel-chested sailors, he backed up until he had nothing behind him but cage.

"Captain..." The man looked around, his head almost bobbing in the effort. A strangled laugh chirped out of him. "I was telling tales to keep your passengers occupied." He held out his hands in supplication while glancing over his shoulder at Finn.

Finn didn't respond.

Valentin nodded at one of the sailors, and the man moved swiftly, the punch landing even faster.

The spy was on his knees before he was aware of what

happened. The second sailor stepped in and used his knee to slam into the downed man's chin. Finn heard bone snap and glanced at Ethan. Based on his grimace, he'd heard it too.

Then the show was over. Though not completely over for the spy.

Valentin had his man and a confession. Finn had a momentary twinge of pity for the man, then it vanished. Life at sea was hard. If Valentin didn't make an example of the man, he wouldn't be able to trust his crew. And that made it dangerous for everyone aboard.

Valentin nodded to one of the men, who unlocked the cage and opened the door.

Valentin spread his arms wide. "Come out and get some fresh air. Then we'll share a meal, and you can tell me about the women you chase." He raised a hand when Finn began to protest. "No. You can't hide this from me. I know the look of men without their women. Besides, it's been a long voyage with men way overdue for a bath. I could use some discussion about feminine pursuits."

When Finn and Ethan stepped out of the cage, the sailors dragged the spy inside then slammed the door shut with a metallic clank.

"I assume you have a decent vintage to go with dinner." Finn faced Valentin. "And I know you're eating better than the swill you've been feeding us."

Valentin laughed as he steered the men to the door. "What Frenchman would sail without a good stock of wine? And the best port. I believe we have one or two things to celebrate this evening. A traitor caught, we're less than a day from England, and we have years of tales to retell."

Valentin placed a hand on Ethan's shoulder. "And perhaps I can get you drunk enough to tell me why Murphy considers you such a valuable passenger."

Ethan just smiled as he shot a quick glance at the man replacing them in the cell. "Will he make it to England?"

Valentin glanced at the man with derision. "Oh, oui. He'll be mostly in one piece. I'll trade him for goodwill and a few coins. In this, he's better alive than dead."

As the men left the room they'd shared for two days, Ethan smiled at Finn. "Green."

When Finn raised a brow in confusion, Ethan said, "Her favorite flower is lavender, but she still favors the color green."

23

───────

AJ dumped the small crate of supplies on the scarred table. When she'd left for town, the table wobbled terribly, yet it was sturdy now. She had to admit, she didn't think Beckworth would know how to fix something so simple, or find it within himself to do it. The young man who followed her from town with a cart carried in another load of supplies and set them on the kitchen counter. He left the last crate on the porch as requested by the older woman who lived in the old, well-cared for cottage.

AJ and Beckworth had arrived in the town of Corsham, five miles southeast of Waverly Manor, just after midday. As promised, Beckworth positioned himself at the remains of an old stone building just outside town while AJ continued on. The town was larger than she expected, and she kept her head low as she noted the different shops, keeping watch for anyone who looked menacing enough to be one of Dugan's men. Once through town, she circled the outskirts before returning to where she left Beckworth.

She'd given it a fifty-fifty chance that Beckworth would be

waiting for her, but she found him lounging on his horse in the shadows of the building. When she trotted up and nodded, he turned his horse down a secondary road. She followed without question, assuming they were headed to the farmhouse he'd mentioned, but they stayed west for a mile before turning south. Beckworth must have changed his mind about his original destination.

AJ pictured being taken to an old, dilapidated wood structure. It turned out to be as old as anticipated but far from ramshackle. The colorful farmhouse pierced her heart when she thought of the cottage she'd shared with Finn in Ireland after their first jump. It seemed a lifetime ago. She pushed the thought away, knowing it would come back to haunt her when she tried to sleep.

The thin but hearty woman, Eleanor, had been genuinely happy to see Beckworth. The shock of that had barely worn off when AJ noted the kind way he cupped her weathered face and kissed her cheek. Who was this man? Then the old Beckworth returned when he shouted at AJ to take the horses to the stables and feed them. Then he took Eleanor's elbow and guided her carefully into the cottage.

AJ grumbled while she took the horses to the stable, removed the saddle from Beckworth's horse, and brushed it down as Finn had taught her. She had to admit, her anger had calmed by the time she finished feeding the horses. She kept her horse saddled since she intended to ride back to town as soon as she figured out what was up with Beckworth and the old woman.

When she returned to the cottage, Eleanor asked her to sit at the rickety table while she poured tea and fed AJ biscuits. The woman was spry for what AJ could only guess was a woman in her sixties, but age was difficult to determine in this century, especially among the working class. AJ glanced around the cottage. The house might be old, but it was well-loved.

Once AJ had been filled with tea and cookies, Eleanor showed her to a small guest room where Beckworth had placed her canvas bag on a chair. Before she left for town, he handed her a list of supplies, which included food, gunpowder, shot, clothing, and some feminine amenities that must be for Eleanor.

They had discussed AJ taking the cart, but since she never handled a horse in harness, Eleanor suggested she ask Mr. Covington at the mercantile to have one of the boys bring the supplies out.

She changed into a dress and tied up her hair. Eleanor gave her a thick shawl to wear and kissed her cheek. The gesture had made AJ more determined to find out what was up between this old woman and Beckworth.

AJ scanned the cottage and found a few other items that had been mended while she'd been gone. Eleanor returned from the garden carrying several vegetables she dumped in the kitchen basin. She crooned over the supplies. The discussion at dinner was all about Eleanor's only son, who had been studying to apprentice at the apothecary before he left for the war. She fretted constantly, and it was obvious Beckworth was equally concerned. He assured Eleanor her son would be safer once they discovered his medical expertise. He was positive the young lad would end up at an army hospital tending the injured. Whether Beckworth believed it or not, he never gave Eleanor any doubt to his claim, and AJ found herself hoping he was right.

Once the old woman had retired for bed, Beckworth pulled a bottle of wine from a cabinet in the living room.

"You shouldn't be taking her wine. I could have stopped at the inn."

"Nonsense. Who do you think gave her the wine in the first place? Besides, she has a cellar filled with bottles of the stuff."

AJ arched a brow. "All from you?"

He shrugged. "Mostly."

"So who is she to you? The two of you seem to know each other quite well."

"Just a dear friend who used to work at Waverly. More importantly, what did you hear in town?"

AJ wanted to dig deeper into the only person she'd met that could bring out a tender side to Beckworth. She'd been positive he didn't have one. But he was right. She needed to stay focused.

"Not much. When I made a comment about hearing the viscount was back at the estate, people clammed up."

"Hmm." Beckworth pulled at his sleeves before drumming his fingers on the table.

"That's all you have to say? Doesn't it sound like they're hiding something?"

"Or maybe they're scared to say anything that might find its way back to them. You're a stranger in town asking about the viscount. You do remember how scary Dugan is, don't you?"

AJ hadn't thought of that. But was that enough to explain the closed lips she'd found in every shop she'd entered? Probably. People from small towns tended to stay close and shut others out, especially if driven by fear of reprisal.

"I should have stopped at the inn. I might have heard more from someone who had too much ale." She leaned in and ran a finger along the wood grain, knowing it was something Finn did when in thought. "I did happen to hear something at the mercantile. I don't think the two women knew I was behind them. A week ago, one of them saw the viscount's carriage on the road to someplace called Hagersham. He returned a few hours later."

Beckworth leaned in. "You're sure they said Hagersham?"

"It's not an easy name to forget. What does that tell us?"

"Not sure, to be honest, but it is interesting."

"Why?"

"There's nothing there anymore except for an old church. Most of that has deteriorated over time. The church was built in the ninth century." He sat back and sighed. "There might be someone in Bath who knows something about it. Hagersham is about five miles east of there. Did either of them say they actually saw the viscount?"

Good question. She had wondered as well, and if she hadn't stayed to eavesdrop for as long as she had, she would have missed the most important piece. "The younger woman swore she saw the viscount poke his head out the window. The carriage had been held up by a cart with a broken wheel. She said the viscount seemed very impatient and yelled at the driver to go around. Her description of ash-blond hair and blue eyes sounded like it could've been you."

Beckworth jumped from his seat to set a kettle of water over the fire.

"Do you know this man who claims to be the viscount?" AJ had a gut feeling Beckworth was holding back, and retired reporter or not, she thought it a good time to toss the question out there.

Beckworth grabbed the edge of the counter, his knuckles almost white. Without seeing his face, AJ wasn't sure how to gauge his response. Had she gotten close to something, or was he just angry that someone claimed to be him?

"I don't know him." Beckworth remained at the counter until the water was hot in the kettle.

Once he poured the tea, he settled back down. His face was haggard, days of confinement finally catching up with him. She considered the situation from his perspective. He'd been gone four months, yet a year had passed him by. Then he discovered someone else had moved into his home, taken everything he'd built, legally or otherwise, and called it their own.

But they were forgetting the important piece of the puzzle, the reason she was here—to find Maire.

She turned the cup of tea in her hands, then broached the topic. "Not once did I hear any mention of anyone staying at Waverly other than this viscount. If Maire was there, where would she be?"

The question seemed to shake Beckworth out of his personal musings. "She could be locked up in the same chambers as before, but it will be difficult to confirm." He stared at the fire, then turned to study AJ. "There is one other place we could try. If she's not there, and if the building isn't being used for anything else, the location may give us a vantage point."

AJ nodded, thinking she knew where he was going. "Are you talking about the old barracks building?'

Beckworth shook his head. "No. The building is too valuable for housing his security force. There's another building on the other side of the property. It's well hidden behind trees and shrubs."

"An old guest house of some sort?" That didn't make sense, even to her.

When Beckworth didn't answer, a shiver crawled up her spine. "What kind of building is it?"

"It used to house holding cells."

"A jail?" AJ tried to play down the rising panic while not waking Eleanor.

He shrugged. "Of a sort." When he noticed AJ's distress, he tried to calm her. "Let's not get worked up. If Maire s there, it will be easier to extract her, depending on the number of guards."

AJ bit her lip, considering their options. They weren't there to rescue Maire, just to confirm if she was on the estate. But if she'd been held in a cell all this time? AJ wouldn't be able to make a decision until they confirmed she was at the estate and could evaluate the situation. *Finn, where are you?* She pushed her tea away. One thing was certain. She'd get little sleep until she knew for sure if Maire was within reach.

24

Leaves rustled behind AJ as she crept toward the next tree. She pressed her body against the rough bark and, closing her eyes, counted to ten to calm her breathing. When she refocused on her surroundings, she caught a flash of Beckworth melding behind the tree she'd just left. He nodded toward the clearing.

She gathered a breath and inched around the tree. Two guards, their backs to her, spoke for several seconds before parting, each striding off in different directions to continue their rounds. That made six guards in all they'd spotted since they began their reconnaissance thirty minutes ago.

Beckworth had woken AJ at first light and promised Eleanor they'd be back in a couple of hours for a hearty breakfast. By the time AJ had dressed in her pants and jacket, she'd found Beckworth walking around the yard, head down, occasionally squatting to pick up a rock or digging through a pile of leafy debris. When he found a rock to his particular liking, he placed it in his pocket and continued on.

She watched him for several minutes before he noticed her.

"Come over here. I have some for you." Beckworth didn't

bother to glance at her before he moved to another section of the yard.

"I know we're somewhat limited on our weapons, but sticks and stones?" AJ quirked a smile when Beckworth lifted his head, his expression serious.

"No sticks. Just the stones." He stuck his hand in a pocket and came out with a handful. "Here. Put these in your pocket."

When she stared at his prized collection, he sighed. "Truly, woman, even with this, you fight me?"

AJ pinched the bridge of her nose. "I haven't had a decent cup of coffee since leaving Baywood. The coffee at the monastery was only passable, and it was deplorable on the ship. I think I'm having withdrawal symptoms, or possibly hallucinations. Searching the yard for rocks was the last thing I expected from you."

Beckworth flashed a breathtaking smile. "Oh, my dear, this will not be the last of my surprises. This is a very old trick that, even in its simplicity, works every time." He scraped another pile of debris with his foot to discover several more jewels he slid into his pocket.

He led her over to a log where a tin mug, a glass bottle, and a wooden crate the size of a microwave had been set up. The lineup appeared to be a makeshift target range. "You seem to have some skill with your dagger. Though I doubt you'd hit your mark every time, especially if you haven't maimed or killed anyone yet."

When she raised a brow, he continued. "And stabbing me twice is not nearly the same as hitting the same mark with a throw."

She planted her hands on hips with a reluctant nod, knowing he was right.

"Your archery skills, on the other hand..." He paused to run his hands through his hair. "Well, you're downright scary. But again, aiming for a target, even if it was inches from my head, is different than aiming for a man's chest."

AJ turned to scan the yard, anything to not lock him in the eyes. "I know."

"Don't pout. It's the same for anyone. If we're in peril, I have no doubt you'll come through. But a split second of indecisiveness isn't just about giving the other person the advantage. That instant of delay could also make you miss your mark."

AJ chafed under the mixed compliment, but he was right. Until she was under battle conditions, there was no telling how she'd react.

"Now, these stones." He pulled a couple out of his pocket and jostled them in his hand as if testing their weight. "These will accomplish two things in surveying our main target—the outbuilding with the holding cells. We must remain quiet. They can't hear us coming nor moving about. If we need to communicate, and hand signals or other gestures are impossible, then we'll use these to gain each other's attention."

"You mean if you're not paying attention to me, I simply throw a rock to wake you up?"

His smile came easily. "Now you have it.'

"And you want to practice throwing rocks?"

His smile faded. "It's not as easy as it looks." He turned, and with almost no thought, threw the rock which struck the tin mug dead center as it went flying. He tossed her a stone. "You try."

AJ knew better than to just throw it, so she used the skills she'd learned with the dagger and bow. Without taking much time to set up, she lobbed the rock at the crate and watched it sail by the target.

He whistled. "Not bad."

"I missed it by an inch."

"Yes. But unlike the dagger and bow, you're not trying to kill or injure me. Please try to remember that. You just want my attention."

She rolled her eyes, but couldn't resist a jab. "I'll try to remember. But I can't predict what might happen in the heat of battle."

"Funny. Now, here's the critical part, and the second reason for the stones. As difficult as it is to say this, try to aim for the largest part of me. If my back is to you, aim for the middle of my back. If I'm turned sideways, aim for the largest surface area. You don't want to rustle tree leaves or make any other sound."

She brightened as she understood his meaning. "If I don't hit you, softening the sound of the rock, someone nearby could hear, giving away your location. If that were to happen, I should throw another one in the opposite direction."

He nodded, somewhat disgruntled. "You're quick for a woman." After she scowled, he threw another rock. "But here's the rub. While this is a simple trick—and works almost every time—it's only good once. Possibly a second time if there are more men or slow-witted guards."

That made sense. A snap of a twig or rustle of branches would bring a guard, but it wouldn't take long for him to figure out the ruse.

Beckworth checked his pockets and, nodding once, motioned to the stable. "The horses are ready. We'll ride to the west side of the estate, hide the horses, then walk south to where the outbuilding is. We stay within sight of each other. Once I give the signal, you don't say a word." He stopped until she nodded. "If either of us is spotted, we run like hell for the horses. Try to stay small when you run. If we're lucky, they'll think us curious boys who've strayed too far from home. Keep riding west until you reach a main road, then cut south. Otherwise, we determine the situation and be back for breakfast within an hour or so."

"Sounds too simple."

"That's where people get lazy. Creeping up on armed men should never be taken lightly."

"I get it," she grumbled.

He laughed. "If we're as good a team as I think we'll be, you'll be back before you know it. And those coffee urges you're having? Eleanor makes the best coffee this side of London."

Now, miles away from Eleanor, she could almost smell the coffee. She winced when something struck her leg. Glancing down and not seeing anything, she turned to find Beckworth smiling at her. Then he pointed behind her. That had been the second time he'd thrown a rock at her. The first time, he'd hit her shoulder, fairly close to the point where she'd stabbed him. He'd shrugged in apology, but she'd caught the slight smile before he'd disappeared into the underbrush for her to follow.

This second rock was her signal to return to the horses. She checked the thick stand of woods and listened. After a moment of nothing but the sounds of chickadees and a few insects, she dodged down a deer trail. She couldn't move as efficiently as Beckworth, so she kept her focus divided between where she stepped and scanning the terrain for guards who might have seen them.

The man was scary quiet in his stealth mode, which explained why it had been so difficult to catch him in Baywood. Ethan had mentioned Beckworth demonstrated the skills of a street urchin. She'd meant to ask Beckworth about it but decided the question broached a personal area she wasn't sure she wanted to know.

When she reached the horses, she crouched behind a small outcropping until Beckworth caught up with her. They waited while their breathing slowed. After five minutes that seemed an eternity crouched knee to knee with Beckworth, he nodded, and they broke for the horses. They walked the horses for a short distance before mounting and running for the farmhouse.

By the time they made it back, AJ was giddy, still laughing as she brushed down her horse.

"Addictive, isn't it?" Beckworth had finished caring for his mount, which was munching on hay, its tail casually flicking the air.

"I had no idea."

"You would've made an excellent natty lad."

AJ gave him a questioning glance.

"A pickpocket."

"A thief? Is that supposed to be a compliment?"

"Most assuredly."

She grunted. "And where did you learn all these skills?" She ran the brush along the horse's flank as if his answer was of no concern.

After a moment of silence, Beckworth took the brush from her and led her horse to its own stall and pile of hay. "Something I picked up while living in London. It was a long time ago." He patted the horse on its rump before closing the door. "I believe I smell coffee."

25

———

"It makes more sense to send letters to the earl and Hensley. They'll both send men, and I won't have to spend time traveling back and forth." AJ leaned back, a hand covering her stuffed stomach. She'd barely breathed between bites of breakfast Eleanor had waiting for their return. Though the cook at the monastery tried, her meals didn't come close to Eleanor's cooking.

Beckworth claimed her zealous hunger was from the adrenaline of their surveillance. Earlier in the meal, he told the two women, "A good heist could make you think you'd been famished for days. I've seen people eat until their clothes no longer fit, plumping to twice their size."

Both women laughed at his tall tales. AJ learned more about Beckworth through his stories than any creative questioning could answer. The fact he seemed nothing more than a flimflam man, a master at the con, shed a light into Beckworth that somehow made his previous actions make sense. Unfortunately, understanding him better didn't mean she agreed with or trusted him. This particular argument about her staying was no different.

He spared her a glance before returning to his second helping of breakfast. "You're only scared of going because you think they won't let you return with them." He spread marmalade on a slice of toast while AJ studied him over the rim of her mug, savoring the aroma of the coffee. Beckworth hadn't lied about Eleanor's touch with coffee.

AJ ignored his comment, having already come to that same conclusion on their ride back from Waverly. Both the earl and Hensley would be too protective to allow her to return, forcing her to remain behind to wait for Finn. "If I stay, I can tell people I'm Eleanor's niece or family friend. If they trust Eleanor, the other townspeople will be more inclined to talk around me. I'd be in a better position to discover something. You're unwilling to go to town, worried someone may recognize you."

"She has a point," Eleanor interjected. "Women know more about the events around town than anyone else." She pushed herself up from the table and set another pot of coffee on the fire.

"I don't need you both bantering at me. This is a matter of safety, not skill or accessibility." Beckworth tugged his sleeves then crossed his arms, the old viscount seeping through.

"How about this?" AJ changed tactics. "Even if I go to Hereford, I should send letters anyway. That way, if I'm held up somewhere, or get lost or whatever, both men will have the most current information." She pushed a fork through the crumbs of her breakfast before Eleanor snagged the plate from her. "We're not even sure who's in the building. What if it's some other prisoner?"

Beckworth nodded, his gaze unfocused as he stared into his cup. "That's a very real possibility. And that's what I'll be confirming while you go for backup. I'll also need to monitor the guards' schedules and patterns."

"It would be easier with two of us. I'll write the notes and post them today. Then we can finish our negotiations." Maybe she'd find some trace of Finn or Ethan in town. If they'd landed in Hereford, they should have been waiting for her here. It didn't make sense they hadn't caught up with her yet.

An hour later, dressed in her plainest gown and letters in her hand, AJ found Beckworth in the barn where he'd saddled two horses.

Beckworth noticed her questioning glance and shrugged. "If you're crazy enough to go to town, Eleanor has given us a list." He scratched his shoulder, then tugged on his sleeves, his next statement forcing a twitch of his lips. "It appears we're drinking more coffee than she'd originally planned."

They rode to town in silence, neither seeming eager to restart their argument. AJ had no doubt Beckworth was piling up reasons why his plan was better than hers. What he said made sense. Finn would have the same argument. Why was her safety more important than Maire's?

When they reached the town's border, Beckworth stopped by the same crumbling building as yesterday. "Remember, keep your head down, post the letters, get the supplies, and get out. No questions."

"I understand."

Before she could move her mount away, Beckworth grabbed her arm. "Seriously. We can't afford to tip our hand."

They glared at each other before AJ nodded. "I get it. In and out." She pulled away from him, ignoring his encouraging—and slightly concerned—expression.

With Beckworth's warning still ringing in her ears, she stopped to post her letters before heading directly to the mercantile. After handing the shopkeeper Eleanor's list, the heavyset man tugged on his ear while giving AJ a curious assessment. The last time she'd been in the store, the shopkeeper's wife had helped her and hadn't seemed to care that AJ was a stranger. She kept her expression friendly, refusing to glance at the door, trying to remember how many steps were required to escape. Then, feeling stupid for being paranoid, she forced a larger smile.

"This looks like Eleanor's handwriting," the shopkeeper finally stated. "But I just sent out a bag of coffee last week. Seems odd she'd need more already." He scratched his protruding belly as he studied the list again before resting his gaze on her.

AJ shifted from one foot to another. Had Eleanor sent a hidden message? Did she feel like a hostage and Beckworth her captor? The woman had seemed genuinely pleased to see him. AJ considered her options, but after further thought, silenced her nerves and stuck with the plan.

"Eleanor is a dear friend. A friend of a friend, actually. We're traveling through on our way north. It seemed silly not to stop for a visit." AJ's voice faded out, stopping herself from further babbling.

The shopkeeper's gaze roamed the shop, stopping for a second on a man in the far corner. AJ picked at her skirts and pushed her hat farther down on her head. When the shopkeeper's gaze fell on her again, he motioned her to a stand of root vegetables she didn't recognize.

In a voice that carried through the shop, he laughed and said, "Oh, no, you don't want to cook it that way. It will taste better in a soup, or maybe a stew." He picked one up and handed it to her, lowering his head and whispering, "These are very dangerous times in Corsham."

Unsure what he meant or how to respond, she nodded. "I imagine so during times of war."

"Men who have left for such pursuits may come home to find what they left behind has been taken."

AJ went still. Was he talking about Beckworth? "War is a terrible thing."

"The best a man can do is to rely on his friends."

She wasn't sure if this man was a friend or not. Maybe the new Viscount of Waverly was holding his foot on the throat of the town. That sounded like Dugan. When she thought back to her trip to town the day before, she'd thought the townspeople somewhat reserved. She'd assumed it was because she was a stranger. Maybe it was something else entirely.

"Friends are always good, but they can be hard to find." AJ waited while the man considered her words.

He flicked his gaze around the store, lingering a second longer on the man who still hovered in the back of the store. "You'll want to get back to your visit. I'll send the boy out with your purchases this afternoon."

"You're so kind." When AJ pulled out a bag of coins Beckworth had given her, presumably from Eleanor, the shopkeeper staid her hand.

"Eleanor has an account. You'll want to be on your way."

AJ reached for the man's hand, giving it a light squeeze. He patted her hand in return, then turned in search of another customer.

On her walk to the door, she felt the eyes of the stranger as if someone laid a heavy hand on her shoulder. Once outside, she hustled to her horse and kept a steady pace as she nudged it out of town. She wanted to look back but didn't dare. Yet she knew they watched her. With her head down, she still managed to notice a few things. A man walked out of the shadows as she neared the smithy. Another man stood from a bench in front of the apothecary as she passed. Had they been waiting for her?

She fought the urge to kick her horse into a run. Every neuron told her to follow her flight instincts, but she managed to keep her mount at a steady pace. *Nothing to see here.* She thought about the time the Romani had left her and Maire in the middle of a vacated meadow. They had found their way to a town, only to fall into Dugan's hands. He must be using the same strategy here, keeping men in town to watch for strangers or suspicious activity. His way of keeping the villagers under control.

Before she reached the edge of town, she couldn't help but glance back. The three men she'd noticed were now on horseback following her. She couldn't lead them back to Beckworth. In a panic, her brain swirled with empty possibilities. The only idea that kept resurfacing was to do the exact thing she'd decided against—riding toward Beckworth. If she rode past without slowing, he'd know something was wrong without having his hiding spot blown. She wasn't going to escape without some form of distraction. Beckworth would need to put his childhood skills to the test.

As soon as she passed the last building in town, she made a left down a narrow road. If the weeds growing through the middle of it was any indication, the road was rarely used. She kicked her horse, frantically searching for the best route that led back to Beckworth's hideout. The crumpled building came into view, and just before reaching it, she yanked the horse toward a copse of trees.

Before the turn, she braved a quick glance toward the building and caught Beckworth's startled expression. Out of the corner of her eye, a huge man appeared out of the shadows from the other side of the building. He was on foot, and when he saw AJ, he began to run.

Dugan's men had surrounded them.

Then the sun cut through the shade.

Lando.

Jamie must have asked Lando to follow her. No wonder neither of them had put up much of a fight.

Then Beckworth tackled Lando. What was he doing?

She didn't have time to consider her question when multiple

hooves refocused her attention. With nothing but her single plan to work with, she continued her path toward the trees. The branches hung low, but AJ kept her head down. After several yards, thinking she'd cleared the trees, she steered the horse down a smaller path.

The horse cut the corner short, raking AJ against a tree. An errant limb caught the sleeve of her dress and dug into her arm. She cried out in pain and didn't see the second branch as it hit her square in the shoulder, knocking her to the left. Her grip loosened on the reins. She squeezed her legs in a last vain attempt to stay on the horse.

The fall played out in slow motion. She slid off the saddle as the horse raced on. Her first thought was to tuck into a ball, but the ground loomed. All thoughts vanished when she landed on her side, and her head slammed into the ground.

The hooves drew nearer. Then she heard nothing at all.

26

A J's feet skimmed along the stone floor. Her arms ached from the rough hands that held her as two men dragged her down the hall, each walking at a different pace. Their grip tightened when they stopped at a door where a third man fumbled for a key. She felt like a turkey wishbone at Thanksgiving. A door scraped open, and they moved on. When they came to a stop at the second locked door, she tried to stand, but her legs wouldn't hold her. Once through the door, the two men continued to drag her to yet another door.

Another man, presumably a guard, glared down at her.

One of the men holding her growled, "Open the door. Dugan's orders. They're to be together for now."

The man hesitated for a moment before something metallic clanked. Keys. Three doors. Were there three different keys? AJ tried to piece things together, for whatever good it would do. Her head ached, and she couldn't remember why. *Did they hit me?*

The door opened to a room darker than the dimly lit hallway. The smell of human waste and mold would have doubled her over if she'd been standing on her own. The men yanked her through the door and unceremoniously dropped her. She remained on the floor, the cold stone, as filthy as it must have been, felt soothing to her aching head.

Stars danced at the edges of her vision when someone grabbed a fistful of her hair, lifting her head off the floor. Stale breath, tinged with something sour, made her gag. A voice whispered, "Welcome to Waverly." Her head slammed back to the floor, then the man placed his beefy hand on her shoulder and used it as a brace to push himself up.

The muffled stomping of boots faded as a door slammed and peaceful silence settled around her. She curled into a ball and tried to focus, but the pounding in her head wouldn't stop, and her foggy thoughts flipped through scenes like a kaleidoscope— the men in town, Beckworth's startled expression, Lando running after her, the trees, then blackness.

They must have brought her to the building she'd investigated earlier with Beckworth. Could there be a second building? The guard confirmed Dugan was involved, so it must have been his men who chased her. Had Beckworth been caught too? Had he led her into a trap? Damn. She'd been careful, but they'd been waiting. She pushed herself up but dropped back down when her vision blurred.

Feet scuffled from somewhere in the cell, and her heart pounded. The guards mentioned her sharing a cell, and the realization drudged up a new fear. When hands grabbed her, she flung her arms out to fend the person off.

"Ow. Stop that. I'm only trying to help."

AJ knew that voice.

"Maire?" The single word barely registered in her own ears, yet the person reached for her again, fingers tentative on her shoulder.

"AJ?" The voice, full of wonder, flooded AJ with relief.

AJ drew herself to a sitting position, stopping partway when the stab of pain became too intense. The room wasn't as dark as she'd first thought. A single candle glowed from a table across a larger-than-expected cell. The accommodations were a far cry from the last time Maire had been a guest at Waverly. Beckworth had kept her housed in an immense, richly appointed room with a grand veranda overlooking the gardens. Now she lived in a pitiful cell where the only light came from a grated window in the door and a single candle flame.

Waiting for her eyes to adjust, AJ surveyed more of the room. A small pallet lay against the far wall—Maire's bed. A bucket sat against the opposite wall, and from the odor drifting from that direction, AJ assumed it was the latrine. She decided Dugan was one man she wouldn't hesitate to shoot through the heart.

AJ completed her scan of the room at the lit candle perched on a wooden table. Two chairs accompanied the table where multiple stacks of books and writing materials covered every inch.

She gazed up at the woman who now stood in front of her. Maire's dress was tattered. Random spots of sky-blue material contrasted with spatters of mud and what looked like blood-stains. Her matted hair hung dull and listless. But for all that, Maire stood tall, her expression full of sorrow and something else AJ couldn't decipher.

Maire dropped to her knees and pulled AJ into an embrace, her tears wetting AJ's cheek. "What are you doing here?"

AJ pulled back, scanning Maire for injuries. "Are you hurt?"

"The blood wasn't mine."

Maybe not, but there was a fresh bruise on Maire's left cheek that made AJ's blood boil. She ran her fingers over the bruise. "Who did this?"

Maire shrugged. "It doesn't matter." She scooted closer. "Let me see your head."

AJ turned her back to Maire but flinched away when Maire's fingers found the tender spot.

"Hold still."

"It hurts."

"I imagine so. It's also bleeding. Let me see how deep it is."

AJ gritted her teeth through the pain, but after another minute pulled away. "Enough. At least until the throbbing stops."

"I think you'll live." Maire sat back, her gaze narrowing as she studied AJ.

After a second or two, her expression softened. AJ wondered if Maire was concerned with the condition of her head. She reached back to touch where it hurt and winced. Maybe she had a concussion.

"Now, tell me why you're here." Maire's serious expression would have made AJ chuckle if it wouldn't hurt.

She did manage a snort. "Isn't it obvious? I'm here to rescue you."

Maire's tinkling laughter reduced AJ's fear that her friend might have gone mad being locked away in the darkness. "After all these months, you haven't improved your skills."

"And I'm glad to see time hasn't dulled your wit."

Silence fell between them. For all the questions AJ wanted to ask, she wasn't sure where to start or how important they were considering their current situation.

"Ethan went to the future." Maire's even tone seemed tinged with disappointment by his decision.

"He was crazy with worry."

"I told him to never do that."

"Then why did you keeping working to perfect the incantations?"

Maire refused to look at her. She picked at the dirt on her dress then pulled at a piece of thread that dangled from her sleeve. "I should have listened to him."

"Who?"

"Ethan."

"You mean you should have let him go with you to Peterstow for the seeds?"

Maire gazed at her like she had three heads. Maybe she did. The throbbing in her head had increased. All she wanted to do was lay down and let the cold stones relieve the ache.

"Seeds? I didn't go to Peterstow for seeds. I went to meet someone about the book."

AJ touched her head. Maybe swelling had impacted her hearing. "What book?"

"He told me to ignore it. To leave everything in the past. But I didn't listen. I had to know."

"Know what?"

"If the book was real."

"I must have landed in Oz," AJ bit out. The pain flared, but she managed to dismiss it. "What the hell are you talking about?"

"Didn't you come here for the book?"

Maybe the darkness had nibbled away at Maire's sanity. "We're here for you."

For the first time, Maire lifted her head. "Who's we?"

AJ glanced around the cell. She couldn't see past the shadows. Was someone lurking? She spread her arms wide. "What? You're still not impressed by my rescue?"

"No."

The blunt answer hurt, but she could see Maire's point considering she was now locked in the cell with her. "Well, actually, Finn and Ethan..." She scratched her head. "I don't know. They should be close, but the jump didn't go as planned."

"You mean they aren't with you?"

"Long story. I imagine we'll have time to discuss it all, but I'm having a hard time keeping my eyes open."

Maire rose and retrieved a cup of water. "Drink all of this. I'll ask for herbs to help with your headaches. Sometimes they bring what I request. Other times they ignore me. For now, staying hydrated is your best option."

AJ drank greedily and held out the cup, feeling like Oliver Twist asking for more porridge.

She shook her head. "Unfortunately, I don't have an endless supply, so I'll need to ration your amount. They only replenish the water once a day."

"What book, Maire?"

Maire returned the cup to the table. She straightened a pile of paper, nudged a book, ensuring each item lay in its proper place. Her shoulders drooped when she finally responded. "The druid's book. The book I'd seen Beckworth with the first time I was at Waverly."

Puzzle pieces clicked together. She finally understood that nagging itch she'd felt in Baywood each time the druid's book was mentioned. When the two women had previously been held as Beckworth's guest at Waverly, Maire mentioned a book she'd seen in the viscount's study. Maire claimed the book disappeared after Finn and AJ arrived. Had the book traveled to France and back again? AJ doubted it. Wouldn't the book have been one more item for the duke to gloat over?

The full picture still alluded her, but she was too tired to keep it in focus. She slumped to the ground and pressed her head against the soothing coolness of the floor. "Start from the beginning. The book was mentioned several times in our search for you. Why didn't Ethan mention he knew about it?"

Maire gripped her hands in the tattered folds of her dress. Her lips pressed into a thin line. "I made him promise to never tell anyone about the book."

"Even us?" AJ couldn't hold back the hurt in her voice.

"I hadn't thought to mention you or Finn. You were gone, pursuing a different path." A ghost of a smile crossed her face. "I always wanted to know if you were both safe and happy." Maire sank to the ground next to her, laying her head on the floor to face AJ. "I'm so sorry."

AJ placed a hand on Maire's shoulder. She was so thin. "Don't worry about that now. We'll tell you all about the future when Finn gets us out of here."

Maire shook her head and clasped one of AJ's hands. "Dugan rotates the men at different times. Nothing can be predicted. The guards never talk when they're at my door. A different servant comes every couple of days to change the buckets and bring writing supplies. Only one of them will tell me anything, and she knows very little. The viscount rarely leaves the estate, but he receives visitors. I'm told the guests are always men, and they partake in secret evening meetings. Only the most loyal of the staff are allowed to serve."

"Have you seen the viscount?"

Maire didn't answer, but her grip on AJ's hand grew tighter. "About that."

Finally, AJ thought. Some answers.

A door creaked from someplace in the building. Maire sprung up, her hands clenching her skirts.

AJ followed but at a remarkably slower pace. "Who is it?"

Maire shook her head and whispered, "Probably a guard with food. Maybe Dugan."

A cold chill ran through AJ. She felt as though someone had punched her in the gut. Beneath that, anger stirred. She wished someone had put a sword through that man when they'd had the chance. Her hand instinctively searched in her pockets, her fingers curling around the dagger. Surprised to find the guards hadn't found it, she'd be foolish to use it without knowing more about where they were being held. The dagger's solid form comforted her nerves, but seconds later, her heart stopped.

She fished in her other pocket, desperate when all she felt was fabric. Her breathing settled with the familiar touch of the

Heart Stone and her wedding ring. Why hadn't the men searched her? They must assume a woman wouldn't have a weapon. She could live with that mistake.

More importantly, the last thing she needed was to lose their only way home. She'd give up her dagger before she'd ever willingly relinquish the Heart Stone.

The women stood side-by-side. Maire's arm slid around AJ's waist to keep her from swaying. Her legs felt like she'd overdone a soak in a hot tub. She gingerly touched her head, wincing at the pain, then studied the blood on her fingers. It was tacky. That was something.

AJ's nerves frayed at the sound of boots on stone, the jangle of keys at the lock, followed by the scraping of the door. The last person she ever wanted to see again ducked as he stepped into the room.

Dugan.

As big, and perhaps scarier, than the last time she'd seen him. A scar marred his left cheek. It wasn't fresh, but it didn't carry the deep fold of his other scar that ran across his forehead. AJ guessed he might have gotten the injury during the battle at the monastery.

He glowered but didn't advance. Instead, he stepped to the side to make way for another man.

The man was slim. His legs, covered in wine-colored breeches, were long but lacked substance. A gold brocade waistcoat hid beneath the buttoned cream tailcoat. The ruffles of his shirt matched the coat. The color of his hair couldn't be determined in the poor lighting with his face hidden in shadows. His thin fingers played at the edge of the dark paisley cravat.

When he stepped into the light of the candle, AJ couldn't hear anything but the rushing in her ears. If Maire hadn't been holding her up, she would have sunk back to the cold stones. The handsome face staring back at her seemed crueler than normal, but the cornflower-blue eyes were unmistakable. How had he gotten so presentable in such a short amount of time? She must have been unconscious during some point of her capture.

AJ's breath rushed out in an angry hiss. "Beckworth."

27

"Beckworth." The second time she uttered his name, the word slithered out like a vile declaration. AJ squinted, partly because her head throbbed and partly because shadows played at the edge of her vision. The relief from the cold stones now gone.

Something wasn't right.

He folded his arms across his chest and studied her. The perusal lingered so long, she shifted from foot to foot, her only desire to collapse and find the comfort of the floor. She forced herself to endure, more as a childish refusal to appear weak to someone she had begun to trust—if only for their mutual goal. The man was more duplicitous than she'd thought. He'd lied to them from the start with his innocent whining about being stuck in the future.

He tapped a finger against his chin as he continued to study her. What the hell was he thinking? Maybe he was formulating a new lie to exert more control over them.

AJ clutched her dress until she felt the edge of her dagger. She dropped her hand, remembering that Beckworth knew she carried one. Yet he hadn't told the guards to take it away from her.

He stepped closer. His calculated perusal was similar to the way he'd studied her when she'd first met him at Waverly all those months ago. Still, something was off. She couldn't put her finger on it.

The silence continued. Somewhere water dripped, and in the distance—birds, their trills dulled behind rock and mortar. Then she saw it. The slight scar on his upper lip.

She stumbled back. Maire caught her arm before she fell.

AJ squeezed her eyes shut, then opened them again. There was no other explanation. "You're not Beckworth."

His high-pitched laugh echoed through the cell. The sound so similar to the duke's, she shivered. She would have taken another step back if Maire hadn't gripped her tighter.

"I can understand your confusion." His voice wasn't Beckworth's, its tonal quality as annoying as nails on a chalkboard. But the resemblance was astonishing. He snapped his fingers with an air of annoyance, and a servant appeared out of the shadows holding a golden goblet. The Beckworth look-alike took the proffered cup and drank, wiping his lips before handing the cup back to the young lad who never lifted his head.

"My physical appearance never sat well with our father." He swaggered around the room, stopping at the table piled with books. He picked up a small stack of pages, flipped through them, then glowered at Maire. His expression of annoyance was a dead ringer for Beckworth. "Instead of disavowing Beckworth for looking like a duke's son, my loving father scorned me for looking like a whore's son." His face turned scarlet, and spittle flew from his mouth. "Me. A duke's son. Treated my whole life like some blackguard."

After a minute, he composed himself. He ran a hand over his hair then fidgeted with his cravat. His color returned to a pasty white, and he lifted his chin. Once more in control. "After fleeing England in disgrace, Mother took ill, and the damp weather on the coast of France only made it worse. I couldn't have been more pleased when Father sent us away to live with Mother's family in Austria.

"Then, the strangest thing. Months later, I received a letter from Father stating he found a way to recover his lost estates in England. After his disgraceful departure, I finally had the upper hand in our relationship. I had the money but required the proper titles. And he owed me."

AJ's head pounded, promising to explode at any minute. She felt like Alice, but she wasn't sure if the man in front of her represented the White Rabbit or the Red Queen. Based on the way her luck had been going, she assumed the latter. With her increasingly foggy hearing, it was difficult to keep up with the man's banter. Though she couldn't stop squinting at the face she'd been looking at for the last week.

When he'd finished strolling around the cell, he stopped next to her. "You must tell me who I have to thank for killing the old bastard." The request must have been rhetorical because he began moving again, seeming to prefer his own voice as he droned on. When he stepped next to Dugan, he rested a hand on the big man's shoulder.

Dugan didn't move. He stared straight ahead with a slight smile—or grimace—it was hard to tell with him.

"Fortunately," the duke's son paused to squeeze Dugan's shoulder before turning to AJ. "Dugan is a loyal asset to Mother's family. He only stayed with the duke because of Mother's request. For some unknown reason, she still loved the worthless dolt."

While the man prattled on about Dugan's worthiness, AJ played catchup. Beckworth was the duke's son, and he'd failed to mention it to her. AJ would have listed that little nugget under need to know. "You look the same age as Beckworth." AJ blurted it out, realizing belatedly by the man's glare that she must have interrupted him. It just surprised her that the duke had been sleeping around. The thought of anyone wanting to bed him made her shiver. Maire's ever-tightening grip brought her out of her musings to find the duke's son eager to discuss the unfortunate situation.

"Beckworth is older by four months. If he hadn't been a bastard, he would have been the one to inherit." He shrugged. "It only makes sense that I should take Waverly and continue as the one true viscount. It is my birthright. It's time that charlatan stop pretending he's someone he could never truly be—a duke's son."

Suddenly, the man she knew as Beckworth solidified. A bastard born on the streets of London, who had somehow found his father. Either on his own or through his father's blessing, he'd risen above his station. AJ recalled the interactions between the duke and Beckworth during the small time she'd spent with them at the monastery. The duke had belittled Beckworth at every turn. Yet from what Finn had told her, Beckworth had come to the duke's aid during the battle.

How the duke's indifference must have festered. She almost felt sorry for Beckworth. He had been nothing but an asshole while playing viscount, but now she understood why. He tried to model himself after his father. Had he been trying to earn the man's respect—or love?

"Beckworth must have meant something to your old man. He gave Waverly to him instead of you. It seems to me you're taking advantage of an empty estate because your dog—"AJ pointed her chin at Dugan—"is bigger than anyone else's. For now."

The women held their ground as the new viscount stormed

toward them, coming within inches of AJ. Spittle settled at the corners of his mouth, his ugly sneer reminiscent of the duke's. He raised his hand, his fingers flexing in and out of a fist, but he didn't strike her.

After a few moments, the newly anointed viscount retreated to the table. He picked up the pages he'd flipped through earlier. He reviewed them again before tapping them on the stack of books, his expression disappointed as he clucked his tongue. "My dear, Maire, you haven't progressed very far."

Maire said nothing.

"You know the arrangement. I'll have to punish you for this."

AJ tensed, but Maire remained stoic. Had this been the ass who had given Maire the bruise on her face?

"Your rations will be cut in half until you provide better translations. These notes say nothing about the druid's stone. It's nothing but ramblings."

AJ shot Maire a glance at mention of a druid's stone. Was there a stone they didn't know about? AJ didn't think Maire would respond. When she did, her words were listless and rote.

"I can only transcribe what's written. It's not my fault the words are nothing but gibberish from a madman."

"Not a madman." The shout forced AJ and Maire back a step. Even Dugan gave the viscount a quick glance before his vacant stare returned to some point at the back of the cell. Did Dugan ever consider this new viscount might be as mad as the lost druid or the duke? The truth was probably that he didn't care. He had the might and men to protect himself.

The duke's son threw his arms up and continued his rant as he paced the cell. "You are transcribing words from the very man who traveled to the future. His words are sacred. They will lead me to my own glorious future. The future that belongs to me, an heir to the druid legacy. The one that was foretold."

"By some old woman with a cup of stale tea leaves," Maire murmured under her breath.

The man's rants worried AJ. Another fanatic searching for a way to use the stones. Had Maire known someone sought the stones before she began her search for this book? Had Ethan? Why did everyone feel the need for secrets?

AJ stepped away from Maire. She wrapped her arms around her middle as a deep longing for Finn and their home almost dropped her to her knees. She reached down, her fingers curling around her pocket. The shape of the Heart Stone replenished her courage. As long as she had the stone, they had options.

When the viscount's tirade stopped, he waved at Dugan before pointing at AJ. "Move her to another cell. Same restrictions as the Murphy woman." He turned to Maire. "Her fate rests with you." His voice rose in that annoying, high-pitched tone. "If I don't see improvement in your translations, her rations will be cut each day until she's living on the meager water I dole out and whatever insects she can dig up." He whirled in a dramatic display of a flapping tailcoat and stormed out.

AJ reached for Maire, wanting to hug her before being dragged away, but Dugan's men grabbed her arms before she took a step. She managed to get a last glimpse of Maire before the door clanked shut. Her friend had simply watched her go. There was nothing else she could do.

She tried to walk, but once again, the men kept a brisk, uneven pace as they rushed her to the cell next door. As soon as they stepped through the threshold, they tossed her to the ground. AJ reached out instinctively to break her fall, but her head still managed to skim the floor.

The sound of the door banging shut brought a gasp of despair. She had to stay positive, but for now, with her head pounding, and the truth of their predicament staring her in the face, all she wanted to do was close her eyes and wish it all away.

She curled into a ball and reached into her deep pocket to close a fist around her wedding ring. Stella would agree this was a proper moment for a pity party. AJ rested her head against the floor, for the moment uncaring if the cell contained a pallet. The cold stone eased the constant ache, and she closed her eyes to the darkness, hoping her dreams held an answer to her dilemma.

28

Tap. *Tap, tap, tap.*

At first, AJ thought a bird might be at the window, but she was positive she'd filled the bird feeders. The soft knocking continued, and she reached for the bed covers to ward off the morning chill. There were no covers. No soft mattress. Then she remembered where she was. She tightened her muscles, pulling her knees up to maintain her fetal position in a vain attempt to stop the shivers.

The tapping became louder.

She pried open an eye. Shadows formed from the filtered light streaming through the narrow window in the cell door. Her first question was how long had she been sleeping. With no answer available, she moved on to her second question. Was she okay? Her headache had subsided, and her muscles relaxed at the good news. Her body was stiff, but nothing seemed broken. She tentatively stretched out one leg, then the next. Just stiffness brought on by the cold. She dragged herself upright with arms as stiff as her legs and glanced around.

She winced at the dull throb in her head, but then the ache eased. With the smallest movement possible, she took in her meager surroundings. Most of the room remained beyond the dim light. To her left, she noticed a pail by the door. After a few shaky steps, she peered into the bucket. Empty. A clay pitcher and a cup sat a foot away. She sniffed the pitcher, then poured a small amount in the cup. Water. She filled the mug and drank it down.

Maire had said the water was only replenished once a day. She set down the cup and turned to frown at the bucket. After taking care of her personal hygiene, she paced the length of each wall. It seemed to be as large as Maire's and filled with the same meager amenities. A thin pallet lay limp in a far corner, her lips curling in disgust at what might be living in it. A table with two chairs hovered in another corner with a candle and a handful of matches. She lit the candle and sat when the added light revealed there was nothing else.

She wrapped her arms around her and tried to think of something other than how cold it was. Not even a filthy blanket. Did they intend to freeze her to death? Her stomach growled. She performed another personal inventory. She had to strike while she had the energy.

They'd dragged her to the cell next to Maire. That would put Maire's room on the opposite wall from where she sat. She picked up the candle and, starting at one end of the wall, worked methodically as she checked each stone for an opening. She'd covered a third of the wall when she found it. A narrow gap between the rocks about a foot off the ground. She placed the candle on the floor and checked for buildup of dirt. Nothing. The hole must have been there for some time, possibly decades.

She knelt and peered through the gap. A dim light was all she could see, but that was something. She thought of calling out, but if there was a guard outside the door, he was sure to hear. Needing to know, AJ hefted a chair and placed it under the grated window in the door. She stepped up and peeked out.

Flames flickered on torches along the wall. Light filled the hall several yards in both directions, including the second gate they had come through. No guards were visible. They may have been positioned earlier for show, but Beckworth and Maire both mentioned the guards were shifted at random.

At least they were alone for now. She dragged the chair back to the table and dropped down to peer through the hole.

"Maire?" Her voice cracked. She cleared her throat before trying again, a little louder. "Maire?"

She dug into her pocket and waited for any sound. If someone came, they'd have to come through the gate, and that required a key which was sure to make a clatter. She pulled out her dagger and worked at the crack, trying to make it larger. The sound of her dagger on stone reminded her of the earlier tapping that had woken her. Had Maire tried to signal her?

She stopped prying at the rocks and began tapping. After a few seconds, she waited. Hearing nothing in return, she tapped again. Then she heard the other tapping. She peered into the hole and saw a blur of a shape.

"Maire?" Silence. Scraping.

"AJ?"

"Yes." *Thank God.* "I'm here. There's a hole here."

"Yes. I found it some time ago, but there's only been a handful of other prisoners."

"There are others?"

"Not currently. But occasionally someone is brought down. They only stay a few days before they're taken away."

AJ didn't like the sound of that. They would need to double their efforts to escape. "Do you know how many guards are usually outside your door?"

"No. But there are usually two when they bring meals and water."

"How often do they bring food?"

"Once a day with the water."

AJ glanced to the clay jar and cup. "I guess they decided not to feed me today."

"They didn't feed me the first day either. I think the viscount is trying to make a point."

"As if the accommodations didn't already make a statement."

AJ dug at the hole. The mortar crumbled from dampness and age. Beckworth never mentioned how long the cells had been there, but the building must have been built long before he'd been born. Had he ever thrown anyone in here?

After some time, and several limited conversations later, she'd managed to enlarge the gap until the two women could hear each other without raising their voices. They discussed the guard rotation and whether any of them seemed persuadable. Maire quickly dashed any hope. A servant came once a week to empty her bucket. The duke's son came about as often to check Maire's progress on deciphering the book.

"Do you have the book with you?" AJ asked.

"No. I only get one page at a time. The viscount has someone copy the words onto a single page for me to work from. I don't think they're given to me in order, or the druid was truly mad. Individually, the pages don't make sense."

"What's with all the other books?"

"They're supposed to have keys to help me with the encryption."

"Do they help?"

Maire laughed. "Not in the slightest."

"It sounds like this viscount doesn't know what he's doing."

"That was my thought in the beginning, but he knows more than he should."

"Does he know about the Heart Stone and the torc?"

"He doesn't seem as interested in those. At least, he hasn't mentioned them more than once or twice. The pages he's given me say nothing of the Heart Stone, but I have seen references to the smaller stones. I think the man might be slightly unhinged. It can be difficult to know what he's searching for."

"I'd agree with your assessment of him, but I can't say we met under the best conditions."

After a moment of silence, AJ asked Maire how she was holding up. Her response made light of her situation, but AJ heard the tiredness behind her words—and the fear. This incarceration was nothing like her time spent with Beckworth.

"We should stop for a bit. I'll tap when I think it's safe to talk more." Then Maire was gone.

AJ returned to her empty table. She considered her trip to town and her attempted escape from Dugan's men. Beckworth's surprised expression confirmed he would have also seen the men chasing her. She bolted upright, grabbing her head at the sharp pain from moving too quickly. When she could think clearly again, the memory of the second man slammed home. Lando. Jamie had sent someone after all. And Beckworth had tackled him, probably saving Lando from one of these cells—or worse.

Could Beckworth and Lando pull off a rescue with just the two of them?

And did she dare wait?

Before they retired, AJ and Maire kept their conversation light, sharing simple memories. When AJ grudgingly dropped onto the thin pallet, she squirmed to find a comfortable position. She thought about the passion in Maire's voice when she spoke of Hereford. The estate had been a home to Maire, even if she hadn't been there long. AJ couldn't help but wonder if Ethan had something to do with that.

Her musings turned to Finn, but before she could summon his image, keys rattled somewhere in the hall. Not close enough to be the door to her or Maire's cell, the sound must have come from the second gate. She tried to recall being dragged down the hall but couldn't remember how far it had been between the two gates. If she hadn't heard anyone come through the first gate, the building must be larger than it appeared from the outside. Maybe the building wasn't that big, and the first gate wasn't locked. Would the outer door be locked from the inside?

Her only advantage would be surprise. Earlier in the day, she'd considered different options, working through each one, weighing their feasibility for success as Finn and Lando had trained her. With enough foresight and the right conditions, she could take out one guard, maybe two if they weren't built like Dugan. She wouldn't be able to kill them, but they'd be down long enough to find keys, release Maire, then get the hell out of the building. Simple. Unless there were more guards down the hall or outside the building, which was likely.

What the hell was she thinking?

She was in over her head.

Even with the odds against them, AJ made a mental note to inventory the guards' weapons. If there was a way for her and Maire to get their hands on them. She was doing it again. Their only true hope was a rescue by Beckworth and Lando. She snorted. Beckworth would be the last person to risk his neck to free them. But with any luck, he'd share his knowledge of the building, and Lando would find a way.

She rolled to her side, assuming the guards were being posted for the evening when she heard keys again. Then the door to her cell squeaked open. She froze. Sucking in a deep breath, she turned toward the scuffle of boots. Two men, outlined by the torchlight from the hall, came to a stop ten feet from her. Each carried a sword at their side, a dagger sheathed on the opposite leg, and a pistol on their belt. Well-armed. They were muscular, but no taller than Finn. They looked like book-ends, both dark-haired and bearded. The one on the left had a scar on his chin. The names Tweedle Dee and Tweedle Dum came to mind.

Why were they here?

The sound of approaching boots provided her answer. The man ducked as he entered the room. He stopped after a few steps and stared down at her. Then he crossed the room to sprawl in one of the chairs. He lit the candle before folding his arms across his chest.

Dugan.

Terror crawled up her spine at the smile that appeared on

his scar-ravaged face. Had Finn felt that fear each time Dugan and his men had visited his cell in the monastery? Would she soon be feeling the same pain he'd felt after each interrogation? They had nearly killed him. Could they do the same to a woman? Based on the ugly grin marring Dugan's face, she'd guess the answer was yes.

AJ pushed herself up until she stood with her chin high, preferring to face this threat on her feet. She wouldn't be an easy target, and though her head thrummed with a dull ache, she kept her spine straight, just like Maire would do.

Dugan nodded, and the guard on the left with the scar—Tweedle Dum—grabbed her arm and pushed her toward the table. Tweedle Dee followed and stood so close behind her, she could smell his sweat. She instinctively took a tiny step forward. His tactic meant to intimidate, and it was working.

"The viscount was surprised to learn of your history with the stones." Dugan studied her for a moment then motioned for her to take the other chair. AJ remained standing.

"I've come here for a chat, Miss Moore, but I won't tolerate insolence." He motioned to his men. Tweedle Dum moved so quickly, she didn't have time to dodge him. He grabbed her arm again and shoved her into the chair. He took a position directly behind her to the left while Tweedle Dee stood to her right.

The quick movement made her head pound, and she squinted at the renewed intensity of it. If Dugan noticed her discomfort, he didn't give any indication.

"That's better. Your obstinance will only make our discussions more difficult. Where have you been all this time?"

When she didn't answer, he leaned toward her, elbows on his knees as he waited. "I think you need another lesson."

Before she realized what he meant, Tweedle Dee moved in front of her and slapped her hard enough to make her ears ring. She had a split second to wonder if her earlier injury had given her a concussion before another slap made her rock in her seat. She raised her arms to ward off another blow, but the man had already stepped behind her.

Dugan leaned back. "Let's try again. Where have you been since the monastery?"

"America," she spat out. Finn always said to stick as close to the truth as possible.

That made Dugan's brows rise. Good. Keep him guessing.

His eyes narrowed. "Why did you return?"

She had asked herself that question on more than one occasion. "I received word that Maire had disappeared. I came to find her."

Dugan laughed. It was a rather unexpectedly pleasant sound. She hadn't thought he could laugh, and if he did, she was expecting something more diabolical. His rich tenor would have warmed her if she didn't know what a dangerous man he was. What had made him such a monster? Or was he a true believer in the stones and the crazy story his new viscount preached?

"Well, you certainly accomplished your mission. Bravo, Miss Moore. See how easy that was?"

AJ had a feeling the questions were going to get more difficult.

Without dropping his gaze, he crossed a leg over his knee. He settled back as if they were old chums sharing stories of their time apart. "Where is Mr. Murphy?"

This time it was her turn to bark out a laugh. "That's a very good question."

With the barest of a nod from Dugan, Tweedle Dee came around and delivered another slap, followed by a punch to her stomach region. She would have fallen if Tweedle Dum hadn't caught her and returned her to an upright seated position. Her head hung as she sucked in deep breaths. Previous self-defense training had taught her to tighten her stomach muscles to ward off a blow, but she hadn't seen the hit coming. Her head ached to a blinding degree. When her breathing returned to normal, she touched her cheek. It was warm, and she'd probably have a bruise to match Maire's by morning.

"Try again, Miss Moore."

She held her arms in front of her body, protecting it from further abuse. But it was her head that worried her. It was difficult to stay focused. Her earlier concern about a concussion faded away with the newer fear of a brain hemorrhage.

"I'm not lying. I don't know where he is."

When Dugan looked like he might give another signal to the guards, she raised a hand. "It's true. He was preparing a ship, but I couldn't wait. I was worried about Maire, so I took the first passage I could find. He was going to follow." She stopped, took a breath, and winced. "I haven't heard from him." She hung her head.

He didn't respond, and she took that as a positive sign. His belief in her words might have come from the soulful tone of her voice. The one that truly wanted to know where he was. Would he find her in time?

"Where's the Heart Stone, Miss Moore?"

Even with her minced brain, she knew she'd have to be convincing in her lie. She touched her head, grimaced, then waited out each second of silence he'd give her. When she finally pulled her thoughts together, she raised her head and sneered.

"Do you still believe in magic?" She shook her head, which was the wrong thing to do. Dugan began to blur, which was a better look for him. Her breath hitched, her diaphragm still sore. "The stones are a fake. Time travel is a fantasy, propagated by a powerful man in a vain attempt to reclaim his lost position." She tried to hold his gaze. "If I came from another time, why the hell would I come back to this?"

That made Dugan pause. Was he a non-believer, following

out of blind loyalty? He was too practiced to reveal anything. He tried another approach.

"Did you leave the stone with the monk?"

When did Dugan leave France? She couldn't think, and this should be an easy answer. They had searched for Beckworth and hadn't found him. But Beckworth was slippery. Dugan might have been able to hide on his own, but with his men? No. He had left town as soon as the battle turned. He was probably gone before Finn killed the duke. Rather than fight for the right memory, she stopped trying. She let her mind wander until she heard Sebastian's calm, even voice. Then she remembered a story he'd told her and Maire, and gave Dugan a partial truth.

"I imagine whatever stones Sebastian collected were scattered to the far reaches, just as the Prior before him did with the stones during the Reign of Terror."

Her tongue seemed too large for her mouth, and talking became a challenge. She'd never experienced a migraine before and found herself hoping for that over a brain bleed. She felt herself slipping and one of the Tweedle brothers pushed her back onto the chair.

Dugan cracked his knuckles and shifted in his seat, once again leaning forward. "Who are you working with?"

"What?" She didn't mean to be an ass. His line of questioning kept changing, and she couldn't keep up.

"I don't think you came here on your own. Who are you working with?"

Darkness blurred the edges of her vision, and when one of the guards, she wasn't sure if it was Tweedle Dum or Tweedle Dee, shook her to answer, she knew she was going to pass out. Before she did, she was able to reveal one last truth, and she hoped she delivered it with an evil grin. "A street urchin from London."

30

Finn crouched behind a thicket of dense shrubs. The guard focused on the ground, glancing up occasionally as if an afterthought. Finn sighed. He hated to have to kill these men, but they were already far outnumbered, especially if Dugan's perimeter forces moved in. He and the others had barely slipped through the line to reach the building.

Watching the man approach, Finn studied his face. Hard as stone, and Finn reminded himself who these men were. Mercenaries who gave no quarter. Without further question, Finn's resolve steadied his hand.

When the guard passed his position, Finn moved behind him. With reflexes sharper than they'd been in days, Finn grabbed the man around the neck and slid the blade into his side. The guard emitted a small gurgle before buckling. Finn dragged the man under the shrubs, then looked around.

He hadn't been seen. He wiped his blade and moved to his next target.

After dispatching the second guard, Finn turned to find Lando watching him several yards over. The big man nodded then disappeared into the trees. Finn moved in the opposite direction, searching for other guards, confirming Beckworth's reconnaissance regarding the number of Dugan's men they'd find. If he wasn't so worried about AJ and Maire, Finn might question the crazy plan Beckworth and Lando had hatched. But the need to rescue the women pushed rational thought aside—and he trusted Lando.

Beckworth was a different story. If the man was working for whoever held Waverly, he had a strange way of showing it. Beckworth had been the first to take down one of the guards. If he was truthful about wanting to take Waverly back, then the stealthy bastard had finally become useful for something.

Once Finn was convinced there were no more guards—for now—he turned for the door to the building. Scurrying through the trees, he almost tripped over two men Ethan must have dealt with.

When Finn and Ethan had found Lando at the inn in Corsham and discovered AJ had been taken by Dugan's men, Finn had immediately blamed Beckworth. But Lando insisted it hadn't been Beckworth's fault. In fact, Beckworth had been helping AJ in her search for Maire. How the hell had they ended up on the same side? And why had AJ been in town alone? He'd have to get his answers later.

Finn pushed his irritation aside as he crept to the building. Beckworth stepped out from behind an overgrown vine.

"Are they all down?" Beckworth whispered.

Finn nodded.

Ethan stepped out from a tall patch of shrubbery. Lando materialized from behind a large boulder. For a small group seeing little action since their battle at the monastery, they had worked well together, taking down double their number. Surprise had been a valuable advantage.

Beckworth pulled out a small ring of keys and, as silent as the thief they all knew him to be, worked the lock. The other three positioned themselves with their back to Beckworth, scanning the area for another patrol. After a moment, Beckworth tapped Finn on the shoulder.

"Let's go." Beckworth slipped into the darkness of the building.

Once they were in the building, Beckworth closed the door behind them. "We have to keep it dark in case there are guards inside." His whisper forced them to huddle close. "There's a gate at the end of this hall, but the lock broke decades ago. I never had the lock replaced, and I'm hoping no one has bothered since I've been gone."

This bit of information hadn't been shared during their planning. Ethan glared at Beckworth and appeared to consider backing up his aggravation with a right hook.

Beckworth held up his hands. "Would you have changed your mind in coming if you'd known this before?"

When no one said anything, Beckworth continued. "If there's a new lock, I'm just telling you I'll need time to pick it. I wouldn't have bothered taking this risk if I didn't think I could get through the gates. There's a second gate about ten yards from the first one. That one will be locked, but I have a key. Remember, keep your eyes open, stay in the shadows, and remain silent. There may be more guards, and everything echoes in here."

Beckworth moved out without waiting for any response. If nothing else, the man didn't dither. The men spread out along the hallway, the torches casting more shadows than light. If there was someone beyond those shadows, they waited patiently for the team's approach. As Beckworth predicted, the first gate wasn't locked, and they slipped through without a sound.

They found no guards when they reached the second gate. Had Dugan thought his outside patrol was enough? Or would they find guards waiting for them when they tried to exit? Finn pushed the thought away for later, refocusing on his frayed reserve.

Beckworth worked the lock in near silence. The only indication that he'd finished his task was the squeak of the gate when he pushed it open and stepped through. He'd barely had time to turn around when Ethan and Finn barged through, both racing to the cell doors. Lando stayed at the gate, covering their backs in case additional guards arrived.

Beckworth told them there would be four cells. Ethan and Finn ran toward the farthest cell but stopped at the third door where a dim light showed through the narrow window. Ethan peered in while he waited, bouncing on his feet, for Beckworth to unlock the door. Once unlocked, Ethan pushed his way in. Finn stayed at the door but nodded at Beckworth to open the other doors.

"Maire?" Ethan's whispered question was answered by a slap and then, after a short struggle, a surprised gasp.

"Ethan?"

That was all Finn had to hear—his sister's voice. "Where's AJ?" Finn's vision slowly adjusted to the dim light as he waited for Ethan to pick up Maire, who struggled to be put down.

"I can walk. Please. I want to walk out of here." Once he set her down, Maire pointed toward the next cell before falling against Ethan for support.

Finn raced to the next cell which Beckworth had already opened. He stepped into the shadows, sword held in front of him. The last thing they needed was a surprise.

No candle burned in this cell, and rather than stumble in the darkness, Finn fetched one of the wall torches before storming back in. The smell wasn't nearly as bad as Maire's cell, but it was just as bare and cold. When he found AJ on a thin mat, curled against the chill with no blanket, he was ready to kill the guards all over again.

"AJ." When she didn't stir, he squeezed her arm, but there was no response. Worry swept him. He rolled her over. The trace of blood along the side of her face and the darkening of what might be a bruise on her cheek sent waves of outrage through him. He tried to rouse her and, after a few seconds, heard a soft groan. Relief flooded him. He felt her scalp and found her hair caked with dried blood. When he pulled his hand away, his anger rose again when he spotted the fresh blood.

He gingerly picked her up and rested her head against his shoulder. He left the torch where it lay and moved as quickly as he dared out of the cell. When he reached the gate, Beckworth stepped out from the shadows.

"What's taking so long?" When Beckworth noticed AJ's unconscious form, his brows furrowed. "What happened? Why isn't she awake?"

"I don't know, but she has a head injury."

"Where are the others?"

That brought Finn to a stop, and he turned as quick footsteps approached. Ethan and Maire emerged from the cell. Ethan supported Maire, who clutched several books and loose papers to her chest.

Ethan shrugged. "She wouldn't leave without them." When he saw AJ in Finn's arms, he frowned.

"Not here. Let's go." Finn turned and raced through the second gate to find Lando waiting for them near the outer door. Lando's expression turned dark when he saw AJ's limp form in Finn's arms.

Ethan and Maire stopped behind Finn. Beckworth brought up the rear but pushed through to stand next to Lando.

"You know there could be an army waiting for us outside," Beckworth calmly mentioned as he ran a hand down his blade.

Lando stepped to the side and gave Beckworth a grim smile. "Only one way to find out."

The group backed themselves against the walls, except for Beckworth. He flung the door wide before jumping to the side. Two pistol shots rang out, and Beckworth sighed. He put his sword away and pulled out a pistol at the same time Lando did. The two men ran out, taking their shots.

Ethan crept to the door, saw Beckworth and Lando engaging the two soldiers. "There seems to only be two, but they've probably sent for aid."

"Then let's go." Finn led the way out, turning left through the brush. A few minutes later, the sound of men quickly approaching made them stop to confirm who followed. The second he saw Lando, Finn immediately turned to finish their escape.

They ran for several minutes before stopping at a group of horses. Lando helped Maire up to Ethan, prying away the books and pages from her grasp.

"Let me put them in the saddlebag, lass. You don't want to drop them on the way."

Lando's reasonable urging seemed to work, and Maire released her stash.

Finn laid AJ in the grass and was about to step away to get his horse when she stirred. He dropped to one knee. "AJ. Can you hear me?"

Her lashes fluttered, and she squinted when she tried to open her eyes even though he'd laid her in the shade of a young birch tree.

"AJ." Finn ran a hand over her cheek and felt her forehead. No fever, and her cheeks were a little pinker than they'd appeared in the cell.

She struggled against the light but managed to whisper, "I fell off the damn horse."

Finn smiled. "Maybe I should have thought to pack a helmet."

Her hand reached up, her eyes open to mere slits. She touched the tip of his chin, feeling her way to his cheek, gently cupping it. "You're real?"

"Yes, yes, he's bloody damn real. Now let's get you both in the saddle before we're discovered," Beckworth griped as he brought Finn's horse over.

"Teddy?" AJ's voice sounded far away, yet Finn could hear her mischievous tone.

"God's blood, you're still a pain in the ass." Beckworth tossed Finn the reins and stormed off to mount his horse.

AJ smiled before she passed out.

Lando picked up AJ as Finn mounted, then lifted her into Finn's arms.

"Let's get moving." Beckworth glanced back from where they came, but Ethan was already scanning the trees. "They'll search the area and the town as well. I don't know what's in those books, but they'll probably want them back." Beckworth led them out of the thicket.

"Horses. At least four, maybe a couple more." Ethan yelled and turned his horse toward the group. Maire held on tightly from behind him but kept her head turned, waiting for guards to appear.

"There goes our first plan." Beckworth glanced at AJ.

"Then off to the next town?" Finn asked. AJ murmured in her sleep. He didn't know the extent of her head injury, but traveling to the next town seemed too far away. They needed a closer place to hide.

Beckworth seemed to have the same thoughts because he shook his head. "No. You'll never outrun them with her unconscious. The plan assumed the women were healthy enough to ride." He stared at distant trees, then sighed in resignation before glancing at the rest of the group. "Do you remember the junction I took you to after we left town?"

"Before you took us back to Eleanor's?" Lando asked.

"Yes. We need to split up. Lando and I will take the main road. We'll try to encourage them to follow our trail. I have a few hidden routes we can use to evade the men, but we'll lead them south before breaking off and returning. I suggest the two of you"—speaking to Ethan and Finn—"split up and stay on the small trails. Head west toward the junction. Once you're there, about five hundred yards to the southwest is an old barn hidden within a large stand of trees. Stay there until we catch up."

"If you don't catch up?" Finn asked what he already knew the answer to.

"Then you're on your own." Beckworth didn't have to say anymore.

Finn swung his gaze to Lando, who smiled back.

"Don't worry about me, my friend. This isn't the end." And with that he swung his horse around, Beckworth close on his tail.

31

Finn and Ethan rode together for several hundred yards before multiple deer trails branched off from their path. They ducked into a dense thicket when they heard horses approach. After several long moments and the sound of voices too far away to be distinguishable, the horses took off.

"They split up." Ethan touched Maire's hands clasped tightly around him.

"Aye. Sounds like some went south following Beckworth, but the others turned east." Finn noticed Maire's stern expression and furrowed brow as she watched AJ lying motionless in his arms.

"You need to take the most direct route to the old barn." Maire turned to check the trail behind them, then peered over Ethan's shoulder at the path ahead. "Take the deer trail that heads west. Ride slow, so you don't disturb the vegetation. Ethan and I can make it look like more than one horse has traveled our path."

Finn cocked an eyebrow and glanced at Ethan, who tried not to smile. "Yes, dear sister. What would we have done without you?"

Her thoughtful expression quickly turned to irritation. "I'm only trying to help."

When they heard men call out, still some distance away, Ethan rubbed her hand. "And it's a fine plan."

Finn rolled his eyes, something he was sure he learned from AJ. He pulled his horse next to Ethan's and cupped his sister's cheek. "I've missed you, sister."

"Aye. I've missed you too. Now be gone." She touched his hand, gave it a swift kiss, then kicked their horse.

The horse took off, surprising Ethan. Seconds later, he slammed into a branch but managed to keep them mounted. Maire's tinkling laughter trailed behind them.

Finn turned his mount to a trail large enough to pass without breaking branches. Before long, more trails appeared. He changed direction often, heading north first before turning onto a random, westward trail. He kept to a slow pace, refusing to jar AJ more than necessary.

He thought about his sister. She'd been too thin, but six months in a filthy cell hadn't diminished her spirit. She was a fighter. Their parents would have been proud. He glanced down at AJ, worry creasing his brow when he noted the dark shadows under her eyes. Her soft moans stopped within minutes of separating from Ethan and Maire. He spoke to her, but she remained silent.

Twenty minutes after his last turn westward, the path edged toward a large stand of birch trees. Several yards farther, a wide, well-traveled road ran north and south. He assumed this was the main road, but he'd turned so many times to remain out of range of Dugan's men, he couldn't be sure.

He urged the horse forward and was almost out of the trees when he caught movement to his left. He paused then quickly backed up. He waited.

A horse's head, hidden within dense brush on the other side

of the road, nudged a branch as it picked at the leaves. If he could see the horse, then its rider could spot him. Finn kept his horse motionless as he considered his options.

AJ began to stir. Of all times. He bent his head. "Quiet love. Stay still for me." He might as well have spoken to the wind because she struggled enough to make the horse take a step sideways into a nearby tree.

The leaves shook. Finn moved the horse back another step. If anyone had seen the branch move, they might think it was no more than a deer. His luck wasn't with him. Three horses stepped from the woods, and the riders weren't farmers. They were a hunting party, and Finn and AJ were their prey.

The men studied the birch trees where Finn hid. He wouldn't be able to escape them. The sound of a horse somewhere in the distant south forced them to turn their heads. One of the men turned, kicking his mount into a run.

Two men were better odds if he'd been alone. He'd have to lay AJ down in the trees so he could fight. If these men were some of Dugan's finest, he might not survive. What would happen to AJ if no one knew where she was? Wouldn't she be better off back at Waverly, even if she were a prisoner?

If he had the Heart Stone, he could take them home. But not knowing the extent of her injuries, the jump could kill her. For once, he was happy he didn't have to make that decision.

He was scanning the trees for the best hiding spot when the sound of a wagon made him look up. It came from the north and traveled at a good clip. The cart was piled with chopped limbs and barrels. The wagon made to pass the two men on horseback until the men forced the cart to a stop.

Without a second glance, Finn turned his horse north and picked up his pace. After a quarter-mile, he turned back toward the road and, careful to study the terrain first, crossed it. Hairs on the back of his neck stood up as he waited for men to call out. But they were alone.

After clearing the road, he traveled west until he found a small path that led them south. After their close escape, AJ had faded again, her body listless against his chest. He leaned down and kissed her forehead. "Stay with me, AJ. We're almost there."

BECKWORTH AND LANDO drove their horses hard, stealth of little concern. They wanted Dugan's men following them—at a distance. Beckworth wasn't sure if the men chasing them were locals, though he doubted it. The one correct thing he'd managed to do when he'd moved to Waverly was to learn everything he could about the estate and the nearest town. He knew the manor inside and out. He'd met most of the townspeople over the years, had studied the surrounding terrain, and knew most of the farms on the outer fringe.

His time on the streets of London taught him that friends came in many shapes and financial standing. His most trusted friends were farmers and merchants rather than the aristocracy he played to as viscount. The superiority he used when he hosted his dinner and hunting parties came from the knowledge he'd gained by working for the duke. His varied roles as a hustler, spy, and occasional assassin taught him many things—how to dress, how to treat servants, and flamed his fascination with art and literature.

When he had the estate to himself, his servants knew a different man. And that difference was what made most of them loyal to him. How loyal was now a valid question. He'd been gone a long time, even with an estate manager to care for things. For now, he would have to draw on friends from town and nearby farms. So far, they'd been eager to help. Considering what he knew of his half-brother and Dugan, Beckworth would seem a fairy godfather.

The knowledge of the area was key to his current dilemma. After racing down the main road for two miles, he veered toward a smaller road and ran his horse against the brush, hoping to make a well-seen path. He turned to glance back and found Lando directing his mount through the brush on the other side of the trail.

Beckworth smiled. The big man was as sneaky and dangerous as he looked.

Another quarter mile and the path widened. A few hundred yards after that, Beckworth stopped. He couldn't hear anything beyond the horse's heavy snorting.

"You hear anything?" he asked Lando.

Lando nodded. "They're not far behind."

Beckworth smiled. "Like whores to Mrs. Brubaker's meat pies."

"I've eaten her pies. We would send boys down to the quarter to buy them by the dozens." He chuckled. "Now I know why they returned with such large smiles."

Beckworth grinned with a dreamy sigh. "Ah, the lasses loved to trade for pies."

Lando nudged him. "We leave these men now?"

"And parting is such sweet sorrow," he recited. At Lando's raised brow, he laughed. "You can learn much about life through Shakespeare, my good man." He directed his horse between two trees before breaking into a trot down a narrow trail. He slowed the horse as he switched from one trail to another. Lando followed in silence.

They kept a steady pace until they reached a wide road. The two men scanned the area before crossing. Four men on horseback sat under an oak tree just north of the junction.

"Damn. I didn't think they'd have men this far west," Beck-worth grumbled.

"All of our work weaving to stay ahead of them gave his men time to get ahead of us."

"It seems Dugan has grown his little army. Surprising with a war on."

"So they're either lazy, or they're mercenaries."

"And some a combination, but these particular men don't appear careless." Beckworth scratched his chin, then glanced at Lando.

"Agreed. We move south and find another place to cross." Lando turned his horse without waiting for Beckworth's response.

Beckworth watched Dugan's men while Lando found a trail heading the right direction. When it appeared no one had spotted them, Beckworth turned to follow Lando. He'd always cursed Murphy for having good men at his back. Now he was grateful.

They crossed the road a mile farther south without incident. After another switchback of trails, Beckworth circled back until they broke out into a narrow field with an old barn. Right under the noses of Dugan's men.

When they reached the barn, Beckworth's shoulders eased as he monitored the path for visitors. The barn carried a vacant feel, but they split up as they approached the aged structure. Beckworth dismounted and, searching the dirt in front of the door, was satisfied that no one had been there recently. He swung the barn door wide.

Lando rode his horse into the barn while Beckworth retrieved his before closing the door behind them.

Lando frowned. "They should have arrived before us."

Beckworth didn't respond as he tied his horse to a post that seemed solid enough. "They're probably just being careful. And they don't have the benefit of knowing exactly where they're going."

Lando grunted in a tone that said he wasn't buying it.

Beckworth couldn't argue the point, but there was nothing to do but wait.

32

Finn walked his horse around the perimeter of the barn, searching for evidence of passage, either human or animal. He'd neither seen nor heard anyone since slipping past the last patrol. Yet, with the barn being so close to the junction, he couldn't take a chance.

He glanced down at AJ, her face peaceful in sleep. The knot in his belly tightened. If she were just asleep, then why couldn't he wake her?

After circling the building, he turned his mount so they faced the door and waited. After a moment, the door creaked, and a man filled the opening. Finn sighed and squeezed AJ closer as he clucked to move the horse forward.

Lando patted the horse as Finn rode by then closed the door. Finn stopped to wait until his sight adjusted to the darkness.

"Thank heavens. We thought you'd been caught." Maire ran to Finn with Ethan close behind, each reaching up for AJ. "Does anyone have any water?"

Finn dropped a skin in her hands then dismounted. He released the horse to find the others tied to a post. He scanned the barn. "Where's Beckworth?"

"He went to look for you." Lando spoke over his shoulder as he peered through a gap in the boards.

The group remained silent and watched Maire pull a tiny, folded parchment from the sleeve of her dress. Ethan scrounged in saddlebags until he found a tin cup. He squatted next to Maire as she poured water from the skin and tapped white powder from the parchment into the cup.

Finn sat on the ground and braced AJ's upper body against his chest. With Ethan's help, Maire forced drops of the liquid into her mouth. After the first few drops, AJ began to drink, though she never opened her eyes. When Finn laid her down, AJ remained unresponsive.

Maire touched his shoulder. "Just give her time."

Fifteen minutes later, Lando shifted at the door. He kept his eye to the boards until Finn heard the horse, then Lando opened the door to admit Beckworth.

"I should have known you'd find your way." Beckworth rode up to the group but didn't dismount. "I've been watching the men at the junction. Definitely not Dugan's best, but they're smarter than most. My best guess is they're unfamiliar with the area, or they would have someone patrolling this barn. Our luck is with us for now."

"Is it safe to leave?" Lando asked.

Beckworth glanced down at AJ. "Probably not, but I don't feel comfortable being this close to them." He pointed his chin at AJ. "And she needs medical aid. The travel on the road has increased, which should keep Dugan's men busy, but when that quiets down in an hour or so, they may begin checking the side roads. I suggest we leave now."

"You have a destination in mind?" Finn asked as he and Ethan stood AJ up.

Finn's spirits rose when she managed to hold a portion of her own weight and squinted at her surroundings. His mood soured as Lando passed an already-sleeping AJ into his arms. Tired of worrying, he eagerly clutched to the slim hope her brief sliver of awareness had given him. Her few seconds of wakefulness were more than he'd seen since leaving the cells.

Beckworth watched the group mount their horses. "I have a thought to the best place to go. Assuming the man's still alive."

"You're not sure?" Ethan's tone testified to his frustration tinged with fear for the women.

Finn battled the same emotions. He was angry, concerned about Dugan's men, and terrified about AJ's injury. However, badgering Beckworth when he knew the area wasn't the best idea.

"I haven't been home for months. It's the best option I can think of." He leaned over his saddle, arms crossed on the horn. "Of course, if you have a better option, I'm all ears."

Ethan and Beckworth glowered at each other until Lando broke in. "You've gotten us this far. We trust you."

Finn's brows scrunched together at Lando's comment. He hated to admit his friend was right, though trust might be the wrong word. They were almost clear. Now was not the time to test alliances, regardless of the strangeness of bedfellows.

Lando opened the barn door then mounted, taking the rear position.

Instead of turning north or south as Finn expected, Beckworth led them farther west, away from Waverly, Eleanor, and the town.

"You're sure about this?" Finn asked as he pushed his horse to ride next to Beckworth.

Beckworth waited a beat then nodded before kicking his mount faster.

Finn let his horse fall back, leaving Ethan and Maire to stay close to Beckworth. Finn stared down at AJ's unconscious form. Deep concern for her marred his happiness at finding her. If only Ethan and he hadn't been stopped by French soldiers. If only she had waited for him at the monastery. He could berate himself all day long and into the night, but it wouldn't change what happened. And regret wouldn't solve their current situation.

Lando followed a hundred yards behind them, occasionally stopping to see if anyone followed. When the group reached a wide road, they had to wait ten minutes until Lando caught up with them. Once Lando arrived and confirmed they were still clear, they crossed the road quickly, then traveled for another mile before turning right down an overgrown deer trail.

"Are you lost, little man?" Lando called out when Beckworth slowed. He twisted his head at something only he heard, then after a second, rode up close behind Finn's horse.

"You need to stop calling me that. And no. I'm not lost. The man who owns this land doesn't like surprises."

"Then why did you bring us here?" Ethan growled.

Maire's head rested against his back, and Finn caught the squeeze of her arms around Ethan's middle. Even half-asleep, she attempted to calm him.

"This is safer than my original choice."

Ethan glanced back at Finn. Neither of them knew the nature of Beckworth's motivation, and with no other option at hand, Finn shook his head. They would keep to Beckworth's plan for now.

When they reached a dilapidated gate, they stopped. Dozens of skulls hung from a massive winter-barren tree. Most were from a mix of animals—dog, deer, boar, and even bear. But several human skulls hung between the others, the bones bleached white from time and exposure.

The gate didn't appear to have worked for decades, but Beckworth stopped in front of it before calling out, "It's Beckworth. I have friends and gold."

The other men shifted in their seats, causing the horses to sidestep.

"I thought you said this was a friend." Finn reined in his mount.

"He is. He's just a bit nervous with new people."

"Maybe we should have tried for a town." Finn glanced at Ethan and Lando. Ethan stared at the skulls and appeared ready to bolt, but Maire studied them. Finn shook his head, knowing her rapt attention to the skulls stemmed from fascination rather than fear or disgust.

"This is a better option." He looked down at AJ. "We need to get her to a safe place where she can be seen by someone with medical experience."

"A witch doctor?" Ethan asked.

Beckworth shrugged. "He's been called that and many other things." When he noticed the men's nervous glances, he heaved a sigh. "I know you lot don't trust me, but if I wanted to do her harm, I had plenty of opportunity before you arrived. And I could have just as easily set you up rather than risk my life to save the women. Now shut up until we reach the cabin. You should be grateful the old codger's reputation for being mad as a hatter overshadows his ability to cure anything." He glanced up at the skulls. "Almost anything."

Beckworth turned away from the group. He'd made a decision on their behalf, and they could either trust him and follow or go their own way. Finn pushed hair out of AJ's face. She should have woken by now. There wasn't any choice.

"I know it's been a while," Beckworth called out. "I'd love to tell you about my travels."

After another minute, a branch rustled, and a lad, somewhere in his late teens, popped his head out from behind a tree. "How do I know it's really you?"

Beckworth chuckled. "Who else would have knocked you from that foul-smelling donkey?"

The boy moved farther out from behind the tree. He tilted his head to one side and scratched his cheek as he thought about Beckworth's response. Then he laughed. "You've been gone a long time. Old Bart thought someone finally hung you."

The lad approached the group, giving each person a long and thoughtful look. When his gaze lit on the woman in Finn's arms, he straightened up. "Is she injured?"

When Beckworth nodded, the boy rushed to open the makeshift gate. They followed him for several hundred yards as the path twisted through the dense trees before opening up to a clearing with a cabin, a barn, and several other outbuildings.

A hunched man limped through the front door to stand at the outer edge of the covered porch. He leaned against a cane as frail in appearance as him. Wrinkles formed the olive-toned canvas of his face. His hair, what there was of it, had faded to a dull gray, but his light brown eyes were as clear and inquisitive as a two-year-old's.

"Well, bring her in. I can't look her over from here."

33

Finn rushed into the spacious cabin, a listless AJ in his arms. He scanned the interior, searching for the best place to lay her down. A kitchen ran along the right side of the expansive interior. A table that could fit a dozen could be used as a last resort. The cluttered living space to his left was filled with chairs, sofas, and various-sized tables. Every surface was piled with books, clothing, or other odd paraphernalia.

The lad who'd led them from the gate had preceded Finn in and now waved at him from another door at the back of the cabin. The back room wasn't large, but it was cleaner than the rest of the old man's house. The lad pointed to the cot on the far side of the room.

Finn laid AJ down then brushed back her hair. Her soft mumbles had to be a good sign. He was surprised he heard them at all over the hammering of his heart. The threat of Dugan's men might not be gone, but they were no longer the immediate concern.

The boy brought a blanket and helped Finn cover AJ. "Bart will be in soon. He's talking with the other woman."

Finn nodded. He sat next to the cot and opened the top

portion of her dress, wanting to ensure her breathing wasn't restricted. He smoothed his hand down the back of her head, grateful not to find fresh blood.

"What's her name?" The boy had moved to a hearth Finn hadn't noticed when they'd entered, and he removed a kettle from the pothook.

"AJ."

"That's an odd name." He poured water into a metal bowl. He added a couple drops of a clear liquid then placed the bowl on a stand next to the cot. He handed Finn a clean rag.

"It's a nickname. Short for Abigail." Finn wasn't sure why he was explaining anything, but the conversation masked his panic. He dunked the rag in the warm water. A slight tingle skittered across his skin where it touched the water, and a pleasant pine scent tickled his nose.

"She doesn't really look like an Abigail. AJ seems to suit her."

Finn could only nod as he wiped dirt from AJ's face, his anger surging when he noticed the bruise on her cheek had darkened. "What's your name?"

The boy laughed. "You can call me Lincoln."

Finn glanced up at him. "That's an unusual name as well."

"I know. Not like Old Bart." He started for the door, then turned. "Bart might seem a bit odd, but he knows his healing." Lincoln shut the door behind him.

Finished with her face, neck, and arms, Finn began the task of cleaning around her head wound. He placed the rag against her hair, gently soaking the dried blood away. He remembered when she'd done the same for him the first time he'd brought her to this century. They'd been crossing the sea to England on the *Daphne Marie* when a storm overtook them. He'd been hit on the head by falling debris, and she'd dressed his wound. He'd been barely conscious, but he'd still been able to feel her warm lips on his forehead.

Once the wound was cleaned, he glowered at the door, irritated by how long it was taking this Bart fellow. He leaned down and kissed AJ's forehead, breathing in the pine scent from whatever had been in the water. "I'm sorry I was late. You wouldn't believe the traffic. I would have stopped at Donna's to get your favorite pie, but..." He stopped and pressed his head to hers. "I miss you, wife. Wake up and yell at me. Tell me about your journey. Tell me how much you missed me, and I'll tell you how sorry I am for bringing us back here."

He reached for her hand and turned it over, running a thumb over her palm. "Maire once tried to teach me how to read palms. I don't think I ever told you that." He ran a finger along her life line. "I never put much stock in it, but I think if Maire were to read yours, she would say this isn't the end. Your life line is strong. We have so many more adventures waiting for us. Wake up, my love." He kissed her cheek when something scratched at his hand.

He pulled back, AJ's hand still in his. Her fingers slowly curled. His heartbeat quickened. "AJ? Can you hear me?"

"Gulls." The single word slipped from her lips before her fingers relaxed.

Finn stood and started for the doorway, then yelled at it instead. "Bart, get in here before I come out there and drag you in by your ears." Then he dropped back into his chair. "Tell me about the gulls, AJ."

THE SQUAWKING of gulls broke through AJ's slumber. The familiar cacophony lasted only a second, but it was enough to force her awake. Everything was dark, but she was too tired to pry her eyes open. Her head ached, but it no longer pounded.

She thought she'd heard Finn's voice just before the gulls.

He'd been carrying her. She remembered being jostled, then the stabbing pain until she didn't remember anything at all.

Her stomach hurt when she breathed, but she couldn't remember why it would. She moved a toe as she took an assessment of her body. Had it moved? She tried another toe and felt resistance. Not knowing what that meant, she moved on to her arms. They reminded her of fallen tree limbs, damp and heavy from winter rains. But other than the light twinge in her belly, her head seemed to be her primary malady.

Then she felt his lips. His warm voice washed over her but only a few words registered—pie, palm, wife. *Finn.* His cedar scent mixed with that of pine. Were they in a forest? Maybe she was delirious from brain damage.

Lips brushed against her forehead, her cheek, her lips.

She reached for him, but her arms wouldn't move. Was that his hand? She was sure of it. Then the gulls returned. Where were they?

"Gulls," was all she managed to say. She moaned, and something warm was placed on her forehead.

Her hair was brushed back, and a languid breath slid against her skin. His cedar scent invaded every cell of her being. It was Finn. Somehow, he'd found her.

"I know you're strong. I know you could have done this on your own." His lips nibbled at her ear as his hand stroked her shoulder. "But I will always come for you."

"Finn?" His name scratched out of her dry throat like sandpaper across fine wood. She tried to open her eyes but couldn't stop the deeper darkness that skirted her delicate consciousness. He squeezed her hand again and yelled something unintelligible. It didn't matter. The only words she'd wanted to hear had already been said. He'd always come for her.

"WHAT TOOK YOU SO LONG?" Finn barked when Bart finally made an appearance, grumbling under his breath.

Maire followed the old man through the door. This was the first time Finn truly noticed her emaciated appearance. His focus up to then had been on AJ. He stood so Bart could exam AJ, allowing Finn the opportunity to fold Maire into his arms. Her twig-like arms hugged him tightly, reinforcing his suspicions that her spine was made of steel.

"It's good to see you, sister."

"You shouldn't have come."

He pulled away and scanned her face. "Of course, we should have."

She wrung her hands as she stared down at AJ. "At what cost?"

He shook her gently until she glanced up, her stubborn expression firmly in place. "She'll be all right. I believe that." He held her gaze. "And what cost was there to you? And Ethan?"

Maire pushed him away, her voice contrite. "It wasn't his fault."

He raised his hands in surrender. "Enough of that. There will be plenty of time to discuss the mess we're in. Right now, we need to get you and AJ healthy."

A resigned grin lit her freshly washed face that was incongruous to the rest of her appearance. Her unwashed hair hung in thick, dirt-encrusted ropes. Filth and dried blood marred her tattered dress.

She squeezed his arm, still able to read his emotions. "Let me help with AJ. I've eaten. I feel fine. Once she's settled, I'll see to my own grooming."

Finn nodded then realized she had been moving him toward the door as she spoke. When he tried to object, her fiery temper emerged.

"You'll only be in the way."

He hung his head, shaking it slowly back and forth. He didn't want to leave AJ. Not until she was stable, and she didn't appear anywhere close to stable.

Maire wouldn't be deterred. "You've done a fine job of cleaning the wound. You talked her into waking, even if it was brief. That's an excellent start. Now let us finish. See to the others. Beckworth is eager to talk to you."

Finn's jaw clenched.

"Brother, I know better than any of you the type of man Beckworth is. And now I can say I've seen worse. He may have kidnapped me, but that's between him and me." When Finn gave her an exasperated look, she waved him off. "I was in his care for almost two years. He kept me like a dove in a gilded cage. That's not how I've spent the last six months. Consider that when you're forced to work with him." She took a step closer, shaking a pointed finger at him. "And believe me on this as well, brother. As much as Beckworth has to pay for, we need him."

Bart, who had been examining AJ, stood up and, with cane in hand, limped his way to the table. He mumbled as he opened a book then glanced up at Maire. "Are you two going to chat all day? If not, can I get some help with the medicines?'

Maire rolled her eyes, a gesture AJ seemed to have taught everyone.

Finn sighed, his battle lost. "It's still good to see you, sister."

He heard her soft chuckle after she closed the door in his face.

34

When Finn returned to the main room of the cabin, he found Ethan and Beckworth glaring at each other from opposite ends of the kitchen table. Lando sat in between them as if playing referee while quietly eating a bowl of stew. It had been good to see his old friend when he'd arrived in Corsham. Somehow, he'd been only half surprised to have found him with Beckworth.

Before going to Waverly, Finn and Ethan had stopped in Corsham. They wanted to confirm if AJ was still in the area. If nothing else, AJ was predictable. She wouldn't travel to Hensley's or Hereford without stopping by Waverly. If she wasn't at the inn, a stop at one of the local public houses might provide news of Waverly.

They visited the mercantile and was on their way to the apothecary when Finn caught sight of Beckworth. The man ran, leading them out of town and straight to Lando. When Beckworth shared the news that AJ had been captured, Finn almost pummeled him before Lando interceded, explaining that AJ's capture hadn't been anyone's fault but Dugan's. And while Finn hadn't wanted to hear the excuses, he could do nothing to change the past.

The rescue plan had been simple, and Finn hated to admit the four of them had worked seamlessly. They had taken the guards by surprise; the mission taking less than thirty minutes. Now, he had time to determine what to do with Beckworth.

"Are you going to tell us what's going on at Waverly?" Finn went right for the heart of the matter as he dragged a chair to the table. He left the empty chair for Maire, hoping in vain she'd come out on her own to eat.

Lando glanced at Beckworth, a troubled frown creasing his forehead. This didn't bode well.

"It seems rather obvious, doesn't it?" Beckworth pointed his chin toward the stack of books and loose papers Maire had insisted on stealing from her prison and were now scattered on the table. "It's the bloody stones. Obviously, there must be something else they want your sister to decipher."

"Dugan isn't the one pretending to be the viscount, is he?" Ethan's quiet tone belied the anger beneath.

"No. That would be someone else." Beckworth stood and dug around a shelf, moving clay jars aside until he grunted with satisfaction. He pulled down a jar that looked like all the rest, then grabbed four mugs. He set them on the table and filled the cups with a clear liquid. He put the stopper back in the jar and passed the mugs around.

"Careful. This is quite strong, but I think it's appropriate for the next part of the conversation."

Beckworth took a swallow, grimaced as it went down, then shook his head like a cat shaking off rain. Then he grinned and rasped out, "Just as I remember it."

Finn glanced at his two friends, who both shrugged before lifting their cups. With watery eyes from the potent smell, Finn tossed back a long swallow, as did the others.

Beckworth waited while the homemade hooch worked its

way into the men's bellies. Seemingly satisfied his audience was well fortified, he began his tale. "I was born in London to a woman who worked for the Duke of Dunsmore. The duke was a charmer in his younger days, and being the powerful man that he was, the young female servants always caught his attention. And he'd bed them whether they were agreeable or not—or so my mother said."

He waited until he saw the spark of understanding in the men's eyes.

"You're the duke's son?" Ethan asked the question, but he was nodding as if certain elements fell into place like pieces of a puzzle he hadn't realized were there.

"After my mother discovered she was pregnant and said something to the housekeeper, she was handed a small amount of money and promptly dismissed. She lived with her sister and cleaned rooms at one of the inns until I was born. It was hard times, and eventually her sister's husband forced us out, claiming too many mouths to feed. We ended up living with three other families in an old shanty just off the Thames. When I was old enough, in order to earn my keep, I learned some skills." His lips curved into a handsome and whimsical smile. "As you know.

"Though we were dirt poor, those were the happiest days of my life. I felt loved, and with my scavenging ways, we lived well enough. Mother thought I'd end up in the military or stowaway on a ship to new adventures. As it turns out, I did spend a couple of years on a ship but found it too confining."

Beckworth took another drink and waited for the burn to stop. "I never cared who my father was. At least not until I saw his rightful heir. Oh, Mother had told me who my father was, but I'd learned early on how it was with the rich and powerful versus those of us that weren't. I didn't question it at the time. That's just the way things were. Then one day I saw the duke as he stepped from a carriage to enter a gentleman's club. He had a young lad by his side. The boy looked to be about the same age as me and could have been my double, we looked so much alike. And just like that, I was obsessed."

"Your brother? That's who has taken over Waverly?" Ethan stared at the table, his eyes unfocused, as if continuing to connect the puzzle pieces.

"Amazing, isn't it? Almost an exact duplicate except for different blood in our veins."

"Wouldn't that make this man the heir to Waverly?" Lando asked.

"Not bloody likely." Beckworth emphasized his response with a fist on the table. "Waverly never belonged to the duke. I made sure there wasn't one iota of a link between Waverly and him. Waverly was my payment."

"Your payment? That's what this is all about. Your due as the bastard son of a duke?" Finn's anger flared.

"Not payment for being his bastard. His payment for the things he made me do. The things his spoiled, worthless heir either couldn't or wouldn't do. Oh, he had Dugan to do his interrogations and beat downs. But he needed someone who could get close, get inside the doors to listen and learn, and sometimes..." Beckworth's gaze shifted down as if in embarrassment. "Sometimes to be a silent assassin. My payment was a title and an estate."

Beckworth glowered at them and took another long swallow. When he could speak, it was with a more humble tone. "I know what you're thinking, and you're partly correct. I saw the riches I could have, but it was my mother who encouraged me."

Ethan scoffed, and Lando looked doubtful, but Finn understood. Not from personal experience, but he'd heard stories from enough Irish bastards to know the tale. "Your mother wanted you to have what should have been yours."

Beckworth met Finn's gaze and appeared heartened that someone understood if not agreed with his actions. "She worked so hard to give me a life. When she saw my half-brother, she got angry. Up till then, I'd never seen a mean-spirited bone in her body. Not until that moment. She knew the duke would never accept me as his, but she thought I might be of service to him. So Mother encouraged me to learn more skills—deadly skills. Eventually, the duke saw it as a bonus."

"How did your brother know about Waverly or the stones? He wasn't at the monastery." Ethan downed then rest of his mug then shook his head. "Never mind," he rasped out. "It must have been Dugan."

Beckworth nodded. "The question I have is why? As far as I knew, my dear brother has been in Austria, living what I'm sure is an aristocratic life. His mother is a blue blood."

"Then what is Maire transcribing?" Lando lifted a corner of one of the books and looked inside. Seeing nothing of interest, he dropped the cover.

"If you want to know more, come back here," Maire called from the doorway. "AJ is awake."

35

AJ didn't think she'd seen anyone more precious when Finn barreled his way into the room. She flinched as she pulled herself up to greet him. He stopped short. His forehead wrinkled as he stared down at her. He took another step, his arms rising then dropping to his sides. She held out her arms, not caring if it jarred her head. All she wanted was to feel his arms around her.

He dropped to his knees next to the cot and brought her gently into his arms. She held on for all she was worth, breathing in his scent, reveling in his strength. Feeding off it. Tears broke through; she'd thought she'd never see this man again.

Knowing everything they were up against, nothing mattered more than having Finn by her side.

He pulled back and wiped her tears away. His signature smile made her heart beat faster. He rested his forehead against hers and spoke in a hushed whisper, "I missed you, wife."

She kissed his ear, her voice just as low. "And I missed you, husband."

He ran a gentle hand over her head. "Does it still hurt?"

"Of course, it still hurts." The reply coming from Bart rather than AJ. "She got a good hit to the head, probably when she fell off the horse. Then it seems someone kept abusing her head whenever this false viscount didn't like her answers. She has some bruising, but it's her head I'm most concerned with."

"Explain," Finn barked, and his jaw clenched.

"I've worked up a tonic." The old man scratched his backside before glancing at Maire. "Well, I suppose I had a little help." When Maire nodded her appreciation, he continued. "She's been sleeping more than she should, even under the circumstances. Now, that could either be the body trying to heal itself, or there could still be swelling. Either way, she needs to stay in bed until her headaches are gone."

AJ fidgeted under the blanket. "I feel fine." When everyone gave her a disappointed glare, she decided now wasn't the best time to fight that battle.

"How long before she can ride?" Finn squeezed her hand when she tensed. "Or maybe a carriage?"

"Didn't you just hear what I said?" Bart's face reddened. He took two steps as if moving closer might help Finn understand him better.

"We heard you, old man." Beckworth sighed. "No one's questioning your skill, but the longer we stay here, the more danger we're putting you in." Beckworth touched Bart's elbow, guiding him toward a chair. "Sit before you fall down."

Once the old man sat and pushed Beckworth away, he mumbled, "They leave me alone. For the most part."

"Yes, but after they've exhausted all other possibilities, they might make an exception. We can't take the chance."

"We came for your expertise." Maire laid a hand on the man's arm, and he patted it. "Now that we have the tonic, I can monitor AJ. If the strain of travel is too difficult, we'll stop."

"I still don't like it," he grumbled. AJ noticed the spunk leave the old man and wondered how long Bart had been trapped in this cabin with only Lincoln for company.

Ethan dragged in a chair from the other room, and Maire seemed relieved to sit. Lando followed with more chairs. They gathered around AJ, but they turned their gazes toward Maire.

AJ couldn't remember seeing her so nervous. "They need to know everything, Maire."

Ethan scooted closer to Maire. Now that AJ knew Ethan's part of withholding Maire's interest in the druid book when he jumped to the future, the two of them appeared to be on trial. AJ had no doubt Ethan would be more than willing to take the fall for all of it.

"Just spit it out. It has to do with the stones, right?" Beckworth's earlier comforting tone with Bart disappeared, replaced by impatience.

AJ had overheard the story he'd shared with the men in the other room. She wondered what would have happened to him if he hadn't been caught in the fog and transported to the future. Would Dugan have come to Waverly anyway and taken over the estate? Maybe killing Beckworth to keep him out of the way? There was obviously no love between the brothers.

"The stones are an important piece, but not all of it. There is a slim possibility the Heart Stone may be of importance."

"What else?" Finn asked. AJ squeezed his hand. This next part was going to irritate him, and she wanted him to stay calm.

Maire sighed and stood to pull the kettle from the fire. She made herself busy preparing tea, her posture rigid as she ignored the group. While she poured the tea, she replayed the story she'd told AJ in the cell, starting with her travel to Peterstow in search of the druid's book. She glossed over the part of Ethan's knowledge of the book, but based on the tic in Finn's jaw, AJ knew he hadn't missed that piece. If Ethan had bothered to tell them about the book when he'd arrived in Baywood, their investigation might have moved faster. But Ethan required Finn and AJ's assistance for more than just finding Maire. He'd known that he would probably require assistance in rescuing her. For a moment, AJ felt her own irritation with Ethan though she understood why he did it. Finn, however, would require more than a few words of apology.

"When I learned the druid's book was real and had been found, I couldn't resist."

"And this *Mórdha Stone Grimoire* is the druid's book?" Lando turned a little gray. "Grimoires are filled with black magic."

Maire returned to her seat, her stoic resolve back now that she'd revealed her secret. "Not all, but you're right. Some can be dangerous, or at least that's what I've been told. But any book that speaks of magic spells and incantations would be accurately called a grimoire."

No one asked how Maire came to know about grimoires, though everyone knew her ability to transcribe old Celtic. AJ had learned about Maire's socialization with the Irish Travellers when they had unknowingly wandered into a Romani camp in their failed escape from Dugan. AJ didn't know much about the Travellers, but she knew some Romani had knowledge of old magic.

"I was only given one page at a time to transcribe. Someone had copied the original text onto the individual pages. Sometimes the writing appeared hurried, making it difficult to read, and one misplaced letter can lead to a different meaning. I'd only seen the book once before." She glanced to Beckworth, who kept a straight face, either not wanting anyone to know he'd once had the book in his possession or he didn't want to derail her. "From what I remember of the book, I've transcribed maybe a third of it. And from what I've seen so far, the druid suggested the possibility of time travel by use of the smaller stones, but I don't know how."

"But we've used the smaller stones to travel from the start." Ethan scanned the group who were nodding in agreement.

Maire shook her head. "All the travel up to this point has been a direct relation of the smaller stones and their connection to the Heart Stone. The incantations were used to bring the stones together—to find each other. This druid's experiments were to use an individual stone to travel through time."

The sobering silence summed up the group's thoughts. Their understanding of the stones to this point assumed the Heart Stone was the required element for time travel. If it was true that each stone had such power on its own, and there were five smaller stones, the druid's book could prove more dangerous than *The Book of Stones*.

"What's this viscount's name?" Ethan asked

"He said something about being an heir to the druids," AJ interjected.

Beckworth snorted. "My ass."

When everyone turned to him, Beckworth waved a hand in a dismissive gesture. "He's gone daft. His name is Reginald Johannes Penwether. He has a small claim to aristocracy in Austria through his mother. The only title he's ever held in England was marquess, and he lost that when our dear father's title was taken."

"All I know is he thinks he's related to some ancient druid." AJ slumped back. Bart shuffled over to hand her a mug of tea. She wrinkled her nose as she sipped it. The earthy smell of valerian root and chamomile smothered the scent of something that left a bitter aftertaste. She would have preferred coffee and then wondered if her brief withdrawal from caffeine made the headaches linger.

Maire's chortle broke through AJ's musings. "An Englishman with ties to the druids? Ridiculous. But AJ isn't wrong. He seems to think he can make himself invincible with the stones."

Beckworth's face flushed with either frustration or anger. Maybe both. AJ couldn't decide. He crossed his arms across his chest and grumbled. "Must be all that blue blood inbreeding. If I'd known I'd have to give away half my brain to be a full duke's son, I wouldn't have wasted half my life trying to impress the sod."

Beckworth's flippant remark on his lifelong struggle for acknowledgment by an arrogant father seemed to take the air out of the room. In a somewhat successful attempt to turn the conversation away from him, he turned to Maire. "So how much of this information have you shared with my brother?"

Maire sighed, her eyes downcast. "Only enough to keep him satisfied."

"Stop." Ethan glared at Beckworth, who shrugged. He grabbed Maire's hand. "You have nothing to be sorry for. You've been held in a dungeon for the last six months."

"Not exactly a dungeon." Beckworth raised his hands in mock defense. "Though I admit not the best conditions. My question wasn't meant as an accusation. We need to know how much Reginald knows."

AJ smirked at Beckworth's use of his brother's common name.

"I kept him appeased for several weeks because the copied text was truly dreadful and when..." She glanced at Beckworth and gave him a conspiratorial smile. "When I finally told Reginald that nothing made sense with the unintelligible handwriting, he reviewed the pages and came to the same conclusion. It was another week or more before he brought me new translations. But I had to feed him something. I dragged it out for as long as I could and, beginning to understand where the translations were going, tried to feed him false information. That worked for a couple of months before he discovered I was holding back. I don't know how he knew. He either had someone checking my work, or he just made an assumption. I'm not sure which."

"No one is blaming you. Giving him false information was perfect." Ethan glared at the others, daring anyone to say something different.

"If Reginald did have someone reviewing your work, wouldn't this person require some understanding of the old Celtic language? Possibly enough to link together what the druid was working on?" Finn asked.

Beckworth considered the question. "He's always been well-traveled, so he could have made some important connections."

"You said the duke's wife is an aristocrat? I'm surprised she stayed with him." AJ couldn't wrap her head around why she'd want to stay with the duke.

"She didn't have the titles on her own, but she did have money. I do believe she loved him from what little I saw of them together, but when he lost his title, and she became his source for capital, the tables were turned. She eventually tired of him, stopped the cash flow, and left for Austria."

Lando, who AJ almost forgot was in the room, spoke up from the corner. "If he has someone that can translate old Celtic, the person must not be well-versed enough."

"There's more to it than just the ability to read old Celtic." Maire glanced down at her hands, brows pinched in thought as seconds ticked by. When she seemed to have her thoughts together, she leaned forward, "The druids weren't ones to write many things down. When they did, it was sometimes written in some form of code that differed from sect to sect. With enough readings of the book, some can correctly decipher the translations. With Sebastian's help, we were able to do just that with *The Book of Stones*, though not all of it. And that was two of us working long days and nights for months."

"So how much does he know?" Finn asked, his tone soothing and non-judgmental.

"I told him the torc seemed to play a part." Maire sat back, her spine stiff. Her expression seemed to dare anyone to challenge her actions. "I wanted to steer him away from the stones, and I knew the torc was well hidden in the monastery. With the war, I assumed travel would be difficult and the port well-guarded."

"That's good," Ethan said and rubbed the back of his neck. "Finn and I have it on good authority the soldiers have a strong presence at the port. Not invincible. Sebastian has his own smuggling operation going under their noses. But it would be difficult to invade the monastery until Napoleon is routed from France."

"And that will be several years yet," Finn added.

"Right." The old man leaned on his cane and pulled his body up from the chair. When Beckworth moved to assist, he pointed the cane at him. "Stop right there. I've been getting up from my chair since I was old enough to walk." He moved to his work table and began grinding herbs.

AJ laid back, suddenly too tired to hear anymore. When Finn leaned close and gazed down on her with a worried expression, she reached for his hand. "I'm all right. Just too much too soon, I think." She reached for her pocket then realized she wasn't wearing her dress. Panic shot through her, and she sat up so abruptly, a jolt of pain made her wince.

"Don't worry. Your necklace and dagger are safe." The mirth in Maire's tone told AJ that her friend had found more than just the Heart Stone in her pocket.

36

Bart limped to the bed and handed AJ a cup. "Drink it all down." He turned to the room. "Everyone out. The woman needs rest."

Finn lingered while the rest of the men filed out. He kissed her cheek. "I'm going to check on the horses, then I'll be in the next room."

AJ smiled up at him, but the movement made her wince. When his smile faded, she placed a finger on his lips before he could say anything. "I really do feel better. I'm just not used to the bright light."

He didn't look convinced, but he nodded. "That must be it." He glanced at Maire but didn't say anything as he stood to leave.

Before he made it to the door, Maire called out. "I don't know why he didn't tell you, but he didn't mean any harm."

"We all pay for our secrets, Maire." He left the room, shutting the door quietly behind him.

Maire sat next to AJ and pointed at the cup. "You need to drink all of that."

AJ swallowed the tonic without pause, assuming she was drinking the same concoction Bart had given her the last time.

She gagged, spitting the last remnants across the blanket. "God, that's awful. What's in that?"

The old man cackled. "If I told you it would taste bad, you'd still be sipping it. Now just lay back and let it do its job."

"To what? Poison me," she grumbled.

"If I wanted to poison you, the tonic would have tasted like honey in summertime."

"Good to know." She laid back and stared at Maire while Bart fussed at his table.

"Where's my ring?"

Maire reached into a pocket and handed AJ the necklace with the Heart Stone and wedding ring. "When were you married?" Maire's lips twitched beneath her stern accusatory stare.

AJ thought back to her impromptu wedding to Finn in their bathtub back in Baywood. "No one knows except my close friend Stella, and that's only because Finn asked her help in picking up the ring. I wanted to wait for Finn so we could tell you together."

Maire hugged her with more vigor than AJ expected, and she grabbed her head.

Maire laughed. "Sorry. It couldn't be helped." She glanced down at the ring in AJ's hands, her fingers clasping and unclasping around it. "It's quite similar to our parents' promise rings."

"That was Finn. He completely surprised me."

"Did you have a ceremony?"

"If you call a handfasting with Celtic vows being shared while naked in a tub a ceremony, then yes." She couldn't help but grin, which only grew wider at Maire's flushed cheeks. "I can't believe you're blushing."

"I can't believe you mentioned my brother naked."

They both giggled until they heard a crash from outside.

When nothing else happened, Maire sighed. "I fear Ethan just paid for his secrets."

FINN STORMED THROUGH THE CABIN, out to the porch, then down the steps. Ethan stood next to Lando and Beckworth. They appeared to be scanning the landscape for threats while reviewing their security measures. The men turned when they heard Finn approach. Without breaking stride, Finn drove a right hook into the side of Ethan's head. The man went down.

Finn marched into the barn and grabbed the reins of the first horse he came to. The saddles had been removed, but they hadn't been properly brushed. He looked around then noticed Lincoln step out from one of the stalls.

"Where are the brushes?" Finn called out, surprising the lad who came running.

On the way, Lincoln picked up a brush from a nearby barrel. "Sorry I haven't gotten them brushed yet. I wanted to get their stalls ready first."

"Don't worry. I prefer to brush my own."

Lincoln fidgeted, moving from one foot to another, a question apparently on his mind.

"What is it?" Finn softened his tone. His anger wasn't at this boy.

"Did you mean to brush all the horses?"

Finn glanced at the other three horses then back at Lincoln. "How about we split the effort?"

Lincoln nodded with enthusiasm. "Let me finish with the hay, then I'll get started."

The barn door opened while they brushed the last two horses. Finn glanced over his shoulder to see Ethan approach, a sheepish expression on his face.

Before Ethan reached them, Lincoln untied the horse he'd been brushing and led it to a stall. When he was out of earshot, Ethan stopped next to Finn, who continued to brush the horse.

"We always seem to be full of secrets." Ethan leaned against a post, arms crossing over his chest.

Finn nodded. "Almost as if we didn't trust each other."

A moment went by before Ethan tried a different tact. "I thought you might run me through."

"The thought had occurred."

Several minutes passed. The silence only broken by Finn's even strokes of the brush and the chuffing of horses from their stalls. Ethan shook his head and turned away.

Finn sighed. "We're fine." He set the brush down and faced Ethan. "I understand why you did it. Just like I understand why AJ didn't tell me about seeing Beckworth following her, or why Adam didn't tell his wife about his gambling debt. Just as I stand by my reasoning for not sharing everything with AJ after our jump—or before it."

Ethan raised a brow at the last admission but waited for Finn's words to sink in. He ran a hand through his hair, and he sounded so tired. "Damn it, Finn. Life was so much easier without women."

Finn's bark of laughter echoed through the barn. His amusement only increased as he thought about the last two years of his life. Then Ethan began to laugh. The chortles growing in unison as the stress of the last two weeks broke free. Falling against opposite posts, they slid to the ground facing each other across the aisle.

"I should have told you something when we were in Baywood." Finn considered Ethan, who wiped tears from his face. He looked haggard. They hadn't stopped for a decent meal or sleep since arriving in England. He waited for Ethan to meet his gaze. "I'm happy it's you that Maire picked."

His friend said nothing. Instead, he stared at his hands resting in his lap. "I don't deserve her."

Finn's signature grin appeared, and he chuckled. "Of course not, man. You're not Irish." Then Finn grew serious. "But there's no one I trust to care more for her than you. If nothing else, that was easy enough to see when you arrived in Baywood. I know the look of someone in pain, riddled with guilt, and unable to do anything."

Ethan nodded. He picked up a rock and turned it over in his hands. "What about Beckworth?"

"I'm not sure I care." Finn would be happy to just walk away from the man and never think of him again.

"We need to do something about this book."

"Aye." Finn rubbed his jaw. The plan had been so simple. Find Maire. Yet, before they'd jumped back, he'd known that if Maire had been kidnapped, there would be more to the story. They should have tossed the blasted stones, torc and all, into the sea. Be damned to Sebastian's preservation of history. And if they could recover the druid's book, would that be the end? He needed to make sure that it was.

Ethan threw the rock down the aisle, and it skipped twice before landing still. "Beckworth seems eager to get Waverly back."

Finn nodded. "And that's the key to him. As long as our plan to steal the book matches Beckworth's desire to regain Waverly, he can be trusted. Otherwise..."

"Otherwise, we find creative ways to convince him that our plan coincides with his best interest."

Finn's grin returned, and he hoisted himself up. When Ethan stood, Finn held out his hand. "Our mission is to steal the book, get rid of it, then get the women to safety. Once and for all."

Ethan shook his hand. "Agreed."

37

A knock on the door woke AJ. She'd barely roused by the time Maire opened the door wide enough to stick her head out. AJ caught a glimpse of Finn's tall figure before Maire whispered something to him then slipped out the door. Finn stepped in.

"How are you feeling?" He closed the door and leaned against it, crossing his arms over his chest. His gaze roved over her as if seeking his own answer.

AJ sat up and performed a self-examination. She was still stiff, but the headache was nothing more than a dull ache. "Better." They stared at each across the room. She broke the contact and studied the tightly clasped hands in her lap. "I'm sorry I didn't wait for you."

"You were right not to."

She lifted her gaze and saw the truth in his eyes. Holding back a smile, she nodded, still unsure why he was across the room inspecting her like she might be contagious. "What happened to you?"

He lifted a shoulder. "You know the story. The fog returned and grabbed us in your wake, just as it did Ethan with our very first jump, and as it did in bringing Beckworth to the future."

"I thought so. But after a couple of days, and you didn't show up, I thought Ethan might have used the revised incantation Maire had translated."

"We weren't sure where it would take us. Following you, if we could, was the better option."

"How far away did the mist drop you?"

"Only a couple of days' ride, but we ran into some soldiers."

She sat straighter, looking him over more thoroughly.

Finn chuckled. "We both survived and made it to the monastery only an hour after you left."

"You caught a ship?"

"A captain I know made port a couple of days later. He has a fast ship, and we docked just shy of Southampton. Then we rode straight for Waverly."

"My goal was Hereford, but Waverly was on the way."

"And the two of you thought you'd be enough to find and rescue Maire?"

Now she understood. He wasn't upset that she'd gone into the past without him. Beckworth had forced her to jump with him. And he wasn't mad that she'd left with Jamie on the *Daphne Marie*. He was mad she'd trusted Beckworth.

"We had similar goals, but they didn't include rescuing her. I didn't think we'd even find her. When we discovered the building heavily guarded, we knew someone important was in there. I was gathering information from town on the chance someone may have seen her." She gave him the most sincere smile she could drum up. "I sent letters to the earl and Hensley. They've probably just received them or should soon." He didn't need to know she had no intention of leaving for Hereford, and she felt horrible for the slight misdirection. She bit at a nail and glanced at Finn. His expression had changed. Any sign of irritation had been erased by something smoldering behind those emerald-green eyes.

"Why are you still standing over there?"

"I'm afraid if I get close, I'll hold on too tight. You need time to heal."

"I'd heal faster if I could hold my husband."

Faster than she could blink, he was next to her. He pushed her to the side of the cot as he climbed in next to her, rolling her half on to him so they'd both fit. The creaking of wood under their combined weight made them both freeze. She giggled while he found the most comfortable position for both of them.

She never thought she could miss someone so much that it felt as if she'd break into tiny pieces. He pulled her close, and she rested her head on his chest, the strong beat of his heart loud in her ear. She wrinkled her nose and sniffed her armpit. Maire must have given her a sponge bath she hadn't remembered. Which left Finn as the one who sorely needed a bath. But she was willing to forgo the smell so she didn't have to release him. He was here, and for the moment, they were all safe.

"I don't think this cot was built for two." AJ snuggled closer.

"Nonsense. We don't require any more space than this." His breathing settled into a steady rhythm.

AJ didn't mind remaining in bed if it meant being next to Finn. She closed her eyes and waited until their breathing became one.

Another knock at the door stirred them both awake.

"Come in." Finn rubbed his eyes and gave AJ a quick kiss on her lips.

Maire poked her head in. "I'm sorry. I gave you as much time to sleep as I could, but AJ should take another potion, and dinner will be ready soon." She moved through the door when Finn and AJ began to rise. When she stepped closer to the bed, she wrinkled her nose. "Someone needs a bath before dinner."

"After." Finn helped AJ to a sitting position.

"Then you'll eat outside. You'll not ruin a perfectly good meal." Maire ground chamomile in a small bowl then added a pinch of a dark powder.

AJ took Finn's arm to stand, wobbled a bit, then leaned against a chair. "I wouldn't mind holding dinner until then."

"Maybe we should have a bath together." His mood had improved with sleep.

Maire handed AJ a mug. "This won't taste quite as bad as the last one. I've added honey, but it's best to drink it down as quickly as you can." She turned to her brother. "This isn't an inn, and we don't have time to heat water for a bath. There's a creek behind the cabin, and considering the temperature outside, I don't think we'll have to wait long for you to finish."

AJ drank the tonic, trying not to gag at the taste. She wiped her mouth, glaring at Maire as she handed the mug back. "You lied. That was just as nasty as the last one."

Maire shrugged. "Then it's a good thing it's the last one you'll need. You can be a bit stubborn about all this."

"Who's one to talk?"

The two women glanced at the door when it banged closed. Finn was gone.

AJ grinned. "I guess a dip in a cold creek overrides our bickering."

Maire laughed then moved to help AJ freshen up. "I wish you'd stay in bed."

"I need to get away from that cot. My body feels like it's shrinking in on itself. I need to move around."

"Your head."

"Is much better. And I need to see if I get dizzy when I walk around. I promise I'll come straight back to the cot if the headache gets worse."

"Then let's get you dressed."

Maire unzipped the duffel that AJ had packed in Baywood.

"Where's my other bag?" AJ asked.

Maire pointed to it, half-hidden beneath Finn's duffel.

"I'd prefer the dress I had on." She glanced around the room. "It's ruined, isn't it?"

"No. It's still damp from being washed."

"There should be another dress in my canvas bag. It doesn't fit as well as the one I had made in Baywood, but it has secret pockets."

Maire rummaged in the canvas bag and pulled out a dark jade dress. "This is perfect." She reached into the pockets, felt around, then turned the dress inside out. She reviewed AJ's handiwork and nodded with approval. "What a wonderful idea." She helped AJ draw it over her head. "We'll have time to modify the pockets in your other dress." She pulled out the trousers and shirt AJ had previously worn. "I think we'll have time to give these a wash as well." She reached into the pockets of the pants and nodded with satisfaction at finding the hidden pockets. "Let's finish getting you dressed. The men have made plans."

38

———

AJ shuffled into the main room to join the group for dinner, her stiff muscles forcing small jerky movements. Lando jumped up, a grin lighting his face. He wrapped her in a bear hug. "I'm glad to see you up and around." He stepped back, his hands gripping her shoulders while he gave her a quick perusal. His smile faded. "You still look a little pale."

She patted his arm. "I'm fine. The head still aches, but it's much better." She glanced around the spacious cabin, surprised by its size if not by the clutter. One corner held two overstuffed bookcases, and more books filled tables, sofas, chairs, and other available space. A single hearth shared duty with the kitchen and the rest of the living area. The place was certainly well lived in.

The smell of stew and fresh bread refocused her attention to the dinner table. Two jugs sat in the middle of the table, and she suspected one held wine and the other ale. "It appears someone got a head start."

"Not by much." Lando pulled out a chair for her. "We waited for Beckworth and the lad to return."

AJ glanced at Beckworth, who stuffed a piece of bread in his mouth, then washed it down. The telltale drip of burgundy slid down his chin, and he wiped it away with the sleeve of his arm. He gave her a wink as she sat.

"And where did you go?" She glanced around to see that no one else ate, though a few drank. Finn hadn't returned from the creek yet.

"All in good time." His smile disappeared as he gave her the same once-over Lando had given her. "How are you feeling?"

Bart poured AJ a glass of wine while she smiled at the others at the table. Maire and Ethan sat across from her, and Beckworth sat to Ethan's right. Lincoln took the seat at the end of the table with Lando to his right. A space between Lando and AJ had been saved for Finn.

AJ responded to Beckworth by addressing the table. "Just so everyone is up to speed. My muscles are stiff but just need time and exercise. I have a dull ache in the back of my head but nothing compared to how it was. I promise to take it easy until the headaches are gone, and if they get worse, I promise to tell someone. Now, are we all caught up on AJ?"

Beckworth chortled. "Not hardly, but it will do for now." He finished his slice of bread and reached for another when Maire reached across Ethan and slapped his hand.

"Wait until Finn returns." Maire glared at him until he sat back.

"Do you know how long it's been since we've had a meal?" Beckworth grumbled.

Maire raised a delicate brow and plucked at her dress, which appeared a full size too large for her.

Beckworth stared into his mug. "Point taken."

The door banged open, and Finn entered carrying an armful of wood, his hair still wet from his dip in the creek. Lincoln slammed the door shut then ran after Finn to help stack the wood by the hearth.

When Finn turned to find AJ at the table, he gave her his own slow perusal, seeming to gauge whether she was well enough to join them. He nodded, more to himself, before he braced a hand on Lando's shoulder to take his seat between the big man and AJ.

"Do your ribs still hurt?" AJ asked.

"Probably as much as your head." He squeezed her knee under the table, which confirmed everything was all right.

Now that everyone was seated, Beckworth stood and removed the lid from the giant pot of stew. He filled his own bowl then handed it to Lincoln. Taking the young man's empty bowl, he filled it and passed it to Ethan. Beckworth continued his task until everyone had a bowl. If anyone found it curious that Beckworth played host, no one openly questioned it. It seemed the man continued to be an enigma to all of them.

AJ had expected the conversation to be stilted, but Beckworth took his role as host seriously and regaled them with stories of his misspent youth. Bart joined in, sharing his own tales and keeping the laughter flowing. By the end, everyone had an anecdote to reveal. When most of the stories included Beckworth, he seemed to humorously accept his part in the misadventures.

While people laughed and emptied their bowls, AJ kept an eye on Beckworth, who in turn occasionally noticed her watching and responded with a brief nod or a wink. Was this the real Beckworth, or was he playing another role? The thought he might be luring them into complacency had crossed her mind until she noticed the strong connection between him and Bart. Then she remembered Eleanor's fondness for him. It was almost as if friends from his past had sought Beckworth out when he moved to Waverly, and he'd made a place for them. Would a man like that betray them? She knew what Finn would probably say. But now that she'd spent time with the man, she wasn't so sure who Beckworth was anymore.

Once the meal was done, the conversation turned serious. Lincoln removed the dishes and refilled the jugs.

Finn focused on their singular issue, directing the conversation as if he were still captain of a ship. "As unbelievable as it seems, the stones continue to be a problem. Now it seems, we have another book full of magical secrets." He nodded to Maire before glancing around the table. He paused when he noticed Bart's empty chair. "Where's Bart?"

"Over here," the old man wheezed, sitting next to the hearth and sipping from a steaming cup. "Some of these books are pretty old. I imagine that fake viscount will be quite interested in getting them back."

Maire rose and raced to the old man's side faster than AJ thought possible. She grasped the edge of the book, but Bart was stronger than he looked.

He wrestled the book from her without losing his place. "Don't worry. I know how to handle a book." He nodded to his bookcase. "I have books older than this, and they're in perfectly fine condition."

Maire relented, but rather than returning to the table, she sat next to Bart and peered over his shoulder as he leafed through the book. Once satisfied he was being careful, she slumped back in her seat, trying to listen to the conversation at the table while keeping an eye on the old man.

Ethan drummed his fingers on the table. "So it seems we have something, this—" He stopped and glanced at Beckworth. "What did you say his name was? Reginald?" Beckworth nodded. "We have something Reginald wants, and he has something we want. Would he be interested in a simple exchange?"

"As important as he believes these books to be, he'll never

willingly hand over the druid's book." Maire wrapped her arms around her middle and stared at the fire.

"Maire's right," Finn replied. "And though it seems he lost his primary translator, with enough time, he'll find someone else."

"What about those pages you brought with you?" Ethan asked.

Maire stood, stared at Bart, and seeming satisfied that the books were safe, returned to her seat next to Ethan. "These were the last pages Reginald gave me. I've kept pertinent notes of my other translations and hid them within the pages of the books." She nodded in Bart's direction. "I thought we might catch a break in whatever I haven't translated yet. I just haven't had a chance to look at them since the rescue."

"And do you have any thought as to whether this druid was mad as so many believed?" Finn asked.

Maire's pained expression spoke volumes, confirming there was cause to worry about the contents of the book. "From what little I've read to this point, this druid was probably the high chieftain of the sect. That would explain why he kept a written record of his discoveries."

A chill swept through AJ, seeing their quick departure back home slipping away. "It seems we have no choice. We can't let Reginald keep the book."

"Why don't we just destroy the stones and the torc?" Ethan asked. "Even if the book remains, the source of power will be gone."

All gazes turned to Maire.

"Would the old monk give us the torc?" Beckworth asked. "He seemed to be a purist. I doubt he'd want to destroy something he was meant to protect." Beckworth picked at his sleeves before tugging one down. "Though it doesn't take care of removing Reginald from my home."

Maire's hands balled into fists, which she tried to hide in her skirts. But AJ had taken note, knowing Maire would resist destroying the stones and torc just as Sebastian would.

"We're not here to help you with family problems." Finn glared at Beckworth then relented. "But you're right. Sebastian won't give up the stones, not unless there was truly no other way."

Beckworth shrugged, unperturbed by Finn's comment. "I'm just stating a fact." He glanced at AJ, seeming to be somewhat apologetic with his next statement. "I'm just reminding everyone of our quid pro quo arrangement. You help me, I help you."

The conversation erupted in angry shouts. Before any real name-calling began, Lando banged his mug on the table, which silenced the room. "We shouldn't do anything before discussing this with Hensley." Lando poured more ale before glancing at Ethan. "I imagine the earl might also have a comment. While I agree this business with the stones is important, I'm more concerned about what this Reginald's end game might be, and its impact on England."

"Lando's right." Finn glanced around the table before resting his gaze on AJ. He clasped her hand. "We don't have enough men to deal with Dugan. We also have no idea where Reginald is keeping the book. We need to gather more intelligence, and we need to wait for the current situation with search parties to calm down. I think we've put our host in enough danger."

"Then we leave for Hereford?" Ethan asked.

Finn and Lando exchanged glances, and AJ understood they had a different destination in mind. It made sense that Ethan would think of the earl, but even with the earl's men, there was only one other person who would have greater interest in this new game. And he had a powerful network at his disposal.

"No. We go to Hensley's." When Ethan appeared ready to argue, Finn held up his hand. "Hensley has better connections. You'll have to trust me on this." His steady gaze moved around the table until he had a nod of agreement from everyone. "And while AJ may look better, I don't want to spend three days on the road. Hensley is within a day's ride."

Ethan nodded. "You're right, of course. But we'll need more horses."

"How about a carriage instead?" Beckworth offered. "It would make more sense. I know it will stand out, but I doubt Dugan's men would think we'd be so bold."

"It would be easier for the women until they regain their strength," Ethan agreed.

"And just where do you plan on getting a carriage?" Finn asked.

Bart cackled from his place by the fire. "You need to have that wheel fixed first. And there's at least a year's worth of dust to remove."

"I can help with the cleaning," Lincoln suggested. He sat up, his eager expression matched the sparkle of excitement in his eyes.

"There's a carriage in one of Bart's outbuildings." Beckworth stood and refilled mugs with wine. "If you promise to return it, I'd be happy to provide it as a show of good faith on my part." He raised his mug. "To our continued partnership."

When no one immediately responded, AJ stood and met Beckworth's mug with her own. Finn shook his head but stood with her, raising his own mug. Everyone else slowly followed suit. While it was clear they only trusted Beckworth to a point, no one could argue the dangers of staying. Their first move was to get the hell out of Dodge and gather reinforcements.

39

Though dusk was hours old by the time they finished their planning, Finn didn't want to wait until dawn to inspect the carriage. AJ watched from the porch as he rode out with Beckworth, Lando, and Lincoln. She scanned the yard for long minutes once they'd left. Satisfied they didn't have any unexpected visitors, she returned to the cabin to help Maire and Ethan clean up. Bart had returned to his office to prepare a medicinal package for their travel.

When the men hadn't returned by the time chores were done, Maire sat with Bart as he flipped through the books she had stolen. AJ watched over their shoulders, but everything was written in Celtic if she remembered the handwriting in *The Book of Stones* correctly. Other than marveling at their binding and colorful artwork, she had little else to comment on.

AJ left them to their own enjoyment and found Ethan sitting at the table, flipping through the pages of Maire's transcriptions. She removed the kettle of coffee from the hearth and set two mugs on the table, pushing the pages aside. She spoke of her travels without him and Finn, filling in details she hadn't shared before. Ethan talked about their capture by French soldiers and the kindness of two shepherd boys. A knot formed in her belly when she realized he and Finn could have just as easily been shot. Finn had laughed about their encounter and subsequent kidnapping by Valentin. He had apparently decided to gloss over the telling of other events.

The idea that their troubles were only beginning brought a tremor of foreboding. She rubbed her arms, shaking it off. But she now agreed with Ethan. Destroy everything except the Heart Stone. And once they got home, they would take the Heart Stone out to sea and toss it in.

"I'm sorry for my deception." Ethan clinked his mug with hers to break her out of her dark musings.

AJ stood to put the kettle over the fire to make coffee and returned with a full jug of ale. With the cold winter night, she wasn't sure which the men would prefer when they returned.

"Now, we're all guilty of secrets." She nudged his boot with her foot. "But it's a bit ironic that you lectured me about my secret while keeping your own."

He had the good manners to look chastised through his grin. Yet, he couldn't hide his deep sorrow. She scooted her chair over so she could lay her head on his shoulder. She grabbed his hand with both of hers. "You're forgiven. You know that." She glanced at Maire, who laughed at something Bart said. "Love isn't something we can explain. Sometimes the things we do for love are the most difficult to apologize for."

"You're a wise woman, Miss Moore." The tension she felt in his grip told her he wasn't free of guilt. His kiss on the top of her head suggested he'd at least started to put it behind him. She leaned back and brushed the hair from his forehead. A little sparkle had returned in his gaze, making him look like the man she'd first had coffee with in Baywood. So much had happened since then—only a few months ago.

The sound of horses stopped the conversation. Ethan ran for

the rifles while Maire helped Bart out of his chair. AJ raced for the back room and collected weapons. When she returned to the front room, everyone had positioned themselves near one of the two windows. She handed Maire a pistol, shot, and a bag of powder.

Maire loaded the pistol then checked the three rifles Ethan had placed between them. AJ crossed to where Bart stood and placed her quiver against the wall. AJ nocked an arrow and blew out long slow breaths, counting to ten then starting over. Between her nerves and how long it had been since she used her bow, she was tempted to loose an arrow or two before anyone entered the clearing.

The horses approached slowly. A few minutes later, a creaking sound followed the sounds of hooves. No one spoke, but AJ could hear the release of breaths as others began to relax their guard. It was possible that Dugan's men could have over-taken Finn and the others, and this was a trap. So they waited.

"There were mice in the hen house but we cleaned them out." The words were shouted from the far side of the yard where no one could be seen, but Bart relaxed his grip on the rifle. He cackled with amusement as he limped to the door. "That's my boy."

AJ gave Ethan and Maire a questioning glance. When Ethan shrugged and lowered his rifle, AJ released the tension in her bow but held on to the arrow.

Bart hobbled out to the porch and lifted a lantern.

AJ had to do a double take. The ugliest carriage she'd ever seen made a protesting lurch into the clearing. The fact the coach hadn't shattered into pieces coming up the rock-strewn drive was a miracle.

Finn and Lando jumped from the carriage bench while Beckworth dismounted and handed his reins to Lincoln. Finn and Lando's horses had been harnessed to the coach.

"You call that a carriage?" Ethan jumped off the porch and walked around it. "It's in such a deplorable condition, everyone will take note of it."

Considering how bad it appeared in the dark, AJ assumed it would only be worse in the light of day. She set her bow and quiver aside to take a closer look. Finn held out an arm to her, and she stepped into his embrace, letting him hold her for as much her sake as his. She drew strength from their connection and instinctively knew Finn felt the same.

"It's not pretty, I'll admit. But it will give us the cover we need to get out of the area." Finn's grin gave her encouragement. He really thought this was a grand idea.

"By looking like paupers?" Ethan asked.

"Exactly," Beckworth commented as he pushed past Lando. He grabbed onto the frame and gave it a good shake. "It's in decent enough shape. You'll look like an impoverished house traveling to visit relatives. It's not that uncommon, and once we have daylight, we can remove anything that looks too fancy." As if to prove a point, he found a weathered tassel on the corner of the coach and ripped it off. "We'll make it look like it's been stripped of anything worth selling."

"I think that's already been done," Ethan grumbled, giving it one last appalling look before ducking into the house.

By the time AJ and Finn strode into the cabin, Beckworth had already found the jug of ale. Maire placed a pot of coffee on the table and poured a cup for herself and Ethan.

"What took you so long?" AJ asked, curling onto Finn's lap, uncaring what others thought. She laid her head on his shoulder, feeling exhausted with the slightest throb of a headache. In all, she lasted longer than she thought she would.

"The wheel wouldn't go back on." Lando filled his own mug with ale.

"The inside of the carriage isn't too bad, but it's musty, and the seats have no padding." Finn held onto his cup of coffee with one hand while holding AJ close with the other.

They'd need a better look in the morning before prioritizing the required work on the coach. So their conversation turned to the roads. They came to a quick agreement with staying on back roads as long as possible before joining the main road toward Bristol.

When Lincoln returned from caring for the horses, he helped AJ and Maire prepare sleeping areas for the men in the large room. Bart was already asleep on the sofa, his rifle next to him. Maire and AJ would share the back room.

Maire placed a pistol next to the blankets she'd laid in front of the fire.

"Don't you think you've been sleeping on the floor long enough?" AJ asked, trying to find a comfortable position on the cot.

"One more night won't matter. To be honest, I can sleep anywhere knowing I'm free." Maire sat on her makeshift bed and poked at the fire. Once the flames sparked to life, she laid down facing it.

Long moments passed.

"Thank you for coming," Maire murmured.

"We love you, Maire. There's nothing to thank us for."

40

A steady rain greeted the group the following morning, tapering off to a drizzle by the time the bags were loaded. In daylight, the coach proved to be even worse than AJ expected, but the gray weather might have impacted her dismal observation. At least the rain had removed the dust. Lando sprinted across the muddy yard, blankets tucked under his arm. With no cushion left in the seats, and with an all-day journey ahead of them, blankets were the handiest items to help soften the ride.

With Maire and AJ the only occupants in the carriage, Finn and Ethan both agreed it would be safer if the weapons traveled inside the coach. If Dugan's men caught up with them, they'd want the weapons handy. No one was going back to Waverly.

AJ and Maire hugged Bart and Lincoln.

"You'll always have a place here whether you're on the run or not," Bart offered with amusement dancing in his eyes. He nodded to Beckworth. "Any friend of Teddy's is a friend of mine."

AJ glanced at Beckworth, but if he was bothered by Bart calling him Teddy, he didn't show it. It seemed a chosen few were among the privileged.

"I suppose I won't be getting a hug." Beckworth laughed when AJ scowled at him. "That's still better than being stuck with a blade." He rubbed his shoulder.

AJ couldn't hold back a grin. "I won't say it's been a pleasure." She scanned the yard and watched Lando jump up to the carriage's bench. He'd be the coachman for the journey. She turned back to Beckworth. "Are you sure you don't want to come with us? Dugan's men must still be searching."

Beckworth shook his head. "I'll stay here for a few days and let Dugan's men tire. Eleanor will send a message when it's safe to return. Besides, now that I've confirmed what's happened at Waverly, I have work to do."

"He'll be watching for you." Finn and Beckworth shared a look AJ couldn't read, but they seemed to have come to an understanding.

"He'll never be watching in the right place." He glanced at Lincoln. "I have my resources, and by the time you return, I'll know who can be trusted."

It seemed neither was willing to shake hands, so they simply nodded before Finn helped AJ and Maire into the coach. Once Finn and Ethan were mounted, Lincoln led them down to the gate. AJ stuck her head out the window, catching Beckworth's gaze as he watched them go. Before they turned from view, he raised a hand in salute, and AJ waved back. She didn't know what to make of him. Friend or foe? Or something in between? Finn was right. For now, they had the same goal, but as much as she wanted to trust Beckworth, it wouldn't hurt to watch their backs.

The first part of the journey was slow going with the rain and muddy road, but by mid-day, the drizzle stopped, and the roads began to dry. Maire had arranged the blankets to provide decent padding on the hard benches, but the ride was still bumpy. They were both thankful when they stopped at an inn.

They ate quickly. The men didn't feel they'd put enough distance between them and Waverly. AJ and Maire were allowed ten minutes for a stroll before Finn helped them back in the coach. Once on the road, AJ immediately complained.

She leaned out of the window and yelled at Finn. "We should have left the coach back at the inn and purchased two more horses. We could've sent a note for Beckworth to retrieve it. I'm feeling well enough to ride."

He grinned. "I wouldn't think you'd want to get back on a horse so soon after falling off one."

She scowled at him. "Haven't you heard it's best to get back on the horse as soon as you can?"

His grin grew wider as he tipped his head to her. "No." Then he clucked at the horse and moved to ride next to Lando.

AJ huffed as she resettled on the bench and crossed her arms. She squirmed and, unhappy with the lump of blankets, pulled one out from under her, and tossed it away.

"You didn't really think he'd let you back on a horse until you're fully healed, did you?" Maire's light tone belied the mischievousness in her gaze.

"Don't start. He's more agreeable in my time period."

"Ah. You can't seem to strip the eighteenth-century man away."

"If we stay here too long, he'll probably burn my trousers and sell my bow."

Maire laughed. "I doubt he'd ever go that far."

AJ grabbed the blanket she'd tossed aside and stuffed part of it behind her back. "I suppose not." She smiled. "I do love that man." She fiddled with the folds of her skirt before steeling herself. "Can I ask you a personal question?" When Maire raised a brow, AJ said, "It's about Ethan."

Before she could finish, someone shouted.

Both women froze. Waited. Two more shouts. The voices were too distant to be Finn or Ethan.

When the coach drew to an abrupt stop, Maire reached for a duffel and AJ for her bow.

"We're traveling to Bristol. Why have you stopped us?" Finn's question was pleasant enough, but AJ knew that tone. Maire's quick glance told AJ she'd also heard the edge in her brother's response.

The women worked faster to remove weapons from the duffels as horses approached. Maire stopped to peer out the left-side window. Even with the gray skies, the brightness still bothered Maire, so they'd dropped the curtain before leaving Bart's. That turned out to be a blessing.

AJ peeked out the other side. "I see one on horseback, about fifteen yards out. He has a musket. He doesn't look like one of Dugan's men unless threadbare is the new uniform of the day. He seems focused on Ethan, who's just to the right of Lando."

She scanned the landscape. The last time she'd looked out the window, they'd been traveling through farmland. At some point, the road had entered a wooded area. The trees weren't dense, but still provided enough cover for riders to hide in.

Maire pushed back from the window and pulled a rifle from the duffel. "There are two on this side. One about ten yards with a pistol. The other one is closer—near Finn. He also has a pistol." She set the rifle on her lap and pushed shot into the muzzle. "I think they're highwaymen."

"Great." AJ raised her bow, but with her right arm next to the wall of the coach, she couldn't pull the string back and still keep her target in sight. "I can't get a shot from this angle. I need more room."

"Let me get the rifle ready, then I'll switch sides with you. Keep your arrow on the man closest to Finn. I'll aim toward the man on the far side of the coach."

"I'm afraid you've crossed into our territory." The stranger's voice was high-pitched but steady. "All we ask is a small toll."

Finn laughed. "I don't remember the king ordering tolls."

"Maybe he needs more revenue for the war effort," Ethan called out from the other side of the coach.

AJ had moved over to the left window in time to see the highwayman spit into the road.

"Let's cut the pleasantries. You know this is a robbery, so I'll ask only once to leave your hands where they are."

Maire used the butt of her rifle to tap the roof of the carriage. When she heard a return tap, she nodded to AJ and pointed the tip of her rifle under the bottom edge of the curtain.

AJ found the positioning from the bench awkward, so she pulled up her skirts and knelt on the floorboard. She nocked an arrow and pointed it toward the man closest to Finn. The arrow hovered an inch from the curtain as she waited for Finn's signal.

"We're no threat to you," Finn said. "We simply want to be on our way. If you take a good look at our carriage, it should be obvious we have nothing of value to steal."

The man studied the coach then frowned. "You might not be as wealthy as most we stop, but I doubt that carriage is empty. Not with the two of you riding guard." He waved his pistol in a lazy arc then turned toward who she assumed was Ethan. It was her best guess since she couldn't see Ethan from this angle.

The highwayman moved his horse a couple of paces closer, which gave AJ a better target. "Tell whoever's in the coach to get out."

Finn glanced at Lando. He must have given Finn the signal the women were ready because Finn's shoulders tensed. If she could see Finn's face, she'd bet her life savings, albeit not that impressive an amount, on the fact that Finn was smiling with his signature grin. She almost felt sorry for the highwaymen.

Finn waited. The only movement was the swish of his horse's tail.

"I said, tell them to come out of there." The highwayman's lips twisted into a sneer.

"I don't think so," Finn responded in a calm, lazy tone.

"We will shoot one of you to prove our intent if necessary."

"Maybe. But probably not before someone in the coach fires."

Hearing the signal, AJ moved the curtain aside just enough for the arrow to be seen.

The man sat straighter, which signaled his buddy to do the same. They glanced at each other, then the first man laughed. "An arrow?"

"I imagine your friend might find a rifle on the other side." Finn's tone had changed. He tried to maintain a hard edge, but AJ caught the lighter note.

She smiled. This was the first time they'd all worked together like this. While the situation was still dangerous, a sense of pride filled her that Finn trusted her and Maire to do their part.

Maire hadn't moved an inch since resting the muzzle on the window, but now she pushed it out farther. She whispered to AJ, "Our friend on this side of the coach looks a little nervous. He's moved his horse back a few steps and is now aiming at me."

"I have a good shot of the lead man. The one behind him has a firmer grip on his pistol, but he doesn't seem to know who to aim at." The highwaymen were now obviously outnumbered, but Finn, Ethan, and Lando were too exposed. She had to wait for Finn's signal.

"I understand that one or more of us may not make it." Finn shrugged. "But I can guarantee you'll be the first one to hit the ground."

The man stared at the window. He licked his lips and moved his horse to his left. AJ tracked the arrow as he moved. For the first time, the man's bravado slipped away. He glanced at his men again before his gaze focused on the arrow.

"Why don't we agree this was just a bad mistake." Finn nudged his horse so he faced the man. "If you put your guns away and ride directly south, through that trail where we can watch you, we'll let you go." He seemed to let his idea settle in before continuing. "Consider this a friendly warning. When we reach the next town, I'll have to send word about this encounter to the local constable. I imagine you'll have a day or two to find a different way to make a living, or at least find a different county."

The lead man stared at Finn as long seconds ticked by. Without another word, he nodded to the other men and lowered his weapon. His two friends joined him, and though they hadn't stowed their weapons, they kept them pointed down. When they began to back away, the three men looked up. At first, she wasn't sure what scared them until she realized they were watching Lando. AJ assumed he must have picked up his own musket, which was already primed and had been laying at his feet.

Clearly outmatched, the men continued backing up until the lead man turned and kicked his horse into a fast trot. The other men followed close.

Once they were far from sight, AJ relaxed the bow and stowed the arrow. Maire laid the rifle on the floorboard and rubbed her shoulders. Her grin was wide. "That felt good."

"Right?" AJ tucked her bow in the duffel when a knock came at the door. She turned to find Finn giving his sister a quick look before locking his sights on her.

"Everything all right?" Finn leaned in, and AJ gave him a swift kiss.

She moved closer. "I know that was dangerous, but at the same time..." She glanced over her shoulder at Maire, happy to see her friend whispering with Ethan. She gave Finn another kiss. "That was so hot."

Finn's laugh made AJ's toes curl. "I admit. Having the two of you as backup adds a new dimension. Now you know why you're in the carriage and not on horseback."

"You are too smart, Mr. Murphy."

"Team effort, Mrs. Murphy." They kissed again before Finn remounted. He glanced up at Lando. "Worked just like you thought it would."

AJ heard Lando's chuckle as the coach moved forward. They didn't stop again until they reached Hensley's manor. When their carriage rounded the circle in front of the stately mansion and came to a stop, the front door burst open.

Mary, Hensley's wife, raced down the steps. "Oh my. Oh my. I've been waiting days for your arrival."

AJ had barely stepped from the coach before the short, plump woman pulled AJ into a tight squeeze. AJ laughed as she hugged the woman back. She was truly happy to see Mary again. AJ had been in a dour mood the last time she'd been at Hensley's. She'd make sure to be the perfect guest this time.

"We hadn't heard from you since we received Finn's letter. We weren't sure when you'd arrive."

"My dear, let her breathe." Hensley's ruddy cheeks puffed out as he caught his breath after chasing his wife down the stairs. His jovial smile instantly made her feel welcome. "It's good to see you again, my dear." Then he was shaking Finn's hand before the two men hugged. Hensley turned to his wife. "It's barely been a couple days since we received his letter."

Mary waved at hand at him, dismissing his response. "I don't care. I've been so worried about all of you." She turned toward Ethan and Maire. "Mr. Hughes, it's so good to see you again. And this time, you have a friend." She grabbed Maire's hands and gave her a quick perusal, much as she had the first time she'd met AJ. "This must be the friend you've been looking for. My dear, you are a beauty, but a bit on the thin side. No worries. Cook will take care of that. I have the best dinner planned. We were supposed to leave for London until we heard you might be coming this way. It's been over a month since I've had a chance to entertain anyone."

"Dear, let our guests at least get out of the courtyard." Hensley extended his arm, which she took as he guided her toward the steps.

Finn and Ethan followed Hensley's example, and the women took their arms as they followed after Hensley.

"It appears you're not quite the last ones to arrive," Mary yelled over her shoulder.

AJ glanced at Finn, who didn't seem surprised by the statement. When she glanced up, she paused before taking her next step.

On the landing, a group had gathered just outside the front door. Jamie and Fitz from the *Daphne Marie*, and Thomas from the earl's guard waited for them.

"Always the one for a grand entrance, Captain," Jaime shouted down, and the men parted as they greeted their friends.

41

True to her word, Mary kept the food flowing. Whether the never-ending banquets were to help Maire recover or to keep all the men in the house satisfied, AJ wasn't sure. But for the last two days, the group had split their time between recuperating and making plans, and not once did they have to step far for nourishment.

Mary kept the house staff busy altering clothes for Finn and Ethan until they were both dressed like country gentlemen in well-tailored breeches, waistcoats and cravats. AJ and Maire each received a new day dress and one evening gown. Hensley tried to stop his wife, but no one wanted to dissuade her from what she seemed to enjoy. And Maire and AJ couldn't keep sharing the same two dresses.

The cold days were accompanied by winter sunshine, and the women found time to walk the gardens while the men went on bird hunts. The hunting party rarely produced any fresh meals. AJ concluded the men had found a way to avoid endless planning sessions in stuffy rooms.

The day after AJ and Finn arrived, Thorn and Dodger drifted in. They'd been in London when they'd received word from Hensley and left as soon as their last assignment was completed. Thorn hadn't changed from his rogue persona. From what Finn told her, the dapper man still caroused in gentlemen clubs when he wasn't performing a task for Hensley. Dodger continued his constant vigil over Thorn. The man had always been a silent observer, but AJ wondered if he'd ever gotten past the loss of Peele at the monastery. Thorn had never replaced his lost bodyguard. Maybe it wasn't that Thorn required two body-guards but that Dodger and Peele had just come as a pair. Either way, it was good to have Thorn and Dodger back with the team.

The team met in the library twice each day to discuss their next steps, but each plan either resulted in more dead ends or harrowing escapes.

Ethan paced around the room while everyone else flipped through books or stared at nothing in particular, lost in their own thoughts. "I think we're getting bogged down by this desire to kill Dugan and Reginald. I'm not saying we shouldn't take the opportunity if we have it, but the goal is this grimoire. Surely, if Reginald doesn't have the book, he'll become less of a threat."

Maire shook her head. She sat next to a small side table where she'd laid out her pages of translations and notes. She kept rearranging them as if trying to make sense of their best order. "He may not be as intelligent as Beckworth, but he's become obsessed. I doubt he'd give up, especially knowing about the monastery. If he has the patience, he could wait until the war with France is over."

"With the smuggler routes, he wouldn't have to wait for the war to end if he has enough coin." Jamie stretched then stood next to Finn, who stared at a wall map of England. "What do you find so interesting?"

Finn turned and smiled at his young friend. "Nothing really. I've been thinking of Waverly's defenses." He leaned against the sofa and crossed his arms.

"We didn't get a very good look since Beckworth already knew where the women were being held. It doesn't have the walls or moat of a castle, yet it will be difficult to breach with the small army Dugan has built."

"A full-scale attack on Waverly wouldn't be taken lightly by the Crown, even with eyes turned toward France." Hensley stuffed a meat-filled pastry into his mouth, then returned to writing letters. Several were already stacked on the corner of the desk.

Thomas leaned over a table on the far side of the library. Fitz, who turned out to be an amazing sketch artist, had drawn a map of Waverly. He'd used Maire's knowledge of the inner house and gardens since she'd lived there for almost two years as Beckworth's kidnapped guest.

Thomas scratched his head. "The only way I see getting into Waverly is to wait for Reginald and Dugan to leave. There will still be men there, but if Beckworth could tell us which servants we could trust, we might be able to send one or two men in."

"Assuming that guttersnipe would be honest with us." Thorn had been unhappy to hear that Beckworth still lived. Then he'd been outraged to learn Beckworth was now helping them. AJ never knew what the bad blood was between Thorn and Beckworth, but Finn assured her he'd keep Thorn under control.

"He can be trusted with this." Lando leaned next to the library door like a sentinel and simply stared at Thorn as if that was all the explanation that was needed.

Thorn scowled at Lando, but when he glanced at Finn, he stood down. "Fine. Beckworth may have duped you with his charm, but I'll be keeping an eye on him just the same."

"Good. You should." Finn stated. "Beckworth has been helpful because he wants Waverly back." He walked over and patted Thorn on the shoulder. "And he hates his half-brother as much as you hate him. So we focus on the book and leave Reginald to Beckworth."

"That's like giving a mouse to a cat." Maire smirked. "Reginald isn't as cunning as his brother, but his little army might be enough to hold Beckworth off."

Ethan nodded. "So that leaves Dugan."

"He's mine," Finn and Thorn both called out, leaving the group to watch which of the two would give ground.

AJ understood Finn's desire for revenge for the torture he'd endured under Dugan's orders. But Thorn's only thought was of Peele. Finn had killed the duke. Thorn's only vengeance would be Dugan.

The two men stared at each other until Finn grinned. "Aye, mate. It's only fair. You get Dugan. But if you miss, I won't wait to give you a second chance."

Thorn, being Thorn, returned Finn's grin with a grand bow and slow smile. "If I miss, it will only be because the bastard killed me."

"Then I'll be sure to clear the debt."

They both nodded, and Thomas cleared his throat. "So back to the problem of getting into Waverly once Reginald leaves."

"It won't work." Maire's gaze turned toward the hearth. Her cheeks held a rosy glow, and the shadows under her eyes were gone. She was still thin, but the new dress, tailored to her new weight, made Maire seem more a pixie than an emaciated survivor.

"Why not, Maire?" Hensley asked, still nibbling appetizers with his afternoon tea. "This Reginald sounds like a man who would travel with a large contingent. That should leave a skeleton of men at Waverly. We'll have to confirm this with Beckworth, of course."

Maire nodded her agreement of Hensley's assessment, but rather than respond with her doubts, she selected a sweet pastry.

She ate her dumpling between sips of tea while everyone waited. AJ suppressed a smile at the men's annoyance, yet no one said a word. One thing about this century—everyone had manners.

Maire wiped her fingers on a napkin and stared up at everyone as though she hadn't known they were waiting. AJ glanced away, afraid she might laugh out loud. Held captive for six months in deplorable conditions did nothing to sever Maire's backbone. And it appeared she wanted to make sure everyone paid attention this time.

"I told you from the start how important this book is to Reginald. So important that he won't let it out of his sight." When the men didn't say anything, she sighed. "If he leaves the estate, the book will go with him."

Thomas threw a pencil across the room. "Well, damn it. That's no good."

"Maybe it is." Finn moved back to the map of England.

Jamie perked up. "Yes. But I don't know if we have enough men."

"You mean to take him on the road?" Ethan asked. He ran a hand through his hair, his pacing continued. "Maybe. We'd still need someone inside, in case this was one time he left the book behind."

"Beckworth would know the hiding places," Maire suggested.

"Assuming Reginald didn't add a few of his own," AJ countered, then turned to Finn. "Where will you get more men?"

"I can probably scrounge up a few men." Hensley picked up his quill and began writing. "Thomas, do you think the earl has any more he can spare?"

Thomas glanced at Ethan, who nodded. "He might have a few more."

"It's still a risk." Hensley sat back, the quill still in his hand. "The men would need to be disguised."

Finn shook his head. "It won't matter. They'll know who took the book."

Ethan seemed to agree. "Even if we take their valuables and make it look like a robbery, no highwayman would take a book."

"At least it's a start and better than anything else we've come up with. Why don't we break and let the idea sit for a bit?" Jamie offered his arm to Maire. "Would you care for a stroll in the garden? I think it's a little warmer today." When she nodded her agreement, he grinned at Ethan, who could do nothing more than nod with a tight smile as they walked past.

AJ stepped next to Ethan before he could follow. "Let Jamie bask in the glow of a beautiful woman. Although I hear he might have a woman or two in some distant ports. It will do him good to spend time with Maire."

Ethan grunted.

"Don't be jealous. She's already given her heart away."

Ethan's silvery gaze locked with hers, seeming to need any reassurance he could get. "We've spent so much time apart."

"She enjoys the attention, and she would never fall for Jamie's pretty words." Finn slapped a hand on Ethan's shoulder. "Hensley has set up the gaming table. I think Lando is interested in winning back some of his money."

Ethan chuckled, and his shoulders relaxed. "Then perhaps I should dissuade him from that notion."

"Nice try, Hughes. But I'm feeling lucky today." Thorn grabbed two meat pies before following Hensley and Lando out the door.

Ethan followed with Fitz, who was already counting his coins.

AJ turned to Finn, something different on her mind. "And did you plan to follow?"

Finn pulled her close. "I'm considering offers."

She giggled and ran a hand up his chest before stroking his

cravat. "I have it on good authority our maid is busy with a task that will take at least an hour."

"Only an hour?" Finn asked as his hands moved down her back.

AJ pulled away. "Let's consider it a challenge." Then she turned and raced for the door, trying to stifle a laugh as she heard Finn chase after her.

42

A J raced through the bedroom door and stopped at the
four-poster bed. She braced a hand on the bed, fighting
to calm her rapid breathing as she waited for the dull ache. The
door shut behind her, and she heard the click of the lock. She
waited, expecting a headache after her short run.

Strong hands ran down her arms before she could turn. "Let
me help with your dress." Finn's hands moved to her shoulders,
and she leaned into the gentle massage. "How's your headache?"

"Barely there." She moaned as Finn's massage melted away
any remnants of pain. She rolled her head to the right, and Finn
took advantage by placing warm kisses on her exposed neck.
Small shivers raced down her spine. They hadn't made love
since the night of their wedding, and her body ached for his
touch.

When she began to turn, he stopped her. "I haven't finished
the buttons yet."

"We only have an hour." Her impatient response came out
like a whine.

"Maids know better than to bang on a locked door." He

kissed the nape of her neck, the tip of his tongue tracing a path to her ear.

"And the men?" AJ questioned.

"Will be busy for hours with their card game. Besides, it's not like they don't know where we went."

AJ felt the heat of a blush, but it wasn't knowing the men were downstairs. This was Hensley and Mary's home. "It feels like we're about to have sex in my mother's house."

With the buttons undone, Finn skimmed his knuckles under the edge of her chemise as he slowly worked the dress open. She grabbed the bedpost and savored the building sensations. The dress dropped to the floor, and he took his time as he peeled the chemise off her, inch by aggravating inch. The cool air brushed against her bare skin, and she gasped when his warm hands turned her toward him, tracing a heated path down her back. She wrapped her hands around the back of his neck and drew him down to press her lips to his.

Their kiss was long, tongues meeting in a slow dance. Finn continued to run his hands up and down her back, leaving tingling sensations in their wake before coming to a rest on her backside, giving it a gentle squeeze.

AJ pushed him back and began a languid process of undressing him.

"Why are you taking so long?" Finn attempted to work the buttons of the waistcoat, but she batted his hands away.

"You said we had all afternoon. I want to savor what's wrapped in all these clothes."

Once the waistcoat was gone, she grabbed the bottom of his shirt and pulled it over his head. She traced kisses across his chest until he growled. He grabbed her, and his kiss made her forget her name for a moment. When he let her up for air, she turned him until his back was to the bed and then shoved.

He landed on the bed, laughing, eyes burning with desire,

and watched her pull off his boots. After a sloppy kiss, she dragged his breeches down his lean, muscular legs. Her smile faltered as she stared at him. He was so beautiful. A little jolt jabbed at her when she remembered how easily they could have lost each other. Finn's laugh died out, and the heat in his gaze increased as he pulled her down to him.

Their lovemaking was swift, and AJ held on, afraid to let go. The ache of their time apart vanished, but not before a twinge reminded her of the danger still ahead. When Finn planted kisses on her breasts, the intoxicating pleasure made everything disappear.

Sometime later, AJ traced lazy circles on Finn's chest as he slept. She shifted closer so she could watch his face, serene in slumber. His eyes fluttered open, and his lips curled into the elfish grin that had captured her heart.

"It had been too long, wife." He leaned up for a kiss.

"Aye, husband." AJ almost purred with his second, more intense kiss. "I never asked. Where's your ring?"

He looked sheepish. "I worried I might lose it. I tossed it to Stella just before we jumped."

"That's good. I was so stupid for putting on the Heart Stone."

"Hush." He sat up and pulled her into a tight embrace. "I should never have left Ethan alone with Beckworth, but that's all behind us." He tipped her chin up. "You know I'll always come for you."

"I know." When the renewed kissing subsided, AJ pulled herself into a cross-legged position. "Maire knows."

Finn said nothing for several seconds. Then he nodded and laid back, hands tucked behind his head as he stared at the ceiling. "She found the ring?"

"When she took my clothes to wash them."

Finn's silence returned, and when she didn't say anything else, his brow furrowed. "And?"

AJ thought back to her conversation with Maire, wishing she could have waited until Finn shared the news with his sister. She nudged his foot with her own and smiled. "Sorry. She was happy. I'm surprised she hasn't said anything to you."

"You know my sister. She's waiting for me to say something."

"Then maybe we should tell everyone tonight. We don't know what will happen once we set our plan in motion. We may have to make a quick exit through the fog. I'd feel better if our friends knew."

"I agree." He grabbed her and rolled until she was underneath him. Her laughter rang through the room. She thought she heard a slight knock on the door before Finn kissed her. Then all she remembered was a slight growl when he yelled, "Go away."

When she next opened her eyes, the room had darkened with late-afternoon shadows. Another knock on the door roused her, this one more urgent.

Finn grumbled as he rose and searched for his breeches. "Just a minute."

AJ pulled the covers up, her body too relaxed to rise.

Finn opened the door to find Ethan pacing back and forth. "Based on the look on your face, you should probably come in."

Ethan stepped in and glanced at AJ. "I hope you've gotten some needed rest."

Her answer was a pillow thrown his way. He smiled briefly before handing Finn a note.

Finn stared at it for a full minute before glancing at Ethan, who shifted from foot to foot, waiting for his response. Finn picked up AJ's chemise and tossed it to her.

"What?" AJ asked.

"It's a note from Beckworth." Finn held her gaze. "Reginald is holding a masquerade ball."

43

After Ethan left, Finn helped AJ back into her dress before he raced down to meet with Hensley. Something had turned their way, but she wasn't sure how a masquerade ball would benefit them. She fussed with her hair and, realizing she'd never fix it without her lady's maid, pulled it back into a small bun.

She was partway down the stairs when the thought hit her. Excitement over a masquerade ball could only mean one thing. She sighed. They were going into the lion's den.

When she reached the last stair, Mary interrupted her musings.

"There you are, my dear. You must have heard there's a game afoot." She steered AJ down the hallway. "They're in the library. I've sent in tea and light refreshment. Dinner won't be announced for another hour."

Mary left AJ at the door to the library and hustled off to stop a maid who'd entered the hallway. She immediately began issuing orders, but AJ couldn't hear what she said over the loud voices of men flowing into the hallway.

After stepping into the room and glancing around, she realized she was the last person to arrive. The team huddled in small groups whispering about Beckworth's letter and what it meant for them. When Hensley noticed AJ, he clapped his hands until the room quieted.

"Wonderful. Now that we're all here, it appears we may have gotten a break." Hensley's commanding voice filled the room, transforming the earlier tension and excitement into a combined sense of purpose.

"And everyone loves a party," Thorn droned, which earned him a few chuckles.

"Especially one with masks," Thomas retorted as more chuckles erupted.

"Though I imagine they'll be asking for weapons at the door," Fitz added.

When everyone began to whisper to their neighbor, Hensley pounded his fist on the desk. His stern features quickly quieted the group. When he had everyone's attention, he smiled. "Now that you have that out of your system, what do we think of this masquerade ball?"

"Just proves he's a rightful dolt," Thorn replied. He'd found a chair where he could sit and polish his sword that was already so shiny candlelight sparkled from it.

"Why a party at all?" Thomas asked. He stood over the same table he had earlier in the day, studying the Waverly map as if some hidden message would appear if he stared long enough.

"And everyone in masks? I don't understand what he's up to." Jamie joined Thomas at the table.

"He needs to meet the neighbors." AJ sat next to Finn and passed a plate of cheese and meat dumplings to him. Dinner might only be an hour away, but she had no doubt Finn would finish his dinner with gusto, regardless the number of dumplings.

"Exactly." Maire selected two sweet dumplings before returning to her seat with a cup of tea. "Dugan rotated guards and servants while I was imprisoned, not wanting any one person to befriend me. But one of the servants was a loyalist to Beckworth. He'd mentioned the townspeople and several estate owners were whispering about the return of the viscount." She bit her lip. "You see, Beckworth entertained often when I was his guest." The word *guest* held a bit of an edge. "If word had spread that Beckworth returned but had turned into a recluse, there would be questions."

"So Reginald has no choice but to engage with his neighbors." Ethan seemed dubious. "But why a large party? Why not just a few guests?"

"He might look like Beckworth," Maire responded, "but on close inspection, he has a slight scar on his upper lip. I suppose that could be explained, but his mannerisms can't."

Finn passed AJ an empty plate, and the soulful begging in his eyes forced her to get up to refill it. She smiled to herself, pleased their afternoon lovemaking had increased his hunger. Finn leaned back, fully relaxed for the first time in weeks. "He wants to show off his ability to entertain. A ball will allow him to do that without having to spend too much time with any one person. His guests will see he's back, and I'm sure he'll have the perfect story to explain away any differences between him and Beckworth."

"The London season has begun." Hensley tapped his fingers, then finished off a glass of whiskey. "Many people have already closed up their country estates, but like us, with the war on, there will be many late arrivals. Anyone near Waverly will be too curious not to attend. This will be their first glimpse inside the estate since the viscount's return."

AJ stood to play hostess, refilling glasses to hide her restlessness. There was nothing she could do to dissuade the team from seeing the ball as the opportunity they'd been waiting for, but she had a bad feeling about it.

When she stopped to pour another two fingers of whiskey for Hensley, he urged her closer. "Don't tell Mary. I promised her no whiskey until after dinner."

"Nothing leaves this room." AJ patted his arm. "Your secret is safe."

"I understand now," Jamie said. "Reginald and Beckworth could pass as twins. Reginald probably threatened the servants from revealing his secrets. He certainly wouldn't fool them for long. But he can't control the townspeople or neighbors, so he has to disguise himself from prying eyes."

"A masterful plan which plays right into our hands." Hensley smiled. "The ball opens the front door. There will be dozens of people, if not more, milling about. But it won't be easy. I have no doubt Dugan will have his men stationed everywhere."

Finn stared off into some unknown place, and AJ knew he was already deep in thought. She'd seen the look dozens of times, in this century and in hers. He could sit for hours as he mentally mapped out each option, considered each outcome. He'd toss out the bad ideas, while rehashing others. This was what he was best at—strategy.

"We won't know for sure." Thomas tapped the map. "But with that many guests, Reginald will probably bring in temporary servants. The number of people in residence for the ball will at least double the number of staff, maybe more. Dugan will have no other choice than to rearrange the guards."

"He won't be able to let too many guards inside." Finn returned to the conversation, but he held on to his faraway gaze. "It will make the guests nervous."

Thomas nodded, his hand tracing the edges of the map. "The question is, how many guards will he place around the manor?

Waverly isn't walled off, and there are dozens of ways onto the estate.

"He's sure to post guards at all the doors." Jamie pointed to several spots on the maps. "These are the main doors that Maire identified."

Maire stood and touched Ethan's elbow. He followed her to the table where Thomas and Jamie stood. She gave the map a thorough review. "I never spent much time in the kitchen other than to visit the herb garden. But I think there was another door on the far side, near the ovens. I think it led outside, but I couldn't tell you where. Beckworth can confirm it."

Thomas made a mark where Maire pointed and circled it. "That's good. Are there any other passages you might have overlooked earlier?"

Maire studied the map. She pointed to another spot in the east wing. "There's a room just left of the small library that Beckworth used as his study. The door was always locked."

"That speaks of mischief," Fitz said.

The other members of the team gathered around the map. Maire pointed out a couple of interior doors that she remembered but had never investigated.

"I'm sorry I didn't mention these before." Maire's expression clouded over, and Ethan stroked his hand down her back.

"Don't worry about that. It's been over a year since you've been in the main house. Take your time." Ethan glared at the men around the table, a clear warning to not push her.

Everyone lowered their gazes and patiently waited. Except for Finn, who quirked his lips and shook his head. No doubt finding it amusing how deeply Ethan had fallen for his sister.

Maire snickered and pointed to a spot on the east wing's second floor. "The only area I always wondered about was Beckworth's master chamber. If you look at the building as a whole, each wing is almost an exact duplicate of the other. They have their own entrances, a grand staircase, and the same number of rooms. Several rooms in the west wing seem larger, but the same could be said of the east wing.

"But there are common areas between them." Lando nodded. "The kitchen mainly, and this room that joins the wings."

"Yes, the main sitting room connects the wings." Maire pointed to an area on the second floor of the west wing. "The master bedroom at the end of this hall is larger than the one in the east wing. It was a well-appointed room but not as grand as mine. It was used for important guests."

"And your point?" Thomas asked.

Maire blessed him with her patient smile.

AJ stifled a laugh, knowing Maire's impish smile was her attempt at politeness for someone who couldn't keep up. If AJ didn't know Beckworth as she did now, she'd be as lost as Thomas and the rest of them to what Maire was getting at.

AJ answered his question. "If you were someone who grew up on the streets and now had a huge estate to call your own, wouldn't you grab the largest chamber for yourself?"

Awareness registered on Thomas's face. "Of course. So why did he decide to take the smaller chamber on the east side?"

"There could be dozens of reasons. Who knows what goes on in his head?" Jaime scowled. "Maybe he wants his guests to see what a magnanimous host he is."

"Quite possible," Hensley stated. "Yet, Beckworth is a sly one." He pointed to Beckworth's chamber at the end of the east wing. "But what's the one thing a street urchin always thinks of?"

Finn laughed. "A second way out."

Fitz slapped the table. "Of course." He elbowed Jamie. "We should've known that. Remember that time in Kilkenny?"

Jamie smiled and rubbed his jaw. "Aye. That was our first lesson to always have an alternative exit. I'd have saved myself from a sore jaw and been two crowns richer." He glanced at

Finn. "Not much different than what you taught us sailing. Always have another route. Just in case."

Ethan sighed. "And there's only one person who can confirm our suspicion."

The name echoed around the room as they mumbled in unison. "Beckworth."

44

———

Two days later, the group assembled in the courtyard of Hensley's estate. AJ stared at Bart's carriage. It looked nothing like it had when they'd first arrived. The coach had been given a new coat of paint, and the embellishments that reflected the wealth of the owners had been replaced. AJ didn't think the updates would bear close scrutiny, but she also didn't see a reason why anyone would give the coach a second glance. AJ's first impression grew when she noted the interior had also been improved with padded bench seats and fresh curtains. If nothing else, her backside would be grateful. Two trunks, filled with AJ and Maire's new dresses, had been loaded into a larger box in the back of the coach.

Mary held a handkerchief and dabbed at her eyes. She'd said her goodbyes earlier but, sorry to see them go, needed to impart final words of sage advice.

"Balls are all about being seen, even at a masquerade ball. I typically remind the younger women to keep their chins raised and backs straight, but with the two of you, that would only bring unwanted attention." Mary tapped her chin in thought.

"So you want us to slouch." The solution seemed simple to AJ.

"Oh, no, dear. That would be almost as noticeable. I think the best would be to keep your back straight but keep your head down as best as you can. And keep moving. Never find yourself in a spot where other women can corner you. They're not your friends."

"More like sharks." AJ remembered her first dinner party at Waverly with Lady Agatha Osborne and Dame Ellingsworth. She'd felt like chum treading water while they picked her clean. She'd been more out of sorts at the time, but that particular memory would never go away.

Mary tilted her head. "I'm not familiar with sharks, but they don't sound pleasant."

"They're cold-blooded fish who swim around and eat everything in sight," Maire explained.

Mary smiled. "Ah, I see. Then yes, that was a good analogy. They are sharks."

AJ nodded. "So if we keep moving, they can't catch us. Sounds simple enough."

Mary's lips turned down. "Don't fool yourselves. A large party might appear an easy way to lose one's self in a crowd, but women can be devious, as you know. There are myriad ways to engage others into a conversation, and the women you'll want to avoid are masters of their craft. Never let your guard down."

Maire squeezed Mary's hand. "I may have only spent a couple of months in London last season, but everything you say is true. We'll take it to heart."

Mary hugged them then watched as AJ and Maire made their way to the coach. When AJ glanced back, Mary waved from the porch before disappearing into the house. Mary had only meant to help, but AJ's stomach did flips at the thought of going to the ball. The plan wasn't set in stone, and she wanted to be part of the plan, but she'd rather face Dugan's men than the local aristocracy.

"Listen up." Finn, who had been speaking privately with Hensley, called the group to order. "We travel as a group and stop at the village west of Waverly Manor. AJ and I will go in first and get one room at the local inn. Ethan and Maire will come in an hour later for another room. Lando will try for a third room if available. The rest of you will stagger in separately, and we'll get you into one of the three rooms. We don't know if Dugan still has men watching the local towns, so be careful."

"Will Beckworth be there before us?" Thomas asked.

"He only said he'd meet us there." Finn raised his hand. "I know. He wasn't forthcoming with anything else. It's possible he wasn't sure when he'd be able to arrive."

"Or he's being an ass like normal." Ethan scowled until Maire laid a hand on his arm.

The group nodded, all expecting the worst from the man. AJ was still on the fence about Beckworth but understood the men's mistrust. For now, however, they were Beckworth's best shot at getting his estate back.

"Then what?" Fitz asked.

"Then we wait to see what Beckworth has uncovered." Finn nodded with the men as the grumbling began. "Look. We're moving forward on very little information, but we know how the game is played. Beckworth wouldn't put anything of value in the note in case it didn't make it to us."

Jamie slammed a fist against the coach. "That's easier to hear when a meager tip comes from someone we trust. We're going in blind."

"I think we all feel the same." Finn turned to Hensley, who stepped to stand next to Finn.

"If you think it's too dangerous to enter the village, find your way to either Bart or Eleanor. You've been given directions to their homes. I know you have concerns, but this is the best opportunity we'll have. I expect each of you to perform your duty."

"WHY DO we always discuss life-impacting plans while stuffed inside tiny rooms?" Thomas mumbled as he pushed Fitz aside to get to the table where he laid out their map.

"Would you rather meet in the stable? At least here we have wine and ale." Thorn, as usual, had commandeered the bed, giving him room to lay his sword across his knee. He hadn't begun to polish it, but AJ knew he'd start once the meeting began. Dodger stood next to the bed, in his usual stance, arms folded across his chest.

Though it was mid-winter, the window had been opened to usher in cooler air to invigorate the stifling room. Squeezing eleven people together in the small space had been a challenge. Maire sat close to Ethan, who seemed to chafe at being unable to pace. He moved to the window to get air, but when he returned to his seat, he ignored it and leaned against the wall behind Maire, his hand resting on her shoulder.

AJ sat by the hearth, and Lando stood next to her like a personal sentinel.

Jamie sat at the table, bumping heads with Thomas as they scoured the map of Waverly, Corsham, and the surrounding countryside. Small circles had been drawn to mark Bart and Eleanor's cottages. Their second map, which depicted the exterior grounds and internal rooms of Waverly, laid partially hidden beneath the first map.

Fitz, accustomed to small places and finding rest where he could, had found a spot in a far corner. He appeared to be sleeping, but AJ noticed an occasional twitch of his lips at some passing remark.

Finn gazed out the window. She'd had little time to speak with him on their trip back. With both her and Maire in better condition, and the interior of the coach updated with better padding, the stops had been infrequent and quick. In those small moments, Finn didn't want to talk, he wanted to hold her and share quick kisses before pushing her back into the coach.

Maire spent most of the ride sharing details of her time in London. She didn't speak of the fashion, hairstyles, or food. Maire imparted important details about etiquette. She discussed mingling with haughty strangers, how to monitor the room for anything out of place, and where to stand in order to scan the room without being cornered or drawing attention. She emphasized keeping open pathways for quick escapes and knowing where all the exits were.

AJ almost laughed. Everything Maire shared sounded like a larger version of the family dinners in Baywood she used to avoid. She would hover where she could make a mad dash out the door if needed. When she thought of her family, it felt like someone had placed a large stone on her chest, making it difficult to breathe. Those family dinners meant everything to her now. She had hoped, once the remodeling of the inn was complete, that she and Finn could host an occasional family gathering and give her mom a break. As each day passed, her future seemed farther and farther away.

She glanced at Finn and found him watching her. His sad expression seemed to mirror her thoughts, and a ghost of a smile touched his lips.

A powerful slam on the door brought conversation to a halt.

The sound wasn't exactly a pounding. More like someone had used a boot. The second hit against the door broke the silence.

The men pulled their weapons, and AJ reached for her dagger nestled within her pocket. When Finn nodded, Thorn opened the door then jumped back.

"Sorry I'm late." Beckworth sauntered in with two clay pitchers. "The lad downstairs thought it time for a refresh."

Thomas growled as he put his pistol away. "Was the grand entrance necessary?"

Beckworth just smiled, lifting the pitchers as if to say, "What else could I do?" before filling mugs.

"Why are you late?" Ethan asked.

"I've been doing a bit of reconnaissance. Fortunately, I don't see anyone that looks like Dugan's sort anywhere in the village, but you can never be too careful. Best you all stay tucked in here for the night."

Thorn, whose sword was still raised, edged closer to Beckworth. "And where will you be this evening?"

"Thorn." Finn's tone gave a clear signal to back off.

Thorn ignored him. "No. I think we have a right to know where our...partner"—the last coming out as a sneer—"is spending his time."

Finn didn't push. They all wanted to know what Beckworth was up to.

"I have my own room down the hall." Beckworth passed by Thorn without bothering to refill his mug. He ignored Dodger, who stared daggers at him.

"And did you plan on sharing the room? It's a bit tight with these smaller rooms." Finn kept his tone even, his patience running thin by AJ's assessment.

"Well, I'm fairly particular about who I share a room with." Beckworth winked at AJ and Maire.

AJ rolled her eyes, and Maire glared, but Beckworth only chuckled when Ethan took a step closer to Maire.

"Maybe if we got back to business." Jamie jumped in to

placate the group. He focused on Beckworth. "I understand your caution, but your message was a little vague."

Beckworth placed the jugs on an end table. "Quite right. Let's get to it then." He strutted to the maps and shouldered his way in until Thomas edged back.

"The situation at Waverly is worse than I thought. Reginald has replaced key staff positions with his own people. My butler, Barrington, has been reduced to a footman. It will probably do the old man some good taking orders from someone else for a while, and it does put him in a position to be most forthcoming with information. I have no doubt he wants his job as butler restored.

"Many of the housemaids are the same, but the housekeeper has also been replaced. The previous one has moved to another house in Devonshire. But Letty and June"—he turned to AJ and Maire—"your lady's maids while at Waverly, are still there and quite loyal to the two of you." He tapped his chin. "The cook is questionable, but she was never one to worry over politics and loyalty. The rest of the servants are too afraid to take a side. Our best bet is to rely on Barrington and the lady's maids unless we can confirm loyalty from the others. But as they say, too many cooks."

"Have you gained any information from them?" Finn asked.

"Enough to know that Reginald organized the ball rather quickly. Several of the larger estates haven't closed for the season yet, and word about the ball spread. Seems everyone is in a flutter to see if I've gone mad."

"I'd be happy to confirm it," Thorn muttered as he stroked his sword with a polishing rag.

"When is this party?" Thomas asked.

"One week from today."

Moans filled the room.

"That gives us little time to come up with a plan." Ethan had a faraway gaze, no doubt mentally reviewing what little information Beckworth had shared.

"Who said we didn't have a plan?" Beckworth rubbed his hands together as if to accentuate a diabolical plot. "I've been doing some research and started a couple of items in motion."

"Without talking to us?" Finn seemed exasperated with the man, and they'd barely begun.

"Time is of the essence, and this will be difficult enough with only three house servants and this rangy group." Beckworth held out his hands in a gesture that asked what else could he do? "I've only spoken to highly trusted individuals."

Ethan and Finn glanced at each other.

"Look, mate." Beckworth sighed and leaned against the wall, hands tucked loosely across his chest. "You know I could care two bits for that book. I'd rather never see nor hear anything about those bloody stones again." When his gaze turned toward Finn, there was bright determination in his stare. "Waverly is mine. I worked for it. I did damnable things to achieve it. It was never owned by the duke, therefore, not some family heirloom for dear brother Reginald to snap up."

"So, we're to trust that you're here because helping us helps you," Lando grumbled, startling AJ by his sudden interest. She'd thought he had dozed off.

"Good God, man, no. Never trust me. But, yes. As long as our paths are connected to a common goal, I'll play my part for our success. Where our paths diverge, I'll go my way, and you go yours. As long as it's not my life for yours, we're on the same side in this."

The men glanced at each other before turning to study Beckworth, judging the worth of his statement.

Finn made the first move, pushing Beckworth to the side, allowing more room for Thomas to step closer to the map. "So, what can you tell us?"

45

For the next two days, the team moved to Eleanor's farmhouse in shifts, maintaining a vigil for Dugan's men. AJ had been happy to return until Beckworth told her about the dress fitting with Dame Ellingsworth. She'd been a nervous wreck ever since, and nothing Finn said made a difference. The last time she'd seen Dame Ellingsworth had been during her first time jump and visit to Waverly Manor. The woman had terrified AJ, almost as much as Ellingsworth's younger friend, Lady Agatha.

AJ shivered at the memory as she watched the landscape slide by. She and Maire traveled north for the fitting, and AJ could hardly wait to get it over with. As they drew closer to the estate, AJ developed the hiccups.

"What's wrong?" Maire chortled.

"Hiccups," she squelched out.

"Yes. They're hard to disguise. Why are you holding your breath?"

"To get them to stop."

Maire's laughter almost doubled her over. "By passing out?"

AJ blew out the air she'd been holding at the same as a laugh erupted, forcing a cough. Maire patted her back until AJ pushed her away. "Enough. I'm having a hard enough time breathing." Maire's unexpected response to her hiccup remedy drained the tension from AJ's shoulders. She was certain Lando could hear their laughter from the coachman's bench, and it took several minutes before they calmed and fell back against their seats. To AJ's relief, the hiccups vanished.

Maire checked her hair and smoothed her skirt as she leaned out the window. "You've been on edge ever since Beckworth told you about the fitting. You were the one who agreed to attend the ball rather than me."

"Only because it made more sense. You know the estate. You'll be better at sneaking around and snooping. And let's face it, no mask will disguise you."

"You're such a flatterer. So what else is wrong?"

AJ bit her lower lip. She hated to appear timid. "It's Dame Ellingsworth. She's a bit of a barracuda."

"You met before?"

"When I was here the first time. Before Finn left for London."

Maire nodded. "I remember Beckworth spoke of her often. Even then, she seemed to be one of the few aristocrats he seemed fond of."

"I wish we knew his ultimate game."

"You don't think it's what he's told us?"

AJ shrugged. "I don't know. Sometimes he seems honest about what he wants."

"And then he slips back into his role of scoundrel." Maire sat back with a heavy sigh. "We may never know. The only thing we can do is hope he doesn't betray us." She glanced to the window. "We're here."

AJ scooted to the window. The estate looked remarkably similar to Waverly, as if a roving architect had traveled the countryside with his satchel of small castle sketches. She snorted. The current-day developer.

"Ready to tread dark waters?" Maire's smile was mischievous as she followed AJ from the coach.

AJ straightened her shoulders and gazed up at the formidable door. "I feel better that you're here."

Maire grasped her hand, and they mounted the stairs together. The door opened before they reached the porch, and a dour-faced butler bowed his head as they stepped through the door. It seemed the main skill requirement for a butler was to wear a permanent frown. She hadn't seen one who could actually smile. Not even at Hensley's.

"Dame Ellingsworth will receive you in the sitting room. Follow me."

The mansion was elegant and competed with Waverly for the number and quality of art pieces. But where Beckworth seemed to have jammed them wherever they fit, Dame Ellingsworth had a lighter touch. Each room as elegant as the last. AJ always assumed Beckworth had picked the most expensive pieces he could find because that had been his perception of being rich. But she had to rethink that. He knew exactly what he had collected at Waverly. After years of being penniless, he'd immersed himself into what pleased him. And he yearned for knowledge. Like his library. It wasn't just for show. Based on their conversations when she'd been his guest, he'd probably read most of the books.

The butler led them to a room the size of Waverly's main sitting room, but it seemed more airy and bright. Probably due to the lighter walls and honey-colored woods of the furniture. Dame Ellingsworth and another young woman sat in front of the hearth hunched over their needlework. Their voices were nothing but a whisper, but Dame Ellingsworth must have been sharing some sordid tale because the young woman kept blushing. When the butler announced them, Dame Ellingsworth bounced up as if she'd been waiting all day for their arrival.

"My dear, Miss Moore. It is so good to see you again." She turned to Maire. "My, what a beauty we have here. Miss Murphy, isn't it?"

Maire extended her a slight curtsy. "It's a pleasure to meet you, Dame Ellingsworth. AJ and the viscount have shared many good words about you."

She waved her hand. "Call me Elizabeth. And I wouldn't believe a thing Teddy tells you about me."

When AJ and Maire exchanged a look, Elizabeth laughed and winked. "I'm more of an old gossip than Teddy would ever let on. That man has always been too good to me."

Another Beckworth fan. Not surprising, since Dame Ellingsworth had seemed a frequent visitor to Waverly. AJ shifted her attention to the other woman in the room.

"Let me introduce you to Countess LaVelle."

After the introductions were completed, Elizabeth motioned for the countess to put her needlework away. "It's such a lovely day, why don't you take a stroll in the gardens. I left a book of John Milton in your room. I thought you might enjoy it."

The young woman's smile faded, but she nodded politely before leaving, a young maid following her.

"Poor dear. That atrocious mother of hers married her off to that despicable old count. He has one foot in the grave, and that child is simply too young for him. I think he's hoping for another heir, but I doubt he has any seed left the way he spread it around over the years."

AJ almost spit out the tea she'd been served, not expecting such talk from a woman of this century.

"No doubt she'll be a wealthy widow soon," Maire suggested.

Elizabeth laughed. "That is the silver lining. Which is why I've been encouraging her to read, but she shows no interest."

She sighed and set down her teacup. "Well, she'll eventually remarry and make lots of babies, and that will be enough for her." She glanced at AJ. "Now, let's see about that fitting."

Elizabeth led them through the estate to a small parlor where a woman was busy sewing.

AJ stopped in her tracks when she spotted the dress on the mannequin. Made of deep russet silk, the cap sleeves were covered in tiny beads the same color as the dress. Lace, also in the same dark shade, covered the bodice before the silk skirt fell away to rest just a few inches from the floor. Though it was all one color, the different textures of the dress took her breath away.

"I didn't think I was supposed to stand out," AJ whispered as she approached the dress.

"It's a beautiful color," Maire said. "It matches your hair and complexion well."

"You can't go to a ball dressed in anything less. That alone would make you stand out." Elizabeth closed the door behind them. "I have no doubt you'll turn heads when you first arrive, so you'll want to keep your head down and pretend the event is more than you're used to."

"That won't be difficult."

Elizabeth chortled. "Once you join the rest of the party, you'll disappear into the crowd. Anyone of your young age, even with a husband or suitor at your side, would be wearing brighter colors, wanting to stand out. No, I think this is the perfect dress for your mission."

AJ flinched at the word, still a little dazed that someone like Dame Ellingsworth would be involved in one of Beckworth's capers.

She spent the next hour playing pincushion. Though the dress made her feel like one of her father's storied queens, she was more than ready to strip it off when the seamstress finally glanced at Dame Ellingsworth, who nodded her approval. Tea had been brought in and the women sat in the corner eating finger sandwiches while the seamstress went back to her sewing.

"I understand you're staying with Eleanor." Elizabeth eyed her guests. "Don't look like I've just spilled some secret. I've known Eleanor for a few years now. She worked at Waverly when she first arrived from London."

"She's from London?" For some reason, that surprised AJ.

"Oh, yes. She joined the staff when Teddy first took owner-ship of the estate."

"And what happened to the first inhabitant of the estate?" Maire asked, a slight edge to her tone.

"To the original Countess of Waverly?" Elizabeth cocked her head. If she noticed Maire's tightening lips, she didn't show it. "I didn't see her last season, but we never entertained in the same circles. Last I heard she had a nice townhouse near Hyde Park."

"I'd heard she was destitute." AJ remembered Finn telling her something along those lines, having to leave Waverly in disgrace.

"Oh, that was her husband. He couldn't manage the clothes on his back and gambled away what little money he had." Eliza-beth sat back, her elbows resting on the chair as she steepled her fingers. AJ noticed for the first time the swollen knuckles she associated with arthritis. If the woman had been afflicted, she hid her discomfort. "The countess had her own money, and personally, I think she was thrilled when the old coot died. She couldn't wait to get back to London. She left most of the estate belongings behind. They were the only things left of her husband, and she wanted nothing to do with the art, books, or furniture. Teddy has been selling off the pieces he doesn't like, but he's careful, researching each piece. I think that's why he seems to know so many people. He's quite the negotiator when it comes to his art."

AJ wasn't sure if she meant the art or his skill at the con. The story did explain the overstuffed feel of the place, and she couldn't argue Beckworth's eye for fine works. She remembered salivating over the Chippendales.

"And Eleanor?" Maire redirected the conversation.

Elizabeth lowered her voice into that gossip tone. "I noticed her right away. She obviously hadn't grown up in service. She tried hard but never had the knack for the proper way to do things in a household. The housekeeper was constantly reprimanding her, but Teddy protected her. He finally confided in me that Eleanor had been raised in a house of prostitution before working as a dressmaker in the theater. She had protected him in his younger days. When he settled at Waverly, he'd sent for her.

He saw right away that she'd never make it in the household. So, after selling off several of the more expensive, though ghastly, works of art the previous viscount had collected, he bought the cottage where she lives." She brushed crumbs off her dress. "They have some sort of arrangement, as he does with several of the townspeople and other small estates. Some are business arrangements, others are some form of protection." She shrugged when she noticed her guests staring at her. "Teddy learned early on that you need friends in many places and not always with the aristocrats. He has a large heart for the working class. Don't let his obnoxious persona fool you. He's a very smart man, though he likes to hide it."

When the tea was done, Elizabeth escorted them to the front door. She picked up an envelope from a side table in the foyer. "You'll need this."

AJ took the envelope and opened it. "I'd forgotten. The invitation."

"You won't get in without it. This Reginald has thought of everything." She hesitated. "When I had this invitation made, I discovered something I don't think Teddy is aware of. There are two different invitations. Yours is the one most have received, including me. But there's another one made on black paper. I haven't seen it. I've only been told that it appears to be an invitation to a secret meeting. It wasn't very specific, just the same place and date as the ball. Though the time was several hours later. The printer mentioned one other thing. A certain phrase that stood out. Something about a druid gathering."

A cold shiver ran through AJ. She could only stare at the invitation in her hands, the words blurring. A hand rested on her arm, and she glanced up to see Maire watching her. AJ put the invitation back in the envelope and managed a brave smile for her hostess. "Well, this should be interesting."

"Be careful, my dear." Elizabeth's concern both comforted and terrified her. "And I don't mean just with Reginald."

AJ tilted her head, not understanding. Did they have something else to worry about with Beckworth?

"Lady Agatha Osborne will be there, and I have no doubt she'll remember you."

46

Finn moved chess pieces around the map of Waverly. The elegant chess set had been a gift from Beckworth, or so Eleanor had told Finn. The white king, a weathered piece of ivory, sat in the middle of the manor—Reginald. The pawns represented Dugan's guards outside the manor, the rooks and knights were guards positioned at the manor doors, and two bishops were stationed close to the king.

Finn's team, in gleaming ebony, were split between the manor and the estate. The black king and queen would be Ethan and AJ, who would be attending the ball as Lord and Lady Beecham. Their job would be to keep an eye on Reginald and ensure he didn't leave the ball. If he did, AJ would signal Letty, one of the lady's maids, to set their distraction in motion.

He considered various entry and exit scenarios, but everything came down to timing and luck. The plan inside the manor had been discussed at length, and the team had come to the same conclusion—Beckworth was right. The book would be in Reginald's bedroom, just as Beckworth's former butler claimed. Nothing else made sense.

Reginald's room was locked whenever he wasn't there, and his valet chaperoned servants when they had to be in the room. The servants' schedules were routine and well organized, but the additional staff brought in for the ball would be Dugan's Achilles' heel—spreading disorder in the manor.

Maire had insisted she be given time to check Beckworth's study, which Reginald still used. Everyone agreed the book wouldn't be there, but she suspected there'd be other items that might explain Reginald's activities. Finn placed an ebony pawn on the map that represented the library. The room, at the end of a short hall, wouldn't be easy to breach and had only one entrance.

Eleanor had devised a plan to get Maire to the room—if they found the time. Finn moved two pieces around the exterior and sipped coffee as he considered the advantages and disadvantages of the change.

"Do you expect to divine a miracle?" Ethan pushed his mug aside. "You've been moving pieces for the last two hours, and we've already been through every possible angle of entry and exit. Unless Beckworth hears something more, this is what we have."

"And I doubt Beckworth will have anything more to share." Thomas stood. "Let's take a break and watch Thorn try to take the young captain in a sword fight."

Finn stared at the map one last time. The tension in his neck abated at Thomas's suggestion, and he grinned. "I would be careful if you're taking bets. I agree young Jamie has been taught by the finest, but no one masters the sword like Thorn."

Thomas shook his head and smiled in return. "It will almost be a shame to take your money." Thomas feigned a lunge. "With Lando's training and Jamie's size, it doesn't seem a fair fight."

Finn's grin widened. "I think I'll take that bet."

Thomas held out his hand, and they shook.

The three men walked out of the cottage to an unexpectedly sunny day. The clashing of swords had been going on throughout the morning as the men trained. Fitz sprawled on the edge of a grassy patch, sweat covering his brow and staining his shirt. The rest of the men had found places to settle while they watched the two men left in the clearing, parrying and lunging with their swords.

The two men wanted to put on a good show, and they danced around the clearing as they displayed their skill. But as time wore on, Jamie's movements became more erratic while Thorn took advantage.

"You're dropping your arm." Thorn sneered.

"That's because it's ready to fall off." Jamie sidestepped, but Thorn had anticipated the move and touched the tip of his sword in the middle of Jamie's chest.

Jamie dropped to the ground as if the sword had gone through. "I yield."

Thorn held out a hand to the younger man. "Your sword is heavier than mine, and with all the extra steps you take to block and lunge, I must give you credit for lasting as long as you did." Thorn laughed at the men's scowls. "You can't argue perfection, my friends." He plopped down on a wood crate and pulled out his polishing rag.

Beckworth stretched out on the far side of the porch and appeared to be sleeping. A single eye opened, then closed. "Dugan's men won't fight fair, so focus on your precision and forgo etiquette."

Thorn ignored him, but Finn saw his slight nod. Beckworth wasn't wrong.

"I'd feel better knowing Hensley was able to send men." Thomas perched on the top step with Ethan. "The earl's men should be here the day before the party. But they'll need rest before the ball."

Ethan leaned against the porch railing and brushed his hair back, face pointing up to the sun. "Worse case, your men should be sufficient to cover the outer perimeter and our escape routes."

"They'll be spread thin if the alarm is called too soon," Thomas argued, then relented. "I'll break them into teams. One to stay on our planned routes, the rest will form smaller groups and track Dugan's men."

Movement from the driveway brought everyone to attention until Dodger broke from the trees.

"Where the hell have you been?" Thorn yelled.

Dodger appeared startled. "I went to get additional supplies."

"That was hours ago." Thorn continued polishing his sword.

"I stopped at the inn for ale."

"I thought we weren't going to spend time in town." Beckworth had risen and stared at Dodger from the top of the stairs. "It wouldn't be good to be seen."

Dodger's face turned red. "I don't work for you. It's bad enough you're here at all." He stormed past the porch toward Thorn. When Thorn stared up at him, Dodger hesitated, then continued past the clearing toward the river.

"Touchy that one." Beckworth sauntered down the stairs. He tugged his sleeves and glanced toward the path Dodger had taken.

Thorn stood. "With reason." He gripped the hilt of his sword, though he kept the tip pointed to the ground.

Beckworth shrugged. "It was battle. And if you recall, I wasn't in charge."

Thorn took a step, but Finn moved into their path. He understood Thorn's need to blame Beckworth for Peele's death. There was bad blood between the two of them that preceded the duke's entry into their lives. But this wasn't the time for personal vendettas. "A couple more days, and we all go our separate ways. Eyes on the mission."

Thorn glowered at Beckworth, who appeared bored with the conversation. Deciding he'd get nowhere with the man, Thorn turned his back on Beckworth and found a spot next to Jamie and Fitz, where he continued cleaning his shimmering sword.

"You'll need to watch your back with Dodger if you plan on surviving this mission." Finn didn't think Beckworth required the advice, and Beckworth's response proved him correct.

"I watch my back with all of you, mate." He glanced at Finn. His expression hardened. "I don't take my safety lightly. Nothing personal."

"Noted." Finn turned to glance at the men. Fitz waved his arms about as he chatted with Jamie and Thorn. By the grins on the men's face, Fitz was spinning long tales.

The men had spent the week in planning sessions and weapons practice. Even with all that, there was too much free time to think about a fancy party that might get them killed. If he didn't have to worry about Reginald or Dugan showing up in Baywood one day, he'd take AJ home right now and leave the book behind. But the slimmest chance of someone traveling to the future and finding them left Finn cold. He had no intention of looking over his shoulder for the rest of his life.

"We could use some fresh meat for dinner," Finn shouted over the side conversations.

As expected, everyone jumped to their feet, except Beckworth, who dropped down to lay in the grass.

"Five shillings each, and the one who brings back the biggest beast gets the pot," Fitz yelled as he picked up his sword and bow.

Finn watched them leave, pleased to see Ethan go with them. The man needed a distraction so he'd stop fretting over Maire and AJ. They had Lando for protection, and the women weren't exactly easy prey—they had their weapons bag with them.

Once the men were gone, and Beckworth had fallen asleep under a tree, Finn mounted the steps. A heaviness fell over him when the mission planning reinserted itself. He returned to the map and chess pieces, wondering which of the kings would be checkmated before the ball was over.

"A druid's gathering? What the hell is that?" Thorn wailed when AJ shared the information from Dame Ellingsworth.

"I told you the man was off his rocker." Beckworth flopped in front of the hearth and propped his feet on a stool. "His delusion of being a druid legacy is becoming tiresome."

"That could be bad news for us," Ethan said, and AJ was surprised when Thomas nodded in agreement.

"How so?" Jamie asked. "If he's busy with these other men, it will give us more time."

"Not if they need the book for their gathering." Finn kneaded AJ's shoulders, and she leaned back, closing her eyes.

She should pay attention, but she was bone tired. The carriage ride for her dress fitting had been long and stressful, first at meeting Dame Ellingsworth, then with worry over Reginald's ulterior motive for his party. All she wanted was a day with Finn. One simple day would restore her spirit, or at least ease her muscles from the constant training. While the men bantered, her thoughts drifted to ways of getting Finn alone. If they couldn't have a day, maybe they could have one evening away from the crowded cottage. She had little time—the ball was in two days.

Tomorrow, they would run through a mock drill of their plan. Each person had to know their own part without question, but everyone else's role as well. Timing would be critical. Finn insisted everyone know where everyone else would be at every step. If the morning went well, they'd finish the day with a last training session. The thought of sore muscles blossomed into a tempting idea.

"What are you smiling about?" Finn warm breath on her ear roused her from her musings.

"Nothing you need to worry about."

He chuckled. "Now you have me worried."

She stretched, surprised to find herself lying in Finn's lap. She looked around. "Where is everyone?"

"Lando arrived with the last of the supplies. The men went out to help unload."

"You should have woken me. I hadn't planned on falling asleep." She sat up, but Finn refused to release his arms. He kissed her ear. "You needed the rest."

"Where's Maire?"

"She's with Eleanor. Something about testing a new disguise."

"And the costumes?"

"They're here as well. Stop worrying."

They took several moments to enjoy each other's company in the solitude. He hugged her tight. "I miss our moments, sitting on the back deck, watching the sunsets."

AJ squeezed her eyes, pushing back the emotions she'd held in check since traveling through the fog. "I miss our baths."

He chuckled. "As do I. Just a couple more days."

He rested his chin on her head. AJ could feel the tension in his hold. The mission never far from his thoughts. She shifted to push farther into his embrace. A small knot formed in the pit of her belly, just a small feeling they were missing something.

"When will your dress be ready?"

"It should arrive the morning of the ball." The pit in her stomach grew larger. She told herself it was nothing more than nerves, but she couldn't shake her earlier feeling.

"Finn..." AJ's odd feeling disappeared when shouts came from outside.

They jumped up. Finn grabbed a musket, and AJ grabbed her bow and quiver from the weapons store they kept by the front door. They both stopped short when they reached the porch.

Dodger and Beckworth rolled on the ground. Beckworth landed a solid punch before twisting away from a crushing blow Dodger planted in the dirt. The other men stood their ground, no one encouraging the two fighters, but no one bothering to stop them either.

Beckworth, lither than the broad-chested man, moved in for another punch, dancing away before Dodger's arms could grab him in a beefy bear hug. Dodger lunged, and Beckworth feinted to his left, but Dodger was prepared. He twisted his body, took another quick step, and swung with a right hook. Beckworth, still more agile, stepped back at the last moment, missing most of the force of the blow. But the punch landed on his right shoulder, the same place AJ had stabbed him —twice.

Beckworth faltered and dropped to his knees as Dodger came in for another attack. But Dodger hadn't expected Beckworth to drop from a punch to the shoulder, and the smaller man followed with a solid punch to Dodger's ribs.

AJ could hear Dodger's grunt from where she stood.

Finn dropped the musket and launched himself from the porch, scrambling for Dodger. The rest of the men, distracted from their enjoyment, followed Finn into the melee to separate the two men.

AJ thought she heard Fitz grumble about how they needed to get it out of their system. She wouldn't be surprised if he'd already placed a bet on the winner.

When the two men had been pulled apart. Lando held Dodger with an arm around his chest, and Ethan held Beckworth by his arms. Finn glared at them.

"What the hell is going on?" he demanded. He wiped his mouth, his hand coming away with blood from where someone had gotten in a blow. He spit before returning his hot gaze to the group. AJ had to admit, Finn still had the capacity to instill some fear.

Jamie and Fitz had both dropped their heads, scuffing their shoes in the ground as if they were twelve. Thomas wore his typical bored expression, though AJ knew he'd been betting on Dodger. Everyone else held sheepish grins, including Beckworth, who yanked himself free from Ethan's hold.

"It seems we still had a few things to work out from our last party." Beckworth spit then rubbed his shoulder, swinging his arm around to test its range.

"I don't care," Finn roared. "You're grown men. Act like it." He turned on Dodger, pointing a finger. "I understand your anger. But this mission is a life and death situation. You're either in this with us, or you're out." When Thorn began to say something, Finn raised his hand. "I don't want to hear it."

He stared at the wagon. AJ noticed his clenched jaw as Finn tried to gain control. Most of the supplies were still in there. One small barrel had been broken and was leaking what appeared to be ale. Fitz noticed and immediately rescued it, which made her grin in spite of the tension.

"Finish this unloading," Finn barked. "And since you all seem to have energy to spare, we'll have an extra weapons drill this afternoon." He glanced up at the porch where AJ and Maire had gathered. "And that goes for you two as well." To demonstrate his meaning, he cuffed Fitz on the ear, then dragged a barrel from the wagon, carrying it to the back of the cottage.

Fitz rubbed his ear and mumbled, "What did I do?"

Jamie threw an arm around his shoulder. "It's more what we didn't do. You were just the closest."

Still rubbing his ear, Fitz griped, "He still has quite the touch."

Jamie laughed as they each grabbed the end of a crate and carried it off.

Maire leaned into AJ. "We thought a week wasn't enough time. I think we'd have been better off with only two days' notice." She turned and returned to the cottage.

AJ sighed. To avoid being assigned a task, she withdrew to change into her pants. Then she thought about the ball and her fancy party dress. Grumbling about her decision, she called for Maire to assist her into a corset. She needed to test her dagger work while wearing the restrictive garment. Just one more thing to add to the growing pit in her stomach. She reached into her pocket to grasp the Heart Stone and her wedding ring. For some reason, neither object gave her the sense of comfort it usually did.

48

AJ grimaced as she dropped to the pallet. Her body screamed from tired muscles, weak legs, and sore feet. The team had run through the mission drills several times, ending early enough to spend the rest of the day in weapon's training. She wanted to curl into a ball and sleep for a week.

She opened her eyes when Finn gently nudged her. "Wake up, sweetheart. It's your turn for a bath."

She rolled over, slowly stretching out her legs. Glancing up, she noticed his grin. "What are you so happy about?'

He brushed a strand of hair from where they'd stuck to her lips. "You're always so beautiful when you wake."

She smiled, that little tingle sparking to life as he bent to kiss her. "How long was I out?"

"About an hour. The men have cleaned up and have found their own corners until dinner."

The mention of dinner reminded AJ of her plan to get Finn alone. She noticed he hadn't bathed yet, and she leaned in before wrinkling her nose. "Not all the men have cleaned up."

He chuckled. "I thought I'd wait for you." His grin was as

magnetic as the first day she'd seen him on the dock in Baywood. Her stomach did a little flip.

"Why don't you get started, and I'll be right behind you." AJ stood, and after stretching her limbs, determined she was in better shape than she'd been before the jump. Her muscles, while still sore, had worked out the kinks during her nap, though a blister was forming on her right heel.

She gathered a change of clothes and stuffed them in her canvas bag, along with a change for Finn. Then she found Eleanor in the kitchen, busily working on dinner with Maire and Ethan.

"Don't you look all domestic." AJ grabbed a carrot from the pile of vegetables Eleanor was preparing and noticed the slight blush to Maire's cheeks.

If she didn't know better, she'd caught a similar blush from Ethan. She wondered where they'd spent the last hour. The need to be close to someone the night before a battle must be instinctual.

"Everything you need is in the basket." Eleanor, a knife in one hand and a potato in the other, nodded toward the far side of the counter.

"Thank you." AJ hugged her until Eleanor pushed her away.

"I can't be responsible when I have a knife in my hands," she warned.

They laughed and went back to preparing dinner as AJ stacked her canvas bag on top of the basket. She hurried to the stables, eager to confirm her earlier tasks hadn't been disturbed. Satisfied everything was still in order, she placed the basket in the straw and fidgeted with its contents. Then she grabbed the canvas bag and ran to the side of the house where the woodshed had been turned into a bathhouse.

She was surprised when she didn't see anyone in her race to

the woodshed. Someone was always around, but the place felt like a ghost town.

A lantern lit the interior of the shed, drawing her attention to the barrel in the center of the cramped space. The barrel was two feet tall and appeared to have been cut to half of its original size. Its circumference was large enough for one person to stand in while they sluiced water over themselves.

Finn sat on a bench, removing his shirt.

"Where is everyone?" AJ asked.

"Jamie and Fitz left for Bart's to meet with Hensley's men, who should be there by now. They probably won't be back before morning. Thomas, Thorn, and Dodger went to a small village north of here to wait for the earl's men. Beckworth had one final rendezvous with his butler. He said he'd be back in time for dinner."

By the time he'd answered her question, AJ had stripped bare and stepped into the tub that was empty of water but still damp from previous baths. Finn had been busy undressing and hadn't noticed. When he glanced up, his appreciative stare made her tingle all over.

"I'm sorry the tub isn't any larger." His voice turned husky, his gaze lit with desire.

She pointed a finger at him. "Don't even think you're going to get lucky in a dark and musty woodshed."

He mocked a hurt expression. "It's been too long."

"I'd rather have my way with you in the middle of the yard for all the heavens to see than in this place." She visibly shuddered until Finn poured a bucket of warm water over her. Not wanting to give Finn any more ideas, she hurriedly washed. She didn't argue, however, when Finn took the rag from her. He worked briskly until he reached her more sensitive areas, then his movements became soft caresses that increased the tingles he'd always been able to incite with little effort.

When her skin was rosy from his task, she took the towel he handed her, stepped on another towel to protect her feet, and quickly dried off while Finn stepped in the tub. Not wanting to miss the opportunity, she donned her plain dress and assisted Finn with his own bathing.

Once they were clean and dressed, he pulled her into his arms and gave her a resounding kiss that curled her toes.

"You've missed a perfect opportunity," he whispered as his kiss moved down her neck.

She pulled back. "Maybe not." She pressed a finger to his lips before he could respond. "I have a surprise."

He kissed her finger, then her wrist. "You know I love your surprises."

She stooped to pick up their discarded clothes. The slap on her butt made her spin around. She arched a brow. "It's going to be like that, is it?"

His grin said it most definitely would be.

She threw the clothes at him and raced from the shed, her giggles erupting as she heard him in pursuit. If anyone had been left to watch her race across the yard, laughing as Finn gave chase, she'd blush to her roots. And she wouldn't care.

She barely made it inside the barn before she was lifted from her feet. Finn spun them around, his breath catching. "And where do you think you're running off to."

She wrapped her arms around his neck, her voice breathy from the run. "Close the doors."

He slowly released her, letting her body slide down his until she stood on shaky legs. Not wanting to waste time, she tugged on one door while Finn closed the other.

"What do you have planned for us in the darkness?" Finn reached for her waist, but she stepped back and grabbed his hand.

The barn wasn't as dark as Finn made it sound. Holes in the

walls and an open slit in one of the outer stall doors provided enough light to make out the ladder in the middle of the open aisle. AJ released his hand to lift her skirt as she stepped up the first rung. Halfway up, the mixed smell of straw, dust, and aged manure permeating the barn made her sneeze. Finn grabbed a leg to hold her steady. His heavy breathing followed her the rest of the way up, and she knew it wasn't from exertion.

The lantern was where she'd left it, and she picked it up, leaving it unlit for now. In a far corner, in the least drafty place she could find, several inches of fresh straw had been laid out. A picnic basket and jug sat in the middle of two blankets that had been thrown over the straw.

They didn't say a word as Finn pulled her into his arms. This time his kiss was slow and seductive. He drew her down to the blankets, stopping long enough to move the basket and jug to a safer spot. Then he began to unwrap her, slowly stripping off one piece of clothing at a time until they were both panting with need.

AJ worked at the ties of his shirt, wanting to take her time undressing him. She missed the feel of his skin on hers, and the slow anticipation of things to come, but goose bumps erupted on her skin from the chill of the barn. Finn pushed her hands away and stripped quickly before drawing her down to the straw bed. He tugged one of the blankets over them, but the heat from his body was enough for her to forget the chilly air.

Neither could stop running their hands over the other, moving to the sensitive places that drove each other wild. This might not be their bedroom at Westcliffe or the cabin of the *Daphne Marie*, but it didn't matter. As precious as those memories were, they were only places. What mattered was him, the feel of their bodies melding as one, and the intoxicating cedar scent that carried the essence of the man.

And for a few hours, they could forget the danger around

them. When he buried his face in her neck and breathed in her scent, she clung to him as if they might not have a tomorrow.

49

AJ opened one eye, then squeezed it shut when the sun pierced her retina. Typical. She'd managed to position herself in front of a small hole in the barn, turning the bright light of morning into a spotlight. She moaned and rolled over, snuggling into the warmth of the man next to her.

Finn kissed her forehead, her nose, and then her lips. "Good morning, sunshine."

She ran a hand through his hair, tugging on the ends. "Mmm. Can we make this last a few more hours?"

"I wish we could, but Jamie will return with the men soon. I'm surprised he's not here already."

"But we have hours before the ball." AJ released a soft sigh of disappointment, hoping it might sway his decision. "I know I'm being greedy, but the team's as solid as we're going to get. Another few hours of training won't change the outcome of the mission."

"Aye. I was more worried about getting you back to the house before the men arrived."

"I don't care."

When he arched a brow, she pinched his cheek. "It's past

time we told them we're married. If all goes well, today will be the last day we'll ever see them. They might as well know we're a permanent thing."

"A thing?" His grin was playful, and he nipped her lip. "I'm a thing now?"

She shoved his chest. "You know what I mean."

He laughed and rolled them until she was on top of him. "I'm not sure I do." His Irish accent thickened. "Perhaps a lass should show me."

An hour later, straw sticking out of her hair, she munched on leftover bread from dinner then sipped from a skin of water. She stared at the jug. Last night had been her last glass of wine on this side of the jump. She wouldn't drink another glass until she was sitting across the table from Stella toasting their safe return.

They were walking hand in hand toward the cottage when the first group of horses approached. Jamie, with Fitz by his side, led a dozen men into the clearing. He gave the couple a wink as he trotted up to Finn. "I'm glad to see someone's had time to relax while the rest of us work."

"You've been listening to Fitz too long if you think a night of cards and dice is considered work," Finn replied. His impish grin matched the twinkle in his gaze.

"Ah, boss, you've left out the ale and whiskey," Fitz complained. "And there would have been debauchery if we had more time."

They laughed as Finn looked past his friends to the group of men. They slumped in their saddles, their unshaven faces and tired eyes speaking volumes.

"Has Jamie discussed the plan?" When a few nodded, he smiled. "Good. There's room in the stable for your horses. And if I can trust my nose, a late breakfast awaits you in the cottage. Eat, then find a spot to get some sleep. We'll gather mid-afternoon to discuss the operation again." He took the time to meet the eyes of each man, and this time, they all nodded in return. AJ would bet most of them had fought by his side before.

"Well, get to it," Finn barked. "Before Lando finds the breakfast table."

That forced a laugh from the men as they scurried to the task.

Finn guided AJ toward the porch where Ethan and Beckworth sat in chairs, their boots resting on the railing. The two men watched the quiet clearing turn into a base camp of fighting men.

"Have a good night?" Ethan greeted them with an exuberance AJ hadn't expected. Maybe he'd found some alone time with Maire. Considering what the next twenty-four hours might hold in store, he seemed too chipper.

Truth be told, considering their plan, they all had to be just a touch this side of crazy.

"It's disgraceful, really. Acting like common alley cats." Beckworth lifted his chin as if personally insulted and stared at the clearing.

AJ twitched her lips. The way Beckworth and Ethan had teamed up to razz them, she had to wonder what they'd missed last night.

A quick side-glance from Finn confirmed he was thinking the same thing.

"I think someone spiked the coffee this morning." Finn mounted the stairs, his grip on AJ's hand tight as he pulled her along. Before they entered the house, Finn stopped long enough to stare down at the two men, who grinned like Cheshire cats.

"And how I spend time with my wife isn't your concern." He pushed through the door with AJ still in tow. She had the barest of seconds to catch the men's shocked expression as she was pulled into the house.

"Are you kidding me? That's how we're announcing we're

married?" AJ blustered, then stopped short when she entered the main room.

Finn pulled her close and kissed the top of her head. "Seemed the quickest way."

She'd already forgotten what they were discussing, unable to take her gaze away from the long table taking up most of the cottage's living space. Her mouth watered at the feast laid out for the team. They'd been lucky Finn had been mad enough a couple days prior to make the men go hunting. Several glazed pheasants and ducks, along with what smelled like roasted pork, were surrounded by potatoes, vegetables, cheese, bread, fruit, and unnamed pastries. Jugs of ale and dozens of mugs filled another side table.

She felt horrible. "They did all this while we were..."

"Stop." Finn squeezed her. "Beckworth brought two women from town last night to help Eleanor. It was arranged days ago. They've been well paid and were happy to help." He pulled her in for another kiss. "We all have our roles to fill."

"Are you going to just stand there, brother, and play house with your bride, or lend a hand like our parents raised us?" Maire's lilt was thick as she hugged AJ. "I could use your help with the porridge, and Eleanor made a fresh pot of coffee for the two of you."

Maire pulled AJ away as Ethan and Beckworth stumbled in, mere steps before Lando.

"What's this about a wife?" Ethan bellowed. "When did you find the time, and why weren't we there?" His expression was somewhere between anger and hurt.

AJ couldn't leave Finn to answer. Not with Ethan. She gazed down at her toes before raising her head to give him her best apologetic smile. "You didn't miss anything. It happened before we jumped. We would have said something, but with Maire missing, then we were split up..."

"Stop. It doesn't matter." Ethan hugged her and whispered in her ear, "As long as you're happy. You know that's all I ever cared about. That and your safety."

AJ stepped back so she could see his expression. "I know. But your approval means everything to me."

"And you have it. No question about it."

Beckworth said nothing but had the good grace to shake Finn's hand. It was an awkward moment, and both men stepped back as if neither wanted anyone to have witnessed the moment.

Lando could only grin and didn't hold back as he grabbed each of them into a bear hug, almost squeezing the stuffing out of AJ.

Maire threw up her hands in false protest. "We might as well make a party out of it." She pushed AJ toward Finn. "Go tell Jamie and Fitz, they'll be hurt if they hear it third hand."

By the time Finn and AJ shared the news with the men, the late breakfast turned into a wedding reception. Fitz and Lando sang sailing ditties, and when several men joined in, others danced with Eleanor and the women from town. The laughter and singing eventually slowed as the men filtered out of the cottage to find a place to sleep.

When Thorn and Dodger returned ahead of Thomas and the earl's men, only a handful of people remained in the house. The table of food looked like a tornado had hit. Mugs and empty plates littered the kitchen and living area. Thorn skewered the remaining carcass of a duck with his dagger and lifted it up, disappointment marring his elegant face.

"So what did we miss?"

50

AJ tugged at the bodice, not remembering the dress being cut so low. Most of the fitting had been a blur, her attention focused on Dame Ellingsworth rather than the elegant gown. The dress had arrived late, just two hours earlier. Fortunately, the gown fit perfectly, or their schedule might have been delayed while Eleanor made last-minute adjustments.

"It's time," Finn called from the door.

When she turned, Finn's lustful gaze heated her cheeks. "You'll put every woman to shame tonight."

Butterflies stirred. All she wanted to do was rip the dress off and spend the rest of the evening in his arms. "I hope your compliment is just the expected praise from a husband. I'm supposed to blend in."

"You couldn't blend in if you tried." He kissed her hand, refusing to release it. "But for tonight, please try your best."

She gave him a quick perusal. Everything about him was black as night—pants, shirt, and overcoat. Nothing to give him away in the light of the moon. She brushed an errant lock from his forehead. His kiss lit a fire in her belly, temporarily chasing the butterflies away. She held on, not wanting to let go.

"Don't worry. I have the stone that Beckworth had been carrying. If we get separated, I'll use it to follow you."

The knowledge they both had a way to time jump if needed should have calmed her, but she still felt a slip of dread.

"By morning, we'll be home in Baywood." Finn's continual words of encouragement strengthened her backbone. "Just keep that thought, keep your head, and everything will go as planned." He gave her another kiss, and she sensed his reluctance to let her go. Then he did, and for the briefest of moments, a deep sense of loss swept through her, followed by a shiver.

She forced a smile. "Be careful." She handed him his thin black mask, and he tucked it in the pocket of his overcoat.

He studied her for a moment, and she was certain she'd caught a glimpse of his signature grin before he grasped her elbow. He guided her through the cottage and out to the waiting coach.

Ethan, standing rigid next to the carriage, gazed off into the distance, his forehead creased with worry. He bore no resemblance to the carefree man from earlier that morning. His brooding eyes, dark and menacing, seemed appropriate for his coal-black ensemble. His hair had been trimmed in a more fashionable cut, and while he may standout with the women, he should blend easily with the other men at the ball once he donned his plain black mask.

She understood his changed mood. His thoughts were of Maire, who'd left with Eleanor an hour earlier. She'd been dressed as a housemaid. Her hair, darkened with henna, had been braided, rolled tightly into a bun, then topped with a white cap fitting for her uniform. Makeup had been applied to her face, neck, and hands, giving her a ruddy appearance, hiding her flawless alabaster skin. Eleanor had proven to be a master of disguise. AJ shouldn't be surprised. Beckworth chose his friends wisely.

Finn scanned the group, then slowed as he reviewed Lando's livery attire. Nodding his approval, he handed Jamie and Fitz two bundles before they climbed into the carriage. Lando waited by the door. He would play the role of coachman—at least until they were all safely ensconced in their positions.

Thorn and Dodger had left with Maire and Eleanor so they could get in place before the guests arrived and the guards were stationed.

Thomas would follow the carriage with Hensley's and the earl's men. After spending all night and morning at an inn, the earl's men were fresh from their long ride the day before, and were eager to work with Finn and Ethan again. Thomas and Finn had briefed them before dividing them into smaller teams. Beckworth suspected Dugan would keep most of his men close to the manor. The team agreed a smaller advance party would move to a position behind Dugan's men. The selected team would be swift and deadly if the need arose. The rest of the men would create a tight perimeter around their inside teams' exit once the mission hit its zenith.

"Come on, princess. Your carriage awaits." Beckworth's mocking tone was softened by a slight smile. She couldn't fully read his expression, but if she had to guess, it was a sense of satisfaction. This would be a warning shot to his brother. If they were lucky.

AJ dragged her feet to the coach, fighting down the building nausea, as she took Ethan's hand to help her inside. She took a moment to give Beckworth the timid smile she'd been practicing all afternoon.

"I'd say try not to get yourself killed, but, well..." She couldn't help the teasing remark.

Beckworth leaned toward her. "You know you'd miss your favorite pincushion."

AJ laughed, unable to resist the man's wit. "That I would."

She gave a quick glance to Finn before her smile turned menacing. "You watch his back, or I'll stick you with something much larger than a dagger."

His smile never wavered. "You have my guarantee."

Unsure of the veracity of his statement, she nodded and climbed into the carriage. Jamie and Fitz sat across from her, and Ethan took the spot next to her.

"I hope you don't mind." Ethan grasped her hand, ignoring the glance Jamie and Fitz shared. "I could use some encouragement."

She tightened her grip on his, then leaned over and kissed his cheek. "She'll be all right. She knows that manor as well as Beckworth."

He nodded and turned to gaze out his window.

AJ, still gripping his hand, leaned toward her own window, hoping to catch a glimpse of Finn. She needn't have bothered. He stepped to the window and stuck his head in.

"Remember, you're only to follow Reginald to make sure he stays downstairs. Signal Letty the minute you think we need to run. We'll go in a half-hour after dark." He glanced at Ethan, who continued to stare out the other window. "Don't take any risks. We don't know which of his guests received the other invitations, so everyone at the party should be considered a danger."

"If this is supposed to be a pep talk, you need to work on it," AJ muttered. But she couldn't take her eyes off him, memorizing every line, every feature. With her free hand, she cupped his cheek. "Make sure you remember your own words about not taking extra risks. If you can't find the book within your allotted time, get out. There's always a plan B."

His response was a hard, swift kiss, and then he was gone, running to his horse. Once mounted, he whistled. The coach moved out with the rest of team following. When they came within sight of the estate, the group stopped. Jamie and Fitz gave her and Ethan a brief smile and words of encouragement before jumping out.

Hearing horses riding off, AJ leaned out the window in time to see Finn turn his horse toward the coach. His smile looked forced, and she returned her own heartfelt smile, giving him a wave. Then he turned the steed and rode off, Beckworth and the advance party falling in behind him. They would approach from the backside of the estate. The remaining men, who would create the perimeter teams, continued with them as the coach drove on.

Ethan's grip on her hand remained as they heard the last of the horses leave them ten minutes later. Only the sound of the coach remained as they turned down the tree-lined drive to Waverly.

51

Maire pressed herself against the wall of a small alcove in the east wing of Waverly. She waited as the two men stormed down the hall, their long winter cloaks floating around their boots. She slowed her breathing, wanting to close her eyes but didn't dare. Had they seen her? She didn't think so.

"You there. Halt." The gruff voice came from only a few feet away.

She glanced down, thinking maybe her skirts had given her away. But they were tucked between her legs as she remembered doing when she'd first dashed into the alcove.

Then she heard a squeak and turned her gaze to the right. A young housemaid had dropped to her knees, her arms, filled with towels, were raised in supplication. Their eyes met momentarily before the girl dropped her head.

"I'm sorry, sir. I needed more towels for the guest rooms, but there weren't any more in the west wing, so I had to get them from the linen closet in the east wing." The young housemaid's voice trembled with fear.

If there wasn't so much at stake, Maire would stab both men

325

in the kidneys. One thing she'd never heard during her long stay at Waverly were frightened servants. While she cursed her time at Waverly, she'd noticed how loyal the servants were to Beckworth. Her only true friend had been her lady's maid until AJ arrived. The servants were loyal because Beckworth treated them fairly, not out of fear. He'd get plenty mad, sometimes so irritated his face turned red when the staff hadn't performed to his expectations—especially during one of his parties or hunts. But the rest of the days, he always seemed to have a kind word. Funny how she hadn't noticed at the time.

Maybe that's why, though she'd spent almost two years as his kidnapped guest, she'd never felt fear. Instead, she pushed him, her anger sometimes getting the better of her. And when she'd pushed too far, she'd been sent to her room like a misbehaved child. Witnessing the servants cower in fear under this new viscount was more than enough to want to see the scoundrel forced from Waverly.

The two men towered over the poor girl, her arms slowly lowering from the strain of holding up the towels. She'd begun to weep.

"Have you seen anyone else come through here?" One of the men leaned down, his tone like granite.

When she didn't respond, he nudged her with his boot. "Speak up."

The young girl's gaze flitted about before it landed on Maire. The girl nodded.

Maire's heart sank as dread rose. The memory of her dank prison cell threatened to suffocate her. She had nowhere to run. She was fast, but the guards would be equally quick despite their bulk.

"I'll not ask you again, girl."

"A man. Dressed like you." She hesitated. "But much smaller. He ran past as I came through the sitting room."

Every muscle in Maire's body relaxed, and she laid her head against the wall, releasing a long, slow breath. The maid might be scared senseless, but she had enough fortitude to lie—and lie well. There'd been no man, but the room the girl indicated led straight to the front entrance of the east wing. If there'd been a man, he'd be long gone.

The two men stared down at the housemaid before they glanced at each other.

"One of the men must have sneaked into the kitchen then worried about being caught," one of the men suggested.

The other man grunted. "He was right to run. Dugan would have his skin for disobeying orders."

"We should make sure. Let's be quick, or we'll be late to our post."

The two men strode past the girl, their pace increasing as they disappeared through the door that led to the front entrance. Once their footsteps receded, Maire rushed out and knelt by the girl, taking the towels from her so she could stand.

"Thank you." Maire returned the towels once the maid regained her footing.

She smiled up at Maire, a twinkle in her eye. "Anything for the rightful viscount." Then she scurried off.

Well, damned. Eleanor had been right. A small resistance had been gathering, waiting for Beckworth's return. They couldn't do it by themselves, but they did what they could in their own way.

Breathing a sigh of relief as the young woman raced down the hallway, Maire returned to her original mission. She waited, listening for sounds of approaching boots. Hearing nothing, she turned the corner that led to the east wing library.

When she reached the main foyer, she slowed. Unsure whether Dugan's men had left, she eased her head out. The entryway was clear, and the door to the library was closed.

She raced across the foyer, thankful for quiet slippers. When she reached the door without anyone calling out, she gathered a deep breath and reached for the door.

52

———————

AJ noticed the dozens of coaches when they reached the circular drive and made the turn toward the entrance. The carriages were parked between the mansion and stables. Exactly where Beckworth said they'd be. So far, so good. And it appeared they were one of the last to arrive.

She glanced down at the mask she gripped in her hand. Its beauty was enhanced by the subtlety of the colors. The single emerald peacock feather, nestled within the rich chocolate spray of pheasant plumes, bore the same deep green as Finn's eyes. The feathers fanned across the right side of her mask, which began just below her hairline and stopped at the ridge of her upper lip. The mask itself was painted with swirls of brown, copper, and splashes of forest green. The colorful effect made it difficult to focus on the woman beyond the mask. When she'd tried it on earlier that afternoon, she expected to feel claustrophobic, but the mask fit like a second skin. She'd worn it around Eleanor's cabin for an hour until she'd forgotten she was wearing it.

After donning the mask once again, she stepped down from the coach, barely glancing at Lando, who stared straight ahead

329

like any proper coachman. Ethan placed a hand on hers, forcing her to relax the grip on his arm. She glanced up to his masked face, taking a brief moment to notice how handsome he was. At least half the room would be ignoring her, the other women's gazes glued to Ethan. She would have smiled if she didn't think she might pass out.

Ethan moved them toward the stairs. "Deep breathes. More oxygen, clearer head."

She took his advice, breathing in until she became light-headed. She changed tactics and turned to her old ally—counting to ten. After the third attempt, she was as calm as she'd ever be.

"That's better." Ethan's brow arched. "But try not to smile like that. You'll scare the children."

She rolled her eyes.

Ethan laughed as they climbed the steps, displaying the intimate chatter of a husband and wife.

"I'll try to find a happy medium," AJ grumbled, but found enough of a timid smile for Ethan to nod in approval.

As suspected, there were only two footmen at the door, and they barely gave the invitation a second glance. A few guests, mostly men, mingled in the foyer, drinks in hand, all in serious conversation. AJ turned Ethan to the right, which led to the sitting room that separated the west and east wings. A cacophony of voices filled the room as guests milled about while others conversed in groups. Women in colorful gowns and matching masks glittered with beads, pearls, and possibly jewels competed with the singular elegance of the finely tailored men behind their simple masks.

AJ leaned toward Ethan. "Finding Reginald may be more difficult than I thought."

Ethan led her to the far side of the room. "Try not to stare. Listen for voices, and watch for behaviors. Notice the doors?"

AJ glanced toward the double doors that led to the east wing. When she'd been here before, the doors had always been open, though she'd been warned to not go beyond them. Tonight, the doors were closed, and two large men stood in front of them. Not only would the guests not get past the doors, but it also removed a possible exit for her and Ethan.

Ethan took two glasses of champagne from a passing server and handed one to AJ. "One sip for nerves, then keep holding it."

She nodded and let Ethan guide her around the room. He kept to the outer edge of the guests, stopping to chat with AJ about nonsensical topics while they listened to the conversations around them. Ethan made her laugh, and the earlier butterflies vanished as she focused on their task.

Ethan winced when her fingers bit into his arm as he guided them to a small group discussing the war. He seamlessly joined the conversation while AJ kept her head down, only raising it long enough to take note of the women. Once AJ was introduced as Ethan's wife from an unknown peerage, the women ignored her. While it irritated her, their quick dismissal of her as no threat worked to their advantage.

After several minutes of polite conversation, Ethan steered AJ through the foyer to the west wing, where the voices grew louder and it became more difficult to get through the press of people. After gazing at so many men, all of them beginning to look similar, she wondered if she'd recognize Reginald behind a mask, regardless of how similar he was to Beckworth. Without thinking, she finished the champagne, then shrugged when Ethan gave her a disproving glance.

AJ pushed him toward the dining room. In her time, it was where most people gathered. She didn't know if it worked the same at these parties, but it was a place to start. The room's long table and sideboards were filled high with platters of food—roast pork, glazed pheasant, succulent ribs of beef, and other savory foods that made her stomach growl. She had been told to eat before the party, but she'd been too nervous. Ethan picked up a plate and selected several pieces of cheese and fruit.

"I can't eat. I'll throw it up." AJ pushed the plate away.

"If I can hear your stomach, so can everyone else. And after drinking the champagne, you need a few bites."

She couldn't argue his point. They found a quiet spot along the wall while she nibbled at the food.

"Where next?" Ethan asked.

"The conservatory is down the hall to the left, but I don't think Reginald would be that far from his guests. Not this soon. He must still be making the rounds greeting his more prominent neighbors."

"That makes sense."

"There's the drawing room and another sitting room, but let's try the library first. It's down the hall to the right."

Ethan strolled slowly, stopping to admire a painting or piece of sculpture. Little had changed in the décor, which AJ had always found overwhelming and gauche. Now that she knew Beckworth had inherited it all with the estate and was slowly changing it out, she developed a different appreciation. Finding a charming painting or impressive sculpture among the rest of the clutter became a treasure hunt. She was almost sorry she wouldn't be able to spend more time here after Beckworth reclaimed Waverly.

When they stepped into the library, she'd barely taken a breath before she spotted him. She didn't know why she thought she wouldn't recognize him—even with the mask, she could be staring at Beckworth. Ethan pulled her toward the other side of the room, where two men played chess. Two other couples watched the men play, so she and Ethan didn't seem out of place.

She couldn't take her eyes off Reginald. If she didn't know

better, she'd swear it was Beckworth standing across the room chatting with several men. His midnight-blue mask accentuated the cornflower eyes, the ash-blond hair, and his handsome face. The two brothers must have taken after the duke in appearance. She idly wondered if she was staring at the likeness of the duke before excessiveness had turned him into the fat, blowhard he'd become. If the duke could turn heads like his sons, AJ could understand why he had a bastard, and maybe others no one knew about.

Ethan casually pointed toward the other side of the room where another group of couples conversed. They strolled toward them, keeping their backs to Reginald. They stood close enough to appear part of the group, but far enough away to avoid being pulled into their discussion. If she ignored the guests in front of her, she could make out bits and pieces of Reginald's conversation.

His voice was high-pitched as she remembered it, even with his low tone. She only caught a few words—conservatory, east wing, midnight. Then she thought she heard something about a surprise guest. Her gaze flew to Ethan's. He'd heard it too. Who was Reginald referring to? Whoever it was, AJ's tremor of foreboding returned.

Ethan grasped her elbow and guided her toward the door where they'd entered. As they approached, Dame Ellingsworth walked in, her gaze meeting AJ's. Without a missed step, Dame Ellingsworth turned immediately to her right. Her voice was loud and joyful. "Oh look, is that Lady Wentworth? I haven't seen her in ages." She moved quickly, then AJ understood why. Two women trailed behind her. AJ immediately recognized one of them, mask or no mask—Lady Agatha.

She must have cringed, or maybe she gasped, because Ethan turned and bent down, partially blocking her view. Whether on purpose or just concerned, his quick reaction was enough to hide her from Lady Agatha, who'd given them a quick glance.

AJ took the cue Ethan had given her and reached up to straighten his perfectly placed cravat. When he bent his head closer, she whispered, "Lady Agatha."

She'd warned him earlier about the obnoxious woman. With barely a glance in the woman's direction, he slid a protective arm around her and guided her to the door. As they passed the group, Dame Ellingsworth's loud voice hijacked the previous conversation, but Lady Agatha turned her head. AJ chanced a last glance in time to see Lady Agatha raise a beautifully arched brow above her mask as Ethan turned them down the hall.

Damn. She hoped Lady Agatha's hawk-like scrutiny had been for Ethan rather than her. AJ clearly remembered the woman's interest in Finn—regardless of her married state. Either prospect could interfere with their plans.

"Where does the door on the other side of the library go?" Ethan stopped next to another couple in the hallway.

"To a study that leads to another hallway."

"So Reginald could exit either direction."

AJ nodded. Then she dropped her head and turned toward Ethan when she spotted another figure approaching.

Dugan.

AFTER DROPPING off AJ and Ethan, Lando drove the coach away from the front entrance. A liveryman pointed toward a large area where dozens of other carriages had been parked. Winter parties at large estates would typically host the guests overnight, but this invitation had been for one short evening. Fortunately for the guests, it was an evening when the moon would be the fullest, so driving coaches home in the dark wouldn't be an issue. With an early start to the evening, the sun had barely reached the horizon, making this stage of the plan one of the most dangerous.

He directed the horses to the farthest side of the field, away from the house and toward the stables. Most of the carriages had been aligned in neat rows, however, some of the coachmen from grander estates had ignored the liveryman and parked where they wanted. This played to Lando's need to get as close to the stables as he could while still leaving an exit route.

Passing an expansive black coach, he circled the carriage around it, so the horses faced the mansion. He waited until he was even with the other coach before pulling the horses to a stop, leaving twenty feet between the beasts.

Lando waited several moments, ensuring all was quiet, then set the brake and jumped down. He stood by the horses, whispering to them and feeding them treats. He watched as another coach moved away from the entrance, but that coachman followed directions and moved slowly to the opposite side of the field.

After another scan of the area, Lando patted the closest horse then walked toward the back of the coach. He surveyed the area. Satisfied they were alone, he knocked on the wooden box where luggage was typically stored. Satisfied he was still alone, he strolled toward the far end of the field where other coachmen had huddled to talk. He stopped at the first coach he came to and leaned against it, pulling off a boot as if checking for a loose stone.

When he glanced back toward the carriage, he caught a glimpse of two shapes holding small bundles racing from the back of the coach. After they cleared the side of the stables and were out of sight, Lando replaced his boot. Rather than meet with the other coachman, he blended into the trees behind the parked coaches and waited.

53

———

The knob turned, and Maire released a heavy breath, relieved the door wasn't locked. The small room was empty, and she scurried in, closing the door behind her.

She leaned against the door and assessed the room. Based on the stacks of paper, inkpots, and dust box, Reginald used this for his office as Beckworth had. When she stepped to the desk and flipped through the snippets of pages, she changed her mind. This might be the second translator's office.

She became more convinced of her assumption as she sifted through the piles, trying to keep them in the same order she found them. They were so disorderly she doubted anyone would notice she'd been there. Yet, even the most slovenly of record keepers had a system and could instantly tell when something was amiss. In this case, she would bet Reginald rifled through the man's paperwork on a regular basis. The new viscount didn't seem the trusting sort. Not that Beckworth had been any different on that count.

After scanning all the pages written in old Celtic, she recognized most of them as the sections she'd already translated. As if confirming her thoughts, she discovered a stack of her own writ-

336

ing. Folding the pages in half, she stuffed them in the oversized pockets Eleanor had sewn in her dress. AJ's inspiration was proving useful.

She found additional pages of Celtic she didn't remember reading but recognized the translator's sloppy printing. These inscriptions must have been copied from the druid's book. She tucked them in her pocket with the other pages. If they didn't find the book, they would at least have a portion of it. And if they stole the book, they'd leave little behind for Reginald to work with. That alone made her smile.

She glanced at the door, concerned by how long she'd been there. It seemed only minutes, but she tended to lose track of time when reading Celtic. Knowing she should leave, she flipped through the pages in the other stacks. They were mostly scribbles, and after reading a line or two of the tiny print, she shook her head. They were wild musings about the druids, and she began to wonder if everyone that worked for Reginald was a bit mad.

Then her hands shook with a new fear when she lifted a book from a stack of letters and recognized two names—Ratliff and Langdon. Ratliff was the man who'd held this century's Heart Stone in good keeping. He'd been killed by highwaymen on his way to Waverly, or so his daughter had been told. Though the daughter hadn't believed the story.

Langdon was the last name of the first keeper of stones. She skimmed the letters, her mind racing with increased apprehension and anger. Reginald knew Ratliff had the Heart Stone. Ratliff was supposed to bring the stone to Waverly, but he must have suspected foul play. Maire assumed that to be the truth behind the man's death. And though his daughter had been right to question what she'd been told, Maire doubted the woman knew his death might be connected to the Heart Stone.

But what did Langdon have to do with this? Giving the

letters another quick scan, she snatched the ones with the most critical information, leaving the rest. She considered putting the letters back. It was one thing to steal pages about the grimoire, but if Reginald suspected they knew about Ratliff and Langdon, the Heart Stone could be in jeopardy. It appeared it already was, so the letters followed the Celtic pages into her growing pockets.

As a last thought, she went through the desk drawers, and finding nothing of import, stepped back to the door. She gave the desk a quick scan. Everything appeared as disorderly as it had been when she arrived. She took a deep breath to calm her nerves, then slowly twisted the knob.

She opened it an inch before she quietly closed it and whipped around. A guard had been stationed in the hallway. Her gaze flew around the room, but she knew there wasn't a second exit. She was trapped.

WHEN THE KNOCK CAME, Jamie let out a breath. His legs had begun to cramp, and he hadn't been in the boot that long. He couldn't move, and the hot breath of the man stuffed next him gave him a slight case of claustrophobia.

"It's about time. I think I've lost feeling in me legs." Fitz's harsh whisper blew into his ear.

Jamie raised the lid of the boot an inch and breathed in the fresh winter air. When he'd first settled into the luggage box, it brought back memories of stowing away on the *Daphne Marie* as a youth. Now, a full-sized adult with Fitz's knees poking into his back, the childhood images rapidly faded.

When he didn't see anyone, he climbed out and dropped to his knees. He grimaced in pain as blood returned to his legs. He surveyed his surroundings, noting that Lando had positioned the coach following Beckworth's suggestion. The only people within sight were a handful of coachmen off in the distance. They huddled around a small fire they'd built to stay warm. The coachmen would be smoking and passing around canteens of whiskey until someone suggested a game of dice. He tapped on the boot and backed up.

Fitz slid from the boot, landing on his feet and squatting, his shorter legs seemingly unaffected by the brief confinement. Fitz grinned before making his own study of the layout. When he glanced back, Jamie nodded.

Fitz reached into the boot and brought out the two bundles Finn had given them, handing one to Jamie. Fitz peered around the coach. Jamie assumed Lando was in place because Fitz was up, sprinting to the other side of the barn. Jamie raced after him.

When they'd reached the far side of the stables, the men dropped to a crouch. They unwrapped their bundles and quickly changed their outer coats for jackets that resembled the livery of Waverly. Jamie left Fitz and moved toward the front of the stable.

He peered around the corner and, finding no one around, strode across the front of the barn as if he belonged there and slipped inside. The lantern was where Beckworth said it would be, and he removed it from the hook, setting it down near the first stall. He gave a sharp whistle then moved deeper into the stables.

He was halfway down the aisle when Fitz stepped in, the shuffle of his boots moving toward the right. Jamie continued on until he reached the two outer doors that were held in place by a heavy wooden bar. He hefted the bar and dropped it to the ground before running back to the front of the stables.

———

MAIRE STAYED BY THE DOOR, listening for movement on the other side. This had been the one weakness in her planning. The room had no other egress. No window. No secret passage. A simple library turned office.

She slumped against the wall with nothing to do but wait. Time ticked by. She had no idea how long she'd been standing by the door. Her feet didn't hurt, and her breathing was still uneven, so she didn't think it had been as long as it seemed. Maire pressed her head against the wall and closed her eyes. She'd had plenty of practice waiting—six months' worth trapped in a cold cell.

"God's blood, but I think I'm lost again." The squeaky voice of an old woman could be heard over the tinkling of silver against silver. The sound of a servant carrying a service tray.

"Where are you going?" The guard in the hall asked, his tone wary.

"Well now, if I knew that, I wouldn't be lost, would I?" came the short retort.

"Where do you think you're going?" The man sounded irritated.

"I was told to take tea up to Dame Ellingsworth's dressing room, but this doesn't look like the right hallway."

Maire readied herself, hand on the knob. This might be her only opportunity.

"You're in the wrong bloody wing, you ninny. Why they thought of hiring help on the same day of the ball is beyond me," the man grumbled. "The whole lot of you act like you've never served in a great house. You should have turned right out of the kitchen, not left."

"I'm so sorry." The woman's voice was edged with fright. "The house is so big. I can't help but get turned around. And now the tea will be cold."

When the loud weeping began, Maire suppressed a smile.

The loud clatter of objects hitting the stone floor was the signal Maire needed. After waiting a few seconds, she twisted the knob and peeked out.

The tray had crashed to the ground on the far side of the guard. He turned away from Maire and left his post, seemingly caught between berating the servant and helping her pick up the mess. Tea flowed around broken pieces of china cups.

"What a fine mess you have. You'll pay for those cups," the guard growled.

"I'm so sorry." The old woman howled, tears streaming down her face as she wrung her hands.

When the guard began to kneel, the old woman looked up, and Maire almost chuckled.

Eleanor continued to wring her hands as she began to mumble. She spared the barest of nods.

Maire slipped out the door, and as she closed it, Eleanor released another pitiful cry and dropped to the floor in front of the guard. "Don't touch that. You'll cut yourself."

Maire wasted no time and bolted to the foyer, expecting to hear the guard call for her to stop. But the only sound following her was the continued wailing from Eleanor before Maire turned left into a drawing room. She found the door Beckworth had told her about. All the time she'd been his guest, she'd never seen this one. It had been built to blend with the wall. A spring lever in the bookcase that edged the door released the lock, and the door swung inward.

Inside the narrow passageway, she inspected the short hallway and could make out the exit in the dim light. When she closed the door behind her, she was swallowed in darkness. Beckworth mentioned candles kept on a nook in case someone had to hide, but she wouldn't waste the effort. Hands out in front of her, she walked as quick as she dared, having forgotten to scan the floor for impediments. She had to get back to the kitchen.

TEN MINUTES LATER, Maire huddled behind the door of a storage room. With a small candle her only light, she held the pages as close to the flame as she dared. After escaping from the library, she'd made her way back to the kitchen without incident. The sound of the party seeped into the basement, a constant hum in a normally quiet house. The kitchen staff never slowed as they continued to prepare food. Footmen scurried back and forth, leaving with burdened trays, returning with empty plates that were taken to the scullery maids who worked with wrinkled, red hands. Keeping her head down, intent on her task, she passed through the kitchen and ran directly to the rarely used room.

After learning about the two sets of invitations, the team knew the primary event of the evening had nothing to do with the masquerade ball and everything to do with a druid gathering. Where Reginald had found willing participants, Maire couldn't imagine, but she admitted to a curiosity to know who would be attending.

The team assumed Reginald would be busy with his dual pursuits, leaving his bedchamber free. The concern was whether Reginald would leave the druid book in a safe place or keep it on his person. They'd know soon.

When Eleanor and Maire had arrived earlier, the house staff had been in chaos, just as Beckworth had predicted. Though Reginald had been at the estate for six months, bringing several of his own staff had only created disorganization and discontent in the household. To make matters worse, for this evening's party, additional staff were hired at the last minute. The staff might appear well-organized, and the house ran well enough on a daily basis. But a major event like a ball required an efficient staff, all trained to work together to make the event successful. Otherwise, someone might find themselves without a job in the morning.

At first, Maire thought everyone was working well together, but within an hour, the gaps and miscommunication became evident. Eleanor, with the assistance of the two lady's maids, worked to widen those gaps by giving the occasional wrong instruction. Soon, little slivers of problems grew to larger ones until staff were running in circles throughout the west and east wings. The housekeeper hustled about in an attempt to bring order back to the house, but it was slow to take hold.

Maire bent her head toward the letter and squinted at the tight, narrow handwriting, attempting to make sense of what she read. Even with the poor lighting, she saw enough for her earlier fear to return. The letters varied in topic, but Langdon was the main subject. The highlights included his personal schedule, when he'd be in London, and who he associated with. Then her heart rate increased, the blood rushing in her ears when she read the last line from one of the letters.

Have good confidence he has the H.S. but need confirmation of location.

H.S.

That could only mean one thing—the Heart Stone.

All the time she'd been held captive, Reginald asked nothing about the Heart Stone. Nothing she'd translated in the druid's book ever referenced it. Anytime a stone was mentioned, it had been one of the smaller stones. The druid had been obsessed by his experiments with a single stone. Had the Heart Stone been a backup plan? This changed everything. Once the team had the grimoire, they'd need to locate this century's heart stone and ensure a new, safer hiding place.

She considered where a safe place might be and the only

person she trusted with something so valuable would be Sebastian.

The knock jarred her, and she dropped the letters. Three soft taps, a long pause, one more tap. Time to move. She picked up the letters, tucked everything back into her pockets, and blew out the candle.

Opening the door slowly, she scanned the hallway. Male voices coming from the kitchen grew closer. They were gruff and loud—guards.

Picking up her skirts, she turned right and ran for the back stairs that led to the second floor.

54

Once night descended, Finn and Beckworth waited another thirty minutes, then left their horses with the men who had followed them. They raced across the lawn to a small door at the back of the east wing and braced themselves against the wall. The shadows created from an upstairs balcony hid them as they waited.

A few minutes later, the door to a garden shed creaked open on their left. The slim form of Thorn took a hesitant step out, seemed to be waiting for his eyes to adjust to the moonlit landscape, then turned his head at the sound of a pebble hitting the side of the shed.

He ducked as he raced to where Finn and Beckworth waited. After another moment, the larger frame of Dodger joined them.

Beckworth turned to the door partially hidden by shrubbery. The door was nondescript, blending with the gray color of the manor. He reached for the recessed handle, found it wouldn't open, and cursed under his breath. "Did my butler have any information about Reginald's evening schedule?" Beckworth fumbled through his pockets.

Finn and Thorn glanced at each other but said nothing. Antagonizing Beckworth wouldn't move him any faster.

"Ah, here it is." Beckworth pulled out a small metal ring with three skeleton keys on it. Using one, he quickly unlocked the door and stepped inside. The rest of the men ducked through the door before Dodger closed it behind them. He fumbled in the dark, and then Finn heard the sound of the flint before the lantern lit the space.

"No," Thorn replied with a sneer, trying to get back to the topic that sent him and Dodger to the party early.

Finn understood Thorn's irritation, since he and Dodger spent almost two hours in the gardener's shed with nothing to show for it.

"Barrington wasn't able to find the footman who'd been assigned to one of the overnight guests," Thorn continued. "If he was worried about it, he didn't show signs of it, but he felt bad about not finding something useful. He did mention several of Dugan's men have been deployed throughout the manor."

Finn glanced at Beckworth. "I can't imagine that's good."

Beckworth shrugged. "Hard to tell with Dugan. He's always been difficult to predict." He stared at the other men then back at Finn. "We're not aborting the mission, are we?"

Finn considered their options, then shook his head. "We could have used more information, but we're already here, and it's too late to pull out the other teams. Let's stay focused."

Finn glanced around. The interior space was larger than he'd expected, measuring more than twenty-feet-by-twenty-feet. Considering it was on the ground floor, there must be rooms on either side that were smaller than those in the west wing, unless that wing also had secret rooms. On the far side of the space, a set of wooden stairs led up through a passageway almost wide enough for a man Lando's size to walk unimpeded.

Finn nodded after everyone seemed to have acclimated to their surroundings. Beckworth started up the stairs, the other three close behind. When they reached the second floor, Beckworth stepped to the side as the others found positions near a door. The passage continued up, but another narrow hallway curved toward the right.

"What's with all the secret tunnels?" Thorn asked as he crouched in a corner, though the ceiling was tall enough to stand.

"Many old estates have servant passages so they can move around the house without being seen. From what I've been able to learn, the manor was built sometime in the mid-seventeenth century. The lord of the manor constantly worried about the estate being overrun, so he added multiple secret passages should he ever need to escape. Some extend to the west wing though they're not as extensive. Only a small number of people know they're here."

"Including Reginald or Dugan?" Finn asked.

"I doubt Reginald knows unless Dugan found out. I never spoke of the passages to anyone but Barrington and Mrs. Calloway, the housekeeper. The last viscount knew, of course, as did his wife. Can't say who they might have told, but for tonight, we should be safe."

"Let's get this done," Finn urged. Time seemed to be slipping away, though he knew they were on schedule.

Beckworth slid his hand along the wall until a light click was followed by the door opening an inch. He pulled it open and disappeared inside.

Finn lit a second lantern and passed it to Thorn. "Give us thirty minutes, then you might want to come see if we're in trouble."

Thorn nodded. "If you feel like leaving Beckworth behind, I think we'd all be okay with that." When Finn grinned and ducked to go through the door, Thorn grabbed his arm. "It goes without saying he should be left so he can't talk."

Finn shook his head. He didn't know what was between those two, and he'd love to hear the tale, assuming they survived the evening. He closed the door behind him until he heard it lock in place. This passage was narrower and lower in height. Beckworth had shuffled down the short hallway, already disappearing through another door.

When Finn caught up, he stood to his full height as he surveyed the master bedroom. He had to admit, he was expecting something a bit more flamboyant for Beckworth. The room held ornate furniture and a massive four-poster bed, but nothing grander than any estate of this size. Somehow, he'd expected everything to be gilded in gold.

"Where do you want to start?" Finn asked.

"I didn't find anything in the dressing room, the dressers, or tucked under his mattress."

The woman's voice startled them both, their hands instinctively reaching for their hilts.

Then Finn relaxed, unable to stop the snarl that erupted. "Do you think you might have called out to reduce the chance of being run through?"

"You've always been so dramatic, brother." Maire slid from the shadows, and Finn had to take a double take. Even though he'd seen her disguise before leaving Eleanor's cottage, it caught him off guard.

"Can you two carry on your family squabble another time?" Beckworth had removed an impressive landscape painting of what looked like Hyde Park. A small recess had been carved into the wall in which an iron box had been placed.

Maire stepped beside him. "Do you have the key?"

Beckworth gave her a withering glance. Pointing at Finn to help, they lifted the box out of the hole and placed it on the floor. Beckworth retrieved the same key ring as before, selecting the smallest of the keys. Within seconds, the lid lifted, and Beckworth pulled out several sheets of paper, two pouches of coin, and several small books which he handed to Maire.

"It's not here." Her tone dismayed as she scanned the room, already searching for another hiding spot.

"You're sure?" Finn asked.

"Yes. These are ledgers, nothing more."

"Give them back." Beckworth wiggled his fingers, impatience edging his tone. When Maire handed them back, he placed everything back the way he'd found them. After they replaced the box and painting, Beckworth waved an arm. "Spread out and check everything—twice."

They split up, Finn taking a lantern from Maire so he could retrace her steps in the dressing room. When he returned to the bedroom, Maire was still rechecking the dressers while Beckworth searched hidden crevices and small trap doors under the floorboards.

"Are all of these hiding places from previous owners of the estate?" Finn asked.

Beckworth chuckled. "Not hardly." He turned to peer inside an ornate jewelry box, large enough to hold several small books.

"I've already checked that," Maire said. "Twice."

When a small click revealed a hidden door behind the box, Maire shook her head. "And?"

"Nothing." Beckworth slammed it shut.

Finn stood in the middle of the room, frustration eating at him. "Perhaps Ethan was right, and Reginald has the book with him."

Beckworth turned in a circle, his face a mask of intent focus as he surveyed every inch. "I don't think so. Maybe I don't know my brother as well as I thought, but I knew the duke. The only time he was willing to keep something that important on his person was when he was ready to flee. Otherwise, he never wanted to be caught with anything too valuable unless surrounded by several bodyguards.

"The party should be safe enough." Maire continued her search, unwilling to give up, though she was now searching in places too small to hold a book. A clear sign his dear sister was just as frustrated as he was.

"I don't think so." Beckworth repeated his earlier opinion as he turned toward the dressing room. "If he's planning a more private party after the ball, and he's as caught up in this druid thing as you say he is, he'll come up here to change."

"Into what?" Finn asked.

Beckworth tugged at his sleeves and walked to the dressing room. They followed him. He removed a white silk robe from a hook by the door. "This."

"Of course. They would wear robes during a ceremony." Maire glanced at Beckworth, somewhat in awe of his foresight.

"One last place." Beckworth stomped to the back of the dressing room. "I didn't think Dugan was aware of this particular secret, but now that I think about it, the duke saw me pry the floorboard up once. It's possible he told Dugan of my known hiding places." At the back of the dressing room, a trunk sat next to the back wall. "Help me with this."

Finn took the other end of the trunk, and they pulled it away from the wall. It was much heavier than Finn anticipated, and he wondered what was in it. Kneeling, Beckworth walked his fingers along the floor, tapping lightly until he found what he searched for. Maire edged closer and held the lantern high.

Pulling the key ring from his pocket, Beckworth selected the largest one and used it to pry the floorboard loose. He pulled out a rusty iron box and lifted the lid.

The three of them stared down at the single item covered with a white silk scarf.

"Bingo," Beckworth exclaimed.

"Bingo?" Maire asked. "What does that mean?"

"An expression I learned from two old sisters and some form of game."

Finn smiled. "Let's be sure it's what we hope it is."

Beckworth handed the silk-covered object to Maire. "You do the honors, please."

With shaking hands, Maire unwrapped the scarf and reverently ran her hands over the cover. "Bingo," she repeated.

"Let's go," Finn said, standing to push the trunk back in place after Beckworth replaced the box then stomped on the floorboard.

They ran back to the bedroom, and when they reached the secret door, Beckworth picked up the lantern he'd come in with.

Finn grabbed his sister's arm when she moved to follow Beckworth. "No."

"What do you mean?" she asked, trying to pull away.

"We haven't heard the signal. That means you have time." Finn took both her shoulders so she faced him. "A small change of plan. We can't take the chance of all of us getting caught. You know this place. Go back the way you came and find your way to the coach."

"That's insane. What if they've already left?" Maire said.

"They won't leave until after the signal. If they have, then find Eleanor. You know she's taking the path that leads to the far end of the estate, but she's not planning on leaving until things have quieted down. You can both hide until then."

She shook her head until she noticed Beckworth nodding.

"You know it's the safest for both you and the book." Beckworth lifted her chin with his knuckle. "Where's that spitfire I've come to know."

She pushed his hand away, irritation sparking her green

gaze. "Fine. But I don't like it." Her worried gaze pleaded with her brother to change his mind.

Finn brushed her cheek with his hand. "I've been doing this work longer than you. It's not unusual to change plans if necessary."

"Why is it necessary?" Maire asked, her hand touching his.

"It's just a feeling. I can't be more specific. I just think it's better for us to split up."

Maire took a step, then flung her arms around him. "Be safe." She kissed his cheek, nodded at Beckworth, and slipped out the bedroom door.

"Was that the truth?" Beckworth asked.

"What? That I think it's better to split up?"

"That you don't have a good feeling about this."

Finn stared at the floor, wishing he had a better answer.

"Maybe we should give her a few minutes, then follow. We can tell Thorn to go back the way they came and meet us at Eleanor's."

Finn considered it. He had no reason for the niggling feeling that crept up his spine. A warning that on any other job he'd follow. But would leaving the same way as AJ and Ethan put them all in danger? He couldn't risk changing the plan any more than he just had.

"Let's go." Finn stepped toward the secret door.

Beckworth shrugged and opened it.

Thorn and Dodger waited on the other side. Thorn seemed disappointed to see Beckworth, but Finn just shook his head, no longer in the mood for humor. He just wanted to get out of the manor.

Dodger led the way down. Beckworth held the lantern high from his spot at the back of the line to help guide the way. Dodger and Thorn had stepped onto the main floor, Finn and

Beckworth still on the stairs, when the door opened. Two men with swords ducked in, one holding their own lantern.

Dugan's men.

Finn backed up first, Beckworth already two steps ahead of him. Thorn reached for his sword as he walked backward to the stairs. Finn stopped when Dodger stepped forward.

Dodger took another step, nodded to Dugan's men, then turned to face Thorn.

55

An odd hoot of an owl stirred Jamie, and he nudged Fitz, who had been dozing. They had taken cover in a dark corner of an empty stall. Two young lads had been in earlier to feed the horses. They'd rushed through their chores, most likely wanting to get back to watch the party from some well-crafted hiding place. Beckworth knew the staff well.

Jamie rose and patted Fitz on the knee before working his way down the aisle. He unlatched the stall doors, leaving them half-open. The horses seemed too interested in eating to notice. When all the stall doors housing horses had been opened, Jamie pushed on one of the large doors in the back.

He held his breath as it creaked open to the night. When he didn't hear anyone respond to the sound, he pushed the other door open. He continued on without looking back, letting the moon guide him as he strolled toward the coach, keeping a steady pace.

Lando was already there, crouched near the carriage door. Jamie turned and hunched down next to him.

Five minutes later, the rosy glow of fire could be seen through the opened doors. Within seconds, the scream of the horses preceded the pounding of hooves as the first horses raced through the door. Jamie tried to count them, but as the fire quickly took hold, the horses blurred by too fast in their panicked urgency to escape.

The carriage nudged forward, the harnessed horses sensing danger amid the screams from the escaping herd. Lando jumped up to the bench to hold the horses. The sound of splintering wood caused the coach to shake again. The horses of the nearby carriage burst forth, the carriage brake unable to hold them.

Jamie stood, first glancing to Lando, who struggled but seemed to have control of the rig. Then he turned toward the barn, amazed at how quickly the fire had spread, worry overtaking him. He thought the last horse had broken free minutes ago. Then, when he almost gave up hope with the billowing smoke, one last horse raced out. A few seconds later, Fitz followed.

He stopped halfway to the carriage, bending over to catch his breath, coughs rattling him. Fitz was covered in black soot, his hair slick with sweat.

Jamie ran to him and caught him under one arm. He pushed Fitz into the carriage and jumped in behind. Within seconds, the coach lurched. He leaned out the window as they raced across the clearing toward the backside of the west wing. Everywhere he looked, driver-less carriages were being dragged away by terrified horses. Coachmen ran after them, a few managing to jump on carriages before the brakes were disengaged by the heaving beasts.

The coach veered to the left, and he fell across the coach, smacking into Fitz, who was still wheezing. When Jamie glanced out the window again, people streamed from the front entrance, some stopping to watch the flames, others racing away from the manor, searching in vain for their carriages.

It seemed the viscount's ball had taken on a more macabre atmosphere. Fitting for a druid ceremony, he thought. Lando turned the coach toward the lake at the far end of the estate then abruptly veered to the left behind a stand of trees. The coach should be well hidden in the dark, well positioned for a quick escape.

When Lando stopped, he jumped to the ground, sword in hand. Jamie retrieved two swords from under the coach bench, handing one to Fitz, whose color was returning beneath the smoke stains.

Horses appeared through the trees. One of the perimeter teams flanked them as they waited for AJ and Ethan.

Several minutes later, the men glanced at each other at the sound of approaching horses. They formed a circle around the coach and waited.

A dozen guards appeared, the horses branching out to form a larger perimeter around them.

How had the guards known they would be here?

"That asshole, Beckworth." Fitz spat the name before he raised his sword, released a blood-curdling scream, and stormed toward Dugan's men.

***

MAIRE STOOD IN THE HALLWAY, wanting to turn back and follow Finn. She didn't feel right leaving him, though she knew her brother's instincts were usually never wrong. With one last glance toward the bedroom, she raced through the hall and down the back stairs. She paused when she reached the first-floor landing. The melodic sound of a quartet could be heard over the chatter of guests.

Finn had been right. The signal hadn't sounded.

She dashed down the stairs and through the kitchen. The

first screams reached the lower floor as she passed a housemaid. Without a second thought, she ran for the outer delivery door. It opened without hesitation, and she slipped out, slamming the door behind her. She leaned against it as she caught her breath, the scream from the guests mingling with that of the horses. She prayed Jamie got them all out.

The lawn and gardens were as bright as if sunlight kissed it rather than the night. Damn Reginald and his druid ceremonies. Why did everything have to be done by the light of the full moon? Seeing no one, she selected the route that kept her close to the trees and hedges.

She reached into her pockets, needing to confirm the pages she'd stolen from the library were still where she'd stuffed them. The druid's grimoire was safely tucked away as well. Taking a deep breath, she ran for where the coach should be.

She never looked back.

ETHAN STEERED AJ back to the library, keeping her in front of him to block Dugan's view. Her nails dug into his arm until he stopped next to a group of three couples. They easily parted to include them in their circle. For the next ten minutes, they listened to the couples share the first parties they would attend when they arrived in London the following week. When Ethan noticed AJ growing restless, he nodded to the group, making an excuse of getting his wife a snack.

After leaving the library, they moved from room to room, constantly on the watch for Dugan and Lady Agatha. When they reentered the library twenty minutes later, Reginald was still there, seeming to hold court as different guests came and went.

Reginald appeared happy to stay in one place while everyone gravitated to him. His ego must be larger than the manor. Tired of constantly moving, Ethan guided AJ to a sitting room where a small quartet played and several people danced. This seemed the best place to rethink their next steps.

Finding a quiet spot, Ethan pulled AJ into his arms and rocked back and forth in time with the music. "How many ways are there to get from the west to east wing?" He smiled down at AJ, and she smiled back as if he were the most interesting man in the room.

"More than the two of us could monitor." Her focus glazed over for a moment. "I doubt he'd go through the kitchens. He doesn't seem the type to hide. He considers Waverly his home. I think he'll go where he wants, when he wants, regardless of his guests."

"So the quickest route?"

She gave it some consideration. "Through the foyer and the connecting sitting room." She hesitated. "Beckworth mentioned a servants' door with a long passage that runs behind the staircases and leads to the east wing."

"Our best option is to stay close to the foyer, working between the dining room and library."

"The sitting room is larger and would be easier to move around."

He considered her idea, but it would be safer in a crowded room rather than a larger room. Easier to move around meant easier to spot. He was about to mention that to AJ when he noticed a lone man slip into the room. He wore evening attire, but everything about his movements told Ethan he didn't belong there. The man scanned the room, his slow gaze scrutinizing each person.

Ethan moved AJ away, keeping behind other guests until he found another couple moving in the same direction. He stuck to them as if they were together.

"Where are we going?" AJ's whisper could barely be heard above the music.

"Someone just came in to search the room."

AJ tensed but kept moving with him. "You don't think they're looking for us, do you?"

"If I said no, would it make you feel better?"

"I'd think you were lying."

"Then we might as well assume the worst."

"I doubt Lady Agatha would have said anything." AJ turned her head to look for the man.

"He was by the door where we came in."

She peered around a large woman with red feathers sticking out of her mask. "He's still there, leaning against the wall. I don't think he's leaving."

The couple in front of them exited through a different door that brought them to the foyer. At least they were where they wanted to be. They'd been lucky the room had two doors. Ethan positioned AJ next to a group of men discussing the war.

"Mark my words, this war will go on far too long. The economy will be ruined," a man with a scruffy beard said.

"Nonsense. Our navy will route them by the end of the year," said a shorter man, wearing glasses so thick his eyes appeared twice their normal size.

"Nine o'clock," AJ whispered.

Ethan made a slow turn toward the direction she gave him until he spotted Dugan. The man wore a scowl as he scanned the room. He ignored the group of men where Ethan had shifted AJ behind the taller men. Another man followed Dugan in, and after Dugan said something to him, he took a position near the door to the sitting room.

When Dugan strode down the hall toward the dining room, Ethan moved AJ toward the back of the staircase. "I don't like the feel of this."

"Are they just being cautious?"

Her question sounded hopeful, but they both knew the answer.

"You think someone betrayed us?" AJ's whisper was a combination of anger and confusion.

He understood her frustration because his own thoughts agreed with her. "I can't think of any other reason for positioning men in each room."

"Maybe they're looking for Reginald's inner circle."

"Maybe."

"How long have we been here? Surely, Finn's had time to find the book."

Ethan didn't respond. If they'd been betrayed, so had Finn.

"Beckworth," Ethan mumbled.

AJ shook her head. "I just don't believe that."

"Who else?"

"We don't know for sure if they're looking for us. And what motive would Beckworth have?"

"Maybe he decided to work with his brother after all."

AJ was still shaking her head when Ethan moved them down the hall. Suddenly, she pulled back. "Where are we going?"

"To the conservatory."

"We're supposed to wait for the signal."

"We can wait for it in the conservatory. We'll be closer to the exit."

"But what if Reginald returns to his room?"

"I think we're beyond worrying about that now." Ethan pushed her in front of him, not feeling comfortable with her behind him.

They came to a group of people amassed in the hallway not far from the dining room, no one moving, all talking while creating an effective roadblock.

In the worst English accent he'd ever heard, AJ pushed her

way through, "Excuse me. May we pass?" If anyone found it strange, they didn't show it. They were all too busy eating, chatting, and tossing back free champagne.

AJ suddenly stopped before they cleared the crowd. Ethan glanced up and swore. Dugan marched down the hall, heading straight for them. He hadn't spotted them, but he would soon.

Before Dugan reached them, a man stepped out from another room and pulled Dugan aside. While Dugan appeared to be issuing orders, AJ tugged on Ethan, pulling him away. She only took a few steps, glanced at the people milling around them, then stepped behind a large fern, dragging Ethan with her.

They stood in an alcove with just enough room for both of them. The fern protected them from curious gazes.

"We should be safe for a few minutes." AJ turned them so Ethan's back was to the fern. "If you stand still, your dark clothing should make a good backdrop for the fern. No one will look back here unless they're truly searching."

"Then we'll be trapped."

"Do you have a better idea?"

"No. But how did you know this was here?"

AJ's expression relaxed for the first time that evening. "When Finn and I were here during our first jump, he pulled me into this very alcove to calm my nerves before meeting Dame Ellingsworth and Lady Agatha." She blushed, and Ethan couldn't help but smile.

"I won't ask how he did that."

"He was quite honorable," She teased.

"Uh-huh," was all he managed before AJ poked him to silence.

When a minute passed, she relaxed. "Dugan just went by, though he stopped for a moment. I think he was searching the people ahead, but he kept going."

They waited five minutes before Ethan felt the urge to move. "We need to get to the conservatory. What's the safest route, even if it's a bit longer?"

Before AJ could provide an answer, screaming started from the front of the house.

"Finally," AJ muttered.

Feet thundered down the hall, everyone racing to the front of the house to see what happened. When the group in the hall vanished, Ethan stuck his head out, looking both ways.

"It's clear." He grabbed AJ, no longer caring about the safest route. His only focus was the fastest way out while the fire in the stables kept everyone occupied.

"If they're on to us, they'll be waiting for us in the conservatory."

They were down the hall where a left turn would take them to their destination when AJ yanked him to a stop.

"Then let's not take the chance. This way." AJ turned right and ran down another hallway before stopping next to an armored suit. She felt along the wainscoting, and a door opened. She pulled Ethan inside the lit passage. "A servant passageway." She took two steps before reaching stairs leading down. "We'll go out through the kitchen."

When they reached the lower floor, AJ pushed the door open, peered out, then stepped into the kitchen. Ethan quickly surveyed the room. The stable fire had emptied the kitchen as it had the hallway upstairs. AJ pulled him through the kitchen, picking up speed as they reached a door beyond the giant hearth.

Ethan didn't bother slowing her down with questions. She knew this manor better than he, and he trusted her survival instincts. When they burst through the outer door, AJ stopped to catch her breath.

They stood in what would be Waverly's food garden, but in

February there was nothing left but withered husks from the fall harvest. Ethan gathered his bearings. The conservatory would be to their left.

They moved quickly but didn't run. Ethan cursed the full moon, a spotlight on their backs. They made it across the lawn before shouts broke through the silence of the gardens. He didn't have to tell AJ to hurry because when the second shouts screamed, "Halt," AJ broke out in a full run, skirts lifted as she made for the trees.

It wouldn't matter how fast they ran, the guards would be on them before they could reach the safety of the coach.

AJ must have thought the same thing because she suddenly turned, leaving the small path and cutting across a bed of dried plants, almost losing her footing.

"Where are you going?" Ethan called out, then almost stopped when the single figure stepped out from the trees. His rapidly beating heart almost choked him.

Maire.

56

"Dodger?" Thorn stumbled back, unaware of the guards edging around the room, his wounded expression revealing a man trying to make sense of everything.

Dodger shifted his gaze. He reached out, palms up as if in offering.

"You betrayed us?" Thorn asked again.

"I did it for Peele."

Thorn shook his head, not understanding. "How is this vengeance for Peele?"

Dodger pointed his chin toward Beckworth. "How could we work with him? With my brother in the ground."

Thorn turned his gaze on Beckworth and spat. "I have no love for that man. I have an old debt that will be cleared one day." His frown deepened, a confused sadness in his gaze. "As much as I hate him, he wasn't the cause of Peele's death. That was the duke and Dugan."

"He was part of it. He might as well have put the sword through my brother."

"So you betray us to the more guilty of the two?" Thorn stepped back, his hand resting on the hilt of his sword.

Dodger staggered, seeming confused by Thorn's response. His eyes dulled, his voice hollow when he finally looked at Thorn. "And now you'd run me through?"

"You haven't just betrayed Beckworth. You've betrayed us all."

"No." Dodger's face lit up, eyes glazed with a madness he'd hidden from everyone. "I have the viscount's guarantee you and I will walk away from this. He said he'd make Dugan pay for his misdeed."

Finn backed up a step, pushing Beckworth with him into the shadows of the passage. He slowly withdrew his sword and whispered to Beckworth, "We need another way out."

Beckworth shook his head but moved another step up the stairs. "There aren't many places left to run."

"Have you gone mad?" Thorn yelled. "This viscount won't punish Dugan. He's his right-hand man." Now he spat at the feet of Dodger. "And you think I'd turn my back on friends. Just walk away while they're butchered. That makes me an accomplice to your betrayal. Do you think I could live with that?"

"You'll see. This was the only way to avenge Peele's death."

"Not my way." Thorn drew his sword, and Dodger answered with his own.

Dugan's men stepped back to let the two fight.

Finn took a step down, but Beckworth grabbed his arm before he could take another. "Thorn. This isn't the time."

"There is no better time, my friend," Thorn called back, keeping his steady gaze on his bodyguard. "I cannot let this stand." Thorn ran at Dodger, his rapier sword swinging madly as Dodger stepped back to block, clearly not wanting to battle Thorn, his mad eyes glazed with confusion.

The room rang with the sound of steel as Thorn pushed his advantage, each swing precise, his feet easily sidestepping Dodger's more clumsy moves.

Beckworth tugged on his arm, but Finn couldn't take his eyes away from the macabre scene. All their plans for naught. A traitor in their midst. He hated it when his sixth sense was right.

Thorn stepped on a broken stone, his step faltering. When he began to fall, Dodger's sword swung wildly. Finn thought Dodger had gotten the upper hand, but Thorn landed on a knee. Before Dodger could bring his sword around, Thorn's sword came up and pierced Dodger in the chest.

The big man poised as if caught in a midair dance. His eyes bulged as they glanced down to the sword buried halfway into his chest. Blood spilled from his mouth. His free hand reached out for Thorn as he fell. Thorn caught him before he hit the ground.

"I'm sorry, my friend. So very, very sorry." Thorn laid him gently on the ground. Tears dripped down his face. He glanced up at Finn. "I'm sorry."

"Not your fault." Then Finn saw Dugan's men step from the shadows. "Behind you." Finn lifted his sword.

Thorn pulled his blade from Dodger's chest, twirled, and caught the first man in the chest. He twisted, lunged, then fell back. Finn moved forward, but Beckworth stopped him again.

"There are too many. We don't have much time." Beckworth tugged at him.

"We can't leave him."

"He's already dead."

Finn knew Beckworth was right. Thorn took another man down, but at great cost. More of Dugan's men entered the room. Thorn was surrounded, but he took down a third man. For a moment, there was a small break in the line, and Finn thought Thorn might get away. Until another man attacked from behind, running his sword through Thorn's back. Thorn stumbled, pushing another man away as he turned. Blood soaked the front of his shirt where the tip of the blade protruded.

He caught Finn's gaze and smiled. With the last of his

strength, he gave Finn a short salute, winked, then turned, burying his sword into the chest of the man who killed him. His revenge complete.

As Thorn fell, Beckworth tugged on Finn again. "Now. Quickly. There's nothing you could have done."

Finn backed away. The horror and loss almost doubling him over. Everyone in jeopardy for something so misguided. How had they not seen it?

They raced up the stairs. When they reached the second floor, Beckworth ducked down a passage on the right. "They'll be on us any minute. There's one last door that might still get us out of here."

"Another secret tunnel? It better be close." Finn kept looking back, the pounding of footsteps growing louder.

"I didn't think to mention it since I didn't think we'd need it." Beckworth raised the lantern then stopped. He ran his fingers over a stone in the wall that looked like all the others. "This is it. It leads down to an underground passage and ends at one of the outbuildings. I doubt anyone is watching that area.'

Finn fumbled in his pocket. "Here." He handed the stone AJ had given him back to Beckworth.

"What are you doing?" Beckworth gaped at him before staring at the stone he never wanted to see again. "Are you as mad as the rest of them?"

"Probably. But if they know our plans, Dugan would have set traps for everyone. Maire may not have made it out with the book. AJ and Ethan..." He shook his head, unwilling to consider what might be happening outside the manor. "You're the only one that knows this place. Knows what happened because of Dodger's betrayal. If they catch us both, we'll be dead. I think I have a way to stay alive, but I need to know you survived. My capture will give you time. You must get word to Hensley and the earl." He closed his eyes, hoping AJ was safe, that he was making the right decision. "Someone has to tell AJ."

"This is madness."

"Just go. We can't both be caught. And, more importantly, they can't get their hands on another stone." He shoved Beckworth into the dark passage, and once the man was through, Finn fell against the door, sealing it. He grabbed the lantern and ran forward. He made it twenty feet.

"Stop, or we'll shoot you where you stand."

Finn turned.

"We meet again." Dugan stood with hands on hips. Two of his men stood behind him, both with pistols. "It's been a long time. You and I have unfinished business." He bent to one side, peering around Finn. "And where did Beckworth run off to? He was always good for that, you know. Running away when the fun was just getting started. But no matter, we'll find him."

Finn dropped his sword, not willing to take a chance against pistols. "How did you get Dodger to go against us?"

"One of my men recognized him at the inn, drinking away the sad loss of his brother. I was surprised how easy it was for Reginald to convince him to our side. But simple minds or mad ones." He shrugged. "Now you and I have a chance to get better acquainted."

"If you knew we were coming for the book, why weren't you waiting for us in Reginald's bedroom?"

Dugan smile faded, and he shook his head. "I hate to admit that the son is as mad as his father. He wanted to see if Beckworth could find the book. I told him it would be too risky, but there's some bad blood between the two brothers."

At first, Finn thought Dugan was referring to Beckworth when he spoke of madness then realized he was speaking of Reginald. So Dugan had noticed the madness. "And still you follow him?"

"I follow my mistress." Dugan straightened. "And if her desire is for me to keep her worthless son alive, then that is what I will do. Now, come with us. I imagine there might be one or two of your team still alive."

When Dugan's two men moved forward to retrieve him, Finn didn't go easily. He punched the first one. The unexpected attack knocking the man flat. Then he caught the other man's hand and bent it back. When the man screamed, Finn slammed his head into the other man's face, then punched him in the kidney. He knew he'd pay for his attack, but the longer it took for him to go down, the more time Beckworth had to get away. His only hope was that Dugan let him live long enough to play his last card.

Something hard hit the back of his head. He fell to his knees. When the second blow came, it barely registered as he fell forward. "AJ," was his last word as darkness descended.

AJ TORPEDOED ACROSS THE LAWN, and though she was running as fast as she could, Ethan's pounding steps were right behind her. She didn't know what was happening. How had Dugan known about their presence at the ball? Her only goal was to get to the coach. Concern for Finn crushed her chest, making it difficult to breathe. She pushed her fear aside, following Finn's instructions—safety first, worry later.

The sound of men yelling for them to stop told her they were too close. Should they dare run straight for the coach, or try to lose the men in the woods and then double back? She'd hesitated too long and missed the footpath leading to the trees. It didn't matter with most of the winter garden mulched into the ground. She barely slowed as she veered from the path. Her foot stumbled over the uneven landscape, but she regained her footing before she fell. The brush of Ethan's hands ready to catch her.

She found the curving path that wound through a different part of the woods. When she glanced up, Maire stepped from the trees.

Her heart dropped to her stomach, landing with an aching thud. She wasn't supposed to be here. She was supposed to be with Finn.

When she reached Maire, AJ led them deeper into the trees before turning back toward the carriage. Ethan grabbed both women, then followed AJ's decision to make their way back to the coach. Maire tugged wildly for Ethan to stop.

"It's too late," Maire cried out. "Dugan's men are already at the coach. Lando and the other men are outnumbered."

"How is this possible?" Ethan cursed.

The men chasing them had temporarily lost their trail. But the guards soon discovered their mistake, and their shouts had turned to where the three of them stood.

"Run," Ethan yelled.

Maire took the lead, weaving through the trees. The ground was scattered with fallen limbs and other forest debris, and both women tripped. Only Ethan's quick reflexes prevented them from falling.

Ethan pulled them to a stop. "We won't be able to outrun them in here."

"We could head left toward where the other teams are," AJ huffed out.

"Not enough time. They're almost on us." Ethan pushed the women behind a cluster of trees that partially blocked them from view. Ethan glanced down at AJ. "We need the Heart Stone."

She stepped back. "Why?"

"You know why."

She shook her head. What was he thinking? "We have to get to Eleanor's."

"We won't make it another dozen yards." He ran a hand through his hair and gave Maire a heartbreaking look. "They're going to catch us. I have no weapons to fight with. They'll put Maire back in her cell, and you as well if you're lucky. I won't survive the night."

AJ recoiled at the thought, but the truth stung. "We should at least try for Finn."

Ethan grabbed her arms, pulling her close so she had no option but to look him in the eyes. "Finn has a stone, remember? He'll be able to follow us. He'll see the fog. Once he knows you're home, he'll know what to do."

AJ glanced at Maire, who was shaking her head. Maire didn't want to leave, might even be afraid of jumping. Who could blame her? She wasn't looking forward to it herself, even to save their own necks.

"AJ. We don't have any more time. We can't let them get too close."

She reached into her pocket and pulled out the necklace. Her hand shook as the Heart Stone swung heavily from the chain. But her focus was on her wedding band. Her heart clenched. She'd arrived in this century without her husband, and now she was thinking of leaving without him. This was all so wrong.

"AJ. Listen to me. Our team is outnumbered. We may have lost half of them already."

The thought of losing anyone sent a jolt of ice through her. Lando? Jamie? The others? She gasped a sob, undecided.

"The fog could be the only thing that can save them."

Her gaze darted to his. The fog was thick, soundless. The men would have a chance to escape if they didn't blunder right into Dugan's men. They would know what the fog meant. They'd have an advantage.

The shouts of Dugan's men grew louder.

God forgive her. She touched the Heart Stone and began reciting the incantation.

"No," Maire yelled. Ethan grabbed her around the waist and held her firm, refusing to let her go, as she beat at his arms.

Ethan took hold of AJ's arm, ensuring they were all connected.

When AJ finished the spell, she reached out for Maire. "It's all right. I hate this as much as you, but this may be the only way to save them."

Maire stopped struggling. They all scanned the woods, watching for the mist.

Dugan's men spotted them and were almost on them when the first tendrils of fog worked their way through the trees, moving fast. By the time the mist had thickened, the three of them had stepped closer until they formed a tight triangle, hands grasping each other.

Dugan's men stopped, unsure what was happening as a silence blanketed the woods.

AJ gave a quick glance toward the men, hoping none were thinking of shooting. She needn't have worried. The men had frozen, mouths hung open, fear widening their gazes as the mist continued to thicken.

It was the last sight AJ glimpsed through her tears as the fog took them.

THANK YOU FOR READING!

But don't go! Keep reading for a glimpse of AJ and Finn's final journey in *The Heart Stone*, Book 6 of the Mórdha Stone Chronicles. Now available to order.

Stay connected with Kim to keep up with next releases, book signings, and other treats by following her on Facebook, her website, or join her newsletter.

THE
HEART
STONE
KIM ALLRED
MÓRDHA STONE CHRONICLES – BOOK SIX

THE HEART STONE

ENGLAND - 1804

Beads of sweat trickled down AJ Moore's temple. The light breeze that stirred the leaves shielding her location did nothing to dry the perspiration. It wasn't a particularly warm day, but the tension from perching in the tree strained her muscles. She'd been staring at the stone building for the last twenty minutes. She was growing impatient but forced her limbs, which were beginning to go numb, to remain still.

Other than the slight rustling of leaves, nothing else stirred. Even the birds seemed to wait in quiet anticipation. The peacefulness was so complete, the twang of the bow startled her, but she tracked the arrow as it flew towards its target, hitting the first guard in the chest. The second guard turned when his partner fell. He bent down which was his dumb luck as the second arrow, that AJ was sure had been aimed at his chest, struck him in the head, piercing his skull.

AJ nocked her arrow, moving her bow from left to right, searching for the other guards. A man approached from the left side of the building, stopping in front of the door when he noticed the other two guards down. He scanned the clearing, musket drawn and ready to fire. Without hesitation, she aimed at the man's chest and loosed the arrow. She knew when the arrow left the bow that she'd lifted her head to soon. Instead of hitting the guard's chest, the arrow pierced his left arm and, fortuitously for her, pinned him to the wooden door. An instant later, a second arrow hit him in the chest, finishing the job.

"Sorry," AJ muttered.

"That's all right, love," Beckworth whispered. "You set up the target for me." He'd been sitting in the crook of a second branch, just off AJ's left shoulder.

She shifted position and gritted her teeth at the painful tingling of nerves in her right leg. Ignoring her discomfort, she nocked another arrow. Fitz had surveyed the area earlier and confirmed six guards, assuming no other men had arrived before their team moved into place.

"Besides," Beckworth rested against the trunk of the tree. "It's good to know you haven't quite worked up the urge to kill anyone."

She glanced at him before turning back to sight her arrow. "Not yet."

He snorted at her clear reference to him. "I know you've been tempted." Then his tone turned serious. "But once you take a life, the world is never quite the same. Make sure the first one you take is worth the price."

She blinked, suddenly quite attuned to her hesitance in striking a killing blow. Hadn't Finn once mentioned something like that, or maybe it had been Ethan. A slight movement in the trees to the right of the building made her twist to take a closer look. Her arrow flew when she saw the tip of a musket point toward a copse of trees where Ethan and Lando hid. A man fell from the tree, an arrow in his shoulder. When he tried to roll away, Jamie appeared out of nowhere and slit the man's throat.

At the same time, Lando moved out of the trees behind another guard who had emerged from the left side of the building, his musket moving from side to side searching for the enemy. The guard barely turned before Lando grabbed him and stabbed him through the neck with his dagger.

AJ stared at the man as he dropped to the ground. She might not be able to deliver the death strike herself, but the fact the rest of her team could with such dispassion didn't faze her.

Not anymore.

One more guard was out there somewhere.

A light gurgle came from their right before Fitz stood, the unfortunate guard at his feet. A spray of blood soaked the front of his leather tunic, more blood dripped from his broadsword. The weapon was a surprising choice for someone of shorter stature but Fitz's muscle-bound chest and arms handled it efficiently.

They waited another five minutes before AJ nodded to Beckworth. He whistled a dove call before they both scrambled down the tree. The team covered the thirty yards to the door in seconds. Jamie and Fitz took a position to the left of the door while the remaining four lined up on the right side.

On a silent count of three, Jamie reached for the door and yanked it open.

Baywood, Oregon - Current Day - About one week earlier

Wind chimes rattled as a cold wind blew in, chased by dark, threatening clouds. Rain would soon lash out. AJ drew the heavy blanket closer, relishing the numbness in her cheeks and hands.

"You should make her come in." Her mother's anguished, hushed voice filtered out through the open window, adding to AJ's heavy heart. Helen hated to see her children suffer. What mother didn't?

"She'll come in when she's ready." Adam's reassuring voice would do little to ease their mother's worry.

"I've made coffee." Stella's voice boomed from the kitchen almost making AJ smile.

Almost.

"She's been like this for a week," Helen crooned. Then footsteps faded away.

When AJ heard nothing more but the crash of the tempestuous waves and the frenzied cries of the seagulls, she closed her eyes. A single tear traveled a lonely path down her cheek, and she let the wind dry it.

Some days, time had no meaning when she did nothing but watch the sea and clouds continue their march toward shore. She considered going into the house but didn't have the energy or desire to rise. Her limbs weighed her down, heavy as stones.

The French doors opened and someone stepped outside. "I'll give you fifteen more minutes, then I'll carry you in whether you're ready or not." Ethan Hugh's tone brooked no argument. When AJ didn't respond, the door closed.

"How's Maire?" Stella sounded close, probably staring out the window at AJ. If AJ knew her friend, Stella would want to shake her. That made AJ almost smile again.

The group had either been silent while AJ lost herself in the coming storm or they had returned from wherever they'd gone because the conversation picked up.

"She's almost as unresponsive as AJ." Ethan sounded tired, unable to do anything to help the women who suffered from Finn's disappearance. "When she's not going through her translations for the hundredth time, or locked in a room with AJ talking about who knows what, she sleeps on the new couch I bought. She won't sleep anywhere else. She stares out to sea, just like AJ."

"It's been a week," Adam said.

AJ tuned them out. She couldn't listen anymore. She knew exactly how long it had been—down to the minute. A week here meant almost three months in the eighteenth century. No one understood the shift in time. She snorted. No one really understood how the druid stones worked at all. The incantations used with the stones to create the fog that took people through time had been guess work from the start. Only Maire, Finn's sister, with the help of Sebastian, a French monk, were able to translate the druid's writing in *The Book of Stones*. The book explained how the stones had been created on an eclipse-darkened night, centuries ago, during a freak lightning storm. Talk about a perfect storm. The book also explained how the druids had created the silver torc to keep the six stones together, amplifying the power of each stone. The problem was that the book had been written in ancient Celtic, and there were very few people who could piece the language together. To make it more difficult, the druids had written in a secret code, hiding the individual words of the translations throughout the text.

Maire had deciphered the original incantations and modified them, making the time travel more reliable—to a point. They couldn't select a specific time or place to go, nor were they certain where they'd arrive when they traveled back in time. Though they had traveled enough times to have a decent guess.

Only five days had passed when AJ returned with Ethan and Maire, though she had spent almost two months in the eighteenth century. Where Finn had been left behind, with no one knowing what happened to him. Her heart clenched as the wind whipped, banging a bird feeder against a post. The early storm, unusual for the dog days of summer, matched her raging anger and deep, unfathomable ache of loss.

Someone had betrayed them. That was the only explanation. Ethan assumed it had been Beckworth, but that made no sense to AJ. Beckworth had fabricated situations in the past, and his earlier actions while working for the Duke of Dunsmore hadn't made him any friends. AJ was convinced Beckworth acted out of survival mode. But had he? His hatred for Reginald, his half brother and full heir to the duke, was real. She was positive about that. And everyone despised Dugan, originally the duke's right-hand thug and now Reginald's man-at-arms.

She considered their last evening at Waverly Manor in England. Their team had sneaked into Reginald's masquerade ball to steal a second book that spoke of the stones. The druid's book, referred to as *The Mórdha Stone Grimoire*, had been written by a druid who had traveled through time. The team believed the man to be the druid chieftain who had written a journal of his time jump experience and continued experiments to repeat his time travel. This book, also written in ancient Celtic, was thought by some to be the ravings of a crazed man.

At some point during the party, Dugan's men had cornered the team. AJ, Ethan, and Maire had escaped through the fog, returning to present day. They had no idea if anyone else made it out. Maire wouldn't have if Finn hadn't changed the plan at the last minute, forcing Maire to take the book and run for the carriage. Had Finn suspected Beckworth? And why hadn't Finn used the individual stone he'd carried to return to the present? If he'd lost it or someone had taken it, Finn would have found his way to France to get another stone from Sebastian. He should have been able to accomplish the trip to France in the three months that elapsed in the earlier century. But he hadn't. No matter how she looked at it, there were only two possibilities. He was either dead or captured.

She ran her fingers over the Celtic etchings of her wedding band that was still bound to the necklace and Heart Stone. When she closed her eyes, she could hear his voice on the wind, see his lopsided grin, a longing in his emerald green eyes, and a lilt on his tongue.

"I'll always come for you, sweet lass."

One week. It seemed like months.

The vibration of her phone jarred her from her contemplation. She opened her blanket to peer down at the glow from the phone resting on her lap.

It was a short text.

"It's time."

AJ blew out a long breath. Finally.

She pushed herself out of the Adirondack chair, hugging the blanket close, the edges dragging on the ground behind her as she entered the house. The group stared at her, probably waiting for her to say something, but she ignored them as she passed the dining table. She marched up the stairs and dropped the blanket on the floor of her bedroom. After changing to a warmer sweater and getting her tangled hair in order, she ran down the stairs, grabbed her purse, and was shutting the front door when she heard Stella's voice call out, "Where are you going?"

She was in her car, screeching out of the parking lot of the inn by the time the front door opened. Through the rearview mirror, she caught a glimpse of everyone standing on the porch before she made the first turn up the tree-lined drive.

Ethan cursed under his breath as AJ sped away. He should follow her, having a fairly good idea where she was going. When he turned to ask Stella's opinion, she'd already gone back inside. Only Adam remained on the porch.

"Come in, Ethan. We need to talk." Adam patted his shoulder then waited at the open door.

"I need some time, Adam." Ethan dropped into one of the porch chairs and stared at the empty drive.

Adam shuffled his feet but after a long sigh, returned inside.

Ethan pulled his jacket closer, thankful the house blocked the wind. He shook his head and stared at the stand of trees across the parking lot. He'd anticipated this moment since their last jump and Finn hadn't followed. He'd known for sure when Finn hadn't arrived the next morning. Would they ever be safe from the stones and those blasted books? Maire and AJ thought he didn't want to go back. That he would just leave Finn for whatever fate had decided.

They should know him better than that, but when he considered his mood this last week, he understood how his actions appeared. No matter how he broke it down, Maire would have to go with them, and he had no idea how to keep her safe. He couldn't follow her everywhere she went for the unforeseeable future. It would grate on her and their relationship.

He huddled deeper into his jacket, the cold wind seeping into his bones. His life had been so simple living with the earl. It was a lonely life. He'd never thought he'd find a woman to share his life. Had never looked for one. The first time he stepped through the fog, he never expected to return home. Now home was anywhere Maire was. And being Finn's sister, Maire would never rest until they found Finn. And he would never let AJ go back alone.

There had only been one option, and he would have to wrestle with his own fears. She might chafe at his actions, but once they stepped through the fog, Maire will have a permanent bodyguard. And if it strains what they have together—so be it. Her safety was more important than his happiness.

He stared at the drive for another hour before the chill drove him back inside. When he trudged back to the kitchen, Stella stood in front of the coffee pot, bouncing with impatience as she waited for the final drips to finish. She glanced at him, her brows drawn down, her expression unsure. When he nodded, the worry lines disappeared, and she returned her vigilance to the coffeemaker.

Helen, who looked pale and withdrawn, struggled to smile. She looked nothing like the sparkling person she'd been at her birthday party which, in this timeline, had been only a week ago. Stella refilled the mugs before sitting next to Helen, patting the older woman's hand. Helen immediately grasped the proffered hand, and studied Ethan, as if she was waiting for the worst possible news.

Adam stood in front of the bay window but returned to his chair when he noticed Ethan had returned.

"Why do I feel you've been planning something behind my back?" Ethan asked as he lifted his cup and tasted the fresh brew. He gazed at the three of them over the top of his mug as they huddled around the table.

"Because you're a smart man." Stella's other hand fidgeted, and she kept glancing at the paper napkins on the table.

Ethan forced back a grin. She was dying to release Helen's grip and return to making her little birds.

"It's not that we've gone behind your back, per se," Adam started.

Ethan waved him off. "It's because I've been too stubborn to listen, is that it?" When no one suggested otherwise, he blew out a sigh. "It's not that I don't want to do something about Finn. I just wanted to give him time to find his own way back."

"So that you wouldn't have to go get him?" Adam asked.

Ethan sat back, shocked at the truth of what they thought of him. "There's never been a question of whether or not Maire and I would return."

Adam and Stella exchanged glances.

"That's not the impression we got from your brooding." Stella hunched forward, her intent gaze trying to read some underlying meaning in his response.

"Maire and I don't belong here." He brushed his hair back, unwilling to voice his true fear. He wasn't superstitious, but he couldn't help believing if he shared his concern for Maire out loud, something horrible was doomed to happen. "I didn't want AJ going back." He shrugged. "I'd hoped Finn would have found a way home on his own. Since he hasn't..."

No one questioned what he was thinking. They'd all known, though no one would say it out loud.

"AJ is stronger than she looks." Helen's calm voice surprised him, but apparently not the other two, who simply nodded in agreement. Helen's cool brown gaze held a steel edge he hadn't expected nor seen until now. "I know something of loss. As much as it still crushes me to remember the day the state trooper came to my door to tell me about Joseph. As horrible as his death was, I had a body to bury. He was there for me to say goodbye." A tear slipped down her face. "It was the hardest thing I'd ever done, burying my husband. But something I had to live through." She glanced at Adam. "For my family."

She released Stella's hand and leaned toward Ethan. "All AJ has been left with is a mystery. Is Finn alive and, for some reason, unable to find his way home? Or is he dead? As much as I don't want her to leave, knowing she may never return..." She paused when her voice hitched and she blinked away the tears. "His loss will haunt her. She'll eventually return to her life, but she'll forever be watching the sea, wondering if her husband will return."

As much as he wanted to argue, he knew Helen was right. Had always known as each day turned to the next and the fog never appeared.

"She'll end up like that old geezer who built the McDowell house. Staring out to sea, quietly going mad." Stella seemed calmer, her hands now free to fold her origami figures.

"Just like the old fool that lived here at the inn, closed off in the upper rooms, still watching for Japanese Zeros long after the war had ended." Adam added. "Only instead of the Zero's, she'll be watching for the fog like we've been doing all week."

"Sometimes I think love isn't worth the pain." Ethan hadn't meant to say the words out loud but he couldn't stop the fear that clamped a cold hand over his heart and squeezed until he could barely breathe. He knew they had to go back, knew Maire and he didn't belong in this time. But Maire's knowledge made her vulnerable.

"Of course it is." Helen barked, waking Ethan out of his stupor. "It's everything—pain, happiness, irritation, bliss, anger, and passion. You can't have just one side of love. It simply doesn't work that way."

Ethan gave her a sad smile. "I know. I think I've felt every one of those emotions since I've known Maire." He moved his coffee cup out of the way and placed his elbows on the table. He hesitated, then decided to tell them the whole story. It was something he should have shared with them as soon as they'd returned, but their focus had been on AJ and Maire. "We haven't told you everything about that evening, other than we had to flee without Finn." He picked up his cup again, more to have something to do with his hands than needing any more coffee. "We'd been surrounded. Dugan's men had been waiting for us."

"Someone betrayed you?" Adam appeared startled.

Ethan nodded. "It's the only explanation."

"Beckworth?"

Ethan shrugged. "Unknown but likely. We had a tight team. Everyone had worked together before. The only team members we didn't know well were the people Beckworth brought in."

"Could it have been someone from that other man...what was his name? Hensley?" Stella laid down the origami, her focus solely on this new information.

"I don't see how." Ethan ran a hand through his hair, then sat back. This particular topic had been just as frustrating as wondering what had happened to Finn. "Hensley's men didn't arrive until the day before the ball. They were told the basics, but none of the details."

"You had mentioned earlier that Dugan's men knew where to find the coach. Is it possible someone spotted it being driven someplace it shouldn't have gone and just suspected something was up?" Adam asked.

Ethan studied Adam. He kept forgetting Adam was a lawyer with a logical mind that would have come in handy when they'd planned their assault on Waverly. "I supposed anything is possible. But the guards were all over the manor, searching rooms." He stopped, remembering something Maire had told him when she first found Ethan and AJ running from the manor.

"Tell us." Stella said, obviously recognizing he'd remembered something.

"It was when Maire ran into us and told us the coach had been compromised. I'd asked where everyone else was. She said Finn had changed plans. He decided it would be better if they split up. He worried about someone catching them with both the book and the stone he carried. So he told Maire to leave the manor a different way and meet us at the carriage. If that was impossible, she was to find Eleanor and hide until it was safe to leave."

"And what does that tell us?" Adam asked.

"If Beckworth was the one who betrayed us, why would he be okay with Maire leaving when both she and the book were within his grasp?"

"My thoughts exactly," AJ said as she marched to the table and sat down several paper bags infused with tasty aromas.

For a moment, everyone appeared startled. They had been so engrossed in Ethan's story, no one heard the car arrive, the front door, or the rustling bags.

"That's why you raced out of here like ghosts were chasing you. Dinner?" Stella chided.

"Not the only reason. I had a few other things to pick up."

They all stood and stared as Maire lumbered into the room dragging two duffels. After dropping them, she moved into Ethan's open arms and kissed his cheek. "We weren't sure Ethan would play along with all his brooding. So we thought it best to wait until we had everything we needed."

AJ pulled paper containers from the bags. "Let's eat. Then we'll share what Maire and I have been up to."

Ethan could only stare at AJ. Her stoic resolve was gone. She moved with purpose, and appeared more vibrant and fierce than she had before the masquerade ball. He knew that look. She was prepared for battle.

THANK YOU FOR READING!

If you can't wait to read AJ & Finn's final adventure, you can order *The Heart Stone* now!

Connect with Kim to keep updated on next releases, book signings and other treats by following her on Facebook, her website, or join her newsletter.

OTHER BOOKS BY KIM ALLRED

The MÓRDHA STONE CHRONICLES series:

A Stone in Time - Book 1

Keeper of Stones - Book 2

Torc of Stone - Book 3

A Stone Forgotten - Book 4

The MASQUERADE CLUB series:

The Lion & the Gazelle - Book 1

The Wolf & the Butterfly - Book 2

The WORLD OF MASQUERADE:

"The Huntress and the Hawk" (novella)

ABOUT THE AUTHOR

Kim Allred lives in an old timber town in the Pacific Northwest where she raises alpacas, llamas, and an undetermined number of free-range chickens. Just like AJ and Stella, she loves sharing stories while sipping a glass of fine wine or slurping a strong cup of brew.

Her spirit of adventure has taken her on many journeys including a ten-day dogsledding trip in northern Alaska and sleeping under the stars on the savannas of eastern Africa.

Kim can usually be found working on the farm, playing with alpaca fiber, or heads down on a new book, constantly surrounded by her fur babies and parrot.

Keep connected with Kim and join her newsletter.

www.kimallred.com